Joe Wm Boyd

27-October-1982

D0914354

A Private
Investigation

Also by Karl Alexander
Time After Time

A Private Investigation

KARL ALEXANDER

DELACORTE PRESS/NEW YORK

Published by
Delacorte Press
1 Dag Hammarskjold Plaza
New York, N.Y. 10017

Manufactured in the United States of America
First printing

Designed by Rhea Braunstein

LIBRARY OF CONGRESS CATALOGING IN PUBLICATION DATA

Alexander, Karl.
  A private investigation.

  I. Title.
PZ4.A3768Pr [PS3551.L3569]   813'.54   80-16647
ISBN 0-440-06834-7

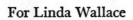
For Linda Wallace

ACKNOWLEDGMENTS

I'd like to thank William and Jacqueline Tunberg for their love and encouragement; Bill and Frances Downing for their common sense and confidence; my agent, Mike Hamilburg, for his loyalty and support; my editor, Cara Scolaro, for her advice and criticism; and Mary Ann for her intuition and perception.

Most of the time a writer must live in a room with a typewriter, a suffering isolation. To have people around him who care about what he creates makes life sweet indeed.

Prologue

Were they on their way home from the airport? Yes, that was it, that must be it, although she couldn't understand why he seemed so ethereal now. Their reunion had been tender. She had been so happy to see him, and he had been his normal loving self.

As they drove along in their old VW, he discussed the campaign and the candidates he knew so intimately now. He held her hand tightly, saying that he wished he could tell her everything, but that she would have to bear with him and not suffer his preoccupations or fears; she didn't deserve to.

Curious, she placed her hand on his leg, glanced at him, then looked back at the road. "Why can't you tell me everything?"

"I don't want you involved, Sara. I love you too much."

"Involved in what?" She turned and stared at him, concerned.

"I can't say." He managed a boyish grin, but it couldn't hide the strain in his face. His eyes were tired. "It's just better this way." His voice was low. "Besides, there's Valerie to think of."

Valerie, their eight-year-old daughter, was fast asleep

on a neighbor's couch while Sara had gone to the airport. When they got home, they would wake her up and surprise her with a midnight snack from her favorite take-out place, and she would be ecstatic that her daddy could stay for the weekend this time.

They crossed the intersection of Lincoln and Rose, passing through the amber shadows of the streetlights, then turned into a Taco Bell two blocks up. He parked in back, told her to wait, started to get out, then hesitated.

"Something tells me to go straight to the office and start my story."

"Now?" She was incredulous. "It's eleven thirty! Andy, what in the world is going on?"

He shook his head. "Nothing."

"Please tell me. You can tell me if something's bothering you."

He held her face with both hands, studying her. "Don't make me lie to you. Ever." He gave her a kiss. "I'll be right back, okay?" Then he slid out of the car and hurried through the shadows toward the front of the taco stand.

She touched her lips where his had brushed them. It had been such a quick kiss, and yet she tingled with feeling. How odd and unusual. Maybe it was the place they were in. She turned and looked back at the dark side-street behind the parking lot. It seemed ordinary. Houses and trees and parked cars, their shapes made soft by the fog. She shifted in the seat and looked out the front window again at the back of the stand. That view was ordinary, too. She wondered. Andy had always told her never to rely on intuition. Why, then, were her lips still tingling? How curious. The feeling was so strong.

She suddenly felt alone; she wished he would hurry.

Why did she feel so isolated? She needed to know what he would not tell her; she needed to know his story. Yes, that was it, she decided. When he came back to the car, she would smother him with love and insist that he tell her. Then he would relax and explain, and everything would come clear. There would be no secrets between them. She sat up alert and straight. Why wait? Her hand touched the door handle.

She heard a car slowly pull away from an intersection. Opening the door, she swung out of the VW and walked toward the Taco Bell.

Suddenly there was a popping noise. Had someone set off a string of firecrackers? No, October was the wrong time of year. A car must have backfired. No, that wasn't it, either . . .

Something was terribly wrong.

And then she was running through the shadow of the stand, angling left and around the corner. She thought she was moving as fast as was humanly possible, but it took forever to get around the side and into the lighted area. Her eyes swept the scene in front of her—in slow motion, it seemed. The boulevard was empty, and the bright pools of yellow from the streetlights revealed nothing. But on the side-street directly in front of her a car was accelerating away in nervous jerks. She turned further to her right. In front of her, brown plastic tables rested on a sea of damp concrete. Then she saw her husband swaying under the harsh neon, listing away from the counter. She glanced back at the car, but now it was moving so fast that she saw nothing distinctly. It rocketed away, its molded taillights flickering dimly, then turned off the side-street and disappeared into the night. The model, the license plate, even the color were a blur. She could recall only the bizarre shape of the car—like an overturned bath-

tub with unusually tiny windows which emitted no light. She was surprised that it was moving so quickly and so gracefully.

She heard a sound and turned again. He was grasping at the counter, hunched over now and retching. His strength seemed to be leaving him. He fell onto the concrete, his body twitching. He pushed up on one arm, shakily, then went down again, face-first with a dull smack.

She uttered a moan, then ran toward him, dodging through the tables with an agility she did not know she possessed. Her mind became crystal clear and began recording the scene with precision. Hysteria—even grief—would have to wait. She knelt beside him on the concrete, her legs becoming wet in the puddle of his blood. She touched his shoulder; it didn't feel like it was all there. Frightened, she looked closer and drew back in horror. A bullet had torn his back apart —only his shirt was holding him together.

He managed to raise himself up again and push at the air with his right hand as if to stop what had already occurred. He wasn't ready to give up; he wanted a second chance.

"Andy," she said delicately, a statement rather than a question.

With a great effort he turned toward her voice. She was sure that he could not see; his eyes had glassed over, yet he continued to hold himself up. His chest heaved, then fluttered. His lips struggled to form words.

"Andy!" she repeated. She put her arms around his shoulders and tried to pull him to her, but he slipped through her embrace and rolled back onto the pavement. Again he tried to speak, but to no avail. His muscles coiled and tensed once more before releasing

the last of his strength in a weak hiss. Then his body went limp.

She leaned away from him, more in awe than in terror. A presence, a brightness rose from him. She moved her arm through it gently, and then it disappeared. Confused, panicked, she look down at him again. He was gray, a mound of death lying still on the rough concrete.

She screamed. She got up and backed away, shaking her head. She screamed again and pounded her knees with her fists. There had been no reason! She did not know why!

Only seconds had passed, yet she had aged considerably, or so it seemed. She looked again, this time beyond him into the Taco Bell. There had been one cook on duty—a soft, brown youth. He had been shot, too, his body thrown back onto a stainless-steel contraption and under the infrared warming lights.

There were no witnesses.

She looked down at her husband, half-expecting him to rise unhurt, as if he only had been acting. But Andy was a corpse now; his blood was turning black. The horror set in; she grew numb. She began to shake, and her teeth chattered. Then she held herself tightly, insisting that she would not lose control or let herself be overwhelmed. The scene in front of her was unacceptable, so she would change it.

She ran the images back in reverse.

She was back at the VW, closing the door, then walking toward the Taco Bell to tell Andy that she loved him dearly and that whatever was going on, there should be no secrets between them. When she reached the side of the building, her spirits lifted. Everything would work out fine this time. She heard the car accelerate away from the intersection again.

She was sure that it would drive right on past and fade away. The chain of events was progressing smoothly this time. She had changed things for the better. There was no more danger.

That sound again. The quick bursts of gunfire. She couldn't stop them.

She rounded the corner. The car was lurching away—Andy crumpling onto the concrete, arms flailing. A confusion of distinct bright colors and images. The soft, brown youth dying, too, bloody holes ruining his white apron. She was running toward Andy, dodging through the tables. Her mind became crystal . . .

No.

She was back at the VW, slamming the door, hurrying toward the Taco Bell, trying to control herself, hoping to God that she could have one last tender moment with him.

A popping noise.

She suddenly remembered the sharp odor of burnt gunpowder. It wafted past her. It was part of the scene. She sighed with resignation. No matter how hard she tried, she could not alter the circumstances. The scene would not erase. The awful outcome remained.

She was back at the VW . . .

It was no use. Nothing to be done. She would cry forever. Or so it seemed.

She screamed.

One

And screamed again.

Sara Scott awoke drenched with sweat in the middle of the night, her scream echoing through the drafty apartment. She thrashed around on the bed until she was free of the covers, then sat on the edge, tense, waiting for the terror to leave her so she could go back to sleep. Her nightshirt clung to her like a cold, wet towel. She shivered, then put her face in her hands and tried to relax by thinking of other things, but her mind would not let go of the memory. She moaned, then went to the window and raised the shade. The view outside provided no escape. The moon was full and yellow and too bright. Despite the mist it cast black shadows that seemed to welcome Sara's torment.

Andy had been dead for almost four years now, and yet to this day no one knew who had killed him or why. She was certain that the mystery nurtured her awful recollections, her nights of solitary dread. If only the truth were known. His death would be explained, and she would be released.

A dog howled. She looked out the window again. The night seemed just to lie there under the fat moon, waiting for her to succumb. The shadows and the occasional shrieks of the mockingbirds were eerie. She pulled the shade down and her terror subsided, but the fear lingered within her. She swore softly. She hated that feeling just as much as she did the initial seizure of panic.

Hearing a noise, she turned and was startled.

Valerie, now twelve, stood in the doorway, silhouetted in the light from the hall. "Are you okay, Mom?"

"I'm fine," Sara replied curtly. "I heard something outside, that's all." She paused. "Didn't you?"

"Mom—"

"Go back to bed, Valerie. You shouldn't be up."

The next morning came hard. Somehow Sara made Valerie breakfast and sat through it silently, drinking coffee and pretending to be absorbed by the morning traffic report on the radio. After her daughter left for school, she showered and dressed in jeans, tennis shoes, and a University of Hawaii jersey. The shirt reminded her of her parents, now retired to a life of rum drinks and surf fishing on Oahu's north shore. They had sheltered her before Andy had come along. Since his death they periodically offered her and Valerie the guest rooms over their carport. Sara steadfastly refused. Rather than accepting charity of any kind, she was determined to put her life back together again.

She went to her old vanity and looked into the mirror. She didn't look much different from the way she had in her wedding picture, which now rested in a shoebox in her bottom drawer, where she kept what little remained of her life with Andy. She had the same brown eyes that sported a touch of hazel. The same long hair, several shades darker. Fair skin. Full lips and a mouth that could look either sensual or philosophic, depending on the occasion. Yes, she still had the same face that Andy had seen. Only the wrinkles were new, although she had to look closely to see them. She rather liked them, anyway, hoping that they suggested wisdom and not just age. She didn't mind being thirty-two; she just hated the thought of having nothing to show for her years.

She stepped back and looked at her curvaceous figure. It hadn't changed much, either. Andy had always called her voluptuous. Magnetic. She didn't know. She didn't think in those terms. Especially now.

She quickly brushed her hair, made up her face, eyed herself critically, and approved. Then she put on her coat and corduroy hat, tucking her hair up underneath. Next, she grabbed her purse, left the apartment, descended the worn steps, and hit the street. The sun cleared a line of dirty palm trees and glared into her eyes. It was hard to believe—here it was late September, and Venice was bathed in bright sunlight instead of smothered in the low clouds that usually filled the southern California sky.

Sara then walked west on Horizon Avenue. The houses stacked up ahead were all decaying wooden bungalows, choked by bamboo, bougainvillaea, and succulents. Seventy years ago they had been the utopian dream of an eccentric millionaire who thought that southern California's Venice would be the ideal location to recreate the Italian Renaissance, complete with gondolas and canals. Well, he and dozens of subsequent movie producers had been wrong. The miles of canals had long since been filled in and paved over, making nondescript, narrow streets conducive to crime. The one or two waterways left were stagnant and used only by flocks of ducks and gulls.

She passed a vacant lot where a house had finally collapsed and then had been removed—over a decade ago. Adjacent to the lot a small two-story cottage glistened like colored glass in a muddy field. Out front, a lady who looked to be eighty-five planted winter flowers in a garden that had obviously been well kept for over fifty years. From her porch in a wheelchair another lady talked to the gardener, making weary yet emphatic gestures. The two appeared to be sisters. Sara nodded but was not acknowledged. That did not bother her. One usually did not make a habit of recognizing strangers in Venice.

On Market Street she continued west, then crossed the main drag of Pacific Avenue and followed Market another half block, almost to where it dead-ended into the Ocean Front Walk and the dirty sand beyond. As usual the salt breeze was tainted with the faint odors of garbage and hydrocarbons. Sara entered 71 Market Street, a substantial building constructed from surplus World War I firebricks. Inside, the foyer suffered from a lack of fresh paint, but it was invitingly wide and spacious. She went up the broad wooden staircase covered with deck webbing. The stairs did not creak— another point in favor of the old building.

She reached the second floor and moved down the hallway with a quick, businesslike stride. Suddenly she stopped. Her eyes narrowed. Easing her purse around to the front of her body, she continued walking at a slower pace, her eyes fixed on the fourth door down on the right. Lettering on the marbled glass read:

207
SARA SCOTT
PRIVATE INVESTIGATOR
BY APPOINTMENT ONLY

The door was ajar. Someone had broken into her office.

Pulling the 9mm Baretta Brigadier pistol out of her purse, she released the safety. She fondly called the little weapon La Belle, because no one ever expected a woman to have a working handgun in her possession. When she peered into her small reception area, her piece was at the ready. No one was there. She looked across the anteroom. Her inner office door was closed, but light streamed through the crack at the bottom—a light that she had not left on. She thought about firing through the door to nail whoever was inside, then recalled she had installed a solid-core oak door to prevent that from happening to her. She sighed. She supposed she could just burst inside, roll across the floor, and come up firing, but she wouldn't want to overreact. She would have to be cleverer. Whoever was in there probably wanted her or something that she had. She smiled. Two could play that game.

"Hello, Miss Scott?" Sara called. "Yoo-hoo, Miss Scott, are you in there?"

"No, she ain't in here," growled a male voice. "But it sure sounds like she might be out there."

Surprised, Sara stepped back. Then she frowned, opened the door, and strode inside, keeping close to the wall. She had La Belle poised.

He half turned. He held a paint roller in his left hand, and with his right pushed the housepainter's cap back on his head. His eyes narrowed at the sight of her pistol, but other than that he seemed unconcerned.

"*Spencer Harris?*" Her jaw went slack. She stared at the large, muscular black man and—for some reason—noticed that he had not spilled a single drop of paint on his brand-new, pressed cap and coveralls. Even his hands were clean. He had been painting as if he were either tap dancing or trying to hide an ambiguous past.

"Next time you come in here, watch your step, dig?" He gestured with his roller. "You done messed up my wall."

She looked. White paint was smeared across the sleeve of her coat where she had brushed against a wet surface. She lowered her pistol, stood tall, and put her hands on her hips. "Just what the hell is going on?"

He resumed rolling on paint, intent upon finishing the back wall of the office, concentrating as if he actually enjoyed the tedious work.

Sara continued staring at him. Around his thick neck hung a gold razor blade on a chain. Along with a Playboy Club key, a cocaine spoon, a Star of David, a Saint Jude medal, several doubloons, a Krugerrand commemorative and a miniature phallus. All twenty-four carat. Every time he moved, he jangled. *The man's wearing Fort Knox,* she mused, then frowned. She noticed that her possessions were not where they were supposed to be. He had jammed all of her potted plants and furniture against the front wall corner by the door. They were piled on top of her scrunched-up Oriental carpet. Her pictures were there, too—her prized Cézanne print of the lady in yellow stacked against the original John Altoon drawings she had found in a condemned building while pursuing a missing person, and the photographic studies of misty seas she had done as a fledgling art student. And face-down at the front of the stack her framed bachelor of science degree, hard-earned at West L.A. State's night school after Andy's death. She loved the decor of her office, the mementos of her personal life. To see them rudely pushed into a corner—coleus leaves and palm fronds smashed between picture frames—made her furious.

"Spencer!"

"Not *now,* girl. I got to get this corner straight."

She glared at the back of his neck, paused for a moment, then dropped La Belle into her purse and set it on the desk behind her. "Well, then, let me help you."

She picked up a paint-laden brush from the roller pan. Then she advanced on the corner, deliberately stumbled and, while falling against the wall, flicked the brush at Spencer. Paint splattered all over his carefully shaven face, broad chest, and lush gold pendants. He slowly turned toward her, globules of eggshell white making freckles on his dark complexion.

"What the hell are you doing?"

"I tripped. I'm sorry." She gestured with the brush. He flinched in response. "It was an accident."

"Put the brush *down,* girl."

She obeyed, then straightened up. "I told you when I first moved in that when the office needed painting, I would do it."

"It ain't your office no more." He removed a linen handkerchief from a pocket and carefully wiped his face.

"What?"

"You heard me."

"What do you mean, it's not my office anymore?"

"You're three months behind in your rent, girl. As of *yesterday.*"

She stepped back and gulped. "So I'm three months behind. Give me a break."

"You got a break last month. Remember?" He bent down and carefully placed his roller on the edge of the pan. "You see, normally I'm a patient man." As he straightened up he eyed her body and made no attempt to conceal his stare. "But the reservoir of my patience has finally gone dry, you dig?"

"Come on, Spencer, just give me a little time. I'll get another case."

"I don't see nobody lining up to bust down your door."

"It's not as if this is the hottest location in town, either."

"I ran an ad in the paper last week. It said, 'Office for rent. 71 Market Street, Venice.' I've already had fifteen calls." He grinned. His teeth seemed ominous. He cleaned the paint off his gold charms and medallions with the handkerchief.

"I'll get your damned rent! You'll see!" She turned, went across the room, and picked up the phone that, miraculously, had not been turned off yet. Sara dialed her answering service to see if there were any messages that might lead to a new client. Whoever answered put her on hold. She stood with her back to Spencer, the phone against her ear, and drummed on the desk with a pencil. While she was waiting she remembered her last case, almost six months ago. Some guy had paid her five hundred dollars to spy on his girlfriends to see if they were cheating on him. It hadn't taken her long to figure out that the guy was a pimp who wanted to know if his women were conducting any business on the side. She got the girls together, told them what he was up to, and gave them the money he had paid her, less expenses. Supposedly they had escaped to the Midwest.

"Triple-A Answering. May I help you?"

"Anything for one by seventy-two?"

"Sorry, Miss Scott, no messages."

She hung up and sighed. No gig. No retainer, either. She turned and faced Spencer, head held high, a defiant glint in her dark eyes.

He was waiting expectantly, his roller poised to

start the next wall. "So what's the word, *wo-man,* you got a job or what?"

"I don't think that's any of your business," she replied with dignity. "And may I suggest that you have yourself and your paint cans out of here by the time I get back?"

"No, no, Miz Sara, you seemed to be confused. You got it all wrong. Twisted," he said, mocking her deep, controlled tones. "May *I* suggest that *you* start moving your personal belongings out of my modest building while you have the time? I mean, I wouldn't want to see you picking them out of the trash, dig?"

"I don't suppose you'll give me till the end of the week?"

"Try the end of the day, girl."

She was so angry when she left her office that she broke down and lit the half-crushed Sherman that was lying at the bottom of her purse. She hadn't smoked in three weeks—more a testimony to her dwindling supply of cash than to her willpower. She knew that Valerie would reprimand her when she smelled the tobacco, but she didn't care. Right now she needed the crutch of a bad habit. She clenched the cigarette between her teeth, straightened up to her full five-feet-six, and stomped down the stairs. *The end of the day, huh? We'll see about that, Spencer!* She went out the back way and crossed the trash-choked alley to her 1972 Pinto sedan, parked in a lot reserved for a maverick film company. The car needed a new paint job, not to mention a new fuel tank if the consumer experts were to be believed.

She drove north on Pacific Avenue, deliberately slowing down to hit the green lights. Red lights were a personal aversion; she had a thing about them.

Somehow she thought of them as bad omens, and right now she needed all the help she could get. When she crossed into Santa Monica, the scenery changed. The street widened. The houses were well-kept here; the shrubbery trimmed. The only dogs she saw were on leash. Even the air seemed cleaner, although one look at the horizon where the smog met the Pacific told her that it really wasn't. She gripped the steering wheel harder and sped up. She was going to look up Claude Casparian; she didn't know what else to do. It had been a couple of months since she'd seen him, but just the thought of him brought back memories.

Memories of her husband. Andy. Tall, lean, red hair, hazel eyes, always bent forward slightly, poised for motion. He had been killed a week before his thirtieth birthday—cut down on the edge of a promising career as a journalist. He had worked for *Rolling Stone*. There had been rumors that he would be promoted when his current assignment was over. They had given him free rein this time—to cover the California gubernatorial campaign and produce in-depth, personalized studies of the candidates and their entourages.

His death shocked everyone who knew him. The authorities launched an investigation. Sara cooperated fully, trusting them implicitly when they confiscated Andy's notes and tapes as possible evidence.

Two months passed. Her parents came, comforted her, helped with the funeral, then returned to their island paradise. Her eight-year-old daughter finally stopped asking questions, realizing that her daddy was never coming home again.

For a long time Sara did not hear from the police. They stopped returning her phone calls; no developments were forthcoming. Yet she didn't lose hope. She promised the memory of Andy that someday everyone would know who had killed him and why. She was certain that it was only a matter of time. She even had her pledge written on his tombstone, despite being cautioned about such eccentricities.

The police closed their investigation, unable to discover a motive for Andy Scott's death or a murder suspect. Sara had accepted their failure philosophically and asked to have her husband's personal effects returned. But all she ever received were apologies. Andy's notes and tapes had been lost somewhere in the massive police bureaucracy and were never found.

Undaunted, Sara had hired Claude Casparian to find her husband's killers after the police had given up. In spite of his reputation as a notorious ladies' man, he was supposed to be a damned good private detective. At first he balked when he found out that Sara couldn't pay. What about her husband's insurance? She had curtly replied that what little remained of the money was supporting her and her daughter. He agreed to take the case when she offered to work for him in exchange for his services. They both learned very quickly that they had different opinions regarding the duties of a secretary, however. The first time he made a pass at her, she laughed it off and reminded him that he was old enough to be her father. The second time, she slapped him, then threw out the 150 proof tequila he had been drinking. The last time, she gave him a black eye and threatened to have him arrested for harassing a female employee. Ultimately they became good friends.

Casparian spent a year on the case and accumulated an impressive dossier on Andy Scott, despite never having access to the notes and tapes lost by the police. He learned everything there was to know about the young man's life except why anyone would want him dead. Everyone spoke very highly of the *Rolling Stone* reporter, including the governor. Then a candidate, he had been planning to offer Andy a job on his staff when the tragedy occurred. Then one day between Thanksgiving and Christmas the detective told Sara that it was no use. All he had done was provide fuel for her memory. He had no leads. He could not crack the case. So it was finally over? He nodded. Crestfallen, she'd gone home, having run out of hope. That night she dreamt of Andy's murder for the first time.

The next day she returned to Casparian's office and began cleaning out her desk. Wait a minute, Casparian protested, he hadn't meant that she was fired or anything. If she wanted, she could stay on for two fifty a week. She didn't want any charity. He spread his big hands. Two fifty a week was charity? He needed a secretary, and if she didn't want the job, he would find someone who did. She had grown to like her job very much, but she wanted more. So she gulped, then stated that she would take the job only on the condition that he taught her the business. To her surprise he agreed, and so their association continued.

She often wondered if Andy were the only reason she wanted to have the credentials of a private investigator. But it was a difficult question to answer. Because of her promise to her dead husband she never allowed herself to answer it honestly.

As the years passed Casparian trained her meticulously, and she repaid him by solving a few of his cases on her own time, despite the additional demands of motherhood and night school.

Her life changed. She got her bachelor's degree in psychology and her private investigator's license, and Valerie no longer needed a baby-sitter all the time.

She said good-bye to Casparian and left to start her own business. He wished her good luck, then gave her his blessings and a case of Lite, which was her favorite beer.

Things had gone downhill ever since.

Two

Casparian's office was just off Wilshire Boulevard, in one of those newer buildings where the windows were permanently sealed against the soft breezes that came in off the bay most afternoons. Sara parked underneath the building and went up the back elevator. She got off at the fourth floor and went down the corridor, humming quietly, her troubles temporarily forgotten.

His door was locked. Was he out? No, not Casparian. He didn't usually go out until night unless he absolutely had to. So, he was probably drinking and didn't want to see anyone. She grinned. She would surprise him. She *loved* to surprise him. Opening the door with one of the keys she kept forgetting to return, she slipped into the waiting room. With the other key, she unlocked the inside door marked Private and silently entered his office. The IBM Executive typewriter she once used was humming, the switch was on, but no one was in the room.

Maybe a jealous husband had finally caught up with him. Or perhaps a spurned lover, although she doubted that, since Casparian had never been known to spurn anyone. When she saw light under the conference room door she was relieved. Of course. He was in there either sleeping off a hangover or on the phone with a prospective girlfriend.

Well, not quite. When she opened the door, she saw Casparian laid out on the sofa. He wore a dreamy smile, but that was all. Astride his naked loins, a plump and pretty dyed blonde moved toward ecstasy, her heavy breasts swinging and slapping together. Sara discreetly backed out of the room and started to close the door but was too late. The lady saw her, stopped moving, and gasped. Casparian opened his eyes, then smiled sheepishly when Sara came into focus.

"Hey . . . Well, I'll be damned." He lifted his head. "How you been? Long time no see." The blonde slipped off him and awkwardly started dressing. Casparian sat up, chuckling, quickly pulled on his pants, and fastened them high on his thick and hairy torso. "Sara, meet Ruby. Ruby, this is Sara."

Sara blushed crimson and didn't know what to say. Ruby left in a hurry, straightening her sweater, which was on backwards, and apologizing about having to visit the ladies' room.

"How'd you get in?"

Sara dangled the keys.

"That's cheating." He took a large swallow from a glass of tequila and stood up. His voluminous trousers were held up by wide, bright-red suspenders. "What can I do for you?"

"Casparian, have you ever considered hiring a partner?"

"Are you kidding?" He was incredulous. "Why pay someone to argue with you?"

"What about a consultant, then?"

"*I'm* usually the one who's hired as a consultant. What the hell are you driving at, Sara?"

"An assistant. That's it. You need an assistant to

help you out because you can't handle the workload, right?"

"Wrong."

Sara grimaced. "You don't need an assistant, then?"

"No."

She hesitated, then thought about her current economic woes and swallowed her pride. "I'd like my old job back, Casparian."

"No." He scowled and ran his hand through his hair, which had the same texture and color as steel wool.

"Why not?"

"You're like a daughter to me, and it disgusts me to think of shacking up with my own daughter."

She didn't immediately understand; her eyes went all wide and innocent. "What are you talking about?"

He gestured impatiently. "Ruby's my new secretary."

"Oh." She sat down next to a copying machine. She looked at the floor and sighed, her disappointment evident.

"What can I say?" he explained apologetically. "It's been a long time coming, but I finally found a rich widow who doesn't mind answering the phone." He offered Sara a cigarette.

"No thanks."

"I mean, she ain't no Victor Borge at the typewriter keys, but at least she'll never have to ask me for a raise."

"Casparian—"

"You should've called me last month. You would've had your old job back in a flash. Especially after the string of turkeys I ended up hiring and firing since you been gone. I wouldn't have known what I was missing, either. But that was last month."

"And now?"

He grinned. "She makes a lousy drink and she's a slow learner, but I like her. She's good people." Then he actually blushed. "Okay, okay! So she's just as horny as I am."

"Sometimes you're a real asshole, Casparian."

He shrugged. "I know." She got up to leave. He turned and pointed triumphantly. "Then how come you buzzed up here and asked for your job back, anyway?"

"I need the money."

He brightened, his demeanor changing from that of former boss to doting father. "Why didn't you say so in the first place?" Crouching a little, he led her to the couch and insisted that she sit down. She perched carefully on the edge, suspicious of the sofa's more central regions.

"Drink?"

"It's a little early, isn't it?"

"Yeah, but it's free." He poured her one and proposed a toast to old times.

"Okay," she agreed. "To the good old days when I was gainfully employed." She sipped the tequila and her eyes watered. "Do you know anyone else in the biz who's looking for a partner?"

"You think I'd turn you on to the competition? Didn't you learn nothing while you was working for me?" He drank. "Why don't you try something else? A different field?"

"I'm not ready to quit yet."

"You'd make a great cocktail waitress."

"Whoopie-fuck," she commented dryly. "Thanks, but no thanks."

He laughed. "Do you remember when I taught you how to break and enter?"

She nodded and could not resist a dutiful smirk. "I still carry that little crowbar for heavy security doors."

"No, no," he said impatiently. "I meant when I taught you how to do it with finesse, with imagination, with class."

"You mean with a credit card?"

"Exactly."

"I still carry Master Charge, too." She lowered her voice. "And for a B and E it works whether it's overdrawn or not."

Casparian roared, then gradually quieted down when he realized that Sara wasn't in a jovial mood. He eyed her critically. "Do you still see that shrink you went to after your old man died?"

"No." She paused. "The guy tried to convince me that the only way to live was to accept things the way they are and to take them as they come. But I won't give up that easily. You know that." She shrugged.

"He gave you some good advice. You should take it."

"Maybe."

He studied her briefly, just long enough to see the wistfulness in her expression, the persisting hope that someday Andy's case would be solved. He reached over and took her hand. "Sara, forget about it, will you? Forget about it and get out of this rotten business."

His gentleness was induced partially by the liquor, but she appreciated it anyway. "I've never given up on anything before in my life, and I don't intend to start now."

"Listen, if I couldn't solve that case, then no one can."

"It's not just that, Casparian! It's me! I *like* being a private detective. The job appeals to me."

"Yeah, but sometimes that ain't enough." He glanced away, playing with his thick mustache and thinking. "Look, can I loan you something?" He turned toward her and spread his hands, playing the benevolent Armenian, even though he hailed from Omaha instead of Fresno. "How much do you need?"

"Aw, Casparian, you know that I want to work for what I get! Besides I owe you too much already."

"Bullshit! You never borrowed nothing from me."

"Well, maybe so, but if that's the case, I sure don't want to start now. I'd rather learn how to cope without loans. That way I won't have to pay you back someday."

"Okay, let's make it a gift, then."

"No," she replied, but she was sorely tempted. "I'm not ready for handouts. Not this week. I came here asking for a job, and if there isn't one, then it's my loss."

"You sure?"

"I'm sure." She got up, gave him a fraternal kiss and embrace. *No, not this week, but if they toss me and Valerie out of the apartment and it gets so that we can't even afford to eat, well then, maybe the week after.*

"Good luck, little girl. I'll be thinking about you."

"Fall by the office sometime. You've never seen it."

"It's a deal." He winked at her. "I'll bring some lambchops and a hookah."

He showed her out. As she crossed the office she waved at Ruby, who had composed herself and was now back behind the typewriter pecking out a report. Ruby looked up, blushed, then glanced enviously at Sara's trim figure, mentally comparing it to her own soft excesses.

Sara left. She wasn't any richer, but she certainly

felt better. Seeing Casparian always lifted her spirits. She chuckled. Visiting him was like going to a store-front church.

71 Market Street.

Sara was worried when she arrived, because while driving back to Venice she had gotten stuck at several red lights. Nevertheless she still felt good enough to put portents out of her mind. She went inside, started up the stairs, and steeled herself to face Spencer Harris. She was determined not to quit bothering him until she had been granted at least a week's stay of eviction.

When she entered her office, she was surprised. Spencer wasn't there, even though all of his paint cans, rollers, and dropcloths remained. *How easy just to shove them all outside, close the door, and then change the lock,* she thought. She grabbed the paint cans and started for the hall. She put them in the corridor and was on her way back inside for the roller pans when she happened to see a woman seated in her reception room, calmly smoking and reading an ancient copy of *Crawdaddy.* The lady was in her mid-thirties, but was made up to look ten years younger. She wore a dark chemise tied at the waist and a big, floppy hat that hid part of her face. She was tall, thin, and stunning. Sara approached her carefully, lest she be a hallucination that might disappear at any moment.

"Hi, I'm Sara Scott. Can I help you?" She sat down on the old couch next to the potted palm.

"Lovely place you have here." The lady smiled and made a sweeping gesture at the decrepit furniture. "Neo-Goodwill?"

"You're an interior decorator?"

"Professional housewife."

"Aha. A jack of all trades."

"Jill," she corrected Sara, an amused expression on her face. "And you're a private investigator?"

Sara nodded and leaned forward. She was all ears.

"May I ask what you charge?"

"Two hundred a day plus expenses."

"Isn't that a little high?"

"I have an established clientele."

"I can see." She nodded toward the outer office door.

Sara followed her look and saw that Spencer had returned and now was scraping her name off the glass. She groaned inwardly, horrified, but when she turned back to the woman, she was smiling sweetly. Sara gestured at the paint cans. "I'm redecorating."

"Oh." The lady's mask of sophistication dissolved into a harder, more serious expression. "I suppose two hundred a day is the going rate?"

Sara smiled. "I'm sure we can work something out."

The woman nervously lit another cigarette, crossed and recrossed her legs, then looked away. "I think I might be needing your services."

"I'm curious. Do I come highly recommended?"

"You don't come recommended at all."

"Oh." Sara couldn't resist a grin. "You let your fingers do the walking through the Yellow Pages."

It was the right thing to say, for the woman laughed, and the sound was genuine and good-natured. As quickly as it had come the tension lifted. "Not exactly. You're the only lady detective listed in the Western Section and I thought you'd give me a better shake on a possible divorce case since—"

"I was a female before I was a detective?"

The woman nodded and smiled.

"I don't know if it helps or not, but at least you can rest assured that I won't make a pass at you." She paused. "Come on in and let's talk about it."

Sara led the woman into her office, took a *Ficus benjamina* out of a wooden chair, and gestured for the lady to sit down. Then she began rehanging her pictures and putting her plants back in their places, actually appreciative that Spencer had painted the walls. She reminded herself to tell him that he had done a good job. "The first thing you should know is that I don't have any use for an Alimony Ann."

"Who's Alimony Ann?"

"The lady who wants out of a marriage so that she can cash a thick check every month and spend it on her Latin American lover, not to mention the condo in the Springs."

"All I want is to find out if my husband's playing around."

"The second thing you should know is that I don't work on consignment."

"Why not?"

"Because it's unprofessional," Sara replied, not mentioning how far behind she was with the rent.

The woman nodded. "And since we're both professionals—"

"I would appreciate a retainer so that I can begin my investigation as soon as possible and put your mind at ease." Sara straightened the Oriental rug.

"Can you tell me a little more?" The woman lit another cigarette. "I mean, about your other cases."

Sara turned. "Absolutely not. Information about my clients has always been confidential." Her heart pounded. "Now, if you think you've come to the right place . . ."

The woman leaned back and nodded. "I like your style. Do you think you could do it in a week?"

Sara's knees sagged and she felt light-headed. She couldn't believe what she was hearing. *Thank God, a job!* She sat down behind her desk. "A week would be fine, Mrs.—"

"Reardon. Mrs. James Reardon." She took a stack of bills out of her purse and handed Sara fourteen hundred dollars, explaining that the money came from her personal savings. She didn't want her husband confronting her with the telltale canceled check.

Sara nodded understanding, discreetly blew the dust off her receipt book, and wrote Mrs. Reardon a receipt with a shaking hand. She took a deep breath and told herself to relax but could not stop a sigh of relief. Then she turned and handed Mrs. Reardon the receipt. "What makes you think your husband's playing around?"

"He's off his feed."

Sara nodded. "I know what you mean."

Mrs. Reardon explained that her husband was a social psychologist. They had been married for twelve years, had no children (she hated kids, he loved them), and lived in a pleasant two-story house on Kingman Road in Pacific Palisades. Lately, however, their sex life had been boring. *Incredibly* boring and then nonexistent. Moreover Mr. Reardon had been coming home surly and uncommunicative every night. Something was terribly wrong.

"One last thing, Mrs. Reardon. Do you have a photograph of your husband?"

"No," she replied, puzzled.

"Then can you give me some idea what he looks like so I don't end up trailing the wrong man?"

"Oh, sure." She smiled at Sara and winked mischievously as she got up to leave. "That's easy. He's the only black man in the neighborhood."

* * *

Sara kicked that one around for awhile, a smirk on her face. She liked the unexpected, and she especially admired people who saved their best for last. She would enjoy working for Mrs. Reardon.

She leaned back in the desk chair, content with the sense of well-being that came from having money in her purse.

Then she heard scraping. She got up, and peeked around her oak door. Spencer had removed her name and title with his razor blade and was halfway through By Appointment Only. He was concentrating hard to make sure that he got all of the paint as well as the faint outline of the letters. Sara waited patiently until he was finished. He straightened up, wiped his brow, then polished the glass with his handkerchief. He inspected the surface and approved. At that moment Sara came into the hall, planted her feet, put her hands on her hips, and faced Spencer.

"Looks good. Clean. You did a good job."

He regarded her coolly and frowned suspiciously. He wasn't used to getting confident vibes from ladies. "Ain't you *gone* yet, wo-man?"

"I really like the office now, Spencer. The painting made a *world* of difference and the color is just *perfecto*. It makes up for the lousy location of the building."

He rolled his eyes with disgust, but couldn't hold back a small grin because he was confused. "Why you talking trash, girl?"

"You've made the place too nice for me to move out. Really."

"Lemme tell you something. There ain't nothing in this world for free, you dig? Nothing."

"So?"

His eyes narrowed. "You trying to tell me something?"

"Yeah. I don't want to move."

"Well—" He studied her and seemed surprised that she wasn't walking away. "If you want to stay here, you got to pay the rent." He thought for a moment, then grinned as if he understood. He gazed at her breasts. "But now, all is not lost, because there are ways and *ways* to pay the rent, you know what I mean?"

"No, I don't."

"If you ain't got the bread, baby, you can always sell some meat, you understand where I'm coming from?"

"I'm sorry, Spencer, I only deal in currency." She handed him six crisp one-hundred-dollar bills. "Leave the receipt in my mailbox."

He was astonished and, for once, at a loss for words.

"And when you paint my name back on, I'd like the letters done in gold, you understand where *I'm* coming from?"

Three

After school Valerie wandered along Main Street, lagging behind her friends, Molly and Karen, who talked incessantly about roller-skating on the Ocean Front Walk. Her eyes were dull, her freckled cheeks pale, and she moved listlessly, her angular frame hunched forward. She was looking down at the grimy sidewalk, lost in her thoughts, remembering the night before.

Momma had the nightmare again.

Valerie had been furious and had sat up the rest of the night in her cramped bedroom, absently picking at the threadbare carpet. Once again she wondered why her mother hadn't been able to save her father. *Why hadn't she yelled? Why hadn't she warned him so that he had a chance to run away? God knows,* Valerie thought, *I would've screamed loud enough to save my daddy's life. Still, why couldn't it have ended then? Why couldn't Momma just forget about it and be normal? Why did she put him first in her life, even though he was dead? What a crock.*

Now, strolling through the afternoon smog, she was confused and frightened. Lately her mother had been having the nightmares more frequently, and Heaven knew where the terrors would lead. Was her mother going insane? Valerie shivered. She wished that they could talk about it, but she knew that her mother would say that she wasn't old enough to understand. Well, dammit, she was old enough to see that something was awfully wrong! There must be something she could do. She was tired of suffering and worrying. And waiting.

She sighed, lifted her head, and swept back her thick red hair. Suddenly the idea came to her. She nodded once, her jaws clenched with determination. *She* would do something on her own. *Secretly.* Yes, she would find out who had killed her daddy and why. No one would know until the time was right. Then she would tell her mother, show her that she *was* old enough, and the nightmares would end.

Valerie felt triumphant until she realized that such a task might be impossible. Did she really have a chance? There was always a chance, and so what if she was only twelve? She was good at secrets, so why couldn't she unlock one that was four years old? Wasn't she the best chess player in junior high and a whiz at jigsaw puzzles where all the pieces were the same color? Of course!

"Valerie? Aren't you *coming*?"

She saw Molly and Karen waiting for her at the traffic light on Brooks Avenue. She gulped. "I can't."

"How come?"

"I'm starting dancing lessons," she lied, then turned and raced toward home.

Once there, she dropped her books on the kitchen table, went straight to her room, opened her closet door wide, and fought her way past the dusty boxes of toys she had outgrown. From behind them she lifted out an antique wooden filing case inherited from her father, carried it into the room, and sat down with it on the floor at the foot of her bed. She opened it reverently, for inside were mementos from her daddy—birthday cards, picture postcards from important places, snapshots of the three of them together, crazy drawings on Taco Bell napkins, and a half-dozen press badges he had given her. Hidden in smaller tins inside the file were things that had actually *belonged* to him—an old tie, a pipe that still smelled of an aromatic tobacco blend, a dog-eared copy of his favorite book, *Fear and Loathing in Las Vegas,* a stack of clippings—newspaper articles he had written, eight-by-ten glossies of him on the 1976 campaign trail, diplomas, and faded ribbons from brief service in the Vietnam War. All these things her mother had thrown out because she said it hurt to have so much of him around. All these things Valerie had carefully rescued from the trash and stashed away.

Having something tangible of her father's made her feel special and more secure. When she touched one of the relics, she imagined that she was holding onto a piece of him. She was trying to know him in death as she never had when he was alive.

She carefully emptied out the file and surrounded herself with the memorabilia. Now her collection would have a purpose. The items were keys, and she was sure that if she put them together in the right sequence, she would discover a clue to her daddy's murder. She began chronologically arranging the postcards her father had sent her when the telephone rang.

Typical, she thought. *Just when I'm getting started. It must be a giant conspiracy to keep me from discovering the truth.* She scrambled to her feet, hurried into the living room, and answered it. "Hello?"

"Valerie?"

"Oh, hi, Mom. How are you doing?"

"Guess what?"

Valerie was momentarily speechless and surprised. Her mother sounded like a different person. She imagined her looking smart and sexy. And *normal. Hmmmm. It must be because she's out in public.* Valerie nodded. Her mother didn't show the effects of the nightmare when she was with other people. You had to wait until she thought she was completely alone to see the haunted look in her dark eyes.

"Valerie, are you there?"

"Sure, Mom, what's up?"

"I got a job, that's what's up!"

After she hung up, Valerie danced around the room, delighted and flooded with relief. Now they wouldn't have to ask for loans and get turned down. Now they wouldn't be thrown out of their apartment. Now they wouldn't have to sell everything in order to eat. Life would get better for them. *Perhaps someone wealthy had hired Momma,* she imagined. *Or this job would lead to another and another after that.* Her mother would become famous, and they could move to a little house in a canyon, because that's where her daddy had always wanted to live.

She went back into her room and gazed at the mementos on the floor. What mystery did they hold? Soon she would find out, but not right now. Her mom had gotten a job and deserved a surprise.

Valerie put away the relics of her father's life, then left the apartment to go shopping.

At the end of the day when Sara got home, Valerie handed her a beer, then led her through the apartment to the back steps outside the kitchen door. She explained that even though it wasn't Mother's Day, *her* mother deserved to relax and let someone else do the cooking. Sara did not object—for once she wouldn't have to make a decision, throw something together, and call it dinner.

Still, she asked, "Are you sure you can handle it, Val?"

"Of *course* I can, Mom! I've been studying this gourmet book."

"Okay, okay." Sara lit a cigarette and quickly explained that she would quit again as soon as the Reardon case was over. Valerie shrugged and went back inside.

Sara sipped her beer and watched the sun set over a new high rise they were putting up on the beach. She lounged against the railing and enjoyed her new sense of well-being. She was sure that depositing money in the bank for a change had a great deal to do with it. Now they could stay afloat for another month or two—maybe three if she really stretched it, although she was tired of living on next to nothing. Still, she might have to for a little while longer. There were bills to pay, but right now life wasn't so bad. She wasn't broke anymore. Valerie was fixing dinner, and the evening promised to be tranquil. Except for . . . She scowled. Why did her thoughts always have to come back to the nightmare. Why couldn't she dwell on more pleasant memories? She closed her eyes, and forced her mind to go further back in time. She smiled. There. She had done it. She was with her father in Colorado Springs. He was on his last tour of duty with the Air Force. They were at the base pistol-range, and he was showing her how to use a handgun. She had developed remarkably well under his tutelage and this time was shooting for a perfect score. Six, seven, eight in the black. Nine. A shout of encouragement from her father. Suddenly the image dissolved. *She heard the next shot while rounding the corner of the Taco*

Bell to tell Andy she loved him. Something was terribly wrong . . .

Sara moaned and stood up on the steps. Opening her eyes, she blinked into the sun, angry with herself. She drained the rest of her beer. Slowly the image faded, but her mood had been ruined.

Valerie stuck her head out the door. "Dinner's ready, Mom."

Sara went inside and saw that her daughter had covered and set the kitchen table. On it were a large salad, a steaming dish of chicken and rice, and a bottle of chilled white wine. Candles were lit, too.

"Oh, Val." Sara brightened and smiled. How could she feel even half-bad when her little girl had gone and done this?

"Did I surprise you?"

"*Surprise!* This is wonderful! Where did you get the wine?"

"Fred at the market on the corner was very happy that you finally got another job because that means you'll be able to pay the bill now. So, he said that we should celebrate. So I said how can my mom celebrate without something to drink? So then he slipped this bottle of wine into the grocery bag and said that it was on him." She paused. "Congratulations, Mom."

Sara hugged Valerie and kissed her on the forehead. "Amen, kid."

Valerie tolerated the embrace for a while, then pushed away and watched her mother pour the wine. "Can I have a glass, too?"

"What about your homework?"

"I've already done it."

"All right. A small one." Sara smiled. "Your spelling couldn't get any worse anyway." She poured Valerie a third of a glass, then sat down and started in on the chicken. She almost choked. The meat was uncooked and had a rubbery texture. She turned her plate around, glanced at her daughter, then tried the rice. It was overdone. It tasted burned. Sara heaped salad onto her plate, grateful that nothing had been done to the lettuce and that Valerie could make a passable dressing. She ate heartily until she discovered a worm munching on a leaf, too. The lettuce had not been washed. Sara pushed her plate away and swilled down her wine, lest she lose what little was in her stomach.

"What do you think?"

"It's great."

"Then how come you're not eating anymore?"

"I'm allergic to turmeric," Sara lied. "Didn't you know?"

"I'm *sorry!* D'you want me to make you something else?"

"No, no, that's okay. I'm fine, really." She got up from the table, grateful that she had something to do. "Be right back." She went to the phone in the living room and called Mrs. Berman, the older woman who lived downstairs. She kept her voice low so Valerie wouldn't hear and complain that she was too old to have a baby-sitter. Sara told Mrs. Berman that *finally* she was working again, so it would be "routine A," which meant that Mrs. Berman would automatically supervise Valerie in the afternoons and evenings if Sara wasn't there. Mrs. Berman wished her Godspeed, adding that she didn't understand why a woman as young and pretty as Sara didn't find herself another husband with a steady job.

When Sara returned to the kitchen, she saw that Valerie was playing with the candlewax, totally absorbed. She sat down at the table and poured herself more wine.

"Mom?"

"Yes?"

"What did you and Daddy talk about just before they shot him?"

Sara breathed in sharply, unprepared for such a question. "Didn't we discuss this before?"

"No, we never did. You always said that I wasn't old enough."

"And now you think you are?"

"Yes."

Sara glanced away and wanted to leave. Then she felt her daughter's gaze and remained at the table. The girl deserved to know. After all, they had lived through an awesome experience together. She took a large swallow of wine and began speaking, despite the pain of the memories.

She talked about how preoccupied Andy had been and how he had refused to discuss it because he didn't want his family involved—"*There's Valerie to think of.*" She patiently explained to Valerie that if her father had not been so close-mouthed and stubborn, then they might have an inkling as to why he was murdered.

"Why?" Valerie asked.

"Because he might have shared his troubles with me, and I would've known something."

Valerie wanted to know how it was being married to such a man. Sara smiled and replied that she'd always known exactly where she stood—which wasn't altogether true, for Andy had an unknown quality about him, a private place inside where no one was allowed. She assumed that fun lurked there. After all, he was always surprising her.

Sometimes he would come home in the middle of the day just bursting with energy. I would be busy, but he would insist on an excursion, then take us to a baseball game or a parade, or a drive in the mountains. Other times he would spend hours by himself, then wake me early in the morning and read me love poems he had composed. How can I describe those moments? They were so beautiful then. They seem like such a waste now.

When the silence grew awkward, Sara quickly talked about the 1976 election campaign and how excited Andy had been to land the assignment. His only regret was that he would be on the road for six months, but Sara knew how much he wanted the challenge and how important it was to him to succeed. Politics excited him. Sometimes she thought it was the power that intrigued him. In any case he'd been offered a prestigious assignment, and so she pushed him to accept.

They only saw each other once or twice a month after that, but at the time she was certain that it was well worth it. So far hadn't everything in their lives been for the best?

The rest was history, and obituaries.

She winced now, thinking how tragically it had ended, and fell silent again. She stared at the remains of dinner. The poorly cooked mess mirrored her feelings about plans and good intentions. She shook her head. The future was then.

"Is that all?" Valerie asked.

"Of course not."

"I want to know more, Mom. I want to know it all."

Sara frowned and wondered why Valerie had suddenly taken an interest in her father. The girl had never asked adult questions before. *Unless—of course! The kid's growing up. Wanting to understand her father's death is only natural.*

Sara drank more wine, but the ache stayed with her even though she was slightly tipsy now. She was tired, too, and didn't want to talk about it anymore. She might get sentimental, and she hated Valerie to see her in such a wretched condition. She passed. "Why don't you tell me what you remember for a change?"

Valerie cocked her head and thought about that for a moment. "He was the tallest man in the world. We had the same color hair. He used to laugh about the gap between my front teeth." She paused. "I remember going to the beach with him and making sand castles that had moats and things."

"So do I."

"Do you think you'll ever get married again, Mom?"

"Why do you ask that?"

"I don't know." She shrugged. "I wonder sometimes."

"Maybe I will and maybe I won't, but there's one thing you should know." She corked the wine. "I have always been capable of great devotion, but the sun rises and the sun sets, and the rent has to be paid whether there's a man in the house or not." She rose from the table. "No more questions, kid. I've got things to do. Tomorrow's a working day." She smiled. "Thank God."

The next morning she awoke early, restless about her new case. She made coffee, then dressed in a blouse and skirt instead of jeans, because she wanted to be able to go anywhere and pass. She left her hat at home, too, not wanting to appear distinctive.

She parked her car in a suitable spot in view of James Reardon's two-story Palisades home. She arrived there at seven, in time to see Reardon get the morning paper off the front steps and then go back inside. Meanwhile she huddled in her coat and cursed herself for forgetting the Thermos of coffee that she'd left on the kitchen table.

James Reardon left his house at nine-fifteen, and Sara picked up the Olympus that was on the seat beside her. She had held it so many times that the metal finish was worn away on the sides. The camera fit into her hands like it belonged there.

A quick glance at the overcast sky told her that the world was still a two-eight. She set the exposure, looked through the eyepiece, and zoomed in to a tight shot. Reardon had a kind face that had gone sour. He seemed rather worried for such an early hour of the day and automatically glanced back as if looking at a large, invisible hand on his shoulder. He nervously touched the knot of his maroon tie. *Focus. Click.* Sara widened out and tracked him coming down the steps and crossing the front yard. He wore a three-piece suit and his slim, brown Naugahyde briefcase seemed more appropriate to an insurance salesman than a psychologist. *Focus. Click.* Sara swung to her left, leaned over, and sighted Reardon through her lens once more. Now on the driveway in front of his garage he brushed the dew off his shoes, checked his watch, then climbed into a black Porche 924. Sara was surprised that he left the car out all night exposed to the elements, not to mention the vigilant eye of professional thieves. It was curious, unless he wanted to be ready to leave home in a hurry. *Focus. Click.* She got one last shot of him just before he drove off.

She gave him a lead of a half block before starting her car, swinging around, and following.

His office was just a few minutes away, in a Brentwood medical complex where the more privileged tenants had private decks and patio gardens. He parked underneath the building while Sara left her tired Pinto on a side-street just off San Vicente Boulevard.

She reached behind her and took a small athlete's equipment bag from the back sea. In it was a cassette recorder—well, what *looked* like a cassette recorder.

Aside from the standard volume, record, rewind, play, and balance controls, the machine had a band for six stations and a fine tuner. Sara pulled up the rabbit-ear antenna, slapped in a fresh cassette, and turned the device on. From an inside pocket of the bag, she took out one of six sinister-looking electronic bugs, each numbered on its base, each possessing a tiny yet powerful built-in microwave booster which enabled the device to transmit conversations over great distances. She selected station three, blew softly into bug number three, saw the decibel meter react, and was satisfied that the machine worked. She placed it on the floor of the Pinto, slipped the bugs into her skirt pocket, hit the street, and headed for the medical building, her stride jaunty and feminine. Bugs. At first she had felt guilty about using what the corporate spooks would term "electronic surveillance." Casparian had given her the machine as a present to get her started when she had gone into business on her own. When she tried to return the stuff to him, he was hurt and puzzled. He refused to take his gift back, then explained by performing a ludicrous imitation of Lynn Swann. While trotting across his office holding a glass of tequila he said that if he, Claude Casparian, were a wide receiver in the NFL and everyone else was using two hands to catch passes, then why should he only use one? Sara had accepted his logic, wanting very much to be a savvy private eye. After all, if she was a real professional, didn't she deserve all the tools of the trade? She rationalized that when she was privy to an intimate conversation, it would be for her ears only. So far she had kept that promise. Too, she had thought of the decade that the country had just sleepwalked through. Electronic surveillance wasn't exactly without precedent. As a matter of fact one could say that

it had become an American tradition. Besides, she
had to admit she was comfortable with the little devices. In a very private sense they made her feel less
vulnerable, because she was in fact making others
vulnerable.

In the elevator she prepared for the next scene as a
method actor would. She leaned into the corner,
hunched over, and wrapped her arms around herself.
She thought of the coldest winter day ever: the snow
iced over and the trees looking like inverted crabs.
Imagined standing in the middle of it with just a
sweater and no shoes. When she walked into Reardon's
office on the fourth floor, she was the classic picture
of a manic-depressive.

"May I help you?" The receptionist was a displaced
New Yorker with a deep tan that was supposed to say
I was born and raised in Encino, but her voice gave
her away. Before Sara could answer, she began taking
calls and putting everyone on hold, whether they liked
it or not. When the phone was lit up and flashing like
a Christmas tree, she turned back to Sara and frowned.
"Yes?"

"I'd like to see Dr. Reardon." Sara didn't just want
to bug his office; she thought that it would be a good
idea to talk to him and, as her landlord, Spencer,
would say, get a sense of where the man was coming
from.

"You don't have an appointment, do you?"

"I was referred by Dr. Holland," Sara lied. "Dr. Will
Holland."

The receptionist quickly flipped through the calen-
dar and then the Rolodex. "I'm sorry. Dr. Reardon
doesn't accept referrals from Dr. Holland."

"I really would like to see Dr. Reardon. Can't I
please make an appointment?"

"I'm sorry."

"Can't you see that I'm in trouble?"

The receptionist paled, went to the inner office door, and opened it. "Excuse me, Dr. Reardon."

Sara faked an outburst of tears and slipped a bug under the telephone.

The receptionist turned back to Sara, smiling weakly. She was confused. "Dr. Reardon normally takes calls this morning, and I know he has the afternoon taken. Would you like me to call the paramedics?"

"What are you talking about?"

The receptionist made intricate, futile patterns in the air with her hands. "He must've used the other door."

"Huh?"

"Dr. Reardon just left." She picked up the phone. "And he didn't even tell me where he was going." She punched a button. "Operator, I have a hysterical woman in my office."

But Sara was gone, too. She couldn't wait for the elevator, so she went down the back stairs as fast as she could move, one hand on the railing, the other inside her purse, holding La Belle. When she reached the subterranean parking lot, she ran to the exit. She paused there, peered around a concrete pillar, and watched the elevator arrive. James Reardon stepped out and hurried toward his Porsche. She was taken aback. If she hadn't seen him earlier, she never would have recognized him. He had changed into jeans and a David Soul and Friends T-shirt. A denim cap covered his bald spot and mirrored sunglasses hid his eyes.

Sara ran back to her car, got in, started it, made a wide U-turn, and was waiting across the intersection from the medical building when Reardon gunned his Porsche up and out of the parking lot. He turned right on San Vicente and drove toward the beach, going through the gears like he didn't understand how to drive. Sara followed, flooring the Pinto. It took a moment to respond, but she was soon flagrantly breaking the speed limit, too. When she had the Porsche in sight, she grinned with satisfaction. Casparian called her a natural shadow. She liked to think that she was a quick and diligent student, wise to the rules of the road, who knew how to anticipate.

She saw the Porsche skip into the left lane between two cars just before Seventh Street. He was making a left turn into Santa Monica. She knew that she would never make the same traffic light, so she turned left two blocks earlier, sped down two more blocks, went right, swung left on Seventh and actually had to pull over and *wait* for Reardon to zip past. She gave him a three-block lead, then moved back into the flow of traffic. She turned on the cassette recorder. Reardon's receptionist was on the phone to her sister in New Jersey complaining about the California weather and the inconsiderate nature of black people, no matter how many advanced degrees they might have. Sara shut her off and turned on KHJ.

They crossed into Venice. There was no welcome sign. Instead, there was a haunting portrait of a woman done in black and white on a wall surrounding an old frame house. The artist had made the eyes big and sorrowful, the smile small and wistful. Sara liked the portrait. She thought it was, like Venice, a study in contradictions. Perhaps so, since recently the face of the woman had been obscured by Chicano graffiti.

They came to a traffic light at Main and Ocean Park. Two hard-core blond surfers in black wetsuits ambled

across the street, boogie boards under their arms. A
graying relic of the psychedelic era sat at the bus stop,
aimlessly strumming a guitar. Sara was amused.
"Venice," she said to herself. "Where the ghetto meets
the sea."

They drove south on Main Street, where there
seemed to be a resurgence of small businesses, if fresh
paint and flags were any indication. None of the strolling shoppers looked like they lived in Venice.

Reardon angled left on Washington, a street lined
with expensive boutiques and antique shops which did
not cater to the locals, either. He drove east and entered one of the largest Spanish-speaking communities
in the state of California. He slowed down and parked.
Sara drove on past and parked in an adjacent alley.
She grabbed her camera, swung out of the car, locked
it, and hurried after James Reardon. He went toward
an old complex of buildings surrounded by tall palms
and a flourishing lawn of devil grass. The buildings
had been painted and repaired recently, in marked
contrast to the rest of the neighborhood. Over the
main entrance there was a sign: The Straighten-Up
Halfway House. And in smaller letters: Partially sponsored by an enabling grant from the California State
Health Department—Substance Abuse Division. *Aha,*
she thought. *Of course.* Just like Mrs. Reardon had
said. The man donated afternoons of free counseling
and therapy to the place. Then Sara frowned.

It wasn't afternoon yet.

Out front there was a temporary stage decorated
with red, white, and blue bunting and campaign posters which told voters to re-elect the governor. Sara
had walked into the middle of a campaign rally.

The crowd was mostly festive barrio residents and
their children, although a few blacks from the Brooks

Street ghetto were present. They lounged on the fringe, listening to huge portable tape decks balanced on their shoulders, perhaps realizing that politics had betrayed them in the Seventies.

Several jaded TV mini-cam crews shared jokes and cigarettes with hard-eyed members of the L.A.P.D.'s Metro squad. Campaign workers were there, too, but what surprised Sara the most was a flock of Japanese tourists that had somehow stumbled upon this authentic bit of urban Americana. Draped in Nikons, they moved as one, using their cameras as if they were a group of anthropologists in the field. Sara didn't feel at all conspicuous now.

She noticed that James Reardon paid no heed to the political rally. He headed straight for the halfway house, and she photographed him going inside. She started to follow him, then took one look at the hostile residents gathered around the front door and decided to wait for Reardon outside. If he were having an affair, she thought it highly unlikely that he'd be meeting his mistress here.

She wandered back toward the crowd and the stage, occasionally taking pictures as if she were a journalist.

The current speaker was a tall and thin man with a pasty complexion and sandy-colored hair. Sara guessed that he must be around thirty-five; he was the epitome of the grown-up California golden boy, who now wore the mantle of power as easily as he did a pair of Levi's jeans. The man acknowledged the Japanese visitors by making an impromptu remark comparing the beauty of Los Angeles to her sister city, Hiroshima. The tourists bowed and applauded.

A mariachi band warmed up behind the stage, then filtered around front. Sara photographed the speaker, who looked and sounded familiar. Curious, she moved through the crowd to get a closer view.

"Ladies and gentlemen, the last word I had was that the governor was still in East L.A. showing his support for the Mexican-American community there and his strong solidarity with California Chicanos everywhere!"

Applause, shouts, and cheers. A Latin riff from several trumpets.

"I promise you that he will be here shortly. And in the meantime it gives me great pleasure to introduce another member of the *only* party, the Democratic Party, and no stranger to you, State Senator Anna Perez!"

The band played enthusiastically, and the crowd roared approval. A petite yet statuesque lady rose from a chair and carefully approached the dais. Before she'd entered the world of politics, she had been a well-known movie actress. There were whistles and catcalls from the audience. She tossed her head and her long hair shook loose. She smiled and waved, as if to say that occasionally she, too, thought of those good, old days.

Sara had never seen Anna Perez in person before, but she felt herself liking her immediately.

Ms. Perez shook hands with the man who had introduced her and exchanged kisses on the cheek. "Thank you, Larry. *Gracias.*" She turned. "Brothers and sisters, *hermanos y hermanas,* let's have a big hand for Lawrence Conrad, comptroller of the great state of California!" She applauded Conrad as he humbly returned to his seat. The audience responded in kind, even though the name of the state comptroller wasn't exactly a household word.

That's why he seems familiar, Sara thought. When Andy was covering the last campaign, he used to talk about Lawrence Conrad quite a bit. That was when Lawrence Conrad, fresh out of law school, had hitched his star to the political bandwagon of an obscure young candidate for governor. Then neither of them had anything to lose and no one took them seriously. Even Andy had not given them a chance, saying that their position was too idealistic, their politics too honest. The Republicans would continue to have the Lawrence Conrads of the world for breakfast. Youth and innocence would be defeated once more.

Had Andy been too cynical? Sara wondered. After all now the young candidate was a seasoned governor seeking reelection; now Lawrence Conrad was comfortably ensconced in the state treasury. If nothing else, at least two people Andy had admired and respected had made it—Lawrence Conrad and the governor.

She did not have time to dwell on this. Just as Senator Anna Perez was praising the invaluable work done by the Straighten-Up Halfway House, Sara saw James Reardon leaving the place in a hurry. She swung around, automatically raised her camera, and zoomed in. *Focus. Click.* Reardon was looking down as he walked. Scowling. His shoulders were hunched forward. He appeared desolate. Why had he come here? Surely not for a counseling session. Maybe to cancel his afternoon appointments? He could have called. She tracked him across the lawn to the street. *Focus. Click.* Then Sara followed, leaving the arena of lofty rhetoric, reminding herself once more that she was no longer the wife of a young reporter. She was a private investigator fighting for survival in a world dominated by pettiness.

Reardon led Sara out of the barrio, through the ghetto, and back to the bustle of Main Street. He stopped at a service station, barged into a phone booth, and made a call. When his party answered, he hunched over, spoke quickly, and looked sideways out at the street. At first Sara assumed that he was phoning his mistress and arranging for a rendezvous, but when he didn't speak for a long time, she guessed that someone had put him on hold. Then he muttered curtly, slammed down the phone, and headed for his Porsche, a study in frustration. Curious.

He drove around Venice aimlessly. Sara had a difficult time following him because she wasn't anticipating. She found it hard to concentrate. Her mind was still at the political rally, with Andy, wondering how their life together might have turned out. Where would they be living now? Would she have had more children? Would they still be so happy together? She could not imagine things any other way. Why did they have to kill him? *Why?*

Reardon sped north on Main across Pico, his car bouncing in the dips. The light changed from green to amber. Instead of accelerating to keep up with him, Sara was compelled to slow down. While staring at the signal she stopped at the intersection, astonished at herself. The traffic light blinked red, and she was transfixed. She gasped.

She saw the infrared warming lights behind the counter. The soft, brown youth was sprawled under them. Dying. Amazed, he watched the bloodstain on his chest getting larger and larger. Andy was on the concrete in front of her, twitching, waving, wet with blood. If only he would stand. She tried to pull him to her, but he slipped away.

Slipped away.

Horns blared behind her. She blinked and looked up. The traffic light was green now, and the street ahead was empty. Reardon had vanished. Sara rubbed her eyes, cursing herself. When her head cleared, she pulled over to the side of the road, her hands shaking badly. The traffic behind her rushed onward. A few drivers paused to shout derisively and make obscene gestures. She looked in her rearview mirror. Her face was ashen and her forehead wet with perspiration. She felt sick with horror.

Red lights. She hated them now.

When Sara got home, she was angry with herself for being so susceptible to the distractions in her mind. She slammed the front door, threw her purse onto the couch, then went into the kitchen and got herself a beer. She sat down at the table and stared hard out the window, her jaws tight. She was determined not to succumb to inner voices anymore.

"Hi, Mom." Valerie sauntered into the kitchen, resplendent in sweatshirt and cut-offs. "How'd it go?"

"Oh, just fine," Sara lied, trying to sound cheerful. "How was school?"

"Okay." She sat down across from her mother. "I got a ninety-two on my algebra test."

"Haven't you been studying?"

"Yeah, but the teacher's trying to make me look bad."

"Why?"

"I don't know. I think he's gay."

"Oh, *Val*—"

"Hey, I found this old postcard from Daddy in my dresser," she announced with forced casualness. "He wrote it to me the day before he died."

Sara glanced at the card. On one side was a picture of the Hyatt Regency in San Francisco, on the other in his familiar scrawl: "Hi, Toodles. I'm very busy, but everything's fine. Someday you and me must ride the glass elevator together and have lunch at the top. Be good to your mommy. Love, Daddy." Sara shuddered and averted her eyes.

"Well?" Valerie asked.

"Well, what?"

"If he was in San Francisco on October seventh why would he fly from *Sacramento* to L.A. on the same day?"

"San Francisco and Sacramento are only a hundred miles apart. Remember your geography? He probably took a bus."

"But why didn't he just fly here from San Francisco?"

"He was covering the *campaign*, Valerie! And campaigns move around, understand? He could've been in *five* cities on October seventh and it wouldn't have been unusual."

"Yeah, but—"

"Will you *please* stop asking me questions about your father?"

"Well, you're not telling me everything! You *never* tell me everything!"

"*Valerie*, leave me alone!" Sara exploded. "I'm trying to relax!"

"Jeez, I'm *sorry!*" She stomped away.

Later, when Sara felt better, she took Valerie out for a hot fudge sundae. They talked of little things; Sara was thankful that Valerie had a tendency to chatter during times like these. The tension drained away. Sara was relieved that the relationship they shared was so resilient. She had a notion that it would be tested again. And strained. She could only hope that their life would not be shattered a second time.

The next morning Sara got up early, showered, and put on the same outfit she'd worn the day before.

While waiting for the coffee to brew she wrote a summary of her first day on the case in her diary, embarrassed when she had to jot down how she had lost James Reardon. Then she filled the Thermos with coffee and put it next to her coat and purse so she wouldn't forget it again. She went into Valerie's room and kissed her good-bye after extracting a sleepy promise that Mrs. Berman and routine A would be obeyed.

Once at the Palisades she parked down the street from the Reardon home. She laid her camera on the seat beside her and took her diary out of her purse. Under *Wednesday, September 4* she wrote, "Second day of the Reardon case. Low clouds as usual. Remember what Casparian used to say before he left his office—'Always look out the window before stepping into the street.' " She put the diary away, poured a cup of coffee, lit a cigarette, and waited. In the distance the mist swirled, revealing some shapes and concealing others.

Sara might as well have slept in, because Reardon didn't leave the house until eleven thirty. She followed him to his office, waited on a side-street, and listened to the tap on his receptionist's phone. He himself didn't speak with anyone, and Sara assumed that he was busy with patients. She endured the boring, nasal tones of his receptionist, making and breaking appointments.

Early in the afternoon, Reardon left his office and, as on the day before, drove around aimlessly. This time, Sara followed him easily and was pleased with her alertness, although the fear of another lapse lay coiled inside her.

Eventually Reardon led her to the Palmetto Club, a dank bar on the corner of Main and Navy in Venice. He left his Porsche out front and made a phone call

from a pay phone before going inside. Sara was gratified. *At last. This is more like it.* Reardon was meeting someone here. She was certain. She stayed in her
car with her camera ready, planning to photograph
whoever left with him.

Nobody came and nobody went, and Sara grew very
impatient after a twenty-minute wait. What if the
phone call had been about something else, and Reardon's girlfriend was already inside? Sara frowned. She
didn't want to risk calling attention to herself, but she
knew she didn't have a choice. She put her camera
under the seat, donned sunglasses, got out of the Pinto,
locked it, then approached the padded door of the
Palmetto Club.

She slipped into the bar, intent upon staying in the
shadows, but had to stand in the doorway until her
eyes adjusted to the dim light. Then she quickly
crossed to a table in the far corner of the room and
sat down. No one had noticed her come in. She took
off her sunglasses and saw that James Reardon was at
the bar, staring off and very obviously alone. Sara was
surprised; she looked around to get her bearings.

The bartender was washing glasses and talking low
out of the side of his mouth. The only thing he seemed
to look in the eye was a game show on the TV. He
reminded Sara of a Richard Nixon caricature. Across
the room from the bar was a pool table bathed in
seedy fluorescent light. Two short-haired, tough-
looking women played eight ball. The older one wore
a shiny leisure suit and was hunched over from years
of booze and humiliation. The younger one had on a
leather jacket and jeans and was overweight. Their
friends sat at a nearby table, glanced at Sara, nodded,
and whispered confidentially. Apparently some of the
patrons *had* seen her entrance.

Sara looked away and blushed. She hadn't realized that the Palmetto Club was a "mixed" bar; if she had, she might have stayed outside. She shrugged again— what was done, was done—but she couldn't help feeling a little nervous. Normally she didn't mind people eyeing her body, but it sure was strange when they were female. Weird.

The bartender was standing over her, massaging her table with his towel. She ordered a Lite, and he brought her a bottle. One of the women punched up the jukebox and got vintage Linda Ronstadt.

> *Well, I lay my head on the railroad track,*
> *Waiting on the Double E,*
> *But the train don't run by here no more,*
> *Poor, poor pitiful me.*

Sara sipped her beer and steadily watched James Reardon. He toyed with his drink and seemed to be deep in thought. Occasionally he checked his wristwatch. Sara was pleased with herself. So far she had not aroused his suspicions, and thank God no one was bothering her.

As if on cue, the lesbian in the leather jacket rolled up to Sara and leaned on her table. "Want to shoot a game?"

"No, thanks."

"It's on me."

"Some other time, okay?" Sara blushed. People were beginning to turn and stare.

> *Oh, these boys won't let me be,*
> *Lord, have mercy on me.*

"Come on." She raised her voice. "I'll even buy you a beer."

"I've already got a beer."

"You scared, girl?"

"Do I *look* scared?"

"No." The woman backed off and grinned. "No, you sure don't look scared, honey, but you never can tell now, can you?"

It was obvious that she was not going to leave. Sara scowled and half shielded her face. More patrons had taken an interest in the scene. Some of them even found Sara's uneasiness amusing. At any moment James Reardon might notice what was going on, and her cover would be blown. She nodded curtly. A game of pool seemed like the only way to avoid calling further attention to herself. She stood, deliberately keeping her back toward Reardon and the bar. She appraised her adversary with a cold stare.

> *Oh, these boys won't let me be,*
> *Lord, have mercy on me,*
> *Oh, woe is me!*

"Eight ball?" Sara asked.

The woman nodded.

"You're on." She went to the pool table, actually looking forward to the game. It had been a long time. When she was a little girl, she had learned how to play from her father and his buddies at NCO clubs around the world.

She quickly glanced at James Reardon, her face hidden by the pool table's overhanging fluorescent, and saw that he was still at the bar. She looked back; her opponent was gazing at her legs. Her skin started to feel dirty. She frowned, went to the rack of cue sticks, selected a number fourteen cue, made sure that it was true, and chalked up. Then she dispensed powder onto her hands, making them smooth for an easier stroke.

Her opponent was engaged in animated conversation with her older friend and didn't notice.

"Break?" Sara asked.

"Naw. You go ahead," she replied generously. "You ought to get in at least one shot."

Her friends laughed raucously.

Sara stalked to the head of the table, leaned over the faded green, and carefully lined up the cueball with the rack. She noticed that her opponent had taken a stance at the other end of the table so that she could look down her blouse. Sara gritted her teeth and shot hard. The cueball blasted the rack apart. Six balls dropped—four solids and two stripes. The other woman paled and was astonished. Her friends were silent. Sara straightened up and smiled demurely after a nervous glance told her that James Reardon was still alone at the bar. Then she continued shooting. She took her time, concentrating hard on each shot. She didn't miss. Soon all that remained were her opponent's stripes and the eight ball. Sara checked that Reardon was still there, then contemplated her final position. A three-rail bank would win it. She quickly sighted and calculated the angles. She gestured at the far corner pocket with her stick, chalked up, leaned, aimed, and shot. The eight ball caromed down the table, miraculously zigzagging through the striped balls, and finally dropped into the far corner pocket like it lived there.

Sara grinned with pleasure. It was nice to know that she could still run the table if she had half an inclination. She looked at her stunned challenger. "I guess your momma never warned you about broads who put powder on their hands." She turned and glanced back at the bar.

Reardon was gone.

* * *

"Oh, *damn!* Not again!" Sara ran to her table, grabbed her purse, and bolted out of the Palmetto Club. She was blinded momentarily by the sunlight, then surprised; Reardon's car was still parked on the street, and he was nowhere in sight. She started to panic, then forced herself to visualize the scene in the bar. James Reardon had been looking at his watch. That didn't necessarily mean that he had been waiting for someone. Of course! He was checking the time because he was meeting someone somewhere *else*. And he had left his Porsche parked out front because he didn't want anyone to know that he had left the Palmetto Club.

The corner was too obvious, so Sara turned and hurried down the gap between the two buildings, vaulting over and around some trash cans. She came out into an alley just in time to see Reardon slide into a red-and-white taxi. She ran back to her car, got in, started it, pulled out into the traffic and turned right on Navy. As she gunned past the alley, one glance told her that she'd guessed right; she saw the cab a block up the alley, turning left. She spun right on Pacific, accelerated, and finally caught the taxi a half-mile north as it curved onto the Pacific Coast Highway. Sara laid back a little so that her presence wouldn't become obvious. She lit a cigarette and wondered about Reardon. Why was he covering his tracks? Decoying? She frowned. All this for an illicit love affair?

Reardon continued north on the highway for another fifteen miles. Just when Sara was beginning to relax, the taxi made a quick turn across the southbound lanes and into the Malibu-by-the-Sea Motel, a series of Art Deco weekend resort cabins that had been built before anyone figured that the land would be worth anything. Because of oncoming traffic, Sara was forced to drive north for another half-mile before she could make a U-turn. She went south, but stopped before she reached the motel office. She left the Pinto behind a pine grove, grabbed her camera, then rushed up a hill that rose between the cabins and the Pacific. She knelt down in a thicket of shrubs and looked around. The taxi was parked down the road from the motel, and Reardon was hurrying toward one of the cabins. He didn't bother to check in at the office. Sara got several zoom-shots of him approaching and entering number two. She gulped and straightened up. This was it; this was why Helen Reardon had paid her. Now, even though she was reluctant to, she might as well get down there, sneak up to the window, and get a few pictures. No matter how many times she had done it before, she didn't enjoy this part. It made her feel like a blackmailing voyeur.

She went down the hill through the dried-out tumbleweeds. The brush scratched her legs, drawing blood; she cursed herself for wearing a skirt. She hopped a rusty wire fence and ran through some ice plant to the cabin. She paused to catch her breath and heard the surf, its pounding muffled by the hill. The afternoon sea breeze blew through her hair and for a moment she felt silly sneaking up to the bathroom window. She should be out on the beach in a bikini without a care in the world. That was the image; unfortunately it did not fit.

She carefully pushed the window open, grateful that it was unlocked and didn't squeak. The bottom of the window was higher than her head, so she pulled two cinderblocks out of the border of an overgrown garden and propped them up against the cabin. She stepped up and peered inside. James Reardon was there, slumped on the bed, talking in low tones to someone else. Then she gasped and stepped back off the cinder-blocks. Now she knew why the paragon of a well-respected, professional black man had been so troubled. Now she knew why he had been so secretive. James Reardon was seeing another man.

Four

Sara blushed with embarrassment. She turned and leaned against the cabin. She never would have guessed that James Reardon was a homosexual. She didn't particularly care one way or the other, but that certainly explained the caution, the decoy, and the motel in Malibu. True, she could be witnessing an act of white-collar crime, but that was doubtful. And if this were a drug deal, it would have been over with a long time ago. Moreover, no self-respecting crook of *any* genre would leave a taxi waiting out front.

Poor Mrs. Reardon, she thought, *that poor lady.* To find out that your husband was cheating on you was one thing, but to find out that he was doing it with another man . . . She shuddered. The lady wouldn't believe her. She would have to prove her discovery. She was going to have to photograph the two men together.

She mounted the cinderblocks again, then rested her lens on the windowsill and waited for the traffic noise to pick up so they wouldn't hear the sound of the camera. *Focus. Click.* Reardon remained seated on the bed, talking to his hands. He projected an intensity that puzzled Sara. The other man came into her picture. *Focus. Click.* He wore a suit, was around forty-three, balding, smoked a pipe, and had a slight paunch. He paced back and forth, and listened. Sara stopped taking pictures and suppressed a giggle. If this was a typical rendezvous between consenting male adults, then society didn't have a damned thing to worry about. She might as well have brought Valerie along. Then the other man spoke, and Sara could overhear the conversation.

"That's impossible! That's the most incredible thing I've ever heard."

"You've got to help me, Alan!"

"Let me think about it."

"*Think* about it? What do you mean, think about it? Come on, man, we go back a long ways together!"

"I know that, James, but still I'm going to need some sort of proof. After all, I have my own reputation to think of."

"You'll get it."

"Then call me tomorrow."

She leaned further into the window to hear better, shifting her weight in the process. Suddenly the cinderblocks slipped out from under her feet. She fell, her camera and chin slamming into the windowsill on the way down. She scrambled up and ignored her aching jaw.

Without thinking, she grabbed the cinderblocks and dropped them back into the garden border that she had originally disrupted. Then she dove for the side of the cabin, huddled there, and cradled her camera as if it were a small bird with a broken wing. Luckily it was not damaged. She peeked and saw Reardon squinting out the bathroom window, looking concerned.

"Was this window open when you first got here?"

"I don't know," the other man replied. "I didn't look."

"Well, why the hell didn't you?"

"Oh, come on now. You're just being paranoid."

"Am I? You heard that, didn't you?"

"Heard what?"

"That noise. That scraping noise."

"I didn't hear anything."

"I'm getting out of here. I'll call you tomorrow."

The door slammed once. Twice. She slipped around to the front of the cabin. Reardon was walking away, heading toward the cab. His partner pocketed something—was it a small cassette or was she just imagining things?

Sara drove south along the coast highway and wondered what she would tell Mrs. Reardon. She could imagine what her report might sound like. *Hey, I've got some good news and some bad news. The bad news is that your old man is in some kind of trouble, and the good news is that he's not a homosexual.* Better not to say anything at all. Better to wait until tomorrow when she would find out what was happening.

She sighed. Right now she needed a break. The day was beautiful, and there was no reason to spoil the rest of it. She turned off the highway and bounced down a narrow road that needed repaving. She drove through wind-bent pines and came out on a broad plain with a row of houses that bordered on the beach. She was going to see Sam Gage; she always visited him when she needed to relax and get away from the day-to-day pressures. His house was at the end of the road, a fitting location. For it had become a refuge to her, a shelter from the storm. Like Sam himself.

Her spirits soared when she saw the place. It was an old, rambling structure, half-hidden by thickets of bamboo and bougainvillaea, yet the house sparkled, for Sam kept it in good shape. Recently he had painted the trim a dark brown, the rest white. Since he worked only periodically as a lifeguard for the county, he never would have been able to afford the place if he hadn't inherited it from his father. He steadfastly refused inflated offers from real-estate brokers to buy the property. They became hysterical when they learned that he owned the house clear. But why should he sell? He was contented; he had his roots there. Sara expected him to spend the rest of his life in the house.

She parked in front of the dead end, left her car unlocked, and hurried along a stone path toward the wooden gate. She hadn't seen Sam in a month or two, though she wondered why she stayed away so long. After all, she really adored the man. Originally he had been Andy's best friend in college. She and Sam never talked about that part of his life, because she always suspected that Sam had loved her from the beginning but had sacrificed his own feelings to remain friends with Andy. She *did* know that they had been opposites and thus very close friends. Andy had been the zealous one, the enthusiastic go-getter. Sam had been the wanderer who had discovered early on the ultimate complexity: the simple life. Each had considered the other a wellspring of understanding, although Andy could never fully understand why Sam didn't want to grab a chunk of the world for himself. Despite philosophic differences the two had been brothers in spirit, and Andy's death had affected Sam as much as it had Sara.

She pulled a string to unlatch the gate and pushed through into a walled patio of old bricks. A lemon tree lived in one corner, spider plants in the other. She crossed the courtyard and went into the house.

Their own friendship had started with Sam's being the protector of his best friend's widow. It had remained on that level for several years, until Sara realized that Sam was the only one in the world that she could really talk to. He became a sounding board for most of her thoughts, although she could never bring herself to tell him about the nightmares. Ultimately he accepted her struggle to raise a daughter and remain dependent only upon her own resources, although she didn't think that he—or any man—would ever fully understand why.

Sex was inevitable. The first time had not been pleasant; they had been drinking tequila and instead of letting herself enjoy it, Sara got these erotic images of Sam and Andy all jumbled up inside her head. For one horrible moment she had equated lovemaking with death.

Since then she had realized that she was a mature woman with certain needs and that she could not ignore part of herself. Moreover, she realized that Andy himself would not have expected anything less of her. So her sex life improved, although it never seemed easy, fluid, or spontaneous. She was never quite comfortable enough with Sam. Their lovemaking was good, but he wasn't Andy. Somehow the memory of her late husband always seemed to inhibit her.

Nevertheless Sara and Sam remained lovers and companions. And when they began to fit, to go well together, she was afraid that he would ask her to marry him. He hadn't, but he did invite her and Valerie to move in for the duration. She had been tempted but eventually refused. She wanted to resolve Andy's death before embarking on a new life. Sam was disappointed, but he seemed willing to wait indefinitely. With a shrug and a grin he had commented that he'd just have to learn to appreciate his solitude.

She was sure that he had. She smiled. He lived alone with two cats.

Sam was not inside the house. Sara crossed the large living room and went through French doors that opened onto another patio. Beyond were sand dunes covered with clumps of ice plant. She knew that she would find him there—in the dunes, where it was still warm because the breeze blew over the top.

He was lying down with his chin up on one elbow, watching the sunset. The sky was pink and red and blue and in some places lavender. The moon was rising, too, now yellow on the pastel horizon. Sara stopped short of interrupting him. She knelt in the sand, swept her hair back with her fingers, and smiled wistfully. *Andy would've enjoyed this. He would've liked the colors, but Andy isn't here anymore.* She closed her eyes and shook her head until her mind cleared. Then she looked at Sam. Since he didn't know that she was there, she had an opportunity to study him. As usual, he wore only a pair of cut-offs, and she couldn't understand why he never got cold. His skin was tanned dark brown and always peeling from the sun. His arms and legs were naturally bowed; though he did not have a swimmer's body, he could stay in the water for hours. His hair was the same color as his skin, only now it sported touches of gray. And his angular face was prematurely wrinkled and always looked thoughtful. Overall he looked like a young ship's captain who had sense enough to stay on shore.

"Hello, Sam," she said in her best gravelly tone.

He turned and looked rather expressionlessly for a moment. "Sara." Then he grinned broadly. "Hey! I was going to call. Where have you been anyway?"

"The same old places." She smiled softly. He got to his feet and she went up to him. He kissed her affectionately, and then they embraced. For a fleeting moment she wished that she had the courage to give up everything and stay with this man. "Oh, Sam."

"You been okay?"

"I finally got another job."

"You always knew you would."

She looked up at him. "Sam, this time I really *didn't.*"

He laughed, leaned away, but held on to her by her hips. "Anything interesting?"

"Two guys in a motel room."

"Jesus. You had to watch?"

"That's what I thought at first, too, but I don't think they were gay. One guy had a story to tell. The other guy said it was incredible."

"What was the story?"

"I don't know. I guess I'll have to find out, as long as I'm being paid."

"You mean you actually stopped off to see me in the middle of a case?"

She shrugged. "I was in the neighborhood, and I wanted to spend some time with you."

"I'm impressed."

"Besides, there won't be any more developments until the man I'm following calls his friend tomorrow."

"A*ha!* The truth comes out! You're not hot on someone's trail right now because someone else said time out."

"Sam!" she protested.

He was serious again. "Whatever you do, take care of yourself. Promise?"

"I promise."

He took her hand and started toward the house. "Can you stay for some dinner?"

"Valerie's expecting me."

"She's okay by herself, isn't she?"

"She's only twelve."

"She'd rather be by herself, then."

"Yeah, but I get worried." Sara kicked at the sand.

"Is there someone you can call. I mean, what about Mrs. Berman? She still watches the kid for you, doesn't she?"

She smiled at him impishly. "You've done this before."

He nodded. "There's this lady that keeps coming around, you see. And she looks just like my favorite female vocalist."

"Now *that's* a compliment." She took his face in her hands and kissed him. Their lips lingered together, and she felt the tension drain from her body. She had been away too long. She remembered when she used to see Sam once a week—so that she could complain about what her shrink had been telling her. She chuckled.

They went inside. Sam moved over to the great old stone fireplace and began laying a fire. Meanwhile Sara called Mrs. Berman. The old lady was delighted that Sara was spending the evening with Sam. Valerie would be no problem at all. Sara hung up and frowned. Sometimes Mrs. Berman seemed just a little *too* accommodating.

Sara went into the kitchen and started preparing a salad, one of the few culinary things she could do really well. Sam joined her. He opened a bottle of white wine, poured two glasses, then made hamburgers with cheese in the center, a specialty he had learned from his father.

"Perfect," she said while chopping a cucumber. "White wine and hamburgers."

"Yeah. I know. I'm such a romantic devil."

They laughed.

After dinner they lay in front of a quiet fire and sipped wine. Sam stroked her back and she gazed into

the coals, totally content, her face flushed from the
heat.

"Don't ever give up on me, Sam—please?"

"Why should I?"

"Don't you get tired of waiting?"

"Hell, no."

She turned and looked at him askance.

"I mean, things aren't too bad the way they are."

"What do you mean?"

He grinned. "I don't see very much of you anymore."

"You're a real comedian, Sam," she said sarcastically. "And here I thought you were going to sweet-
talk me right out of my clothes."

"What I meant was, if you're not around, then I
can't take you for granted."

Her eyes opened wide and she laughed with surprise. "You *are* a silver-throated fox, aren't you?"

They kissed gently. She turned and let her body fall
against his. Her nipples tingled where they touched
his chest. It always started this way. She lay back on
the hearth, put her hands under her head, and closed
her eyes. He reached under her shirt and gently
touched her breasts. Lulled, she imagined she was
swaying. Then Sam moved his hand to her belly and
traced out words with his fingertips. She couldn't
translate what he was writing, but it didn't matter.
She laughed lightly. One of the things she really liked
about him was that he always made love with a sense
of humor, thus imposing a slight distance. She supposed that it wouldn't work any other way.

"Wouldn't you rather be riding a mule on Molokai?"
he whispered into her ear.

"No, Sam, I wouldn't."

"In that case . . ."

They undressed each other. Sara thought vaguely

that his bed would be more comfortable, then forgot about it. This was much more romantic. More fun. She admired his body, now silhouetted by the fire. It looked weathered, but powerful. He knelt in front of her, smiling. She touched his face and when he put his finger over her lips, she bit it playfully. Then he came down to her and she pulled him inside her and kissed him deeply, hoping that for once the bliss would overwhelm her. She caressed his back. His muscles were hard; they felt clean. *This time. Maybe this time.*

No.

She realized that her responses were mechanical. She couldn't get it quite right. She shuddered but not with passion. *Andy. The memories, they wouldn't go away.* Tension was building inside her head. She was angry at herself for conjuring up those images at a time like this, but she couldn't shake them. She wanted to scream out in frustration but concentrated instead on matching his movements, which were coming faster now. She longed to catch his passion and let it consume her. If only . . .

She lifted her hips. She strained but could not force it. The moment passed. She fell back and accommodated him.

Sara felt good when she left, despite her vague disappointment. As she drove south on the coast highway she listened to the eleven o'clock news on the radio. The feature story was the governor's quick campaign swing through the southland and his controversial speeches in East Los Angeles and Venice, where he called for an unconditional federal amnesty for all "undocumented immigrants" who had been living in the state of California for more than five years. The real bombshell came, however, when he stated that he defended the state attorney general's decision that there would be no further prosecution of recently acquitted labor leader Carlos Espinosa. In the governor's opinion, fresh allegations of jury-tampering and the intimidation of witnesses were simply not supported by the evidence. He did not comment on the unexplained deaths of dissenting farmworkers which had prompted the original charges against Espinosa. Sara turned off the radio. Politics seemed unfathomable. Unreal.

She hadn't liked saying good-bye to Sam, but there was no way she could ignore her responsibilities. Namely, Valerie. But deep down Sara realized that her daughter wasn't the only reason she left Sam. She would love to sleep with him and wake up in his arms sometime. Just once, even. But what if she had one of her bad nights? What if she woke up screaming? She shuddered at the thought.

She drove faster, wondering about Valerie again. She was sure that Mrs. Berman had put the child to bed and that everything was fine. Still, she got nervous if she was away for too long. After all, Venice was Venice, wasn't it?

She left her car parked in front of the apartment complex instead of in its usual place behind her office building. She hurried upstairs, let herself in, and was relieved to see Mrs. Berman on the couch. She bid the old lady good night, then went in to see her daughter. Valerie was curled up in bed, looking angelic. She had fallen asleep over a thick Gothic romance. Sara smiled and was overcome with tenderness. Right then she loved Valerie more than anything else in the world. *There's nothing more beautiful than a child sleeping peacefully, especially when the little girl is your own.* She went over to her daughter and gently pulled the covers up to her chin. Valerie stirred in her sleep.

"Night, Val," Sara whispered softly. She turned off

the bedside lamp, then padded into the kitchen for a glass of water before she went to bed. She saw that Valerie had left a note taped to the refrigerator next to the usual grocery list. It read: "You're already forgiven for not taking me to see Sam, too. I hope at least you said hi for me. I said hi to Mrs. Berman for you. No phone calls. I hid your Shermans in the freezer. The binomial theorem is a breeze. Luv, Valerie. OOOXXX."

Sara was delighted. She folded up the message, intending to save it. And before she left the kitchen, she taped up her own reply. "You're a peach! Luv, You-Know-Who."

Then she went to bed and for a long time just lay there, reviewing the day and thinking fondly of Sam. She wondered if he would make a good father for Valerie. He seemed to have infinite patience. She wondered if . . .

Sleep came over her and she did not dream.

The next morning when Sara got out of bed and saw the scratches on her legs from the tumbleweeds, she decided on combat clothes. So, after her quick shower, she donned a dark-brown blouse, faded jeans, boots, and her corduroy hat. She brewed coffee, made a succinct entry in her diary, then briefly stared at *Thursday, September 25.* What would this day bring?

She drove to the Reardon home in the Palisades, parked down the street, poured coffee, lit a cigarette, smoked, and waited. At eight thirty James Reardon left his home, the picture of distress. He looked gray and haunted. He got into his Porsche and drove off. Sara followed him easily. He parked in his usual spot under the medical building, but instead of going straight to his office, detoured to a Shell station on the corner. She watched him go into the phone booth.

Why would he call from a pay phone when his office was just next door? Simple. He didn't want the number he was calling on his phone record. He probably didn't want anyone listening in, either. Interesting. She knew that he hadn't discovered the bug on his receptionist's phone because it was still working.

Reardon hung up and immediately made another call. Sara nodded shrewdly. The first call had been placed to whomever Reardon had met in the Malibu motel, for he had said that he would call the next day. Label him man A. The second one was to another person that man A had turned Reardon on to. (For help, perhaps?) Label him person B. And person B was probably at the other end of a long-distance call, because she saw Reardon drop a whole series of quarters into the box. He talked for a good five minutes.

Then he made a *third* call. Man A, person B. . . . *Hmmm,* she thought. *What was this phone call about? And to whom?* Someone local, perhaps. A person C maybe?

Reardon finally went up to his office. Sara waited in her car by the parking-lot exit and listened to the tap on the receptionist's phone. Nothing was happening, although the receptionist's voice sounded hysterical. Sara figured that the woman was upset because Reardon hadn't even said good morning to her.

A half hour later Reardon's Porsche suddenly hurled up and out of the parking lot. He turned left, then left again, tires squealing, and rocketed off, going east on San Vicente. Sara was amazed. It was only a little after ten.

She started the Pinto and raced away from the curb. She ignored the stop sign and swung onto the boulevard, narrowly threading her way between a line of oncoming cars and a smog-belching RTD bus. There were the usual irate screams and blaring horns, but she went right on by and caught Reardon just as he turned east on Wilshire, although she had to run a red light to do it.

He maneuvered through three lanes of cars and got onto the northbound San Diego Freeway. Sara followed, concentrating hard. Chasing an erratically driven Porsche wasn't so easy. Reardon stepped on it and began weaving through traffic. He was going at least seventy-five, and there were no highway patrol officers in sight. Sara cursed and bit her lip nervously. The man was driving like a maniac. She hoped that he wouldn't kill himself. Or her.

He turned onto the Ventura Freeway, still speeding and zigzagging from lane to lane. Sara stayed right with him, concerned that he might have realized he was being followed. Then she shook her head. She knew what evasive driving was, no matter how badly done. Reardon wasn't trying to lose her. He was just in a hurry to get somewhere.

He left the freeway at Vineland and went north. It slowly dawned on her that she knew where he was going. *Sure, that was it—the phone calls he made.* If the second one had been long distance and Reardon had wanted to continue the conversation *in person,* then he certainly wouldn't have left town on a skateboard. The third call had been for reservations.

She was proud of her logic. Reardon had led her to the Hollywood-Burbank Airport. She wouldn't be left behind, either; she was prepared for such eventualities. She always carried an overnight bag in the trunk.

Reardon turned into the parking lot just before the terminal, took a ticket at the automatic gate, then drove toward the multi-level parking garage. Sara slowed down, timing it so she was entering the lot just as he disappeared inside. She went through the gate and sped down the lane, but just before she got to the

ramp, a neon sign flashed SORRY, LEVELS FULL, and a
red arrow directed her to park outside somewhere on
the asphalt. She frowned, followed the detour, but
was relieved when she found a space very close by.
She got out, hurried around to the Pinto's trunk, unlocked it, and lifted out her overnight bag. Slamming
the trunk closed, she turned and ran into the parking
garage, hoping that she wouldn't lose Reardon again.
Her eyes swept over the ground level and did not see
his Porsche. He must have parked up on level two
or three. Suddenly she stopped and turned in a complete circle, scanning the area once more. The sign
at the entrance had said that the enclosed parking was
all taken. Then why did she see at least ten empty
spaces? She looked at another sign, this one above the
up ramp. This one flashed USE LEVEL TWO. For a
moment she was puzzled. Something was wrong, wasn't
it? She sprinted to the stairs, went up, but grew cautious when she reached the door to the second level.
She slipped through it and eased into the shadows so
that she would not be seen. Her heart pounded. Curiously no one was on the second level except for a
short, slim lady with long, dark hair who was wearing
the dusty-rose jumper of a PSA stewardess. She was
carrying a shopping bag and had her back turned to
Sara. Why was she standing there—on the edge of a
half-empty parking level partially hidden by a pillar?
Was she waiting for James Reardon? There was an
eerie silence, and then Sara heard a trunk snap closed.
She moved to her left and saw James Reardon leave
his Porsche and start toward the elevators at the other
end. Something told her not to follow right away. She
waited; she noticed that he was carrying his briefcase
and a small suitcase. His shoes scuffed on the concrete
and the footfalls did not echo.

Sara glanced back at the stewardess, who was also

watching Reardon intently. She spoke into a tiny two-way radio, and Sara knew for certain that something awful was happening. She heard a car starting down below, screeching tires, and then the hard, urgent sound of an engine accelerating much too fast for the inside of a parking garage. Before she could warn him, a car catapulted up the ramp and roared toward Reardon at high speed. She gasped with horror. He turned; his face was a mask of surprise and terror. He was caught in the open like a stray dog in the middle of an interstate highway. He hesitated, not knowing what to do. He raised his arms as if to protect himself and screamed, but the sound could not be heard over the loud whine of the engine. He dodged two steps to his left and then the car hit him.

For a split second he was pinned to the right front fender, arms flailing. Then the car crushed him against the wall.

He fell to the concrete, his chest and midsection flattened. The car swung to its left, fishtailed away from the wall, and vanished down the exit ramp.

Reardon had been set up. Now he was dead.

Five

Sara was paralyzed. Time stopped. There was a sudden hush, a feeling of isolation. Her mind filled with images of Reardon being murdered in slow motion. *He hit the wall with a thud, then smacked down onto the concrete like Andy had at the Taco Bell.* The images overlapped and blurred together. The nightmare had become reality all over again, and she fell to her knees retching, too sick even to scream. If this was life, she wanted to die. Yes, why didn't the car come back so that she might throw herself under its wheels and end her miserable existence? *Wait a minute! That car . . .* She put her face in her hands and moaned with terror. She would never forget the molded shape of the car that had taken Andy's killers away from the scene. Was the car that had crushed James Reardon the same kind? The same one? Or was she making connections that did not exist? She opened her eyes and looked up. The parking level reeled in front of her. Reardon's body had not moved. She blinked. *He and Andy were one. The car lurched away down the side-street. The car fishtailed across the parking level, then vanished down the ramp.* The images repeated, split apart, came together, finally faded like dust on the wind. She gasped for breath, shut her eyes tightly, and fought to control her mind. *Get ahold of yourself, Sara. The car, the coincidence— it's nothing more than a hallucination. That's the only logical conclusion.* She nodded quickly. *I have witnessed two deaths in my lifetime. A car was involved in each of them. If I had seen ten deaths and a car had been involved in each of them, then that still would not be unusual. But the shape,* an inner voice cried, *that car . . .* Sara drove the notion back into her subconscious, then gathered her strength and stood up.

Suddenly there was the sound of many cars in the parking garage, most of them on the entrance ramp below, but none of them had reached level two yet. Sara guessed that the neon signs were working correctly again. Her mind was clear now, and she looked in front of her. Virtually no time had passed since Reardon had been crushed and the car had vanished. She started to dash toward Reardon's body when she heard the click-clack of wooden heels on the concrete. She turned and saw the PSA stewardess also hurrying toward the body. The stewardess grabbed both the briefcase and the suitcase, stuffed them into her shopping bag, then started away.

"Hey, *wait!*" Sara yelled.

The stewardess spun around, looked back at Sara and blinked. She was astonished. *Caught.* And then she ran for the elevators. Sara went after her, moving hard down an aisle. When she saw that she wasn't going to beat her to the elevators, she took a shortcut through the interminable rows of cars. One hand frantically dug for La Belle in her purse. With the other she guided her way forward, then vaulted off the front fender of a car into another aisle. She managed to shorten the distance considerably, but when she finally got her pistol out, the lady had vanished into the stairwell behind the elevators.

Sara charged down the steps, but the brief chase had taken its toll. She came out on the ground level panting and cursing herself for her smoking habit. The stewardess was a good seventy-five yards away, hurrying into the main terminal, effortlessly swinging the large shopping bag as if it were full of stuffed animals.

Must be a goddamned track star, Sara muttered to herself. She raised her pistol, aimed, then lowered it, realizing that if she fired, she'd be in real trouble. She wisely put La Belle back into her purse. Then she sprinted for the main terminal, determined not to lose her.

Once inside, she headed for the reservation desks, dodging around knots of people. She thought she saw her and was about to yell for her to stop when, much to her dismay, she saw half a dozen PSA stewardesses, all going in different directions. Sara stopped and considered the situation. *Where would she go? To a lounge? No. A gate? Yeah.* To a flight that was just leaving—the perfect escape.

Sara ran across the main lobby and turned up a long corridor which opened into a concourse. There were lots of people around; several airliners were loading and unloading.

Aha! *There* was the stewardess—up ahead, standing in line for the walk-through x-ray security check. She was short and slim, and she carried a large shopping bag, but her long, dark hair was what gave her away. Sara came up behind her and grabbed the shopping bag.

The stewardess turned. "I beg your pardon?"

She pulled away, but Sara hung on to the bag. It ripped. The contents spilled out onto the floor, and a bag and a briefcase weren't among them. Surprised, Sara looked at the stewardess's face and realized that she had accosted the wrong person.

"What in the *world* do you think you're *doing?*"

Sara hurried back the way she had come, her chin held high. She paid no attention to the stares of the bystanders who had seen her molesting a stewardess, but she was relieved when she was out of the terminal. She was angry with herself, though. She hadn't been able to catch the one person she knew to be part of a conspiracy. She hadn't even had the presence of mind to read the license number of the car that had killed Reardon. But the vehicle had just *appeared!* It had . . . *So what if it happened fast, Sara? You're supposed to be a professional!*

She began shaking as she waited to cross the street. Was the car that crushed Reardon the same one that had been at the scene of Andy's death? No. That was impossible. Then why had it seemed the same? She must find out. But how? Her jaw muscles tightened; her eyes narrowed with determination. How else?

By solving James Reardon's murder.

The Burbank police had arrived in force and sealed off the entire parking area. As a result traffic was at a standstill. Bewildered drivers didn't know where to go or what to do, so most of them just stopped. Horns blared. No one paid any attention to a white-gloved policeman who tried to sort through the mess of cars.

Sara crossed the street and ambled along, acting like a curious bystander. The police were interviewing everyone who left the parking lot. They took license numbers. Off to the side lounged a team of paramedics, not needed. She overheard a sergeant complaining about hit-and-run fatalities. He was frustrated by the apparent lack of witnesses. Well, she wasn't about to talk to them. She recalled that Andy's notes were still lost somewhere in police archives. Just for that reason she probably would never learn if there was a connection between his death and James Reardon's. She had no way of knowing what Andy had done during his final days. Thus there was no evidence that she could base a comparison on. And the police were to blame for that.

She watched them wheel Reardon's body out of the parking garage and load it into an ambulance. The ambulance left, followed by several squad cars. Most of the police remained, and Sara saw a heated discussion between an officious lieutenant and a slim, blond-haired man who wore the brown uniform of airport security. She moved closer so that she could hear.

"Why wasn't I consulted on this?" asked the security officer.

"Technically this parking lot is in our jurisdiction," the lieutenant replied.

"Yeah? Well, I want it opened up right now." He gestured at the traffic jam. "Those people don't have any place to park!"

"We're conducting an investigation. There's been a hit-and-run homicide. Now will you get away from me?"

After the police had finished and gone away, traffic returned to normal. Sara finally left the airport, feeling guilty. She had been following Reardon for two and a half days, observing his strange behavior. Why hadn't she anticipated something more serious than an illicit love affair, especially when his haunted air of preoccupation had reminded her of her own? After all, she had known that Reardon had been going somewhere in a hurry to tell someone something. The man Reardon had met called the information incredible.

Sara knew at once—that was where she would begin. The Malibu-by-the-Sea Motel.

But first things first. No matter how distasteful, there was unfinished business to tend to. She pulled into a gas station. After the car was gassed up, she went into the phone booth and closed the door.

"Hello?"

"Mrs. Reardon?"

"Who's this?"

"Sara Scott."

"Oh, great, I was hoping you'd call. I've been worried. So what's up?"

"Do you mind if I come by your place? This isn't something I can say over the phone."

Helen Reardon wouldn't stop crying. She was sitting across from Sara in her bright country kitchen, folded over the oak table, her face in her hands, her body racked with sobs. Sara held her arm and hand tightly, and for the moment kept silent. She sympathized, recalling her own grief when Andy was killed. She had been on the brink of madness then. She had been in the awful position of loving and depending on someone who was no longer alive. She didn't want to know—but she understood her helpless despair.

"What will happen now?" Helen Reardon whispered.

"The police will come."

"Then I can bury my husband?"

"Yes."

"And then I'll really be alone." Her voice trailed off.

"Mrs. Reardon. Please."

"I don't even feel like crying anymore. I just . . . feel . . . *cold.*" She began to shiver uncontrollably. Sara took her coat off the chair and placed it around Mrs. Reardon's shoulders, but it didn't help. Her teeth were chattering. She stuttered and made spasmodic gestures. Her face paled. Sara knew that she must do something. Helen Reardon was going into shock.

So Sara talked quietly of life and death. She mentioned the early years with Andy and how she had quit college to marry him when she was nineteen. Everything was so simple then. She found it easy to lie back and let him make the decisions, especially after Valerie arrived. She became totally dependent and loved it. Her existence, except for the minor irritations of childrearing, might as well have been perfect.

Then came that horrible night. October 7, 1976. Everything changed. She was forced to survive on her own. She had to get a job and later, when it became a career, there were even more troubles. So, she understood what Helen was feeling.

When Helen Reardon finally looked up, eyebrows raised in a question, Sara nodded and told her that, yes, her own husband had been murdered four years ago.

Mrs. Reardon was more resigned than stunned. Her grief sobered her and she seemed to accept the situation. She asked for a cigarette. Sara gave her a Sherman, then lit one for herself. They smoked in silence for a while. Sara could feel a closeness developing between them, a bond. It suddenly occurred to her—no matter how improbable it seemed—that they now had a common cause. Sara placed her hands on Helen Reardon's shoulders. "You're going to be all right."

She nodded almost imperceptibly and wiped her

eyes dry. "How could I have doubted him, anyway?"
She straightened up and looked at Sara. Her face was
anguished, but her voice was steadier and more controlled. "What could I have been thinking of? I mean,
just last night I told him that I had to know what was
going on!"

"What did he say?"

"That I shouldn't worry. That I should get together
with the girls or something."

"I'm sorry."

"I pushed it, though. I kept after him and finally
I accused him of cheating on me. For a moment he
was hurt. Then he got ugly. I didn't know what to do.
He started shouting at me!"

"What was he—?"

"He kept saying that he didn't want me involved."

"That's all?" Sara asked. Her voice sounded tiny
and far away. Andy had told her the same thing just
before he was killed. She shuddered.

"That's all." Mrs. Reardon sighed heavily. "It certainly doesn't matter anymore, does it?"

"You can look at it that way if you want to."

"Well?" Her voice quavered. "How did you handle
it?"

"Not very well." Sara put out her cigarette, her
mind racing, her hand trembling. "Mrs. Reardon, I
want to find out who killed your husband and why."

"But . . . but what about the police?"

"They'll tell you that James Reardon was killed
accidentally by a hit-and-run driver."

"Won't . . . won't you tell them otherwise?"

"If it comes to that. But they won't believe me. Or
you."

"What do you mean?"

"There is no motive. If there was any evidence, it
was taken by a girl in a stewardess's uniform. All we

can say is that your husband was behaving strangely and meeting another man in a motel room."

Mrs. Reardon scowled. "That doesn't sound very pretty."

"I'm sorry. I think it's best if we just leave the police out of it for now."

Mrs. Reardon sighed heavily again. She seemed relieved, yet strangely distracted. Sara briefly studied her and wondered if she was hiding something.

"I don't know how much I'll be able to afford."

"I'll work for nothing if I have to."

"But why?"

Sara started to tell Mrs. Reardon about the car with the tiny windows and the odd shape, the car that had crushed James Reardon, the car that she thought . . . She hesitated. Mrs. Reardon would think that she was crazy.

"Let's just say that I owe it to you."

"Huh?"

"I should have known your husband was afraid for his life, Mrs. Reardon."

"*I* should have known." She looked down. "Is . . . is there any way I can help?"

"You can go through your husband's things for me. We do need evidence. But whatever you do, don't blame yourself." Sara rose. "I'll call you every day and tell you how I'm doing."

Her client nodded. "All right." Then she forced a smile. "Don't you think it's time that we were on a first-name basis?"

"Sure."

"Good luck, Sara."

They shook hands.

"All due respect, Helen, but I hope I don't need it."

* * *

Sara went back to her apartment. She unloaded the film from her camera, then took a battered metal case out of the closet. Since she was no longer trying to find out if the unfortunate James Reardon had a lover, she doubted that she would need her camera. She smiled at the worn Olympus affectionately; it had always served her well. She put her camera away, then went into the bathroom, which also served as a makeshift darkroom. Carefully she developed and printed the film, then nodded with satisfaction. She had two good pictures of man A—the person Reardon had met at the Malibu motel.

Before she left the apartment, she sorted through her cherished collection of business cards, selecting a plausible temporary identity. Valerie had suggested the gimmick to her after watching James Garner get away with it in *The Rockford Files*. Since then she had habitually picked up business cards. One never knew when one might have to submerge and go incognito. Right now she couldn't think of a better reason than the investigation of James Reardon's murder. She would have to be careful.

Arriving at the Malibu-by-the-Sea Motel, she parked in front, got out, and noticed a shamefaced man in a suit and tie scurrying toward a cabin. A plump black hooker swung alongside him, making loud comments about the great weather and love at the beach. Sara went into the office.

The manager was a small man around fifty with a face that told the world he was an ex-boxer. From the looks of him he had taken quite a few hard left hooks. He seemed completely indifferent to her femininity. That was good; that would make it clean.

"Excuse me, sir. Did this man check into your motel yesterday?" Sara showed him the photographs.

He blinked. "Maybe."

"I'd like his name and address, please."

"Who the hell are you? Wonder Woman?"

"No, but I am with the Federal Bureau of Investigation." She held a business card close to his gnarled face which identified her as Ms. Beverly Gianelli from the Los Angeles field office.

He studied it. "So what?"

"I'd appreciate your cooperation."

"Go tell it to the Marines," he sneered, acting like he'd been waiting for years to say that to someone.

"I don't have their phone number," she replied sweetly, "but I could make a quick call to the vice squad regarding your latest visitor."

He stepped back. "Come on, lady! Give me a break! I have a reputation for protecting my customers!"

"Even if they're foreign agents?"

His eyes widened. He pointed at the photograph. "You mean this man is into espionage?"

She nodded authoritatively. "He works for the oil companies."

The manager whistled, then took a registry card out of a file, held it up, and read it. "Alan Rosenus. I hope you nail the dirty bastard."

"Address?" she asked, Bic pen poised.

"There ain't none."

"What?"

"Look for yourself." He dropped the card on the counter in front of her.

She did. There was a name, a scrawled signature, and in the address space the terse information: *"Los Angeles Times."*

"Oh," she said with surprise. *"That* Alan Rosenus?"

She headed back toward the city with just enough time to get to the newspaper before its offices closed, if traffic was light on the Santa Monica Freeway. Alan Rosenus, huh? She wondered what he would have to say for himself. And James Reardon. Rosenus had been a respected reporter on the *Los Angeles Times*'s political beat for many years. His name was familiar to Sara because Andy had been an avid reader of his articles. Her husband had violently disagreed with almost all of Rosenus's views but had admired his lucid, deft style and his brilliant logic. She smiled wistfully. Andy would probably still feel the same way. Just recently she had read some of Rosenus's opinions. He still stood alone—a beacon of conservative thinking at the edge of the tide. He was sharply opposed to the administration's tax and budget proposals, terming them another "something-for-nothing" step along the road toward an "unworkable society." But he saved his best shots for the governor, calling him the best tap dancer he had ever seen, "especially when he's performing 'The Empty Rhetoric Rag.' " Sara couldn't help laughing—she didn't think that there was anyone or anything in the state government that Rosenus liked. She wondered if he ever had anything good to say about those in power. Then she raised her eyebrows and frowned pensively. Maybe that line of thinking wasn't so damned whimsical. Maybe that was why James Reardon had wanted to talk to Alan Rosenus in the first place. It certainly was a question worth asking him.

She parked near Times-Mirror Square and hurried into the editorial building. In the lobby a receptionist was screening visitors, so Sara waited in the shadows until several other people arrived. While the receptionist was busy talking on the phone and checking credentials, Sara slipped past her and into the elevator. She went up to the city room and sashayed down the rows of desks like she belonged there. Most of the reporters had left for the day, but Sara did spot one diligent young woman pounding away at a typewriter.

"Is Alan Rosenus around?"

"That way." She gestured over her shoulder, barely looking up. "Boardwalk and Park Place."

"Thank you," Sara replied, snitching the woman's business card from the holder next to the nameplate. She kept walking until she came to the partitioned offices where the elite worked. She found Rosenus's cubicle at the end of the corridor and slipped inside. Instead of the political reporter, a droll, sour-faced man with long hair sat behind the desk reading the *Herald-Examiner.*

"Is Mr. Rosenus here?"

The man looked up in surprise. He leaned back and let his eyes linger. "I don't know the tune, but for you I can fake it."

"Huh?"

"Rosenus left a couple of hours ago. A friend of his was accidentally killed this morning. My name's Thomas. Art Thomas. Can I help you with something?" He checked his watch. "Say yes and I'll buy you a drink."

"I really do have to talk to Mr. Rosenus."

"Oh." Thomas shrugged and lost interest. "I doubt that he'll be back until next week. He was pretty shaken."

Sara knew that she couldn't wait that long. She swept her hair back with an idle hand, then pushed it up under her hat. "Maybe I could call Mr. Rosenus at home?"

"Good luck getting his phone number."

"You wouldn't have it, would you?" Sara smiled sweetly while searching Rosenus's desk with her eyes, a move Casparian had once considered patenting.

"Nope." Thomas got up, dropped the newspaper into the trash, and put on his coat, preparing to leave. "Why don't you just leave a note?"

Meanwhile Sara had found what she was looking for. On Rosenus's cluttered desk blotter was an opened envelope from the Mark Taper Forum. She read the front of it upside down. A scrawled note said, "Get two tickets for the 4th." Next to the scrawl was an address: "Mr. & Mrs. Alan Rosenus, 2107 Stanley Hills Drive, Los Angeles 90046." She straightened up. "That's okay. I'll come back."

His eyes narrowed. "Who are you anyway?"

She couldn't resist it. "Penny Lane."

"Huh?"

"You know. Like the song?"

When Sara got back to her car, she dug out her Thomas Brothers map book. A quick check told her that 2107 Stanley Hills Drive was a narrow, winding street that led into the hills above Laurel Canyon.

She maneuvered onto a freeway near downtown Los Angeles with much trepidation. The traffic was backed up in all directions, and the smog made the twilight seem apocalyptic. She realized that she was driving on one of those stretches of the southern California highway system where you really don't know which freeway you're on until—in many cases—it's too late. She steered carefully through six lanes of cars to the Santa Monica freeway interchange, passed up the Santa Ana, Harbor, Hollywood, and Pasadena freeways, and crawled west with several hundred thousand other motorists. She turned her lights on.

An hour later she left the freeway and drove north on La Cienega until it bumped its head into Sunset Strip just past a burnt-out massage parlor. She turned right and made the short jag along Sunset Boulevard past the Continental Hyatt House where, legend had it, more than one frenzied British rock group had ripped the fixtures off the walls for souvenirs. Once beyond the glut of talent agencies and rock-and-roll billboards she turned left onto Laurel Canyon Boulevard. A quarter mile later the city was left behind, and Sara found herself amid giant eucalyptus trees. On she went past the rural digs of well-heeled professionals who craved the tranquility of the canyon yet needed the closeness of the city in order to make a living. Once she and Andy had wanted to live in Laurel Canyon. They were going to move to a small place on Alta Vista with a view, but the landlord said no, preferring the business of a blond-haired cocaine dealer who could afford double the rent that they were willing to pay. They had stayed in Venice. She sighed. *Contradictions.*

Sara went up Stanley Hills Drive in low, her Pinto taking up more than half the road. Entering the two-thousand block, she doused her lights and parked on a private side-street called Kress. Then she slipped an electronic bug into her coat pocket, intending to monitor the private conversations of a respected political reporter for talk of James Reardon. She took La Belle out of her purse, checked the weapon, put it back, then quietly left her car and crept toward the Rosenus house, a good seventy-five yards away. At the edge of a redwood fence she paused to get her bearings. She heard crickets and smelled sage and ivy. For a moment she was reminded of . . . She frowned. Now was no time for memories. Alan Rosenus, despite his reputation, might very well have been involved in the murder of James Reardon. A narrow walkway led through a Japanese garden. She followed it quietly, her boots making no sound on the stone path. She didn't know exactly how to approach Alan Rosenus, other than to be careful to keep her hand inside her purse holding La Belle at all times. She came to a hedge and peered around it. There was a small lawn. Beyond was a wooden porch and the house.

No lights were on.

She paused to think. There was a car parked out front, but that didn't necessarily mean that anyone was home. Maybe she should take a closer look. She glanced around cautiously, took a deep breath and darted across the lawn to the refuge of an oak tree. Thus hidden, she peered at the house again. Curiously, the French doors to the front porch were wide open. Light organdy curtains trembled in the slight breeze that blew through the house. *There must be a window or a door open on the other side,* Sara concluded. She went up the steps, hesitated on the porch, listening. All was quiet. She stared through the doors but could see only blackness.

She waited a minute longer, then decided to take a chance and go inside. It wasn't as if she were really breaking in—Rosenus might as well have left a key in the street. She stepped across the threshold and shivered. Darkness. She could not even see her hand in front of her face. She imagined shapes and sounds and felt cold. What if Rosenus really did have something to do with James Reardon's murder? What if his friend Thomas had called him and he was waiting for her here in the darkness?

A noise.

She gasped and flattened herself against a wall. She listened hard. The noise came again, and it was nothing more than the oak tree brushing against the side of the house in the evening wind.

Nevertheless she took La Belle out of her purse and released the safety. Then she eased along the wall, her right hand groping for a light switch. Her heart was pounding. She couldn't see a damned thing. The silence was oppressive. Yet suddenly she *knew* someone was in the room with her! She felt it and her skin crawled. She began to tremble. She sidestepped along the wall faster. Her foot hit the side of a bookcase and for an instant she thought that the loud report was the sound of a pistol firing. She gasped again and almost went to her knees. Then she arched around the bookcase and came to the corner of the room. Her hand found something cold and metal. It jangled, but she didn't pull away, for it was the cord of a swag lamp. She located the switch and turned it on.

Now the entire length of the room was visible. It had wood paneling and a stone fireplace. In front of her on the floor was a suitcase, its contents dumped out and scattered around. She blinked. She was surprised that she hadn't tripped over the stuff. When she looked past it, she saw a form that at first resembled an oblong pile of clothes. She moved closer. There was blood on the floor. *Oh, God.* She was right. She *had* been in the room with someone, only now that person was a corpse lying face-down in his own blood.

Alan Rosenus had been blugeoned to death with a fire poker.

Six

Recently.

The body was warm and rigor mortis hadn't set in yet. Sara went through Rosenus's pockets but found nothing. Then she discovered that her hands were shaking. She saw that there was blood on them. His She inadvertently caught the scent and was reminded of kneeling beside Andy. Death had touched her again. Though she tried to avert her eyes, she was compelled to stare at the corpse. She gasped. Had the body moved, or was it her imagination? Something clicked inside her head. *Andy was lying in front of her, dying. He grunted, then hissed, his strength ebbing away. He went limp, merging with the concrete. His aura rose and left him. The blood around his corpse turned black.* The recollection vanished, and Sara realized that she was quietly sobbing, trying to embrace the limp body of Alan Rosenus. She lurched back; her knees were wet with his blood. Her stomach churned. She gagged, scrambled to her feet and ran to the door for fresh air. She stood there, her chest heaving, wanting to leave, but knowing that she couldn't. There was detective work to be done. No matter how ghoulish, she must investigate.

There would be clues. Keys. Pieces to the puzzle.

And this was one crime that she was either going to solve or die trying. She dug into her purse, took out her gloves, and put them on. Then she strode resolutely back into the room. She walked over to the suitcase and began examining the contents. They seemed to have been packed in a hurry. None of the clothes had been properly folded. At the bottom of the pile was a small cassette player. She inspected it, then went through the clothes again and the compartments along the side of the suitcase. She frowned. No cassettes. She sat back, closed her eyes and thought a moment. That was it. Rosenus *had* recorded the conversation with Reardon in the Malibu motel room. And that cassette undoubtedly would supply the motive for both murders. Thus Rosenus's cassette equaled Reardon's briefcase. Both contained incriminating evidence. Both were in the hands of the killers. The motive for this particular murder, then? Simple. Rosenus knew what Reardon knew.

Which was . . .

She sighed and got to her feet. Which was what she, Sara Scott, was going to have to unravel for herself.

She went over to a desk in the corner of the room. There was a notepad by the telephone. Rosenus had scrawled "BOAC Flight 37. Leaving 10:30 P.M." He was leaving the *country?* She looked back at the suitcase. And on such short notice? Apparently he hadn't found out that his life was in danger until he learned of James Reardon's death.

Sara quickly went through the rest of the house. The murderer had left it a shambles. Ironically he had spared her the task of opening all the cabinets and drawers. They had been emptied out and picked through. In the bedroom the dressers were overturned, the closets ransacked, the bed upended. Jewelry boxes lay scooped out, broken, and smashed. She paused to think—she hadn't found a wallet in any of Rosenus's pockets. There hadn't been any valuables in the suitcase, either. The killer wanted the police to think that the motive for the crime was robbery. Sara grimaced. No amateur had done this job. She shivered and went back to survey the scene in the front room. *Hmmm.* A cassette player with no cassettes. None anywhere.

Well, someone's got a tape somewhere. And on it is one hell of a story.

At that moment a car drove up and parked out front; a door opened and slammed. Sara turned and ran through the house to the back door, went outside, crossed a patio, then worked her way through shrubbery and trees to the front. She stopped and peered around the corner of the house. A woman came through the gate carrying a stack of boxes. Her stride jaunty, she whistled happily. Mrs. Rosenus, no doubt, and she had been shopping. She went up the steps, then abruptly stopped. The open front door surprised her. The whistling stopped. "Alan?"

Sara felt a pang of sympathy. Tears welled up in her eyes. The lady's world was about to be shattered. She didn't know it, but she was stepping into an endless nightmare. There was no way to prevent it.

"Alan?" She sounded anxious. "Are you here, honey?" She seemed to be a little afraid now. "Alan?" She went inside. There was a long pause. "Alan? What's the matter?" The boxes fell and clattered on the floor. "Oh, my God! *Alan?*"

And then Sara heard the long and awful screams that echoed out into the night, gradually fading away. Mrs. Rosenus collapsed into a paroxysm of sobs. Sara wished that she could go and console her. Counsel her. Tell her what to expect. Maybe just hold her hand, embrace her. Tell her over and over that there was someone who cared. But she could not.

When she heard Mrs. Rosenus yelling into the telephone for help, she crossed the lawn, went through the garden and out the gate to her car.

Perhaps it's better that she's alone now, Sara thought as she drove away. Maybe she would get used to the emptiness quicker, although that was unlikely. Bone-tired, disgusted, and tense, Sara drove home, her expression glassy-eyed, her body tense and close to the wheel. She'd heard it all before, and she'd hear it again. Right now there was nothing to be done.

Mrs. Berman wanted to take Valerie shopping, but she begged off, saying that she was way behind in her homework, an excuse that happened to be true. Only when Valerie went upstairs and into her room, schoolwork was the furthest thing from her mind. She got the wooden file out of her closet and once again placed the mementos of her father around her on the floor. She had gone through all of them; she had read all of the postcards and the newspaper clippings and even her old birthday cards. Nothing struck her as unusual or suspicious. She stared at them for a long time, then finally sighed. No clues. Not even a hint. She needed more.

In the hall closet she looked through the boxes stored behind the sheets and towels. Mostly they contained her mother's old school books, baby pictures, and other junk. There was nothing even remotely connected to her father.

Next she went into her mother's bedroom and searched. *Surely Momma saved something. She couldn't have thrown out everything. She wasn't that heartless and cruel.* Valerie went through the vanity drawers. *There. Finally.* Underneath some old panty hose in the bottom drawer was a black shoebox. She took the find into her own room, opened it reverently, and sorted through the memories of her parents' life together. An embossed invitation announced the marriage of Andrew Brigham Scott to Sara Martin. Sara *Martin?* Valerie made a face. Her mother's maiden name seemed strange now.

She looked further and found wedding pictures. A hotel key from somewhere in Mexico. A birth certificate and other documents, including a last will and testament leaving everything to her mother. There was a marriage license, too, and a couple of college degrees. Then she found a sheaf of papers folded together and tied with a purple ribbon. This was something. She knew it. Her heart pounded. She gulped and with shaking hands untied the ribbon. What secrets were in these pages that her mother had chosen not to share with her? She unfolded the papers and was awestruck. She gazed at them.

Love poems.

Some were neatly typed, others had cross-outs and erasures, some were serious, others were embellished with handwritten humor. Practically all of them were stained with her mother's tears.

Valerie began to read. For the first time in her life she understood why her mother could not shake off the memory of her father and why she was still haunted by his death. Their life together, if the poems were any indication, had been beautiful and intimate.

> *Sara in the sun*
> *my eternity*
> *I hold a lock of your hair*
> *and rejoice*
> *for it sparkles with life.*

Valerie became absorbed in the poetry, studied the words and conjured up idyllic images of her parents together. She was in the process of memorizing her favorite, a happy poem written the night she herself was born, when she heard her mother trudging up the stairs.

"Oh, *no!*" *How did it get so late?*

She jammed everything back into the shoebox, put away the mementos from her own collection, and had just managed to stash it all in her closet when her mother walked in the door.

"Valerie?" Sara called as she dragged herself into the apartment.

"Hi, Mom." Valerie came out of her room, blushing and looking sideways.

Sara studied her and wondered what was going on, then forgot about it when her daughter came over and embraced her. "Hey, what did I do right?"

"Nothing. You're just my mom."

Sara smiled and tossed her purse onto the couch. "Where's Mrs. Berman anyway?"

"Home, I guess."

"When it gets late, you're supposed to stay with her."

"I had homework to do. Besides, I knew you'd be home any second."

"But, Valerie, what if I *hadn't* come home?"

"You always come home, Mom."

"That's not the point," Sara replied anxiously, thinking of the murders and, suddenly, her own vulnerability.

"I'm sorry."

Sara shivered, then sighed. She couldn't fight it right now. She got a beer out of the refrigerator, went into the living room, and dropped onto the couch.

Valerie followed, studying her mother. "Jeez. You been to a funeral or what?"

"Of sorts."

"You look wiped out."

"I am."

"How did it go today?"

"Fine." She did not sound convincing.

"That bad, huh?"

Sara looked away from her daughter's gaze. She considered lying, then rejected the idea. She had shared too much with Valerie. The girl deserved to know. *But how do I say it without scaring the hell out of her? How do I say that I might be in over my head and then tell her not to worry? By skipping the details? Yeah. I'll try.*

Sara straightened up, set her beer down on the coffee table, then matter-of-factly explained that on this, the second day of the Reardon case, she had witnessed two murders. Valerie got all small and quiet and serious. She curled up on the couch and looked at her mother as if she were watching the news on television. Sara continued. She was certain that the two murders were related, but she had nothing to tie the pieces together. And she had no idea where the mystery would take her.

"That's scary, Mom." Valerie had grown pale. She tried to hide her fears behind her normal inquisitiveness. "How are you going to find out who did it?"

"The way your father always used to tell me how to do things."

"Deductively?"

"Right. Find out how, then let the evidence lead you to the who."

"Daddy wasn't a detective."

"He worked like one, though."

Valerie's face crinkled up thoughtfully. "Are you afraid?"

"No," Sara lied.

"Are you excited?"

"Very much so. I'm finding out if I can do something that I've never done before."

"You mean like learning how to read? For the very first time?"

"That's it, Val. If I can figure this one out, everything'll come clear. I'll have a future, too."

"Really?"

"Yeah." Sara got a faraway look in her eyes. "And there's more."

"More?"

"I don't know how to say it, but we might be putting the worst of our lives behind us."

Valerie looked down pensively. "It hasn't been so bad, Momma. But whatever you do, don't get hurt, okay? I don't want to have to stay with my grandparents. Even if they do live in Hawaii."

Despite her exhaustion Sara didn't sleep late. Once again she had been spared her nightmare. She shuddered. The experience she'd had yesterday more than made up for anything she had experienced in the privacy of her own bedroom.

She took a long, hot shower, but when she had finished, her eyes were still red and scratchy. She brushed her hair out, pleased that at least it still shone. Then she dressed in clean combat clothes and went to her office. She started the day with her usual cigarette and coffee, while summarizing the third day of the Reardon case in her diary. Under *Friday, September 26* she wrote, "Weather continues abysmal, but am on the threshold of opportunity. Another Casparian maxim which is apropos: If you're good enough, crime doesn't pay them, it pays you."

She put her diary away. *If you're good enough.*

Grumbling, but determined, she took a fresh legal pad out of her desk and printed across the top, "List of Possibles." Then she recorded everything that had happened in a logical sequence. She hated to work like this; it was so methodical. But Casparian, like Andy, had always insisted that evidence ruled. True, intuition might seem more interesting, but ultimately it was a siren song heeded only by the amateurs. Sara did it their way, printing, "James Reardon's strange behavior."

He avoided his own receptionist. He didn't spend enough time at the Straighten-Up Halfway House to provide psychotherapy for a gnat let alone an addict. He didn't tell his wife a damned thing. He used a pay phone instead of the one in his office. He drove like a man possessed. He met a political reporter in a motel room. He went to the airport as if on impulse, and there whatever was on his mind caught up with him and crushed him to death. Then his things had been taken. Finally his accomplice (if that term was correct) had been murdered.

Sara paused, considering the evidence. She put her pen down and stared at her Cézanne print. Maybe she should have stuck with photography. All she had now were unanswered questions. Where was Reardon going? Who had he wanted to see, if anyone? She rubbed her eyes. She thought hard. There was one thing she could do. She could check out the PSA stewardess who had taken off with Reardon's luggage.

She gave La Belle the usual perfunctory check, threw a fresh pack of cigarettes into her purse, and started to leave.

She was reaching for the doorknob when Casparian —of all people—swaggered into the office, his broad shoulders brushing against the potted plants. He dropped his hat on her desk and sat down in a chair. The wood creaked and groaned.

"Nice place you got here. But I wouldn't give you a dime for the neck of the woods you're in."

She laughed. "That's what you always say. Want some coffee?"

"Yeah, sure!" He raised his eyebrows, acting like a father who was surprised that his kid could boil water without an instruction manual. She got a clean cup out of her waiting room.

"Hey, who's that black guy gliding around downstairs? The one with the country's gold reserves hanging from his neck?"

"The landlord."

"I've seen him someplace before."

"Where?"

He thought for a moment, then shook his large head. "I don't know." He touched his temple. "It'll come to me someday. I never forget."

"His name is Spencer Harris."

Casparian chuckled. "That don't mean nothing. Yesterday, it could've been Harris Spencer."

She picked up the Thermos, then remembered that she had drunk all the coffee, so she filled his cup from a pint of tequila she kept in the bottom drawer of her desk. She handed it to him with a sly smile. "What brings you here?"

"I was worried. I wanted to make sure that you hadn't been thrown out of your office. Do you still have money problems?"

"No, I got a case."

"Great!" He took a swig from the cup and was momentarily taken aback but smacked his lips with appreciation. "*Some* coffee." He grinned and winked.

"Must be mountain grown." He gestured. "So tell me, tell me, tell me!"

"About what?"

"What else? Your new gig!"

She did, although she left out her speculation about the murder vehicle because she wasn't sure whether it was a hallucination or reality, and she didn't want Casparian to tell her she was seeing things. When she described what had happened to James Reardon at the airport, he began to listen carefully. His frowns got deeper, and when she finished, he stared at the ceiling for a long time and sipped the tequila slowly while reflecting.

"Okay," he said and rolled his shoulders back. "Let me see if I got this straight. This broad thinks that her old man is fucking around on her when actually he's running scared. He tells something to some other dude who tapes it."

"Uh-huh."

"The other dude puts him in touch with a third party, and he arranges a contact."

"Uh-huh."

"So he goes to the airport to catch a hop, only at this point the bad guys are on to him and he gets snuffed."

"Uh-huh."

"The other dude finds out his friend is dead and realizes that he's in danger because he knows just as much as his friend did and the worst is coming true."

"Uh-huh."

"So he tries to split and gets nailed before he can get out the door."

"What do you think?"

"Somebody doesn't want something let out of the proverbial bag."

"I figured that much out on my own, Casparian!"
He patted her on the shoulder. "Well, good for you.
I always knew that you'd make a great detective. You
was a natural. You got dynamite moves." He handed
her his empty cup. "Yes, thank you, I will have a
second cup, only don't tell Ruby, okay?"

Sara poured him more tequila. "What would you
do next?"

"If I was you?"

"Yeah."

"Go to the police."

"*What?*"

"I know, I know. You don't want to have anything
to do with them because they screwed up your old
man's investigation and lost the evidence, right?"

"That's right."

"Well, one mistake a long time ago doesn't make
them incompetent, and if you leave them out of it, you
could get your sweet little ass into some bad trouble."

"Casparian!"

"Sara, there are murders involved!" He spread his
big hands in a benevolent gesture. "And I don't want
to see you get hurt."

"Casparian, you are *not* my father!" Although just
then he sure did remind her of her dad. "And I am
not going to the police!"

"You're making a mistake."

"Maybe so, but like you say, I've got to grow up
someday."

He got up and paced. "Yeah. I suppose so." He
sighed. "Well, at least you're not chasing Andy's ghost
around anymore."

She cringed inside and then changed the subject.
"So what would you do next?"

"You mean now that we've eighty-sixed the police?"

"Right."

"I don't know." He drained his cup. "I think I'd get drunk and ponder real hard about how badly I needed the money."

"What do you mean?"

"You're going to end up a walking, talking, breathing target, Sara. Some hit man out there is going to have his cross-hairs trained right between the nicest pair of tits I ever saw. Yours."

"*Casparian!*" She blushed. Then a tremor of fear ran from her toes through her groin and into her belly.

"I'm sorry. I didn't know how else to put it."

"I can keep my eyes open! I can deal with it!"

He shook his head. "Okay." He touched his forehead. "All right." He shrugged. "You need any help, I'll be around."

"Thanks."

"And I mean it. Anything at all. You *call* me, Sara, understand? I'm on your side."

"I promise," she whispered.

He kissed her on the cheek and squeezed her hand. Then he turned and rolled out of her office, his bulk slipping gracefully out the door.

Sara just sat there, staring at the wall, suddenly worried about her own safety again. She wished Casparian hadn't said anything. She didn't want to continue her investigation with the constant fear that someone was going to nail her from behind—not to mention that she might walk right into something with her eyes open. She sighed and tried to shake off the apprehensions by wondering if she had forgotten anything. She scanned her List of Possibles, frowned, thought for a moment, then added, "Mrs. Rosenus." She nodded grimly. If all else failed, that was another place to start, another person to ask about the missing tape.

But right now she intended to see what she could learn at the airport. She left her office and headed for her car. Halfway across the alley the back of her neck tingled with fear. Was someone following her? No, it was all in her mind; there was . . . She was compelled to spin around and look behind her. There was nothing there except the dirty brick of the building, and she hated herself for succumbing to an imagined terror.

She climbed into her car and slammed the door. *Well, if nothing else, Casparian would say that there really was something for me to be afraid of. At least this time I didn't hallucinate.*

"Thank God for small favors," she muttered ironically as she drove off.

On her way to the airport she stopped at Helen Reardon's house, knocking softly once, understanding that frequent human contact was the only thing that would keep her out of a psychiatric hospital.

Helen answered the door. She had the big, floppy hat on even though she was indoors. It was tilted forward to hide her eyes, but Sara could see that the lady had taken a turn for worse.

Helen served coffee in the den where the shutters were drawn. She could not stop her hands from shaking; she seemed to have no strength left. Leaning forward, Sara put her hand over Helen's.

"Helen . . ."

She pulled her hand back and turned away. "I didn't find anything, Sara."

"Hey, that's okay. You did your best."

"I went through all of his things, and I didn't find anything!"

"It's all right. Really."

"You don't know what it's like sitting in this house!"

"I do know what it's like."

"I keep hearing the phone ring! I keep expecting him to walk in the front door or ask me to bring him a drink! I keep seeing him, Sara! In every damned room!"

"I know."

"I haven't slept at all!" She collapsed into sobs. Her body convulsed. Sara went to her, held her, and stroked her hair until she felt her relax and regain control of herself.

"I'm sorry. I just can't help it."

Sara handed her a box of Kleenex, then spoke softly. "The more you cry now, the less you'll cry later. Believe me. I know."

Helen nodded.

"Right now there are no days or nights. You're just doing time on the planet Earth, and it's awful. I know that, too, God how I know that. You think the world is mocking you because everything's alive and all you can think about is death. Things will get better, Helen. You'll make them get better."

"But how . . . where do I start?"

"You have to take each day as it comes. You set up a schedule and you stick to it. Rigidly. You create moments for yourself and you live from one to the next. And finally, when you can cope, you get the hell away from here on a long, extended vacation." A pause. Sara shifted uneasily, realizing that she herself had never felt good enough to take a vacation, and it had been four years.

"I'll try."

"You won't try. You'll just do it." She sighed. "Is anyone helping you with the funeral arrangements?"

"James's mother and father are coming out from St. Louis."

"What about your folks?"

She just shrugged, shook her head nervously, and looked away.

"Have the police been here yet?"

"Yesterday evening," she whispered. "I felt so stupid when they asked me where he was going. And I had to tell them that I didn't know. They said, no problem —James's receptionist would know. Will she?"

"No."

"And you were right. They . . . they said that more than likely his death was a tragic accident. They hoped their investigation would turn up something."

"I hope so, too," Sara said sincerely. She lit a cigarette, inhaled, and reflected. Then she gritted her teeth and leaned forward. She had to ask. She had to get it over with. "Helen? Did your husband know a man named Alan Rosenus?"

She was startled, but responded openly. "Why, yes. They had been friends for a long time."

"Did they see each other often?"

"No. As a matter of fact the only time I ever met Alan Rosenus was on our fifth wedding anniversary."

"When you were going through your husband's things, did you find any references to Alan Rosenus?"

"No! Should I have?"

"Alan Rosenus was the man your husband met in the motel."

She was shocked. "James didn't tell me *anything!* Why would he confide in Alan Rosenus?"

"I don't know," Sara confessed. "But Alan Rosenus was murdered yesterday, too."

Helen's spirits faded again, and Sara cursed herself for not breaking the news more gently. She convinced

Helen to take a sedative and go to bed, then left for the airport.

"Hello! Can I help you?"

"I certainly hope so." Sara returned his smile. She made a fluid gesture and instinctively curved toward him.

He looked at her body, gulped, and perished the thought. He wore the brown uniform of airport security. Three stripes on his sleeve indicated that he was a sergeant, and his nameplate revealed that he was in charge of operations. "I'm Don Barrett," he said, extending his hand.

She recognized him as the blond-haired man she had seen arguing with the police lieutenant the day before and was pleased that he was so obviously attracted to her; that would make her task easier. She shook his hand and let her fingers linger just a second longer than she normally would have. He was close to thirty and seemed bright. His blue eyes showed just a touch of red around the edges. He was too thin, but that was definitely more appealing than the other extreme. She briefly wondered what kind of lover this man would make, then averted her eyes and blushed. *What a dumb way to begin an investigation,* she thought. Now was no time for idle fantasies. She looked at him again. He was still smiling at her, but he had a hangdog expression that seemed comical. She burst out laughing.

He shrugged. "Was it something I said?"

She introduced herself as Cathy Coulson from the Banker's Life Insurance Company and handed him a business card.

"I liked the handshake better." Then he read the card. "You? An insurance investigator?"

"In the flesh."

"I'll say."

She forced a frown. "Are you always so . . . accom-modating, Sergeant Barrett?"

"No. Usually I don't even talk to the guys who work here." He laughed. "But you can call me Don."

His laugh was so infectious that she was charmed by it and momentarily forgot why she was there. She relaxed and looked into his eyes as if he were an old friend. Seconds passed. Then she blushed again, embarrassed by her lapse in concentration.

"So . . . so what are you investigating?" he asked, trying to be helpful.

"The death of James Reardon."

He frowned, squinting at her. "Are you sure you have the right airport?"

"He was killed yesterday."

"Oh. The hit-and-run victim?"

She nodded.

"The police are looking into that one. You should talk to them."

She hesitated. "Whatever."

He sighed reluctantly. He didn't want her to go. "I wish I could help."

"Maybe . . ."—she gave him a questioning look—"you could tell me what flight he was booked on?"

He brightened. "Why sure, I can do that much for you." He opened the half-door, and she stepped behind the counter. "For you, no problem at all." He led her into a large, windowless room. "You think that maybe the guy was killed deliberately?"

"We always like to check, even though the police are calling it an accident."

"I wouldn't know."

"Huh?" she said, surprised.

"They don't talk to me and I don't talk to them unless it's unavoidable."

"Why?"

He grinned. "Professional jealousy, I suppose."

"Oh." She looked around at the sophisticated electronic equipment. "Wow. This is some place."

"We do take our work seriously."

"Hey, I'm not screwing you up, am I?"

"Are you kidding? I run this operation."

They went to a small computer console that was in the center of a desk. Barrett indicated an overstuffed office chair, and she could feel his warm hands on her back and shoulder as he helped her into it and stole a look down the front of her blouse. She looked up at him inquiringly and smiled.

"Okay. What was his name again?"

"James Reardon."

He pushed several buttons, and the machine came to life. "And . . ."

"The accident occurred just after ten thirty, so what do you think? He had an eleven o'clock flight?"

Barrett nodded, hit a couple more buttons, then leaned back and waited. The console screen lit up with the information, and he was satisfied. "Sure enough. Western Airlines flight seven-A."

"Where to?"

"Sacramento."

She raised her eyebrows, although she probably would have been surprised no matter what Barrett had told her. "I wonder who he knew in Sacramento?" She looked away and reflected. Her mind raced, trying to think of a way to ask about the woman who had run off with Reardon's luggage, without blowing her cover. Barrett was gazing at her and waiting patiently. She knew that he liked her. She could feel the chemistry. Was he trustworthy, though? She gulped and turned, her eyes wide and innocent. "Don, I—"

"Only if you'll have lunch with me."

Caught unawares, she hesitated and was speechless.

"The food is actually good for an airport restaurant. And the chili is homemade. I swear to God."

"Don . . ." She scowled at herself. She hated to be in this position. "Don, there's something . . ."

"I already know. You've got a steady boyfriend."

"That, too, but . . ."

"So?" He shrugged. "Hell, for all I know, you might be married, but the least you can do is give yourself an opportunity to turn me down *after* you've heard my fascinating life story."

Suddenly, a security guard burst into the office, his face ashen. "Sergeant Barrett! Please, you . . ."

"What?"

But the man was gagging. He jerked his head toward the door, turned, and ran out of the room. Barrett went after him.

Curious, Sara followed the two men out of the office. They were up ahead, hurrying along the south corridor, their footfalls echoing. She ran after them. They went through a security door, turned down another corridor, then descended two flights of stairs to a darker lower level with Sara in pursuit. As she got closer she heard the cries of someone in distress.

She eased around a corner. A shaft of yellow light came from an open doorway, and she could hear Barrett talking in low, urgent tones. She tiptoed to the doorway, gulped, then peered inside. It was a janitor's room. A black cleaning lady was huddled on a chair, sobbing at her discovery. The guard was on the telephone, and Barrett was staring across the room, not moving. Sara followed his eyes. There was a bank of metal lockers. . . .

The body of a woman had been stuffed into one of them; she had been stabbed to death. Sara gasped. She recognized the corpse. It was the same woman who had taken James Reardon's luggage and run away. Only then she was wearing the uniform of a PSA stewardess.

Now she wore nothing at all.

Seven

Sara turned and hurried away from the gruesome scene before Barrett and the guard even knew she was there. Instead of going back the same way, she went in the opposite direction, following an exit sign. Voices from the janitor's room echoed behind her but soon faded in the corridors.

Numb and unable to think straight, she made a wrong turn and was soon lost underneath the airport terminal. The corridors were not well lighted, and when the horror of the dead girl subsided, she became afraid. Remembering Casparian's warning, she imagined that the killer was still stalking the area. The back of her neck tingled. She quickened her pace, continually looking behind her. James Reardon was dead. She shivered. Alan Rosenus was dead. And now this . . . The girl in the stewardess uniform grotesquely stuffed into a cleaning locker. *Everyone who knew what James Reardon knew has been murdered. Am I next? Are they looking for me right now? Are they waiting for me up ahead? Or are they following me?* She spun around. No one was there. The walls shimmered. The empty corridor seemed ominous. *Oh, God, get me out of here!* She ran.

On the verge of panic she came upon a flight of steps that led to a fire door. She hurried up them and burst outside, grateful to be in the sunlight again.

She made her way to the street, figured out where she was, then took a shuttle bus. Two men got on with her and sat down across the aisle. She watched them carefully, her heart pounding. She could not calm her terror. If someone was after her, how would she recognize them? How would she know? She would get no warning.

She got off the bus and hurried into the parking garage. So far she wasn't being followed. She took the elevator, thankful when the door closed and she was alone inside. She shut her eyes, leaned against the cold metal, and wondered about Andy. *Before you died, did you know that they wanted to kill you? Were you afraid like this, too? Why didn't you tell me? If only you had told me . . .*

At level three she left the elevator and hurried toward her Pinto. A car was coming up the ramp. She gulped, but kept walking. The tires screeched. She told herself the sound was normal. She was nervous anyway. The car turned onto her level. Helpless to protect herself, she began running. The vehicle accelerated in her direction. She sprinted to her car and cowered behind it, her chest heaving. Then she looked back.

A VW sped right on past, the driver innocently hunting for a parking space. She straightened up, unlocked her car, and climbed in. Her hands were shaking badly. *Jesus Christ, I've got to get ahold of myself! I can't be so fucking impulsive. I can't let my imagination run wild! After all, if they knew that I was on the Reardon case, then I'd probably be dead already, given how fast Rosenus and the girl were killed. So they're not after me now, and they may never be. Quit being hysterical and calm down.* "Okay,

okay, okay," she whispered to herself, then started the Pinto and drove off.

She went to James Reardon's office. There was a notice on the door, signed by a trust officer of the Crocker Bank, the executor of his estate, announcing the recent tragedy and giving a date for the reading of the will. Sara took several business cards from the box below the notice, then went into the office and spent several hours going through Reardon's files, appointment book, and Rolodex. She found nothing to explain why Reardon was going to Sacramento. But that wasn't unusual. Reardon had gotten a name from Alan Rosenus, and that was that.

On her way out she removed the electronic bug from Reardon's phone. She didn't know how much they cost nowadays. But she sure as hell wasn't going to leave one around monitoring the silence.

Next she drove to the Straighten-Up Halfway House in Venice. She parked off to the side and walked around to the front. Glancing behind her to check that she wasn't being followed, she unlatched the chain-link gate and walked through it. When it clanged shut, the residents who heard the sound turned and stared. Sara hadn't noticed them before—they'd been hidden by long shadows of eucalyptus and palm trees. With their closely cropped hair and starched denim fatigues, they all looked alike. *Conformity,* she mused. *The wages of crime and other bad habits.* There was, however, a power in the collective identity that sauntered toward her. For *them,* that is.

She hurried along the walkway, aware that some of them were following her. She quickened her pace, but restrained herself from running, even though she was afraid. There was no reason to be. She went up the front steps, across the porch, but just before entering the building, she turned and looked back. They were all staring at her. Their faces blurred, merged. She blinked. *She saw only the face of the soft, brown youth behind the counter, astonished that he was dying. Andy. Already dead. What will become of . . . ?*

Trembling, she found herself at an information counter in a large room lit by naked fluorescent bulbs. She forced herself to look around and saw that she was surrounded by bilingual posters which warned against drug abuse. Gradually, she steadied herself. She glanced up at the lights and studied the room. There was no sound. *Strange,* she thought. The room was empty, even though there were three desks for secretaries. She looked for a service bell to ring. There was none. While she waited she examined a brochure and became absorbed. The house was a way station for junkies, most of them ex-convicts, who had kicked the habit, but weren't quite ready to be let loose on the streets. The place provided psychotherapy, Methadone programs, educational courses leading to a high-school diploma and beyond, athletics, recreation, religious, and arts-and-crafts programs. If they so desired, the residents could even work. The halfway house had its own light industries and even boasted its own fleet of trucks.

Sara was impressed. No wonder James Reardon had volunteered to work here.

"You must be a visitor, yes?"

Startled, she dropped the brochure and looked up. The man standing close to her was swarthy, squat, and powerful. His long-sleeve shirt clung to his muscles, and he wore brand-new double-knit trousers. Sara's eyes were drawn to his broad face, black hair, and dark, inscrutable eyes. He was grinning, his hands on his hips. She nodded and managed to smile, awed by the power this man exuded.

He spread his hands; the gesture was practiced. "My name is Jorge Martinez. I am the director and co-founder of the Straighten-Up Halfway House. How can I be of service, Miss . . . ?"

She handed him one of the business cards she had taken from outside Reardon's office. The card identified her as an assistant vice-president, trust division, Crocker Bank. "Bryant. Connie Bryant. I was wondering if you or maybe one of your associates could answer a few questions about the late Dr. James Reardon?"

Martinez's expression did not change. He sighed and replied in impeccable English, appearing to be deeply saddened. "James Reardon was a brilliant therapist, dedicated to helping others. He got results. He fought against apathy and despair—the most terrible diseases of poor people—and that is the highest compliment I can give a man. So what else is there to say?" He smiled wryly. "Except that I have been placed in the unenviable position of having to find a replacement for him."

"I'm sorry."

"No more than I."

He looked at her closely, then spoke gently. "What, may I ask, is the basis of your interest in the late James Reardon, Miss Bryant? Perhaps you are related to Mrs. Reardon?"

"No."

"A mistress, then?"

"I am the executor of Dr. Reardon's estate."

"Of course." He nodded as if that explained everything. "Please convey my condolences to Mrs. Reardon the next time you see her."

"I'd be happy to."

"Listen," he said, his tone suddenly light. "Since you're here, would you like me to show you around? So you can see for yourself some of the remarkable rehabilitation projects that James Reardon was involved in?"

"Why not?" She smiled and gravitated toward Jorge Martinez. She did not feel uncomfortable when he took her by the arm in order to guide her through the office. Once beyond double doors that said GUESTS NOT ALLOWED, they passed lounges, recreational facilities, counseling rooms, stairways to dormitories and not one but two chapels. Eventually they came out into a garden plaza where the walls were decorated with bright murals painted by the residents of the halfway house.

"James Reardon started that," Martinez commented with a sweeping gesture. "He thought that it was a way for a person to simultaneously express his feelings and regain a sense of pride in his accomplishments."

"Impressive," said Sara, staring at the haunting portrait of two men, one black, the other brown, who were shaking hands while standing in a sea of blood.

They crossed the plaza. Martinez waved at several groups of men who appeared to be asleep and did not wave back. Sara had to hurry to keep up with his frenetic pace. He seemed like he wanted to be everywhere at once, continually spouting enthusiasm for his successful programs.

They came to a building that housed several workshops. Men were making everything from jewelry to ceramics and wood products. Beyond a high fence was a large shed, labeled SHIPPING AND RECEIVING. Trucks with the logo SUHH were being loaded. Martinez zealously pointed out efficient workers whom he insisted were well along the path to model citizenship. Then he suddenly stopped, swung around, and faced Sara. He was smiling.

"But surely you didn't come here expecting to discuss, say, how many tax dollars it takes to produce one reformed junkie, now, did you?"

"It is an interesting question," Sara replied seriously.

"But not to the point."

"What do you mean?"

"You say that you're the executor of James Reardon's will. Why would you come here?"

"There's a question about his assets," Sara lied. "It seems that the day he died, he made a large withdrawal from his life savings."

Martinez frowned and looked puzzled. Sara was gratified that her falsehood seemed convincing to a man who was undoubtedly as shrewd as he was intelligent. "Go on," he said.

"Obviously, we would like to know what happened to those funds, so we are talking to everyone who was associated with Dr. Reardon."

"I had no idea that the Crocker Bank was such a responsible organization. What have you found out?"

"Well, Mrs. Reardon, for one, thinks that her husband may have been killed for his money."

"Has she spoken to the police?"

"Yes," Sara replied smoothly. "And so far their investigation hasn't discovered anything unusual. James Reardon was a hit-and-run victim. Another accidental casualty chalked up to negligent homicide."

"Yet you continue to ask questions because of the money, is that it?"

Sara smiled weakly. "We have an obligation."

"Of course you do." He nodded fiercely. "I only wish

I could be of some assistance, but I know nothing of James Reardon's personal life."

They walked on in silence for a while, and Sara heard the shouts of several men who were enjoying an intense game of volleyball. "Still," she asked, "did James Reardon have any enemies that you might know of?"

"James Reardon was a saint, Miss Bryant. He was loved by everyone. To my knowledge he led a model life." He turned, a messianic glint in his eyes, and pointed at some men who were straggling toward the mess hall. "If you like, why don't you ask some of his patients?"

"Thanks, but no thanks." She grinned ruefully. "I don't think I'd get anywhere."

"A wise decision. Men who pass through these portals understandably become nervous when asked about someone's death, whether accidental or not."

"I really appreciate your cooperation. I hope I haven't been a bother."

"Someone as pretty as you is never an inconvenience. Would you care to stay for dinner?"

"I'm afraid I can't."

He shrugged. "Why don't we go out then?" He leaned close, resting his hand on the small of her back. "Frankly on Fridays the food here is lousy."

"Maybe some other time," she stammered, blushing at this sudden display of charm.

"Definitely," he said. Then he escorted her back through the house and across the great expanse of lawn to the front gate. "Call me next week," he said brusquely.

"What?" She was astonished.

He gently touched her cheek. "I'm a very busy man. And if Connie Bryant were in the mood to drop by,

I'd want to make sure that I was here to see her." He turned, quickly walked away, and waved his fist over his shoulder, a sign of both affection and solidarity. *"Hasta luego, novia."*

Sara drove off quite amazed by her encounter with Jorge Martinez. He had not even sounded like a Chicano until he'd said good-bye to her in Spanish. She frowned. *So the man was glib in two languages? So the man had several different personalities, all of which were magnetic?* That still didn't shed any light on her quest for a murderer. Or did it? *Hmmmm.* She pursed her lips. Something didn't fit. According to Jorge Martinez, James Reardon had been a great and brilliant man. What about his strange behavior then? His preoccupation? Had she been the only one who noticed? She had seen Reardon skip two afternoons of work at the halfway house. Why hadn't Martinez said anything about that? Didn't that fact suggest that the dedicated therapist had been shirking his duties? She concluded that while Jorge Martinez didn't yet qualify as a suspect, he certainly deserved consideration.

She pulled into Jerry's Liquor Store on Main Street, bought cigarettes and a can of iced tea. On her way back to the Pinto she sensed that she was being watched. *They knew.* She whirled around fearfully, but saw nothing. Then out of the shadows wheeled a vacuous teenaged weirdo on rollerskates and wearing 3-D glasses. Sara reacted with a shiver, then sighed, but was not relieved. As she hurried across the parking lot she glanced around compulsively.

From the open-air pay phone next to the carwash she called her service. The only message was from Mrs. Berman. Sara felt a twinge of panic. *Has something happened to Val?* She fumbled in her purse, found another dime, and called.

"Valerie is just fine," said Mrs. Berman. "My nephew in the garment business from New York is in town and wants to take us to dinner. Can Valerie go?"

Sara smiled and was relieved. "Only if she doesn't wear cut-offs."

"What do you think I am, a *schmeltzer?* I wouldn't let her wear those to the bathroom. No dress, no dinner."

Sara was laying back on two large pillows, sipping a beer and gazing into the dying coals of a still very warm fire. She had just told Sam everything. As a result she felt drained.

He wasn't. Distressed, thoughtful, he paced behind her in the great old room. "You might have told me sooner."

"I'm sorry. I've had trouble convincing myself."

"What about Valerie?"

"She only knows about the murders. I didn't tell her that I might be on to her father's killers. Needless to say, she's worried about me getting into something that I can't handle."

"And you?"

Sara turned and looked at him. "Come on, Sam. If I wasn't worried, too, I wouldn't be here."

He stopped pacing and sat down beside her. He put his arms on his knees, rested his chin on them, and stared into the fire. "Do you think that you could be in some kind of danger? I mean, right now?"

"No," she replied flatly.

"How do you figure?"

"If they were on to me, I'd be dead already."

He stared at her, his eyes black in the dim light. He

looked surprised and held her tightly by the shoulders. "Forget the Reardon case."

"I wish I could, Sam. You don't know what the last two days have done to me." Her voice trailed off to a husky whisper and quavered slightly. "I'm seeing things. Everywhere. It's all I can do to get out of my car and walk somewhere without making a complete circle to see who's behind me. Goddammit, Sam, I'm *scared!*"

"I want you to quit."

"I can't! You know that!"

"I said *forget it!* You don't owe Andy anything!"

"Okay, fine, but what about myself?"

He shoved her back against the pillows, turned, and stared into the fire again. "You're impossible, Sara. You're goddamned fucking impossible!"

"What do you mean, impossible?" She rose up indignantly. "I've always listened to you, Sam! I've always put up with your habits! Why can't I be allowed to close the book on a bad time in my life? Finally?"

He looked down and shook his head sadly. "Do you really believe that you're chasing the same people who murdered Andy, Sara? Do you really believe that?"

"Sam, I don't know! All I'm saying is that I have to find out!"

"Do you know what the odds are in a situation like that?"

"No." She smiled grimly. "But would it make any difference?"

He didn't respond. He ran a hand through his wiry hair. He thought for a moment, then got up, went over to the hearth, and pitched two fresh logs onto the coals, one eucalyptus, the other pine. They caught fire immediately and crackled loudly. He came back, lay down beside her, and kissed her tenderly.

She looked up at him. Tears formed in her eyes. She felt grateful. "You understand, then?"

He nodded and smiled "I can't let you do it, Sara."

She recoiled. "Sam!"

"I can't let you continue."

"What the hell are you talking about?"

"By yourself, that is."

"*Oh, no!*" She pushed away from him and rolled over. "*Oh, no!*" She got up and retreated across the room.

He came after her. "Sara . . ."

She turned and stood her ground, her dark eyes flashing. "No way, Sam Gage! You are not going to involve anyone else in this, you understand? Not the police, not Casparian, not *anyone!* And if you repeat one word of what I've told you, I'll never speak to you again as long as I live! That's a promise!"

Except for the fire popping and hissing, there was a long silence. The two stared at each other, the dark room between them. For a moment the space seemed insurmountable, but then Sam breached the gap with four long strides and a quick grin. He took her by the arm.

She pulled away. "Sam, I meant what I said!"

"Hey, Sara, take it easy, okay? I wasn't going to call anyone else."

"Huh?" She looked at him suspiciously. She was puzzled. "But, you—"

He placed his fingertips over her mouth and stopped her in mid-sentence. He spoke quietly. "For the first time in my life I am going to commit myself to something other than the mindless pursuit of simplicity."

"Sam . . ." Then she realized what he was saying and her mouth fell open.

"We're going to do it together."

She looked at him, her eyes sparkling. "Sam! You don't know a damned thing about my kind of work!"

He assumed a self-effacing expression. "I don't know a damned thing about any kind of work."

"Well, then?"

"I owe it to you."

"You don't owe me anything."

"We're friends, aren't we? And what about Andy?"

"But, Sam, you'll just get in the way!"

"Maybe I will and maybe I won't. But there's one thing you don't want to overlook."

"What?"

"I was trained to save lives. Remember?"

Saturday, September 27.

Sara finished her obligatory summary of the day before, poured herself coffee from the Thermos, lit a cigarette, and called Helen Reardon.

"How are you?"

"I'm feeling better," Helen replied bravely.

"You *sound* much better."

"Thanks. Have you made any . . . any progress?" she asked hesitantly.

Sara scowled. Why did she sense that Helen Reardon wasn't telling her everything? It must be the tone of voice. The grief. She cursed herself. She had no right to suspect her client; there was no reason.

"Have you?" Helen Reardon repeated breathlessly.

"Yes. I found out that your husband was on his way to Sacramento."

"Why on earth was he going there?"

"I assume he was meeting someone. I think he wanted to tell someone something very important."

"Why wouldn't he just make a phone call?"

"He did that, too."

"If only he had told me what was happening." She sighed. "I feel like such a failure!"

Sara shifted in her chair. "Do you know anyone in Sacramento who was a friend of your husband?"

"Let me think—"

"*Or* Alan Rosenus?" Sara leaned back and waited. The silence was heavy and awkward, but she didn't want to say anything else. She wanted a clean, direct response.

"I'm not sure about Alan Rosenus," Helen began haltingly. "I mean, I'm not sure that he knew her, too. I'd only be guessing."

"Who?"

"Anna Perez."

Sara scribbled the name on her notepad. *Sure. That was the state senator who spoke at the rally the other day. But there's something else. I've seen that name somewhere else.*

"She wrote James a letter of commendation last year for all the volunteer work he'd done," Helen explained.

"Thanks, Helen," Sara said quickly. "I'll call you later." She hung up, looked on either side of her desk, saw her purse on the floor, picked it up, and hurriedly went through it. She took out the brochure that she'd gotten at the halfway house yesterday. She quickly scanned the names listed on the inside cover. She nodded firmly.

Anna Perez was the *politico* who ran the board of directors.

Eight

Of course! Sara exclaimed to herself.

James Reardon had been on his way to see Anna Perez. She was a state senator. She had clout. She would be a logical choice for Reardon to turn to, especially since he did volunteer work at the halfway house. Sara wagered that Alan Rosenus had known Anna Perez, too. Sure. He had been a political reporter, hadn't he? Maybe James Reardon and Alan Rosenus had agreed that Anna Perez would be perfect as a sounding board.

She got the phone number from information, then called Anna Perez's office in Sacramento. An assistant with a heavy Latin accent answered, listened to Sara's request for an interview, and apologized. Just yesterday the senator had left to spend another two weeks in Los Angeles. Sara hung up, thought for a moment, and frowned. That didn't make sense. Why would Anna Perez go back to Sacramento on Wednesday, then return to Los Angeles on Friday? Would a campaign swing take her back and forth like that? Or did it have to do with the death of James Reardon? She'd find out soon enough.

Someone was knocking on her outer office door.

Startled, she reached into her purse for her pistol, then shook her head, disgusted with herself. If there was an enemy out there, he sure as hell wouldn't knock.

Or would he?

Her heart was pounding. She moved against the wall by the door, pistol in hand, swallowed hard, and called out in a tiny voice. "Who is it?"

"Sam."

She sagged with relief, put La Belle away, then unlocked the doors and let him into her office.

"Sorry I'm late."

"Sam, you're a volunteer, remember? You don't have to punch a time clock." She turned to face him and was speechless. Although pleasantly surprised, she gaped at him.

"What's wrong?" He looked down at himself. He was wearing light denim slacks, a sports shirt, and a sweater. His hair was brushed and his shoes were shined.

She emitted a rare giggle. "I don't think I've ever seen you wearing real clothes before."

"Would you like me to drop my pants?"

"Please don't. Someone might recognize you."

He chuckled and poured himself some coffee.

"Don't get too comfortable," she said while she gathered up her purse. "We've got to track down State Senator Anna Perez."

"Oh?"

She briefly explained why. Sam took the phone book, flipped through it, and found the address of the senator's district office. He tapped the page with his finger. "I've passed by here a few times."

"Where is it?"

"In a shopping center in Mar Vista." He grinned. "Between a Von's Market and a Bank of America."

"The lady senator is definitely not stupid."

* * *

Sam drove Sara to Mar Vista in his old but immaculate MG convertible. He was fond of saying that he waxed it as often as he did his surfboard.

While he waited outside she entered the office and was confronted by a massive receptionist-cum-legislative assistant named Hector Bolinas. His flesh rolled over the arms of his desk chair and his jowls resembled soft-brown icicles. Every time he moved, the buttons on his tentlike shirt seemed ready to pop.

"May I help you?"

Sara lowered both her eyelids and her voice, exuding charm. "Hello. My name's Dianne Ryder. I'm a reporter for the *Los Angeles Times.*" She handed him the card she had swiped from the newspaper's cityroom the day before. "I do features for the View section."

He grinned expansively. "Oh, how nice."

"I'm doing a piece on the energy crisis, and I wanted Senator Perez's views."

"I'm sure that she would love to speak with you, Miss Ryder," he said, "but I'm afraid she isn't in right now."

"I can wait," Sara replied sweetly.

He made a practiced gesture of sympathy. "She won't be back until late this afternoon."

Sara made an appointment, then went back outside and told Sam. He was philosophic about the delay. "So we have a five-hour wait."

"We can drive over to the Marina and have a leisurely lunch," she suggested, then suddenly thought of Andy. A month before his death they had lunched at the Marina and he had dispassionately told her to prepare for success. She wondered, then quickly looked at Sam, hoping that his presence would keep her mind off the memory.

"We could drive to San Diego and have a leisurely

lunch," he replied sarcastically. "Don't you think you should've called first?"

She blushed. "Sam, if we're going to be working together, I'd appreciate you *not* reminding me of my bad habits."

"Oh, okay. You mean, like your impulsiveness?"

"*Sam!*" She scowled at him, then got into the car, and he drove away. She lit a cigarette and threw the match out the wind-wing.

"You've been smoking too much, Sara."

"I didn't want you to get the wrong idea, Sam."

"Huh?"

"I didn't want you to think that I was perfect."

Lately State Senator Anna Perez had been suffering from a dearth of attention—a condition not uncommon to state officials in the middle of their terms—so she was hungry for publicity. Sara had to wait only fifteen minutes before she was ushered into the private office.

"It's a pleasure to meet you, Miss Ryder."

Sara studied Anna Perez. Her hair was black, highlighted with touches of gray. Her figure was still voluptuous, and her smooth complexion disguised the fact that she was close to fifty. Her mouth was sensual, and she had a voice to match—she could have made even a weather report about a blizzard sound lush and tropical. But Anna Perez's most remarkable feature was her green eyes. They commanded one's full attention. They were glamorous.

Anna Perez had played the smoldering sex kitten from south of the border long before she had been elected to the state senate, and she had lost none of her magnetism. If anything, growing up with the desperate Hollywood scramble for survival had probably been the best training Anna Perez could have received for a career as a legislator. It was no surprise that this lady had won an election and was becoming the cause célèbre of the local Democratic party. She was a minority woman who had made it; an underdog who had won. She was smart and tough. And she wore sex appeal like a summer blouse.

"Shall we get started?" Anna Perez asked patiently.

Sara questioned her about the Straighten-Up Halfway House. The senator brightened and praised her pet project. She insisted vehemently that the state should provide a larger appropriation for the institution. After all, what other private or public program could say that it had rehabilitated eighty-five percent of its quota of society's rejects?

"Since the halfway house has been so successful, Senator Perez, I guess you must be deeply saddened by the loss of one of their key personnel."

Perez's eyes flickered with surprise. Then her face became expressionless. "You must be referring to the recent death of Dr. James Reardon."

"Yes," Sara nodded quickly, pen and notebook poised.

The senator sat down behind her desk, lit a cigarette, and inhaled deeply, then scrutinized Sara thoughtfully. Her eyes narrowed. "The loss is tragic, no question about it. James Reardon can never be replaced, although I am quite confident that those in charge at the Straighten-Up Halfway House will find someone eminently qualified to carry on his splendid work."

"James Reardon was on his way to Sacramento when he was killed," Sara stated flatly.

"I didn't know," Perez replied.

"Do you have any idea who he might have been going to see?"

"I've only spoken with the man once in my life, and that was over a year ago."

Sara smiled thinly. "Well, you'd certainly know if he'd had an appointment to see you, Senator Perez, wouldn't you?"

"Of course I would, but I've been in Los Angeles."

"The day James Reardon was killed you were in Sacramento."

The senator stiffened, and a distinct edge came into her voice. "I thought you came here to discuss the energy crisis."

"You wouldn't happen to know who might want to see James Reardon dead, would you, Senator Perez?"

The lady slowly rose and leaned on her desk, her jaw muscles clenching. Her eyes never left Sara's face. "I certainly would not!"

"Then there's Alan Rosenus. He was a friend of Reardon's."

"The political reporter? What about him?"

"He's dead, too."

"I didn't know."

"There was an obituary in the newspaper. You do read the *Times,* don't you, Senator?"

"Religiously." Perez pushed a button next to her telephone. She was furious. "I am also a personal friend of the publisher, whom I intend to call and recommend that he fire a certain reporter named Dianne Ryder!"

The door opened, and the huge Chicano rolled inside. "Yes, Senator?"

"Show this *gusana* out, Hector."

Sara was angry with herself. She had used the wrong tactics with Anna Perez, not anticipating that the senator could be so quick and tough. The hoped-for verbal slip about James Reardon hadn't been forthcoming, nor had any measure of cooperation. Instead she was left feeling unsure of her next move.

She stabbed a forkful of salad and chewed voraciously. There were other problems, too. Somehow she would have to make sure that a certain Dianne Ryder did not get fired.

"Well, you don't work for the *Times* anymore," said Sam.

Sara drank her wine. "Whoopie-fuck."

"What'd you say, Mom?"

"You weren't supposed to hear that."

"Oh. Okay."

"It's just that your klutzy mother got an exclusive interview with Senator Anna Perez and came away with nothing."

"You guys." Valerie pushed her plate away and wiggled in her chair, moving closer to Sam. "Don't you ever talk about anything else?"

"Sure," said Sara, after swallowing a bite of her cheeseburger. "What we're—"

"I know, I know." Valerie nodded her head with disgust. "What you're going to do next."

"Can you think of a better way to pay the rent?"

"I'm not big enough to worry about paying the rent." She gave Sara a disparaging look, then got up and carried her plate to the kitchen sink. "Want to play some chess, Sam?"

"You're on, hot stuff."

"Really?" Her eyes widened and she beamed.

"Give me five to finish eating."

"I'll go set up the board." She vanished into the living room, ignoring her mother's withering glare.

Sam munched on his salad, then smiled wistfully. He turned to Sara. "You know, I love that kid."

She placed her hand over his. "Sam, not now, okay?"
He nodded reluctantly. "Okay."

"If you're going to help me, you have to keep me
thinking about the case. I worry about Valerie too
much as it is."

He frowned and lapsed into a thoughtful silence.
A few minutes later he straightened up and snapped
his fingers. "Hey, I got it! What about Mrs. Rosenus?"

"I called her while you were cooking the hamburgers."

"Oh."

"Her mother answered. She's under sedation and
won't talk to anyone."

"Understandable. So where does that leave us?"

"With no leads."

"Okay, so we're back with Anna Perez. Do you think
she's the one James Reardon was going to see in
Sacramento?"

"I don't know, but something tells me we should
follow this up."

"And not admit to ourselves that we have in fact
reached another dead end which could be damaging to
our morale?"

"Precisely." She wagged her finger. "After all, she
could lead us to the killers now, couldn't she?"

"There's only one problem."

"What?"

"I don't believe the good senator will ever talk to
you again."

She gazed at him, but her face showed no expression.
"We'll bug her house."

He was astonished. "What?"

"The only way to find out if Anna Perez has any
knowledge of the murders of James Reardon and Alan
Rosenus is to listen in on her private conversations."

Just the thought made her feel stronger already. Her confidence grew. She straightened her shoulders, feeling much less vulnerable.

"Jesus." He shook his head and turned away. "That makes us just as bad as them."

"Who's *them*, Sam?"

He looked back at her and raised his eyebrows. He did not immediately comprehend.

"Them is us, Sam. And us is them."

"But—"

"Sweetheart," she said softly. "What else can we do?"

He forced a smile, then shrugged comically. "I don't know. Go into teaching?"

"Be serious."

"You ready, Sam?" Valerie called from the living room.

"Almost."

"Jeez, you eat slow."

He got up from the table. "Hang on, kid, I'm on my way."

"Sam?" Sara looked up at him, her eyes open and inquisitive. "Are you with me in this? Totally?"

He nodded slowly.

"Now's the time to pass. If you want to."

"No. There's Andy to think of." He paused. "And you."

She felt relieved, then excited. "I'll start getting ready. Believe me, Sam, this is going to help us a lot."

"How the hell are we going to find out where she lives?"

"You know those maps to the homes of stars that they sell on Sunset Boulevard?" She finished her wine. "I've got stacks and stacks of them."

"Very clever, but what if someone catches us in the act?"

"That's the chance we take. Although I read in the

paper that her husband is on location in Canada with a movie he's producing. More than likely she'll be home alone."

"What if she has live-in help?"

"You're going to find that out up front." She winked at him. "When whoever answers her door listens to your eloquent motorist-in-need-of-telephone-to-call-emergency-road-service speech."

"Hey, wait a minute!"

"We'll leave around eleven."

He didn't have a chance to respond, for Valerie was yelling at him from the living room again. "You going to play, Sam? Or are you chicken?"

He threw up his hands, then grinned and returned Sara's wink. "Nobody calls me that!" He strode out of the kitchen.

Valerie hovered over the chessboard on the floor, her hands flitting about, adjusting pieces and making sure they were perfectly aligned and facing in the proper direction. When Sam came into the living room and sat down next to the board, she leaned toward him and squeezed his hand. "Thanks," she whispered.

"For what?"

"Helping Mom."

He smiled at her. "Don't mention it." He patted her head and winked. "I've been worried about her, too."

Valerie rocked back on her knees. "You go first."

Sam obliged and pushed a pawn.

Valerie groaned. "Dumb move!" She dropped down onto her elbows and studied the board, her face barely six inches from the pieces but her mind far away from the game. She liked being close to Sam. She liked the faint smell of the ocean which always accompanied him. It seemed reassuring. She liked his tan; she liked his strength; she liked the touch of gray in his hair.

Sometimes when they walked along the beach, she would pull him a good distance ahead of her mother so that people would think that it was just the two of them. She scowled and blushed and played with a chess piece. She was getting nowhere.

"Are you that good?" Sam asked sarcastically. "Or that bad?"

"O-kay!" She moved her queen's pawn to the center of the board. He hesitated briefly, then pushed another pawn. Her mind raced.

"What was my daddy like, Sam?" She moved a knight.

"What was he *like?*" He paused. "What a question. I guess I'm not sure. I know he loved you a lot, though. He had a special place in his heart for you. I think he envied your childhood."

"How come? He was a kid once."

"Yeah, but he grew up poor. In the shadows of the milk and honey. From what he told me, he was struggling to survive and never had a chance to enjoy being a kid."

"There's not an awful lot to enjoy, if you want to know the truth."

Sam moved a rook pawn two squares forward. "Your turn."

She brought out her other knight. "What else do you remember about Daddy?"

"Lots, but surely you've heard it all before, Val."

"Are you kidding? Mom never told me everything."

"About what?"

"You know! About him dying. I think she keeps it inside, but doesn't know what it is. I don't think she'll ever know unless someone tells her."

He moved another pawn. "And I think someone's imagination has run wild."

She looked at him, her eyes wide with indignation.

"How many times have *you* been woken up in the middle of the night by my mom's screams?"

He frowned with surprise and studied her, weighing the resentment and the uncertainty. "Never."

She looked down at the board and automatically pushed another pawn, creating a phalanx.

"How often does your mom—"

"Too often," she replied quickly. "Your move."

He did so. She responded by sliding a bishop forward, capturing one of his pawns. He moved again. She picked up her knight and took another pawn— which he had left totally unprotected—leaned back and sighed as if she were bored. He methodically moved a rook forward, and she captured that, too, moving her knight with a flourish.

"You're easy, Sam."

"I wasn't expecting Bobby Fischer in drag," he replied with forced lightness.

The game continued. Sam moved forward because there was no point in retreating, and Valerie danced her pieces back and forth, relentlessly cutting a swath through his men while picking his brain.

"Who did you know first? My mom or my daddy?"

"Your daddy."

"Did you always love my mom?"

He grinned shrewdly. "I do now."

"Did you and my dad fight over her?"

"People only do that in the movies."

"Come on, Sam!"

"Don't ask questions I can't answer, kid."

"Well, I trust you."

"I trust you, too, but there are limits to everything."

She dropped down onto her elbows again, cupped her chin in one hand, and stared at the board, wondering what Sam knew about her father's death. She was certainly at an impasse. The postcards told her nothing. The press clippings told her nothing. The . . . *Sam and my father were the best of friends, so everyone says. Maybe Daddy told him something that he didn't tell Mom.* She looked up expectantly, then glanced back at the board and took Sam's remaining rook with her queen almost as an afterthought. She rose to her knees, an innocent expression on her face. "Do you know why they killed him, Sam?"

"Val . . ." He held her hand. "If I did, don't you think I would've said something a long time ago?"

She shrugged and felt flustered. "Sure, but I just thought that maybe he said something to you before it happened. Maybe you forgot, I don't know!"

"I hadn't seen your dad or your mom for three years."

"Oh." She blushed and looked away, absently playing with the chess pieces she had captured. "Well, did you ever *wonder* why they killed him?"

"Of course I did. Sometimes I still do."

"And?"

"There is no reason."

"There *has* to be!" She cried in anguish. "I mean, I've read everything he wrote, I've read all the letters, I've read the stuff they wrote about him, I've seen the pictures of him shaking hands with people . . . Everybody liked him, Sam!"

"I know," he said softly.

"Well?"

"Maybe everyone wanted something from him, too."

"Huh?" She looked puzzled.

"I don't know if it means anything, but your father was a very ambitious man. Sometimes ruthlessly so."

Sara called Mrs. Berman and asked if she wouldn't mind staying with Valerie for several hours. Mrs. Berman reluctantly agreed, then proceeded to give Sara a twenty-minute lecture on proper motherhood versus staying out all night for immoral purposes. Sara protested that it was part of her job. If that was the case, Mrs. Berman commented, then Sara would be better off unemployed.

Next Sara broke the news to Valerie.

"Momma, I want to go too."

"You can't."

"Why not?"

"We've been through it already. Tomorrow's a school day, and you should've been in bed two hours ago!"

"I want to go with you!"

"For the last time, Valerie Scott, the answer is *no!*"

Her daughter began weeping softly. "Please, Momma!"

"Come on, Val, don't do that! Mrs. Berman's going to be here soon."

"I'm not a *baby!*" she cried. "And I don't want a baby-sitter! I want to go with you!" She curled up into a ball, put her face in her hands, and quietly wept.

Sara felt terrible, and her daughter's tears were only increasing her anxiety. She wrung her hands and turned to Sam. "Can you talk some sense into her?"

"I don't know."

"Try, okay?"

He nodded, went over to Valerie, sat down beside her, and stroked her back. She shrank from his touch. "Go away, Sam! You won't even finish playing chess with me!"

"You won the first two games," he replied. "What more do you want?"

"For you guys to take me with you!"

Sara put on her coat, then looked at Sam and gestured at her watch and at the door. He glanced back at her and shrugged. She sighed, went over to the couch, and sat on the other side of Valerie.

"What is this?" Valerie exclaimed into the pillows, her voice muffled but still indignant. "Two adults against one preadolescent?"

"Honey, it's really better if you stay here."

"I don't want to."

"Val, don't make me angry. You have to."

Valerie raised her head. Her face was tear-streaked and swollen, and she glared at her mother. "You won't tell me the real reason, will you?"

"What do you mean?"

"You don't want me to go because something might happen!" she cried.

"Valerie! That's not true!"

Yes, it is. Yes, it is, Valerie told herself over and over while she stared at the chessboard, playing a mindless game of hopscotch with the pieces. Her mother and Sam had left, and so far she had ignored Mrs. Berman, who was sitting on the couch engrossed in a Rosemary Rogers paperback.

Gradually Valerie's bitterness faded, giving way to the helpless fear that always made her feel lost and tiny. She glanced at Mrs. Berman and could not hide the anguish in her expression.

With a sigh Mrs. Berman put her book down and patted the couch beside her. "Why don't you come here and tell me about it, pumpkin?"

Valerie bit her lip and shook her head.

"It won't kill you, will it?"

"Why should I talk to you? You don't care, either!"

Mrs. Berman shrugged. "Okay, so go ahead and sit there like an angry turtle and snap at your chess pieces."

"Well? All you want to do is read your dumb book!"

Mrs. Berman raised her heavily penciled eyebrows and looked at Valerie over her glasses. "If that was true, I'd have a much easier time concentrating in my own apartment, wouldn't I?"

Valerie fidgeted and blushed. "O-kay." She sighed, got up, went over to the couch, and sat down. She stared across the room while Mrs. Berman waited. Then she crumbled, put her head against the old lady's shoulder, and cried. When she could talk, she quietly explained that her mother was on the trail of some murderers and that she was scared out of her mind that something was going to happen and she would end up an orphan.

Mrs. Berman held her and patted her and reassured her, saying that Valerie shouldn't worry because Sam was with Sara. "He's a good man, Valerie, a strong and wise man. Your mother will be safe with him. And so will you, if it ever comes to that."

Valerie nodded, but she still felt uncertain. "I just don't want to be left alone," she whispered.

"You'll never be left alone, pumpkin, and that's a promise."

Sara was silent during the drive to Beverly Hills, still thinking about Valerie's protests. She didn't know exactly what was going to happen at the senator's house; she didn't know how dangerous it might be, but she was certain that Valerie would be fine with Mrs. Berman. Finally she spoke. "I'm sorry."

"What for?"

"The unpleasant mother-daughter scene."

"It's understandable."

"Why?"

"You love her and she loves you."

"Oh, okay," Sara replied resentfully. "You think I'm

being overprotective just because she's all I've got, is
that it?"

"That wasn't my interpretation of it at all."

"Well, then?"

"All I meant was that Valerie knows that you're up
to something risky. She wanted to come along because
she's worried about you."

"I just don't want anything to *happen* to her!"

"Sara, she doesn't want anything to happen to you,
either."

She slowly turned her head and stared at Sam. Her
mouth fell open. "Oh." Her voice sounded small. The
sudden realization came hard, but it was nice to hear.
She had kept her own fears bottled up; she hadn't discussed them with Valerie, but the girl had sensed
them, anyway. Valerie cared. She wanted to help, to
do what she could, even though she was only twelve.
That was genuine. Sara smiled and felt warm. She enjoyed a rare moment of understanding: Valerie's yearn-
ing to grow up was in part a desire to make sure her
mother was all right.

"Sara?"

"What?"

He touched her hand. "You're a very private person."

"Yes."

"Someday I'd like it very much if you'd tell me what
goes on inside your mind."

Her ears burned. "But why?"

"Because I don't want anything to happen to you,
either."

Sara smoked one more cigarette while she checked
herself out, looking over her dark, nonreflective clothing. She briefly wondered why Sam had asked about
her private thoughts. She shivered. No matter how

close she and Sam were, she didn't think she could ever
tell him about the dream. But for the present she'd
have to put that subject out of her mind. She was
working now. There was no time for self-indulgence.

They rounded another corner and parked up the
street from Anna Perez's house. Sara showed Sam how
to operate the cassette in the Pinto's back seat, em-
phasizing that it wasn't much different from a regular
tape recorder. Satisfied that he understood, she took
the bug that corresponded to station six and presct
it on the mother machine. Just in case, she pocketed
a few more, then turned and looked at him expectantly. "Ready?" she whispered.

"What if there's a big dog or something?"

"He'll bark and we'll pass."

He nodded and gulped.

They swung out of the car and moved quietly along
the sidewalk.

The Perez residence wasn't the most elegant in the
world, but then again it wasn't the most modest either,
considering that the average sale price for a home in
the neighborhood was two million five. Like most
Beverly Hillsian creations, the architecture was eclectic
at best, hodgepodge at worst. It was a three-story
Moorish structure with Angelican landscaping. One
light shone from a bedroom on the top floor. Sara
looked over the house and grounds critically, then decided. The time seemed right. She touched Sam on the
arm. He turned.

"If it's her, just act natural. If someone else answers, lean against the wall."

He nodded and gulped again. He was pale; his face
showed strain.

"Hey, are you sure that you're up for this?"

"Let's just get it over with." He turned and went up
the walkway toward the front door. Sara hurried

across the lawn to a tree by the side of the house that she could watch from.

Sam rang the doorbell. After a moment the porch flooded with yellow light. A full minute passed. Finally the door opened a crack, and he began talking and gesturing. He did not lean against the stucco. Sara sighed. *All systems go.*

She ran along the side of the house through a small orchard of breadfruit trees. Then she slipped through a picket gate, angled around another hedge, and stumbled upon a swimming pool. There she stopped short, gasping. One foot froze in midair, the other on the edge. She felt herself rocking. Falling. Flailing her arms, she managed to keep her balance, but just barely. She backed into the hedge, took several deep breaths and recovered her composure. So much for overconfidence.

She skirted the pool warily, crossed a patio, went through a garden, then down an arcaded walk. A set of double French doors stood before her. And behind her all was quiet and peaceful and clear. No snarling watchdogs, not even a tomcat on the prowl. This was as good a place as any. She peered at the lock. It was so simple a child could have jimmied it. There wasn't even a deadbolt to complicate matters. She made a mental note to warn Anna Perez about her lack of security when this was all over. Then she popped open the lock with a credit card and was about to push open the door when she sensed that this was much too easy. She stepped back, looked up, and breathed in sharply. She'd almost been disastrously careless. On top of the door frame a magnetic alarm was attached to a tiny wire. The Perez household was protected by a professional security system—tied in, no doubt, to a master "electronic sentry" at the Beverly Hills Police Department. If she opened the door and broke the connection, the board would light up, and the dispatcher would be on the radio with a priority call for a burglary in progress. Sara scrutinized the little rectangular device, then nodded. She knew how to bypass it. She had brought along extra bugs just in case she would have an opportunity to plant several. *Well, one would serve right here.* She took one out of her pocket, inspected it, then gingerly held up its magnetic belly. On tiptoes she carefully placed the bug against the end of the alarm. It stuck, creating another magnetic field. So, when she pushed the door, the alarm would be fooled; its magnetic field would remain intact, even though the circuit was actually broken. *Casparian, wherever you are, thanks for making me memorize all that boring stuff that we kept getting from Westinghouse just because you once worked for them as a security consultant, okay?*

She opened the door, slipped inside, and found herself in a formal dining room. She listened and heard the muffled sound of Sam's voice at the front door, then moved along the side of the room and eased through a swinging door into the kitchen. And stopped. There were five doors, all of them closed. She didn't want to take the time to try each one, so she looked around and located the pantry. The top of the large cabinet was slanted diagonally; that meant there were steps on the other side. She opened the adjacent door and saw nothing. The blackness seemed to creep out and touch her. Trembling, she fumbled in her purse, took out a penlight, and switched it on. In front of her was a back staircase. She closed the door behind her. A musty odor told her the passageway was never used. She went up, panning the light beam back and forth, moving quickly but cautiously. The stairs were steep and narrow, and she couldn't let herself trip.

Six levels up the steps ended. *This must be the third*

floor. In front of her was a door, but before trying it, she paused to let her rapid breathing subside. The door, like the staircase, was probably never used and would creak when opened. Once again Sara dug into her purse, this time producing a hotel-size bar of soap. She rubbed the hinges with soap, then held her breath and slowly pushed the door. No creaks. She closed it behind her. Now she was in a wide and spacious wood-paneled corridor. At the far end light came from beneath a door. Sara hurried toward it, her heart pounding with both fear and excitement. She heard Sam downstairs on the telephone, dragging out his contrived conversation, and figured that she had ample time.

She slipped into Anna Perez's bedroom and was not surprised by what she saw. The room was done in white and light-blue pastels. The bed was round and canopied, and had been recently occupied. A fire crackled in the small fireplace, and an FM station played soft music. A bottle of wine and a goblet rested on an oval table between the bed, the fireplace, and a love seat. *Ah, yes, the good life.* Sara allowed herself a smile. *What a way to get ready for bed.* All that was missing was a purebred cat stretched out in front of the fire, purring.

Sara saw the telephone, a cream-colored Princess model, on the nightstand beside the Tiffany lamp. She crossed the room, perched on the bed, picked up the phone, and had it apart with just a few quick turns of a small screwdriver. She removed bug number six from her pocket and placed it next to the amplifier. She replaced the plastic telephone cover, screwed it down tight, put the phone back on the nightstand, and got up to leave. But as she started across the room, she froze. The water was running in the bathroom, behind that door.

Someone was in there.

She was about to bolt for the corridor and the back stairway when the front door slammed downstairs. Obviously Sam had just been shown out and Anna Perez would be on her way upstairs. Sara moaned. She might be able to get out of the house without being caught, but she doubted that she could leave without being detected. If she were seen, then so much for the bug. She hurried toward the door, then abruptly stopped again. Anna Perez had reached the second landing. Now there wouldn't even be a chance to escape! She whirled around and stared at the bathroom door. Heavy footsteps fell on the thick shag carpet.

The bathroom door started to open.

Panicked, Sara took one last look behind her and saw a louvered closet door slightly ajar about fifteen feet away. She ran for it, dove inside, and pulled it shut just in time. Then she slowly straightened up, trying desperately to quiet the sound of her breathing. She crouched and peered through the slats, shocked by what she saw. She had met this man before, yet she never would have expected to see him strolling out of Anna Perez's bathroom.

Jorge Martinez crossed the room and stopped at the side of the bed.

Nine

He was frowning suspiciously. He turned his powerful body, looking nervously in all directions, seeming to sense that there was an intruder in the room. Sara saw his muscles tense and bunch under his shirt. His movements were cautious and poised; he was ready for anything.

The phone rang.

"Just a minute!" Anna Perez called out from below. "I'll get it down here."

Martinez sat on the bed, leaned back on his hands, and appeared to relax. He whistled softly through his teeth as if trying to tell himself that he was just being paranoid. Suddenly he cocked his head toward the hallway and listened. There was only the faint murmur of Anna's voice on the telephone. He cast a wary sidelong glance at the door and then reached into his shirt pocket and extracted a small vial of cocaine. He unscrewed the cap, shoveled into the powder with the attached spoon, and sniffed. He repeated the process twice for each nostril, then put the vial away, threw back his massive head, and gasped with pleasure.

Sara's eyes narrowed. *What is the director of a halfway house for drug abusers doing snorting cocaine on the sly? In a lady senator's bedroom while her husband's out of town, no less.* Sara was so astonished, she almost forgot she had nearly been caught bugging the room. If only she had her camera. Talk about digging up evidence for a divorce case! *My, my, how things change,* she thought. Like Casparian used to say while rubbing his hands together greedily, *Right now you got the whole* schmooka *laid out in front of you, Sara. Take what you need and leave the rest. Only don't blow it.*

Jorge Martinez and Anna Perez? What an unlikely combination, Sara thought. The senator was still uptown and bright lights, whereas Martinez reminded her of reformed neon. The only thing they seemed to have in common was hypocrisy. But Sara did not have time to speculate, for Anna Perez came back into the room. She was wearing a modest housecoat and had just put on fresh make-up. Instead of being ready for bed, she looked like she were set to do a Revlon commercial. She sauntered over to the table, leaned over it, and let her breasts swing out of the housecoat. Unconcerned, she picked up her wine, sat back on the love seat, sipped, and held the glass close to her lips.

Martinez tilted his head toward her. "Who was that at this hour?"

"At the door?"

"Yeah."

"Some man was having car trouble and I let him use the phone to call Triple-A. Poor guy."

He shook his head. "You ought to be more careful. If I was you, I wouldn't do things like that."

"In *this* neighborhood?" she chuckled.

"You're a senator now." With a sudden burst of energy, he bounced off the bed and paced. "You know this city's crime rate!"

"What's that supposed to mean?"

"Nothing." He giggled and sniffed. "I'm just saying that you should be very particular about who you let inside your house."

Amen, Sara said to herself.

Anna smiled and lowered her eyelids. *"Mi casa, tu casa."*

"Hey, I like that!" He went over to the love seat, sat down, and kissed her. Their mouths lingered together. "Who was that on the phone?"

"Henry."

"Henry?" He jerked back and started buttoning his shirt. "Why the hell didn't you say something?"

She put her hand over his and stopped him. "Don't worry, *querido,* he's still in Canada. I told him I'd call him back later."

Martinez sat back, but he wasn't relaxed. His hands twitched compulsively; Sara guessed it was the cocaine. His pupils were dilated, too, so that when he smiled at Anna Perez, he appeared to be looking right through her.

"Canada." His voice was thick. He laughed low. "That's a good long way off."

She nodded. He put his hand inside her housecoat and rested it against her breasts. Neither of them moved or spoke for a long time. Then Sara could see Anna's chest rise and fall as her breathing quickened. She returned Martinez's intense stare, only now her eyes were glazed over as if he had hypnotized her. She slowly shook her head.

"You're incredible. All you have to do is put your hand on me and I'd do anything for you. Such a gift."

"I feel the same way, Anna."

But Sara could tell that he was lying.

Then she began to feel uncomfortable. Martinez was pulling Anna Perez toward the bed. Sara knew what was going to happen, but she could do nothing about it. *What the hell.* She had never been a voyeur before. Life was full of little surprises.

Martinez jerked Anna's housecoat off and roughly shoved her so that she fell back onto the bed. He leaned over and ran his hands across her body like a pianist practicing for a solo performance. She went all soft and supple for him, whimpering with anticipation as he knelt between her legs. She arched her pelvis, reached down, and tried to pull his face against her groin. He pushed her hands away and grinned up at her, his lips curled with disdain. Then he stepped back and slowly undressed, ignoring her whispers for him to hurry. Once again he knelt between her legs, this time making contact. She jumped, shuddered, then gasped. He might as well have been pushing buttons.

Sara was disgusted, and she felt a twinge of sympathy for Anna Perez. She wasn't observing an act of love; this was sexual manipulation. Martinez refused to let Anna touch him; he insisted upon total subjugation. Anna Perez might as well have been an animal. Instead of caressing her, he played her—searching, or so it seemed, for a tune that he had heard before. He was physically aroused, but he was clearly not enjoying himself. *Then why do it?* Sara could guess. Anna Perez was a senator. Martinez wasn't on top of her riding for pleasure. He was between the thighs of power. He held the reins. This must be his way of insuring that he could do as he damned well pleased within the good senator's sphere of influence.

Had she just solved her case?

Anna tensed and wrapped her arms and legs around her partner. She arched upward and her body convulsed as she climaxed. Then she unfolded and went limp like a dying flower.

Martinez lay down beside her and put his hands

under his head. She glistened with perspiration, and the reflection of the fire made gold patterns on her light-brown skin. Her eyes were closed, and she wore a beatific smile. *She looks beautiful,* Sara thought. *She probably even feels beautiful.* The irony of it. How could a woman as experienced as Anna Perez engage in something so personal, so intimate and *not know* what was really going on? *And to think that women were always thought of as the manipulators.* She shuddered, wondering if she had ever been deceived like that.

"Was it good for you?" Anna Perez whispered, her voice used and husky.

"The best time ever," Martinez lied.

"You're just saying that."

"Come on, Anna," he replied with mock indignation. "You know you're fantastic."

"Really?"

"Really."

She smiled smugly, like a child. Turning over, she took two cigarettes from the nightstand, lit both, and handed him one. They smoked in silence.

When they finished their cigarettes, she embraced him from behind, pressing her body against his back. "Darling, I'm so glad you can spend the night for a change."

He sat up, pulled away from her, and swung his legs over the edge of the bed. "I'm sorry, Anna, I can't. Tomorrow's going to be a very heavy day." He began dressing. "I have to be there early."

"So? It's not as if I don't have alarm clocks in the house."

"Anna." He turned and leered at her. "I need *sleep.* I have to be *despejado y despierto,* you know?"

"What's so special about tomorrow?"

He buttoned his shirt. "I have to find a competent volunteer to replace Doc Reardon. Otherwise the entire counseling program is going to turn to shit."

"Oh." She was suddenly self-conscious about being naked, so she put on her housecoat and sat primly on the bed. "He was a good man, wasn't he?"

"The best."

"What a shame."

"Yeah."

"Him and that reporter."

Martinez turned. "What reporter?"

"Surely you know. The guy who hated the governor."

"No. Who?"

"Mr. Rosenus of the *Los Angeles Times.*"

"What about him?"

"He's dead, too."

"What's that got to do with Doc Reardon?"

"Weren't they friends?"

"I don't know. Were they?"

She shrugged. "Someone said that. Or maybe I read it somewhere."

He slipped his feet into a pair of alligator-skin halfboots. "I don't know about any Mr. Rosenus, but I do know that Doc Reardon is dead, and I've got to find someone to pick up the slack."

"Can I help?"

"No. I have to do this myself. Doc Reardon was a very special guy who needs a very special replacement. Someone worthy of his memory."

She went to him, embraced and kissed him. "Good luck." She looked at him and smiled. "When will I see you again?"

"Soon." He pinched her cheek. "You know me. I can't stay away."

"Sometimes I wish I could feel guilty about our affair."

"Why? I mean, how can it be wrong when we're so totally honest with each other?"

She smiled and took his hand. "I'll see you to the door." They left the bedroom and started down the hall.

Sara pressed her head against the cool enamel of the louvers, relieved that she hadn't been caught. Now that they had left the room, the risk she had taken, the danger began to register. She was momentarily overcome with fear. *What if Jorge Martinez is involved in the murder?* She shivered, for she could see herself caught in the open like James Reardon, the car with the tiny windows and the sloping curves rocketing toward her and slamming into her—crushing her against a wall of rough concrete.

When Sara heard them reach the second-floor landing, she eased out of the closet and crept across the bedroom. She paused at the door and listened. They were almost to the first floor now. She hurried along the hallway to the back stairs, opened the door, closed it behind her, flicked on her penlight, and descended the steps two at a time. She was crossing the kitchen before they had even gotten to the foyer. She paused again and strained to hear. They were at the front door now, talking in low voices. Sara gulped, went into the dining room, and started across the hardwood floor for the French doors.

Creak. Not once, but twice.

She was paralyzed. Her heart pounded. She listened intently, but apparently Anna Perez and Jorge Martinez had not heard, for there was no sudden hush or quick movement in her direction. The muttering voices continued. Sara tiptoed forward, walking as though she were on a tightrope, holding her breath, and praying that she would not give herself away.

Finally she was outside. She closed the French door, reached up and removed the bug from the alarm, then hurried away from the house as quietly as she could. When she reached the swimming pool, her fear increased. She shivered; the back of her neck tingled with cold. Was someone following her? She turned quickly, but could see only blackness. She sidled around the hedge, grateful now that the house was out of sight.

Someone stepped out in front of her.

She gasped and fell back against the hedge, frantically pawing inside her purse for her pistol.

"Shhh!" The figure grabbed her by the shoulders.

"Let go! Please, let go!"

"Sara, will you shut up? It's me! Sam!" he whispered desperately. She sagged against him, buried her face in his chest; her heart was beating madly.

"Don't you ever do that again, Sam Gage."

"Hey! I was worried about you!"

"You were supposed to stay in the car!"

"*You* were supposed to be in and out of there in five minutes!"

"Did you hear what was going on?"

"Of course I did! And as soon as I knew that something was wrong I started looking for a way to get into the house in case they discovered you."

"Oh, Sam." She touched his face.

She spared him the knowledge that if he had succeeded, he would have ruined everything—not to mention bringing Beverly Hills' finest down on their heads. "Come on," she said softly. "Let's get away from here."

Hand in hand they moved quickly to her car. They got in and Sam drove away. Sara looked into the back seat and saw that her cassette machine was turning.

She glanced at the decibel meter—nothing. That meant that Anna Perez was alone with her thoughts. Sara turned and stared blankly out the side window. The sex scene she had witnessed kept recurring in her mind, and she felt depressed. She had always admired Anna Perez for being a scrappy politician who tenaciously supported humanitarian causes. She had always viewed the senator as a potential leader in the critical decade to come. Sara lit a cigarette and smoked it ferociously.

So much for public images.

The truth. Anna Perez was vulnerable and morally bankrupt. What did the woman say to her husband anyway?

"Well?" Sam asked, interrupting her thoughts. "Was it worth it?"

"I suppose so."

"How do you figure?"

"Aside from everything else, I don't think that she or Martinez knows what really happened to James Reardon. If they did, they would've been completely candid with each other or they wouldn't have said anything at all."

"You don't think that they could've been lying to each other?"

"No. Anna Perez was too pathetic *not* to tell the truth."

"What about him?"

"It's possible, but I doubt it." She sighed. "He was preoccupied with acting interested."

"Then he *was* lying."

"Yeah, but only about how he felt."

"Are you sure?"

She shook her head. "No."

"So then he's a suspect."

"Nope, he's as clean as punch until we get some evidence."

"What do you think, then? That they're both innocent?"

"So far."

He snorted. "I'm not holding my breath."

A beep came from the back seat. Sara turned and saw the decibel meter registering. She increased the volume. Anna Perez was on the phone to her husband in Canada. She sounded warm and sincere. She said that she missed him very much and would fly up to be with him in an instant except that her work was piling up. She went on for another five minutes. Finally Sara couldn't stand it anymore and turned off the recorder.

"Politicians!" She held her nose and waved her fingers. "Whew!"

"Doesn't exactly make you want to run right out and register to vote, does it?"

She sat up very straight and affected a lofty air. "No, but we could drive up to Hollywood Boulevard and paint a scarlet *A* on her star."

Sam looked at her, his eyes wide. "You're amazing."

"I am?"

"You pick the strangest times to make light of it all."

"I suppose," she replied and stared out the window. "I just get so damned tired of sorrow."

They arrived home at a quarter to one. Sara helped Mrs. Berman down to her place, said good night, then went back upstairs and checked on Valerie, who was sleeping peacefully. She woke her daughter, kissed her on the forehead, and smiled. "See, honey? I'm okay."

Valerie blinked, realized that she wasn't dreaming, then hugged Sara gratefully. "Is Sam okay, too?"

"Sam's okay, too," Sara whispered.

Valerie smiled, then turned over and went back to sleep.

Sara went into the kitchen, took two beers out of the refrigerator, then moved her tired body into the living room. She gave one to Sam, who was now stretched out on the sofa.

"You're a doll."

She sat cross-legged on the floor, sipped her beer, and looked pensive.

"What a night, huh?"

"It's not over yet, either."

"Oh, come on." He waved her off with a disgusted gesture. Then he thought of something and brightened. "Unless, of course, you're referring to the one and only leisure activity in the world that I could possibly be ready for."

"Conversation?" she said sweetly.

"Jesus, Sara," he groaned. "It's one in the morning!"

"There's also something I haven't told you."

"Whoopie-fuck," he replied, imitating her.

"Sam, when Anna Perez was out of the room, I saw Martinez snort enough cocaine to get an elephant wired."

"So? All that does is put him in the mainstream of American society."

"But they were lovers. Why wouldn't he do it in front of her?"

"Like you said, she's a politician. She probably disapproves."

Sara shook her head and frowned. "You're missing the point, my dear."

"I am?" Reluctantly he sat up straight, then took a swig of beer. "Look, so the guy does cocaine. He could shoot up and it wouldn't prove anything."

"It bothers me, that's all."

"What bothers you?"

"He's the director of a halfway house for the rehabilitation of drug addicts!"

"He also provides stud service for at least one lady politician, and that doesn't prove a damned thing either, Sara!"

"God, sometimes you can be thickheaded, Sam!"

He spread his hands. "Well?"

"Don't you see? What about James Reardon? What if he knew that Jorge Martinez used cocaine?"

"Are you saying that Reardon was killed because he was attempting blackmail?"

"I doubt that James Reardon was capable of anything illegal. All he had to do was *know* that cocaine was available in the director's office."

"If it was."

"*Assume* that it was, dammit!"

"Okay, okay, Sara." He gestured and backed off. "I'll assume that Martinez kept his kit and stash right next to the help hotline and did lines between phone calls. What next?"

"Don't you think that Martinez might just be a little sensitive? I mean, what if word got out? The state would cut off funding so fast that he wouldn't even have time to file for bankruptcy!"

He grinned. "The way you make it sound, Martinez would be a fool to use anything stronger than coffee."

She grinned right back. "Nobody's perfect."

"I guess not."

"All I'm saying is that just his knowing that Martinez used cocaine could have been the reason for James Reardon's death."

He stared at her, suddenly comprehending. "Dammit, Sara, why didn't you just say that in the first place?"

Her dark eyes flashed. "Because I didn't think of it until just a second ago."

"Now that's worth consideration, isn't it?"

"Yeah." She nodded. "And you can take it one step further, too."

"You mean, maybe Martinez is dealing?"

"Think about it."

He did, then sighed and finished off his beer. "So how are we going to find out?"

"That's a very good question, my man."

"One thing for sure is that the tap on the senator's phone isn't going to tell us anything. Especially since he hides his habit from her."

"Good point." She picked at the label on the beer bottle, absorbed in her own thoughts. She didn't see his eyes brighten; she didn't see him lean forward, suddenly alert and excited.

"You got any of those nasty little things left?"

"What?" She looked up and she knew. "Bugs?" Tension began building inside her. She was afraid for him and afraid of what he was going to suggest, yet she understood that something had to be done. "Sam . . ."

"The name you use for them isn't right."

"What?"

"Bugs buzz. They can fly, too."

"Huh?"

"Why don't we call them aphids?"

"Aphids?"

"Sure. They don't make any noise. All they do is sit there and suck. Now why don't you give me some?"

"Sam, you're not going to do what I think you are. Are you?"

He nodded.

"But how?" She dreaded what was coming next. "You're not exactly the living embodiment of a man with a drug problem. Martinez wouldn't let you get past the front door!"

"You'd be surprised how terrible I can look after a few days of concentrated effort."

"But that's insanity! You won't know what you're doing!" Then she wasn't so sure. "Will you?"

"Someone has to do it, Sara, and I'm afraid that you don't qualify."

"What do you mean?"

"A, you've already been there and B, women aren't allowed as residents at the Straighten-Up Halfway House."

She was momentarily speechless.

"So if you have any bad tequila, break it out."

Sara did not appreciate Sam's lighthearted attitude about infiltrating the halfway house. She pointed out that even if he could look like a wasted junkie, he would still be suspect because none of the other residents would know about him or his past. He would be watched carefully. He wouldn't have a chance to bug the place. His plan was foolhardy. And if he got caught, God only knew what they would do to him. Nevertheless, he remained adamant. They argued until the first light of dawn began to show through the kitchen window. Ultimately there was nothing that Sara could say to dissuade him. And she was forced to admit that he did have a chance of pulling it off.

Still she did not want him to go. "You won't listen to reason, then?" she asked, exhausted.

"No."

"Sam, if you love me, you won't do this."

"Sara, I'm only doing it *because* I love you."

"You'll get hurt. I know it." A tear rolled down her cheek. And then another.

"I can take care of myself." He kissed the tears away, but it didn't matter. She began to cry in earnest. He knelt beside her and tried to comfort her, but she

simply put her face in her hands and sobbed. He held
her tightly and they rocked back and forth. Finally
she lifted her tear-stained face and looked into his eyes.
Behind them she sensed his compassion and devotion.
Her heart went out to him. She kissed him then, full
on the mouth, and pulled him down onto the floor so
that she could feel him next to her. Their kiss grew
more intense. She slipped her hands under his shirt
and held on to him tightly. His hands gently found
her breasts, then worked their way inside her jeans.
She moaned. Her mind slipped; she began to forget
where she was. Nothing mattered. Was she floating?

She felt cool air first on her back and then on her
buttocks and legs—he was undressing her. She felt
flushed with excitement, and she trembled. She felt as
though she had no control over her own hands. She
opened her eyes long enough to see that they were
eagerly taking his clothes off. Why was she so de-
tached? She had never felt this good before. She broke
the kiss and took a huge breath. Then another. *This
time. Maybe this time.*

He kissed her face and neck, then her breasts. She
moved against him, closed her eyes, and just drifted.
She opened to him totally. She welcomed him for what
seemed like . . . Her mind slipped further.

*Andy's face is above me. His red hair is damp from
exertion. He kisses me, but not with his tongue. Then
he nuzzles my breasts playfully. I bubble with laugh-
ter, only not for long, because he has his hand between my legs, caressing lightly, and I whisper, telling
him I love him.* She mouthed the words, then opened
her eyes and was surprised. *Strange.* He wasn't there.
She glanced down and saw Sam kissing her belly. She
rested her hand on his face. He slid further down,
kissed her thighs, and then, at last, gently placed his
mouth over her. *Warmth.*

She closed her eyes and let the feelings of pleasure rush through her. She didn't want it to end just yet, so she tugged on his hands and he came back up and kissed her mouth again, their bodies flush against each other. Then she couldn't wait, so she reached between them, grasped his erection, and guided it toward her. He moved into position above her, tensing for the moment, and she opened her eyes to say hello. *"Hello, yourself," Andy says, smiling down at me. He kisses the tip of my nose, mouthing something funny like he always does, because it keeps love in perspective just before the serious stuff begins. I feel so good. I'm giggling. He knows I can't wait anymore. There. Ahh. I feel him push inside me, and his warmth is delicious. I open my legs until we're both comfortable. Then I slowly begin moving, relishing the velvetlike sensations.* She lifted her head and gave him a lovebite on the shoulder. *How odd,* she thought. *His smell has changed.* She looked up and saw Sam. His weathered face was concentrating on the moment. He did not see her. His hands stroked her flanks. She felt him moving between her thighs, and the warmth was just as wonderful as it had been the instant before. Identical, perhaps? To what? *Andy slips his long arms around me and actually lifts me to him, even though he doesn't have any leverage. Where does he find the strength? His mouth is on my breasts, my neck, my mouth. Then he gasps. I'm gasping, too. He's panting. I match his breathing. We're moving faster. I say yes inside. I agree, I want, I accommodate. I urge him to hurry. All my muscles tense. I can't stop!* Sam groaned. He buried his face in her hair. He held her tightly by the shoulders. Sweat ran off his body and mingled with hers. She gasped.

Andy. Sam. She could no longer distinguish between them. She wanted to scream for help, but to whom?

She was puffing up with tension. Memory pressed hard against reality. There was no release. *Sam. Andy. Will you give me peace? Please?*

Her mind was gone. There were no more images or thoughts. She moved wildly beneath Sam, yet it was her and *them.*

All was one.

He poured inside her and she climaxed. The tension drained away.

Finally.

They lay together, listening to their breathing subside. Her arm rested against his, and she could feel his pulse just as she could hear her own heartbeat. And at this moment she really believed that she had a future. *Could sex be an omen?* If so, maybe her days of living with the past were numbered. She smiled, relaxed and utterly satisfied.

Suddenly she remembered Sam's questions about her private thoughts and knew she wanted to confide in him fully. They had become so close, so important to one another. He deserved to know everything about her—even about the core of dread that haunted her so. She needed his understanding. She turned toward him, letting her body graze his, then rose up on one elbow and looked down at his face, so resolute, so peaceful now.

"Sam?" she whispered.

"Umm?"

"Sam, I . . ."

"What?"

She rolled back onto the floor and stared at the ceiling, chewing her lip and frowning with frustration. *I can't tell him. It's not over with. Sure, he probably would understand anyway, but how can I possibly describe the emptiness, the terror that eats away inside like acid? I must, though. I have to try again.* She rose up once more, only to discover that Sam was sleeping. She touched his face, but he did not stir, and so she lay back down beside him, sighing.

When the dawn became morning, she finally woke him and told him that they better get up because Valerie would be awake soon. They kissed tenderly, then separated to dress, and Sara went into the kitchen to get the coffee going. She looked out the window and saw that the low morning clouds were unusually dark. Rain, perhaps? It was that time of year, wasn't it?

Later when he was at the door, she touched his lips and gently reminded him that he was taking part of her with him.

"I think I know."

"Then you better be awfully careful."

"I will. I promise."

"I love you, Sam."

"I love you, Sara."

"We'll laugh a lot when it's over." She turned to go back inside.

"Aren't you forgetting something?"

She went and got him three of the tiny microphones. She smiled at him, no longer sad. "It's against my better judgment, but what the hell." She handed them to him. "Just be careful."

He started down the steps. She waved good-bye, then quickly closed the door to keep out the cold air. Just then she longed for summer; it seemed light-years away.

She wondered if she would hate herself for what she had just done, but there was no way of knowing.

Ten

Sunday, September 28.

Sara wandered aimlessly around the apartment, her mind tired and fogged from no sleep and a lot of thinking. She wished that she had told Sam about the dream; she wished she'd had the strength. Still, she hated to admit her problem, hated to have to admit how it obsessed her. It wasn't fair to Sam. After all, he wasn't waiting for *that* Sara, was he? But it really doesn't matter, she thought. The moment for the revelation had passed. Sam had departed on his mission. And all she could do was wait. She cursed inwardly. She did not like her future to depend upon her crippled psyche or someone else's actions, but she only had herself to blame. She could have told him about the dream. She didn't have to let him go off thinking that everything was all right. She shook her head and couldn't think about it anymore. She poured herself a mug of coffee, then went out onto the back steps, sat down, and lifted her face to the fresh morning breeze. She lit a cigarette and watched the mist rise off the streets and buildings. She felt better instantly. There was traffic in the distance and the inevitable sound of foghorns. She hoped Sam was all right.

Valerie was making noises in the kitchen. Soon she came outside and stood behind her, squinting at the daylight. She was wearing her faded light-blue robe and slippers and holding a steaming glass of milk and coffee with both hands. "Hi, Mom."

"Hi, yourself." Sara squeezed her leg affectionately. "You sleep well?"

"Yeah." Valerie's face crinkled up into a smile. "Thanks for letting me know when you came in last night."

Sara took Valerie's hand and pulled her down onto the steps beside her. She put her arm around her. "Are you okay today?"

Valerie nodded. "I'm sorry about last night."

"So am I."

"How'd it go anyway?"

"All right." Sara wagged her head. "But not perfect."

"Did Sam go home already?"

Sara looked away, then turned back to Valerie and quietly explained why Sam had left and what he hoped to accomplish. Valerie frowned.

"Something could happen to him, couldn't it?"

Sara nodded. Once again, Valerie deserved to know the truth. But did she deserve to share the agony of waiting? *Yes, that, too.* Sara pulled her closer. *We've been through it before—here on the edge with nothing left but ourselves. We can handle it again, can't we? Perhaps.*

"Can you stop him, Momma?"

Sara thought for a moment. Why hadn't she asked herself the same question? Or did she really want to? "Yes, I suppose I could."

"How?"

"By taking myself off the case."

"Why don't you then?"

"Quit, you mean?"

"Yes."

"I don't know. I've never given up on anything. I never really considered it."

"Well, could you?"

"There's Mrs. Reardon to think of. And . . ."

"What about Sam, Momma? What about you?"

Yes, indeed, what about me and my responsibility to her? Why am I stubbornly going on with this? Am I being self-indulgent? She gazed off into the mist and shook her head. *No. I want release. Sweet release.*

Valerie placed her hand on Sara's knee and looked into her eyes. "Please, Momma?"

"I'm sorry. I can't just walk away from it, honey."

"But why not?" the girl insisted.

"Because I have to find out!" Sara exploded.

"Find out what?"

"Who killed your *father!*"

Valerie stared at her mother, astonished. Then she seemed slightly confused. Finally she looked down and fidgeted with the sash of her robe, pulling threads out of the terrycloth.

"Val . . ."

Valerie looked up, her eyes shining with tears now. They embraced tightly, and Sara could feel her daughter trembling. She supposed that that was both a sign of love and of a need to be protected. She wondered if she could continue on the Reardon case and still provide refuge for Valerie. She sighed and nodded with determination. She must.

"Really?" Valerie asked in a whisper, her eyes wide. "You can do that?"

"I don't know, honey. Sometimes I think I'm going crazy."

"There is a chance, though?"

"A slight one."

"Oh." Valerie thought. "You mean a long shot."

"Yeah."

"Then you have to do it, don't you, Momma?"

Sara nodded and rocked her daughter back and forth while staring off into space. She had never felt closer to Valerie—except, of course, when they had shared the grief of Andy's death.

"Do you think . . . ?"

"What, Val?"

"That when this is all over you'll . . . you'll be normal again?"

Sara shuddered and looked away. She paused for a moment and listened to the early-morning traffic noise, muted by the fog. Then she faced Valerie, a hint of desperation in her eyes. "I want you to know that I'm doing this as much for you as I am for myself. Although we loved each other very much, you meant more to him than anything else. He would have made a wonderful father for you. He would have taken you places and showed you marvelous things. He loved to play, and when we were alone, he wondered about what you would like or what you would want to do. If he were still alive, your life would be very rich and full, Valerie. I don't think you would lack for anything. We both deserve to know why he was taken away from us. And I . . . I apologize for being so obsessive about this. If nothing else, it's been because of him. I loved him so."

Valerie was amazed, and tears rolled down her face as she shook her head slowly from side to side. "But he loved you, too," she insisted. "He loved you more, didn't he?"

"I don't know. There was a wall. There was a part of him I didn't know." Suddenly Sara breathed in sharply and covered her eyes, for she had just realized that she was searching for a side to Andy that she had never known. Could she find it in his death?

Terribly confused, Valerie hung on to the railing and pressed her tear-stained face against the faded wooden slats. *But what about the poems he wrote her? How can she say that he loved me better?* She gasped. *What if Momma doesn't like me anymore? What if she runs away or something? God, no, don't blame me, please, Momma!*

Valerie turned back to her mother, reached out, grasped her arm, and hung on to it tightly. "We can do things together, too, can't we?"

Sara nodded hesitantly. "Yes. I'd like that."

"This afternoon, Mom?" She asked urgently. "We can go to the pier for some hot dogs or fish and chips or . . ." Her voice trailed off.

"I have to work."

"But today's Sunday, isn't it?"

"It doesn't matter."

"Mom!" she cried.

"Tomorrow, Val. Tomorrow we'll go to the beach, all right?"

"What about school?"

"You can skip school for once if you want to."

"Okay." Valerie looked her mother in the eye. "You're on."

After her conversation with Valerie, Sara allowed herself the luxury of a long, hot shower. When she got out, she toweled down and felt invigorated. She dried and brushed her dark-brown hair. It shone and fell in curls below her shoulders, and she noticed that it was longer than she normally liked to wear it, but that was all right. Long hair made her appear more feminine, and in her world that translated as *more vulnerable.* Good. She'd take an advantage any way she could get it. She went into the bedroom and dressed in powder-blue corduroys and a white turtleneck. She put on dark lipstick, then selected a knitted wool, navy-blue hat. She adjusted it so that it just shadowed her eyes, making them appear mysterious.

She left the apartment and went down to the Pinto, which was parked a half block away. She got in, started it, and drove off, frowning wistfully. Lately she had been forced to pass up her morning walks through the shabby streets of Venice, and she missed the sights. Perhaps it was just as well, for the Venice she had learned how to survive in was dying. Now if you walked, you were likely to be run over by New Wave crazies on roller skates wearing Frisbees. And she hated to see, up close, the inevitable bulldozing of seventy-year-old bungalows for the new rough-out monstrosities of the "affluhip."

She turned down Horizon Avenue and had to brake hard for several stray dogs that ambled across the street. Some things never changed.

When she got to her office, she poured herself coffee from the Thermos and checked with her answering service. *No calls. Typical.* She lit a cigarette and picked up the phone again.

"Helen, it's Sara. How are you today?"

"I think I'm feeling better. I made it to the supermarket and back without crying last night."

Sara couldn't resist. "Obviously, then, you didn't look at the prices."

Helen laughed for the first time in days, and Sara felt that she had already accomplished a great deal. Then Helen's voice turned sober. "Any news?"

"None. I just wanted to make sure that you were okay."

"You're not keeping anything from me, are you, Sara?"

Sara frowned thoughtfully. "Shouldn't I be asking you that question?"

"I beg your pardon?" Helen's voice stiffened.

Sara raised her eyebrows. Her client sounded overly sensitive, didn't she? Then Sara decided not to push it since she had too many other things to do. "Forget it. I'm joking, that's all. Why don't you get out today—go shopping or see a movie?"

"That's a good idea."

Sara hung up. She finished her coffee and stubbed out her cigarette. While getting ready to leave she noticed that her potted palm and coleus were drooping, and she remembered that she hadn't cared for her plants since the Reardon case began. As she watered them and picked off a few dead leaves she thought about Sam. His mission was taking a lot of pressure off her. It was nice to know that if she were so inclined, she could leave it all up to him. For a brief moment she felt that she was a woman with options. But she understood that until she could put Andy out of her mind, she would still be tormented by the darkness in her mind. She shivered, then left her office, locked the doors, and hurried away.

Instead of lifting, the mist turned into a light drizzle. Crouched on the hillside above 2107 Stanley Hills Drive in Laurel Canyon, Sara cursed herself for not having brought a raincoat. Usually she kept the fold-up plastic kind in her purse, but she must have misplaced it. She took off her wool hat and used it to wipe the rain off her face. Then she rung it out and put it back on. Her teeth were chattering, but she was determined to maintain her vigil over the Rosenus residence.

An hour later she was relieved to see a matronly woman dressed in enough transparent raingear to repel a typhoon leave the house, get into a Cadillac Seville, and drive off. When she had first arrived, Sara had spotted her and correctly assumed that she was Mrs. Rosenus's mother, who was taking care of her daughter. Sara realized that talking to the bereaved widow would be hard enough; getting past her mother would be downright impossible. So she had decided to wait until Mrs. Rosenus was alone. Granted, she was drenched, but it wouldn't be for nothing.

She hurried down the hill to the side-street, wiped the mud off her shoes, straightened her soggy clothes, then strode around the corner. She stopped short. There was a For Sale sign in front of the house that hadn't been there before. She pushed through the gate, crossed the garden and lawn, then went up the steps to the front door. She had decided to be straight with Mrs. Rosenus, since she really had nothing to lose. She doubted that using her real name would put her in danger. Besides, if she had to get in touch with Mrs. Rosenus later on, then she couldn't very well pass herself off as someone else. She knocked sharply and waited.

A young woman opened the door hesitantly and looked out with the expression of a curious child. She was partly hidden in darkness making it difficult to see her. Yet Sara was surprised by her youth. She had pale skin that resembled milk-white porcelain. Her eyes were green, and her straw-colored hair had probably not been brushed in days. In odd contrast her lips were heavily rouged, and mascara was swept up under her eyes. She wore a chemise with nothing underneath, and her feet were bare. Obviously she had made no provisions for the chill. In fact, she appeared to welcome it, just as the black-feathered boa thrown loosely around her neck seemed to acknowledge death.

Sara took a closer look. The woman's eyes were dilated and she was swaying slightly. She was obviously on pills.

She swept her hair back. "What do you want?"

"Mrs. Rosenus?"

"Yes." Her mouth made a tiny, brittle smile.

"My name's Sara Scott. If you don't mind, I'd like to ask you some questions."

"Are you from the police?"

"No. I'm a private investigator." Sara showed the photocopy of her license.

Mrs. Rosenus studied it, thought for a moment, then looked up at Sara. "Is this about Alan's will?"

"No."

"You don't represent my husband's ex-wife?"

"I didn't even know he had an ex-wife."

She was surprised. She looked down, slightly embarrassed. "You're all wet!"

Sara frowned. "May I come in? I mean, when I stop dripping?"

"I'm not supposed to talk to anybody."

"I'm on your side, believe me."

"But I'm tired of not talking to anyone," she said conspiratorially. "My name's Judith." She turned and crossed the room.

Sara stepped inside, closed the door behind her, and followed.

The light was better now, and she saw that the young woman was actually quite beautiful, despite the obvious strain she was under. Judith made a sweeping gesture to a chair by the window, not far from where her husband had been bludgeoned to death. Sara glanced nervously at the spot and was glad that no traces of blood remained. She sat down and looked around. The room was immaculate. The windows were open, and the air was heavy with the smell of wet sage and eucalyptus. Sara shivered. She was freezing.

Judith came out of the kitchen with a fresh pack of cigarettes and a small wastebasket. "It seems like I do this ten times a day." She lit a cigarette, then compulsively emptied all of the ashtrays in the room. "Alan was a good man, Miss Scott."

"I don't doubt that."

"You're from the lawyer's office, aren't you?"

"My client's name is Helen Reardon."

There was no response.

"You do know Helen Reardon, don't you?"

"I'm sorry. Alan and I had only been married for six months."

"What about James Reardon?"

"I've never heard of him, either."

Sara leaned forward. "Your husband never mentioned a man named James Reardon to you?"

She shook her head.

Sara pressed on. "He didn't tell you he had a meeting with James Reardon in a motel room?"

"What are you talking about, anyway?" She frowned and snapped at Sara. "My husband didn't go running off to motels with anyone! And what, may I ask, does this have to do with Alan's estate?"

Sara glanced out the window. Mrs. Rosenus was in a nervous state. She'd have to be handled carefully. Sara turned and gave her a warm, reassuring smile. "Judith, Alan Rosenus and James Reardon were good friends. Your husband taped a cassette of a conversation he had with James Reardon."

Apparently Sara had not chosen the right words, for when Judith Rosenus stood up, her hands shook and her voice quavered.

"I really did think you were from the lawyer's office, but obviously you're not. I'll have to ask you to leave." Sara looked contrite. Her smile asked forgiveness. She spoke softly. "Okay, I'm sorry. So your husband never told you about James Reardon. Forget I asked."

"No matter what you think, there were no secrets between us!" she cried. Her voice hung in the air, then broke like shattering glass. "Now will you please leave?"

"I didn't mean to imply that your husband kept anything from you, Judith, okay?" Sara paused. "You and Alan were evidently very close and very much in love."

Mrs. Rosenus was on the verge of tears. Her mouth was trembling; her face was twisted as if it were about to crack. "I don't know who you are or what you want, but I'd like you to leave my house right now."

"Mrs. Rosenus, you must listen to me," Sara replied in quiet desperation, "and you must listen carefully. Your husband was killed because he knew something that somebody didn't want him to know. James Reardon was killed for the same reason."

"Please get out."

"Judith . . ."

"If you don't leave, then I will." She started to walk away. Sara got out of the chair, caught her by the shoulder, and turned her around.

"Do you understand what I'm saying?"

Judith Rosenus shrank from Sara's touch. "My husband was killed by a common thief! Now will you please leave me alone?"

"Who did Alan Rosenus know in Sacramento?"

"Everybody."

"Who did he trust?"

"Nobody."

Sara backed away. Suddenly she didn't know what

to say; her composure had vanished. Judith Rosenus wept. She did so without apparent effort. Her sobs were fluid and easy and not accompanied by physical pain. That had all been used up.

"I'm sorry," Sara managed to say. "I really am."

"Please get out."

"Look, I'd like to go through your husband's files. It's very important."

"If you don't leave right now, I'm going to call the police."

Sara took one of her cards out of her purse. "Someday soon you're going to wonder who really was responsible for your husband's death."

Judith looked up at Sara; she seemed to be curious and puzzled despite her tear-swollen face.

"And when you're ready, you'll want to talk to me." She put her card on the circular coffee table and sat down again. "I understand how you feel, too."

"What do you know about it?" Judith wrung her hands tightly and held them against her chest.

"I was married to a newspaperman once."

"So what does that prove?"

"He was killed, too. A long time ago. I sympathize, I really do."

"I don't particularly care if he was executed!" she shouted, her face twisting up.

Sara gasped. She stared at Judith Rosenus, her eyes black and angry, her mouth agape, her hands clenchinto fists, then letting go. Letting go. She blinked and her mind slipped. Judith Rosenus's green eyes became the tiny windows of the car lurching away down the side-street. *Smoking guns were pulled back inside. The car rocketed away, its molded taillights flickering dimly. Andy was grasping at the counter, hunched over and retching. He was dying now, suspended in that awful hiatus where pain replaced time. He had been executed.* Sara was screaming, pounding on the arms of the chair. She looked up, fighting for breath, suddenly realizing where she was. Judith Rosenus was huddled against the wall, terrified, her eyes wide, her hand to her mouth. She had seen it all. Panicked, Sara sprang up from the chair and started toward her.

"What's the matter with you?" Judith cried.

"I'm all right now! I'm okay!"

"Get away from me!" She cringed, her voice quavering with fear.

Sara stopped, hesitated, then turned and hurried out of the house, frightened and unsure; the nightmare had finally gone public.

When Sara got back to her office, she called airport security and asked for Sergeant Don Barrett, identifying herself as Cathy Coulson from the Banker's Life Insurance Company. The operator put her on hold. She leaned back in her chair, crossed her legs, and waited. Since he was a security officer, it did not surprise her that he was working on a Sunday. Actually she was glad he was there, because she felt guilty about taking advantage of him and wanted to apologize. He seemed like a genuinely nice person—someone who was trustworthy.

"Cathy!" He came on the line both strong and breathless. "I was going to call you!"

She gasped. *Thank God he hadn't.* "Don, my name isn't Cathy Coulson, it's Sara Scott." She explained that she was a private investigator working for Helen Reardon and that neither of them wanted to get involved with the police.

"I'm not a cop," he replied curtly. "I work for the FAA."

"I know, but . . ."

"Should I be angry?"

"Oh, Don, it's nothing personal, believe me. It's the way I work. I just have to be careful, that's all."

"So why tell me now?"

"I tried to tell you the other day!" She blushed and felt foolish. "Besides, what if you'd called the wrong person?"

Suddenly he chuckled. "Maybe I will. Cathy Coulson might be better looking than you."

She laughed appreciatively. "Anyway, I just wanted to say that I was sorry."

"Is that all?"

"I didn't get a chance to say good-bye."

"You ought to be damned glad you didn't wait around."

"I read about it in the paper."

He hesitated. The energy went out of his voice. "It was a mess."

Sara took a deep breath. "Who was she, Don?"

"Another illegal alien. Her name was Marta Fontana. Last year, she was arrested for prostitution in Sacramento. No known friends or relatives. A real mess, I tell you."

Sara was scribbling furiously. "Any idea who did it?"

"Are you kidding?" He laughed derisively. "The city police are investigating. They haven't even found her clothes yet."

Sara shivered. *They're not likely to, either.*

"But if it's all the same to you, I'd just as soon change the subject."

"No harm, no foul?" she asked tentatively.

"No harm, no foul." He chuckled. "I like that. I like that a lot. Hey, why don't we get together sometime?" He sounded animated again. "Maybe have dinner and take in a movie."

"What about my boyfriend?"

"What about him? At least you're not married."

"I've got a kid."

"Kids I can handle. Husbands I can't."

"Don, my boyfriend matters."

"Sure, he matters. Boyfriends always matter."

"Then why are you asking me out?"

"Because I can tell about you."

"You can?"

"Work always comes first with you, right?"

"Okay, I would agree, but—"

"Then if that's the case, what kind of relationship can you have with the guy? I could be wrong, but I'll bet you don't see him that much."

She held the phone away from her ear and stared at it. She could still hear his voice.

"So in the near future when he's gone and you're looking around for someone new to play with, give me a call, okay?"

She nodded into the receiver, speechless.

"I mean, if life was a won-and-lost column, you'd already be ahead by two favors and one deception. You know what I mean, Sara? If that is your real name." He hung up.

Sara slowly put the phone back onto its cradle. Astonished, she stared across the room. She hardly knew the man, yet he had seen right through her. What did she and Sam have to offer each other if they were always putting each other off for other priorities? Sure, they talked occasionally and made love, but they never went anywhere together or did anything that could be called fun or even eventful. Why? She grimaced. She knew why. Andy remained a higher priority. She remembered their wedding day. At the reception she had observed Andy and Sam in intimate conversation and assumed that one friend was congratulating the other and wishing him well. Sam had borrowed money to fly to Hawaii for the wedding, yet had seemed so lost and forlorn. Caught up in the excitement, she had never bothered to analyze the situation. Had Sam loved her then but remained silent out of respect for his best friend? She had taken his affection for granted during that time. Was she doing exactly the same thing now? Yes. Andy still controlled both their lives and probably always had. But Sam had volunteered to help her solve the Reardon case. She shuddered. No, not really. They were both serving the past, the despair, watching helplessly as it wedged between them. And she had used work as an excuse!

Work? Damn! She had to let herself rest; to forget it for one whole day. If she couldn't be with Sam, well then, maybe she and Valerie would have a good time. She got up, grabbed her purse, and headed for the door. Suddenly she stopped, went back to her desk, snatched up the note she'd just written and studied it.

Marta Fontana, huh? No known friends or relatives. Undocumented hooker. Who knows what else you probably did in order to survive.

Sara dropped the note into the Reardon file and closed her desk drawer. She hurried out of her office, suddenly longing for a taste of the cool salt air that blew in off the ocean just after the sun went down.

The next day came peacefully enough, although like the morning before the mist did not rise. When Sara got out of bed, she felt thick and woozy, but she ignored the symptoms. She was also undaunted by the gray skies. Valerie questioned the wisdom of going to the beach. Sara replied that they would go shopping first, wait for the fog to lift, and then spend the afternoon enjoying the sun and surf, which was okay with Valerie.

Sara was pleased. She couldn't remember the last time she had gone shopping with her daughter. True, there were the inevitable trips to Sears, but those didn't count.

This time they took a real shopping trip, to the Fox Hills Mall, a giant, space-age complex of stores which was, needless to say, not within the funky confines of Venice. Sara bought Valerie a pair of jeans that would withstand the school's asphalt playing field, a flannel shirt for the coming winter, new dress shoes, even though Valerie disdained anything more formal than sandals, and a pretty party dress for no particular occasion at all. Then Valerie insisted that her mother buy something for herself. Sara agreed.

Because she loved hats she splurged on a burgundy velvet bowler that she wore out of the store, tilted slightly forward. Valerie said her momma was crazy and didn't mean it. She laughed a lot and blushed; secretly she was very pleased. And more than one man turned to stare, although Sara wasn't sure whether they were looking at the hat.

They went home for lunch, and Sara prepared Valerie's favorite sandwiches. When she sat down to eat, however, Sara didn't feel hungry.

"You know, Mom, you sound funny!"

"I guess I'm getting a cold." *It was all that waiting outside in the rain yesterday.*

"I know." Valerie shrugged and took a large bite. "But at least it's not serious. I mean, you could be getting cancer."

"Thanks."

Sara found a pint of brandy on the top shelf behind two dusty cans of sauerkraut. She took it out and placed it on the counter along with honey, lemon juice concentrate, cloves, vitamin C powder, Tabasco sauce, and eucalyptus oil. She mixed a little of each in a tall glass, added brandy, then regarded the concoction triumphantly.

"Do you know what you're doing, Mom?"

"Of course I know what I'm doing. This recipe was handed down to me from my great-great-grandmother."

"When? Last week?"

"Don't get cute, kid."

"You sure it isn't a cure for athlete's foot?"

Sara took two large swallows. The stuff went down all right, but when it landed in her stomach, there was a silent explosion. *What in the world did I drink?* She gave Valerie a withering look and forced a smile. "You know, you may be right."

"If I were you, I wouldn't drink the rest of that."

"Just straight brandy would be better for a cold, wouldn't it?" Sara emptied the mixture down the drain, rinsed out the glass, and poured in three fingers of liquor.

"I was thinking more along the lines of a time-release Dristan."

"That's the trouble with your generation." Sara tossed her head back, along with the brandy. Her eyes watered. "You have no concept of reality."

"Huh?"

"Life without pills or TV." She poured herself another shot. "Remind me to stop at the liquor store."

"Shouldn't you just go to bed, Mom?"

Sara frowned. "I'm not *that* sick."

"In that case, they ought to hire you to do all those NyQuil commercials. Could've fooled me!"

"So I've got a little cold. Enough, kid. Get your beach towel."

"Momma, you can't go to the beach. You're sick!"

"The hell I can't."

Valerie raised her eyebrows. "I'd hate to be presumptuous, seeing as how I'm only twelve, but aren't you being childish?"

Sara blushed, but she was unwilling to acknowledge her daughter's insight. "I said that I'd take you to the beach and I plan to do just that."

"But you're sick!"

"I've never felt better in my entire life."

"Okay, but it's all cloudy and yukky outside."

"By the time we get there, the sun'll be out. Don't you want to go?"

"Sure, but . . ."

"You never complained when your father used to take you to the beach!"

Valerie stared at her mother, mouth open and suddenly on the verge of tears. Then she gulped, turned, and hurried out of the room, her head down, her long red hair loose and falling over her shoulders.

Sara was immediately ashamed of herself. Was she angry that Valerie had taken such an uncommon interest in her dead father the past few days? She didn't know what had prompted her to make such a cruel remark.

On their way to the beach Sara apologized, and Valerie said that she understood, even if she didn't. They parked at the end of Windward Avenue, crossed the Ocean Front Walk, and trudged over the wide stretch of sand. Sara sat a good distance back from the water and watched as the fog got thicker, but she was not dismayed. *After all,* she told herself, *how often can you go to Venice Beach and have it all to yourself?* Even the black bongo players, normally rooted near the ruins of a pier, were gone, not to mention the winos, the nudists, or the occasional Canadian tourists lacking in good sense.

Valerie was down at the water's edge looking for seashells. She didn't find anything of interest except an Asahi beer-bottle cap, which she had never seen before. She showed it to her mother.

"How odd that you should find this here at the shore." Sara winked mischievously. "Perhaps you would like to save it for your charm bracelet?"

"Maybe it came all the way across the Pacific Ocean, huh, Momma?"

"Maybe, but more than likely it made the journey from Davy Jones's Liquor Locker on Pacific Avenue."

"Awww, Mom."

Sara laughed gleefully. "Are you going in?"

"Are you kidding? The water's cold enough to break your kneecaps."

"The air's a little chilly, too, isn't it?"

"How come you always sound like a limey when you've been drinking?"

"It ain't the booze, honey, it's the turmoil in my nasal passages. And just think how lucky we are. The British have to deal with that condition all the time."

"How much longer are you going to sit there?"

"Are you suggesting that we leave?" Sara asked with mock hauteur.

"Yeah." She looked critically at the sky and then the ocean. "Before we get hit by a tidal wave or something."

"And, I presume, while I can still drive."

They didn't go home. Whether it was the brandy or not, Sara wasn't sure, but she began to feel depressed, and Valerie wasn't asking questions anymore. She drove aimlessly, making no attempt to avoid a string of red lights that seemed to trigger a growing sense of dread inside her. She didn't fully understand the change, for she had been enjoying her daughter's company immensely. But now she felt powerless to control the car. She had made no conscious decision to drive anywhere in particular, yet she found herself following a vaguely familiar route, as if led by an unseen force. The fog appeared thicker now, the low clouds darker. She automatically turned into the parking lot for the Charles Dietrich Memorial Park, oblivious to the concerned gaze of her daughter. Without a word she turned and nodded to Valerie, and the girl got out of the car.

They followed the walkway into the far reaches of the cemetery and were swallowed up by the mist. Neither spoke, and soon they were standing hand in hand in front of a simple white gravestone marked:

ANDREW BRIGHAM SCOTT
1947–1976
* YOU SHALL BE AVENGED *

Sara stared at the slight mound in front of the marker and realized that she had forgotten flowers. She closed her eyes and wished him a beautiful bouquet, wherever he was, brushing away an involuntary tear. Then she became pensive but didn't allow herself to become maudlin. She didn't feel the inclination to cry. There were too many things to be sad about.

She didn't like being drawn to a cemetery just because she had had a good time with Valerie. It was morbid. Barbaric. There was so little joy in her life. Why must those times always be painted with shadows? Sara scowled. She wished she understood.

She stared at the ground in front of her, then walked

around the slight mound to the headstone. She touched the cold, wet marble and shivered because the sensation matched the way she felt inside much of the time. How unnatural—to be so familiar with death.

She didn't want to be here, yet she knew that she would continue to make the journey to his grave. The dream would keep her coming back. The promise, etched in stone. The obsession. The inner voice that always reminded her that she hadn't found his murderers yet. *Goddamn you, Andy Scott! Why couldn't you have told me something? Did you think that you were loving me by not sharing the trouble you were in? Can you see what this has done to me, how it has consumed me? You had your reasons for not talking to me about it, I suppose. But if you haven't already, give me a sign. Please. I love you.*

Nothing. There was no sudden wind or anything else, not that it was expected. The mist remained and water dripped from the tree branches. Nothing.

Except her promise to him: YOU SHALL BE AVENGED, chipped in marble. She could never forget that legacy. She was determined.

She looked away, her mind wandering to the Reardon case. Reardon had been on his way to see someone when he was murdered. *Had Andy, too, known someone special in Sacramento? Hmmm.* Like Alan Rosenus, he would have been acquainted with many people in the capital city. There must be someone in particular, though! Sara had racked her brain many times in the past; now she tried again, but no names came to mind. *If only Andy had said something before he died!* Would she ever know? Or was she condemned to visit this grave for the rest of her life, mouthing the words below his name?

"Mom, I'm cold."

"So am I."

They walked back to the car and got inside. Sara took several swigs of brandy before starting the engine and turning on the heater. Then she smiled at Valerie and had the courage to make light of it all.

"Hell of a family reunion, wasn't it?"

Eleven

Sara spent the evening trying to drown her cold in brandy. She got so looped that she agreed to play chess with Valerie, even though she would have been no match for her if she'd been sober. Valerie tried to even the odds by making blatantly stupid moves, but Sara could not be underplayed—she'd been drinking since noon. Her tongue sufficiently loose, she told Valerie how she and Andy had first met.

It was during the summer vacation after her sophomore year in college, late in the day on Sunset Beach near her parents' Oahu home. She had been reading all afternoon when a boy several years older than she sat down and began talking quietly about the beauty of nature and how sad it was that man didn't fit. She listened and was charmed by his relaxed manner. He introduced himself as Sam Gage, but he didn't get much further than that because they were joined by his best friend, Andy Scott, fresh off a surfboard. Andy lightheartedly proclaimed that despite the absence of twenty-foot swells, his trip to Hawaii was finally worth it since he'd just met Sara Martin. And not once did he lower his eyes or relinquish her attention.

She thought that she must've fallen in love very

quickly, for from that day on she and Andy were inseparable. Silent and dignified, Sam removed himself from consideration and stayed in the role of best friend, although he wasn't around much after that.

When her parents asked if she wanted to finish school before going off with this young man, Sara said no. She couldn't imagine living without Andy and the excitement he had brought into her life so suddenly. They were married at the end of the summer. With donations from friends and relatives they managed a brief honeymoon in Mexico and then set up housekeeping not far from where she and Valerie were living now. Venice was cheap then, and they lived modestly while Andy finished his graduate work at UCLA.

Sara fell silent and let the memory fade into the back of her mind. "I think I'd better shut up."

"You don't have to, Mom," Valerie replied, fascinated.

"If I keep talking, I'm gonna get silly and start bawling or something." She squinted at her half-empty glass. "And if I drink anymore of this stuff, I might kill more than just a common cold."

When she woke up the next morning, Sara could hardly breathe, let alone move. In addition to her cold she had a splitting headache from all the brandy she had consumed. She got out of bed, moaned, rubbed her pounding temples, but did not fall back on the bed. At least she could stand. She left her bedroom and staggered into the kitchen, wiping the heavy film of cold and sleep from her eyes. A cup of coffee and some orange juice made no difference. Her chest hurt, which made her feel weak. She collected herself and headed for the shower but ran into Valerie in the hall.

"Mom! What are you doing out of bed?"

"What do you think? I'm getting ready for work."

"You can't go to work! You look terrible!"

"I'll wear lots of make-up," she replied dryly. "And your cut-offs."

"Awww, Mom, come on! You're sick!"

"All I'm trying to do is finish a job and keep a client happy, Valerie."

"That's *not* all you're trying to do!"

"Okay, okay." Sara coughed again and doubled over with pain. She made it into the bathroom, and one glance at her haggard face in the mirror told her that Valerie was right. She went back to bed.

Before she left for school, Valerie brought her mother a Thermos of hot tea with lemon and honey, a small transistor radio, and a few vials of tetracycline which Mrs. Berman had accumulated over the years, thanks to her Medi-Cal card.

Sara washed down three pills and a handful of aspirin. She huddled underneath the covers and tried not to breathe too deeply, lest she bring on a spasm of coughing. Then she turned on the radio and listened to a discussion on a morning talk show about the governor's campaign for reelection. The host of the show praised the governor's diligent attempts to make a better life for all Californians, while the guest commentator argued that things kept getting worse. The host blamed the problems on the state legislature and the federal government.

Sara struggled to concentrate, but it was no use. Her mind drifted and she slept.

Late that afternoon when she woke up, she automatically turned over to see what time it was but could not open her eyes. She remembered her cold, then pried her eyelids apart, blinked, and saw that it was almost five o'clock. She had slept that long? Sitting up straight, she was overcome with dizziness, but at least her headache was gone. She poured herself more tea, then swallowed three more tetracyclines, and dropped back onto her pillow, wondering if Sam were all right. She stared at the ceiling, and her thoughts turned to Valerie. She frowned. *Where is she anyway?* Sara cocked an ear but heard nothing in the apartment except the wheeze of her own lungs. Usually Valerie listened to disco music while she did her schoolwork late in the afternoons. Maybe she wasn't home yet. Sara got out of bed. Shivering, she slipped into her robe, suppressed a cough, and shuffled down the hallway. She was about to go into the kitchen when she noticed that Valerie's door was closed and a light shone from underneath. She reached for the doorknob, intending to say hello and tell her daughter that she was feeling better.

Valerie had come home from school several hours earlier. When she saw that her mother was fast asleep, she hurried into her room, closed the door, and got out the wooden file filled with her father's relics. Ever since her mother had told her that she might be on the trail of her father's murderers, Valerie had been itching to take another look at them for a possible clue. She had everything spread out around her—the postcards, the clippings, the pipes, her mother's shoebox, the love letters. She was so close—she knew that something was going to click, and the mystery would be solved. *Yes, this time. This time, and Momma won't ever be worried again.* She picked up the stack of newspaper clippings and studied them.

"Valerie?"

She gasped and whirled around, but it was too late. Her mother was standing in the doorway, staring at her, puzzled by what she saw. Valerie felt her face grow hot. *Caught.* Caught amidst all the relics of her father, and the worst part was that some of them were stolen from her mother, who was now swaying in the doorway, her face showing anger as the scene registered. Valerie covered her eyes; she was paralyzed.

"Valerie Scott?" her mother croaked. "Valerie Scott, what on earth is this all about?" She sat on the bed and stared at Valerie's careful arrangement on the floor.

Valerie knew she had to say something. She looked up and saw that her mother's face was twisted with grief and anger. She opened her mouth to apologize, but no sounds came forth. She looked away and absently picked at the carpet.

"How dare you take his . . . his things from me! How dare you!" With a trembling hand, she snatched up the love poems and held them against her chest. She seemed terrified now, and all the color had drained from her face. Suddenly the love poems went flying as Sara jumped down onto the floor in front of her daughter, grabbed her by the shoulders, and began shaking her. "Answer me, damn you! Answer me!"

Valerie pulled away. "I'm sorry, Momma, I'm sorry! I was trying to help you find out, that's all!"

"You were trying to take what little I had left, that's what you were trying to do!" She picked up the shoebox and gestured with it. "This is the love of my life! This is your father! He can fit into this box! Do you have any idea what an awful feeling that is? Do you?"

Valerie shook her head and started crying.

Sara threw the box down. Shaking, she turned, picked up the love poems and put them back into the box. From the middle of the stack a document fell out and fluttered to the floor.

Valerie saw that it was her father's death certificate. Sara snatched it as if it were a lost poem, briefly glanced at it, then did a doubletake, horrified. She cringed, dropped the death certificate, and backed away.

Valerie stared at her mother and did not immediately understand what was going on. "Mom . . . ?" She might as well not have spoken.

Sara's eyes darted around as if there were something else in the room. She put her hand to her mouth and moaned. "Andy," she said hoarsely, then fell to her knees, pulled the shoebox onto her lap, and held it. She screamed once.

"Momma, stop it!" Valerie cried. "Momma, stop it! Please?"

Suddenly Sara blinked, looked up, and focused on Valerie, her body shaking, her eyes wide with fear. "Don't you ever take my things again!" She gathered up her memories, placed them in the shoebox, and hurried from the room, slamming the door.

Valerie did not move for a long time. She wondered what she should do, how she should apologize. Finally she decided that the best thing was to do nothing at all. She knew that her mother had slipped away into the dream, and that frightened her a great deal. Before when she had been worried about her mother going insane, she had always dismissed her fears as nothing but her imagination. No longer. She would have to be very alert from now on, and very careful.

Wednesday, October 1.

Sara felt good enough to start working on the Reardon case again. She ate a light breakfast and avoided conversation with her daughter. With acute embarrassment she recalled yesterday's scene and her loss of control. It had made her wonder if she should seek help of some kind, but she had rejected the notion. She had neither the time nor the money.

When she got to her office, she brought her diary up to date, then called her service. No messages. She thought about visiting Jorge Martinez again. She might be able to catch a glimpse of Sam at the half-way house. Would Martinez suspect her? She smiled grimly. Not if she gave him the come-on, he wouldn't.

The telephone jangled as she was on her way out the door. She jumped but answered it quickly. "Hello?"

"It's me."

"*Sam!*"

"I can't talk long," he whispered.

"Are you all right?" she asked breathlessly. Her heart was pounding.

"Never mind. None of that matters."

She nodded quickly.

"I think I'm onto something."

"What?"

"A reason someone would want both James Reardon and Alan Rosenus dead."

"I know, I know. *What?*"

"Hold on. Someone's coming!" A long, static-filled pause. "Go ahead."

"Is it cocaine?"

"Something worse. Far worse. Wait a minute! They're coming back!"

She heard the phone being covered, probably by his jacket. Tremors of fear ran down the back of her neck. She closed her eyes and gritted her teeth. *God, let him be all right!*

"Okay," he whispered, breathing hard. "It's all clear again."

"Is Martinez involved?"

"I don't know, but I don't think so."

"Sam, just what is it that we're talking about anyway?"

"I can't go into it now. It's too complicated and too goddamned dangerous."

"Listen, will you get out of there?" Her voice quavered.

"I was planning to. That's why I called. Meet me at the beach house around six this evening."

"Why then? Why don't you leave right now?"

"I've got to place a few of these aphids first."

"I'd rather have you in one piece! Please, Sam?"

"Look, I'm all right. Really, Sara. I just have to stay careful, that's all."

She shook her head. "I don't want anything to happen to you!"

"Believe me, I'm fine."

"Okay." She was reassured only because she wanted to be. "Still, I'd feel a lot better if you got the hell out of there now, Sam."

"I thought the whole point of this little excursion was to get some evidence."

"Evidence of *what?*"

The phone went dead.

Sara kept holding it to her ear for what seemed like a long time. She was astonished. Sam had succeeded. *He's actually done it!* Still she was afraid for him and felt frustrated that she had no way of communicating her concern. She stared at the receiver. After thirty seconds the dial tone was replaced by an annoying beep and then a taped message telling her to please hang up, please hang up now. She did.

She sat up straight and furiously scribbled down the gist of her conversation with Sam, then compared what he had told her with her notes. She frowned. She was compelled to cross off two items from her List of Possibles. One was "cocaine dealing"; the other was "Jorge Martinez is our man." Still, she had to restrain herself from calling Helen Reardon to tell her that her husband's murder might be as good as solved.

Sara became restless in the confines of her office, so she left and went around the corner to the Sidewalk Café, a place that she liked for its decent food rather than for its policy of catering to the chic crowd. A waiter who resembled a pained imitation of Elton John wheeled over on roller skates, and Sara ordered a salad.

From her table she observed the activity on the Ocean Front Walk. A vendor selling soft pretzels and bagels went by. He was passed by cyclists who should have been on the bike path but couldn't find room among the roller skaters. There was a collision between a drunk and a skater who wore headphones and mirrored sunglasses. A crowd gathered and a tourist took pictures. Then a cop arrived, wearing the distinctive attire of the beach detail—shorts, blue-and-white L.A.P.D. T-shirt, white socks, tennis shoes, black gun-belt, and baseball cap. As he got off his ten-speed he was cheered. He shooed the crowd away, helped the drunk to his feet, wrote the skater a citation, and left to answer a call on his radio. Things returned to normal. Another vendor went by hawking Mexican ice cream. An elderly Jewish couple bought some, then went to a bench and sat down to enjoy their treat. They were obscured by another wave of cyclists and skaters who instinctively vied for territory like ocean predators.

After lunch Sara went through five cups of herb tea and checked her watch over and over. She tried to read the Venice *Beachhead,* but she had trouble concentrating. She took up watching the bustle on the Ocean Front Walk again but was soon bored. The small dramas played out by bit players were endlessly repetitious.

Mercifully five o'clock came, and she drove out of the infamous little beach community, heading north.

Later, on the Pacific Coast Highway, traffic began to back up. She looked ahead and saw that the Cal-Trans people had closed off a lane for no apparent reason. *Typical.* She slowed to a crawl and moved along in first gear. Her thoughts turned to Andy's death. She wondered if Sam would have anything to say about that. She hoped so, but she was pessimistic. She shuddered involuntarily. Undoubtedly her search would continue and she would relive that awful moment again and again. If only there were some way to avoid another scene like the one she'd had with Valerie. If only she could be forewarned. She couldn't take much more; she couldn't bear the thought of slipping into the dream and not coming back. *Would that be next?*

Maybe not. There was still hope. There was Sam.

The highway opened up again, and she accelerated to a normal speed. She gripped the steering wheel tightly. Soon she would be at the beach house, in Sam's arms, listening to what he'd found out.

She maneuvered into the left-hand lane, went around several more curves, then glanced in her rearview mirror. No one was hard on her tail, so she switched on her turn signal and slowed down. The little-used turnoff was about five-hundred yards ahead. In the road in front of her a wave of traffic was approaching from the opposite direction. In the onrush of vehicles was a car that was similar to the one that had crushed James Reardon. As it sped by Sara strained to get a second glimpse. She blinked. A flash of blue. *Those tiny windows again, and the car lurching down the side-street, then rocketing away while Andy was dying, falling into an eternity of concrete. She glanced back. The car suddenly appeared again, and someone inside was pointing at her. The guns were swinging in her direction, and she had no place to hide.*

A blaring sound.

Sara snapped back to reality and quickly glanced in her rearview mirror. Behind her a driver was leaning on his horn, waving at her and mouthing obscenities. She swung left across the highway onto the narrow, rutted road that led to the beach, her hands shaking, her stomach churning. Overcome with nausea, she was forced to stop, open the car door, and retch.

When her sickness passed, she was left gasping for breath, and her eyes stung with tears. She wiped her face clean with a tissue, blew her nose, then stared out at the trees ahead of her. That car had been blue. *So what?* The shape of the car. That was unmistakable. The car in her mind was identical to the one that had passed her on the Pacific Coast Highway.

What did it mean?

There was no use speculating. There was no way of knowing if the car had been the same one. She put the Pinto in gear and sped down the dirt road, driving through a half mile of pines until she emerged from the trees. Then everything opened up. The houses sparkled in the sun against the ocean. She felt better, knowing that she was about to be reunited with Sam.

After parking in her usual spot in front of the dead end, she got out of the car and hurried along the stone path toward the gate. The bougainvillaea was losing its leaves in preparation for winter; its naked, sun-bleached branches reminded her of a giant eagle's nest. She entered the patio, and strode across the old brick and into the house. In the kitchen she paused, hoping that she would hear him, but the only sounds were the muffled surf and the distant whine of a small plane.

"Sam?" she called tentatively. "Sam?"

She moved to the threshold of the living room and looked around. He wasn't there. One of his cats, the Abyssinian, was somewhere in the house yowling. That did not strike her as strange; he always yowled when he wanted human companionship. Did a lonely Abyssinian mean that Sam wasn't there yet? Of course. She was early. She looked across the room and noticed that the huge beige cat was now at the French doors to the patio, pawing the glass to get in. She couldn't hear him, but she could see his mouth open and close as he meowed plaintively. She frowned. Neither Sam nor the trusted neighbor who fed the cats when he was gone would be likely to leave one cat out and one in. So Sam might be around somewhere.

She decided to look for Sam on the beach, just in case he was already there. When she opened a patio door, the beige cat meandered inside, his tail curiously at half mast. Sara went outside past the small, neglected garden, up the wooden steps, and then out onto the sand. The breeze was surprisingly cold; a refreshing change from the house. She hugged herself to keep warm and started walking through the dunes.

"Sam? Sam, are you out here?"

She trudged along until she was past the dunes and on the edge of the beach. She looked in all directions but saw no one. Gulls circled. Kingfishers ran with the tide, hunting sandcrabs. The sun was two fingers above the horizon, reflecting gold off the water. The sense of peace and harmony was overwhelming. Except within her. She would not experience it until she was reunited with Sam. She turned and started back toward the house.

She was out of the dunes and almost to the steps when she noticed that the back door to the garage was ajar. Her eyes narrowed. Had the door been like that before? Or had Sam arrived while she was out on the beach? No. He would have seen her car and come looking for her. She hurried over to the garage, hesitated, then grabbed the handle, and pulled the door all the way open.

"Sam?" She looked inside. The dark space smelled of polyurethane and surfboard wax. When her eyes adjusted to the lack of light, she saw his MG convertible. She frowned with concern. Sam *must* be home if his car was in the garage! She quickly glanced behind her, then went over to the car and placed her hand on the hood.

Faintly warm.

If he had just arrived, the engine would have been hot and making ticking noises. So he had been here for a while. But where was he? She moaned, spun around and started to run from the garage. *Are they here? Have they trapped me in this dark place? No, please, no!* She stopped, took La Belle out of her purse, and released the safety.

She was suddenly afraid again and did not know why. She was not threatened; nothing could harm her now. Or so it seemed. She walked outside and quickly looked around. The atmosphere was foreboding despite the peaceful surroundings and idyllic sunset. Was she in danger? She held her pistol at the ready, then calmed herself. She considered the logic of the situation. If Sam's car had been in the garage for an hour or more, then . . . Then he must be sleeping! Of course! He was probably exhausted after his long ordeal. Instantly relieved, she put her pistol away and started back toward the house. How could she have been so dumb? Why hadn't she looked in the bedroom before?

She went in through a patio door and quietly closed it behind her. The Abyssinian was still yowling. A bad sign. If *she* were trying to sleep, she would have killed that cat by now. She hurried across the living room, trying not to worry, even though she knew there was something ominous about the sound of the cat's cry.

"Sam?" she called softly. She hated to wake him if he was sleeping. She looked at her watch. "It's almost six. I hope you don't mind if . . ."

She walked around the corner, down the hall, and into the bedroom.

Sam was not there.

The windows were closed tight and locked. The bed had been made and was neat except for the wrinkles where the cats had been sleeping. Sara spun around in the center of the room. She was shaking. The fear returned. She looked behind her. Across the hall from the bedroom the Abyssinian was sitting by the bathroom door, yowling steadily. The beige cat was nowhere in sight.

"Sam?"

No response.

"*Sam?*" She shook her head in disbelief and put her hand to her mouth as if to hold back a terrible premonition. "SAM!"

She ran to the bathroom door, opened it, and burst inside. She stopped short and gasped, then lurched back against the wall, horrified.

Sam was doubled up on the floor as though he were broken. His right hand was holding his throat, frozen there. His normally calm features were twisted with unspeakable agony. His left arm was sprawled away from his body.

A disposable hypodermic dangled from his flesh just above the forearm, the needle sticking up through the skin.

* * *

She screamed.

She slumped and covered her face with her hands, as if that would erase the ugly picture before her. *Sam is dead. They've killed him, too. They've taken him away from me. He is gone. They've left me to grieve for the rest of my days. God, if you have any mercy, please let me go insane so I will not feel anything.* The tears began to flow, but she forced herself to look at Sam. Her body was trembling, but no matter how painful, she had to accept the scene before her or she really would go crazy.

Wait! She gasped. Was that his leg twitching? She dropped to her knees beside him and placed her ear on his chest. She could not hear a heartbeat. She touched his temples. He felt cold. She thought her fingertips felt a very faint pulse, but she wasn't sure. It could have been her own racing blood. She pushed back one of his eyelids and looked carefully at his pupils. There was no discernible reaction; she couldn't tell whether he was alive or dead. She reached into her purse, pulled out her compact, and held the mirror above his mouth. She waited, staring at the small square of glass for what seemed like the longest time.

Then—yes, there was no mistaking it—condensation appeared on the mirror.

Sam was breathing. He was alive.

If she didn't do something, though, he would be dead very soon. She gritted her teeth and pulled the hypodermic out of his arm. A drop of blood appeared where the needle had been. There were traces of a muddy substance inside the syringe. She had never seen the stuff before, but she had heard.

Someone had held Sam against his will while someone else had injected him with an overdose of heroin. *Someone? Someone else?* There were bruise marks on his upper arms vaguely resembling handprints; he had been restrained. *Who would do such a thing? Why not just put a .357 Magnum to his head and get it over with?* They probably had done that, too, only instead of pulling the trigger, they had pushed a hypodermic plunger.

She ran to the telephone in the kitchen and called the paramedics. Then she got a glass and a container of salt. She hurried back into the bathroom and glanced anxiously at Sam. He looked worse. She loosened his clothing to help his slow, irregular breathing, then filled the glass with warm water and salt. A saline solution was what you were supposed to give victims of a heroin overdose. Soaking a towel with cold water, she placed it under his neck. With a washcloth she swabbed his face, fervently hoping that he would regain consciousness and drink the salt water.

"Please, Sam, please," she whispered. "Wake up! Come on, wake up!"

She shook him. He was limp. She applied more cold water to his face, but there was no response.

"Damn you, Sam, you are not going to die! I won't let you die! Now wake up! Please!"

She shook him violently. She slapped his face until her hands stung, but he did not react. Her determination waned, and she began trembling again. On the verge of panic she moved around behind him, hoisted him up onto her lap, and cradled his lolling head. She lifted the salt water to his lips and poured it into his mouth, but most of it dribbled down his chin and neck. She tried several more times, but the same thing happened, so she stopped, not wanting the liquid to get into his lungs. Once again she bathed his face with cold water. Once again, to no effect.

"Please, Sam!" she whispered urgently. "For God's sake, please wake up!"

She felt totally helpless. Her lover was dying in her arms. She imagined that she could see his life slipping away; it was a faint aura that lifted and hovered like invisible lace, then faded. *I've been here before. I've been in this awful place many times.*

She burst into tears, convinced that further efforts at reviving him would be fruitless. She had failed. *There was nothing to be done.* And she couldn't stand it anymore. She gently laid him back down on the floor, got up, and ran to the telephone. As she dialed she forced herself to stop crying. It rang seven times before she got an answer.

"Yeah, it's me," the resonant voice crackled. "I was just on my way out. So what's up?"

"Casparian, it's Sara! Goddammit, I need your help!"

The paramedics arrived in less than five minutes, escorted by a short motorcycle cop who was all boots and helmet. They went to work, first slapping an oxygen inhaler over Sam's face and giving him an injection of adrenalin, then affixing intravenous tubes to his arms, one of them containing a heroin antitoxin with a saline base. Next they hooked Sam up to a small computer which would give them accurate indications of his vital signs. They punched a few buttons, got a readout, and exchanged anxious looks.

"I'll call in," said the lanky white paramedic to his black partner.

Sara saw the escort cop standing in the hallway. He pulled off his gloves, then took out a pen and notepad. The sound of his boots echoed on the tile when he came into the room. The black paramedic glanced up at him, then continued working on Sam.

"Another OD?" asked the cop.

"Yeah."

"Smack?"

"Yeah."

"Good stuff?"

He checked Sam's blood pressure, which was dangerously low. "It's that brown stuff again. Uncut."

The cop scribbled notes.

"Motherfucking Mexican shit." The black paramedic looked around like he wanted to spit.

The cop caught Sara's eye and nodded curtly. Sara delicately stepped around her beloved Sam and reluctantly followed the cop. She didn't want to talk about anything.

The cop interviewed her on the patio next to the lemon tree. Though she ached to sit down, she didn't complain. His questions were snide but routine; he did not suspect her story. She was almost grateful for his arrogance. That meant that he had already made up his mind; he took her for a pathetic dumb broad who was hopelessly mixed up with a junkie and a loser. He did search her for heroin, however, then told her that she was free to go, but that she should expect more questions later on.

The cop mounted his bike, started it, and roared away. Just as the paramedics were wheeling Sam outside Casparian's tan Mercedes diesel screeched to a stop next to Sara's Pinto. She met him in the middle of the street, where the lights from the van flashed red and the radio crackled as if it were charging the skies with electricity. He enveloped her in his huge arms, and she buried her face in his massive chest. He patted and comforted her, stroking her hair paternally. Over her shoulder he watched the paramedics hurry to get Sam into the ambulance. Their movements were professional, fluid, and urgent. Casparian shook his head sympathically. He had seen this many times before, and he could tell that it was serious.

"Where are you taking him?" Casparian asked.

"St. John's."

"Is he hurting or what?"

"He don't know nothing, man. He don't even know what planet he's on."

"Think he's going to make it?"

"Not if I stand here talking to you, brother." The black man vaulted into the back of the ambulance, which was rolling before he got the door closed. They sped around a curve and vanished in the trees, engine and siren howling.

Sara pushed away from Casparian. He tried to hold her, but she wouldn't have any of it. Wisely he did not interfere. Her head held high, she walked around the house to the edge of the sand and stood facing the breeze from the ocean. It felt so good and cool. She wept, the tears flowing freely down her cheeks. Casparian put his arm around her.

"I'm sorry," she whispered.

"Hey, it's not as if you didn't know the guy, Sara."

"I guess we should go, huh?"

"Yeah."

"How long will it take to get there?"

"We got all night."

But does he?

Sara leaned back in the plush passenger seat, shut her eyes tightly, and tried to drive that thought from her mind. She listened to the Mercedes glide along the Pacific Coast Highway, doing a good seventy-five. She forced herself to review everything that had happened since late that afternoon so that she would not forget it. First, the car she had seen just before turning off the highway for Sam's. At the time she had refused to speculate; she had been too shaken to trust her own eyes, and she had blamed everything on the dream. Now, she knew. *It was the same car that crushed James Reardon, wasn't it?* She was certain. *What about Andy's death, though? Was the car also the same one that had fled the scene of his murder?* She frowned. She didn't want to make that connection; she was afraid that her imagination was distorting reality. Still, she knew the coincidence would nag at her, and that she would not be able to put that possibility out of her mind. However improbable, it could be true.

She sighed. One thing she was sure of. Never again would she have any questions about the shape *or* the color of the car that had sped past her on the Pacific Coast Highway.

Casparian gave her a quick glance, then looked back at the road ahead. "Want to tell me what happened while it's still fresh in your mind?"

She laid her head back on the seat. His request reminded her that Sam was dying. She fought back the tears.

"Look, you don't have to if you don't want to."

"No . . ." She took several deep breaths before she could continue. "No, I mean, I want to talk. It has to be said."

"Want a drink first?" He pressed a button. A panel in the dash slid away to reveal a small bar. It held several pints of liquor, four glasses, and even a small ice-maker. Sara was surprised. Casparian chuckled. "I keep forgetting that you've never ridden in this baby before." He gestured at the Jose Cuervo Conmemorativo. "There's plenty of ice, but if you want water, you'll have to cry into it."

She just took a drink and passed the bottle instead. She felt better. Then she settled back in the seat again.

"The last time I talked to you, two dudes had been

snuffed because somebody else didn't want something said. Obviously you didn't go to the police."

"Look, Casparian—"

"Is tonight's deal related to that or not? Because if it is, the police are going to be very interested."

She sighed and nodded. "Okay." Then she brought Casparian up to date, sparing none of the details except her own very private speculations about the dark blue car. And when her throat got dry, she refreshed it with his smooth tequila. Finally, just as they were climbing away from the beach and turning down Wilshire Boulevard in Santa Monica, she finished her story. Casparian took several long pulls from the bottle and contemplated what she had told him. Meanwhile Sara stared out the window at the sodium-halogen lamps which lit up the streets with an eerie glow. She swept her hair back, lit a cigarette, and watched the smoke as it was sucked out the wind-wing in quick puffs.

He finally spoke. "So we got another dead body and one on the way, right?"

She gulped and nodded.

"And you think that the one who's responsible runs a halfway house to dry out junkies and shacks up with a lady politician on the side, right?"

"I don't know for certain."

"Do you realize how crazy that sounds even if the dude *does* snort coke?"

"I said I wasn't sure, Casparian!"

"Let me run it down one more time." He gestured with the bottle. "Sam Gage decides to go undercover for you because he loves you and he wants to help you out. He calls you up four days later, says that he's on to something far worse than cocaine, then crash-lands at the beach with a needle in his arm and enough horse in his bloodstream to derail the Southern Pacific." He forced a laugh. "And you say that the director of a state-funded rehab center is behind that?"

"Yes."

"You been watching too many reruns of *The Rockford Files.*"

"Well, somebody at that place did it!"

"Prove it."

Her eyes widened. "What do you mean?"

"Wake up, Sara, you're a private investigator. You even got a license. So stack your chips on the right squares."

She stiffened, then thought quickly. "Sam was supposed to bug the phones, Casparian! Maybe someone saw him! He was supposed to come out of there with some evidence, too! Obviously he got caught!"

"Evidence of what?"

"A motive for the murders of James Reardon, Alan Rosenus, and some poor girl in a PSA uniform!" she exclaimed, pounding her fist on the dashboard.

He pursed his lips and frowned. "I'm sorry. You lost me."

"Okay." She nodded fiercely and swallowed hard. "This is it. They followed him home. Someone held a gun to his head while someone else shot him up with the same stuff that he had taken from the halfway house!"

"He took smack as evidence?"

"Yes! Don't you see? James Reardon found out that they were dealing heroin from the place! He told Alan Rosenus, who—"

"I know, I know. The elusive connection in Sacramento. And your man Sam Gage confirms all this and gets nailed for his troubles."

"That's absolutely right!"

He sighed and threw up his hands. "You got problems."

"Huh?"

"You got problems, even if it went down like you said it did."

"What do you mean?"

"The evidence."

"What about it?"

"It's inside Sam's body. It doesn't exist anymore."

Sara slumped back in the seat. *I hadn't thought of that.* She stared out the window. She knew the implications of what Casparian had just said, but she couldn't face them yet. They were just too overwhelming.

"It doesn't matter anyway," he commented brusquely. "You would've had one hell of a time proving that a baggie full of smack came from a halfway house in Venice. He could've got the stuff in Pacoima. You got anything else to go on?"

"No."

"You sure?"

"Yes." Her voice sounded small and wistful.

"Shit." Casparian turned right on Fourteenth and looked for a parking space. "Even if he did manage to place some of those bugs, the house has probably been swept clean by now."

"No one will believe me, will they?"

"You know what it looks like, Sara? It looks like Sam was a junkie who got ahold of some uncut smack. That's all. End of story. Pure and simple."

"Whoopie-fuck." She thought for a moment. "What am I going to do?"

"If I was you, I'd lay low for a while."

"You know I can't do that!"

"They're going to be gunning for you now, little

girl. For sure. You got to figure that your boyfriend told them you was involved."

"He wouldn't." But she knew that Casparian was right. She would have to play it that way. She straightened up and regarded him with a cool expression, feeling suddenly strong inside. "I don't have a hell of a lot more to lose, though, do I, Casparian?"

He shrugged his shoulders and muttered an Armenian curse for which there was no translation.

"Well? Do I?"

"Just your life."

They parked, then went into the waiting room of St. John's Hospital emergency ward. Near the information desk a giant color TV was suspended from the ceiling. Most of the visitors were vacuously fixated on a game show; others were trying to read.

Sara identified herself to the admitting nurse, then got some coffee from a machine and sat down next to Casparian for the long wait. She stared at the double doors in front of her. Somewhere behind them overworked minions of the medical profession were trying to save Sam's life.

Except for a trip to get cigarettes and pastrami sandwiches they spent all night at St. John's. Around seven thirty the next morning they were approached by a young intern named Meurer, who told them that Sam's condition had stabilized, although he remained comatose and on the critical list.

When they left, Sara noticed that the sun was shining for a change. Her thoughts turned to the job ahead. At least she had one thing going for her. Whoever had given Sam the overdose of heroin had left thinking that he was dead. That simple fact could be Sara's trump card.

If Sam lived.

Twelve

Knocking.

Sara didn't hear it. She was sprawled on her bed, tangled up in the sheets and blankets, her face half-hidden by the pillow. For quite some time the mid-morning sun had been streaming in the window. A fly had been buzzing her face, too, yet she slept on despite these annoyances.

The knocking continued persistently, and gradually Sara stirred. Her mind was flooded with images. *Andy on the concrete, dying, finally comfortable and cold amid a sea of blood and spilled soda. Juxtaposed, Sam in agony on the bathroom floor, his hand clutching at his throat, the needle in his arm. The images became one, then split apart and multiplied. They overlapped and fused together, the bodies now curiously faceless, blurred.*

She finally awoke, screaming low and hoarse. Her voice rose to a wail, then faded, and she was left gasping for breath as she jerked free of the sheets and blankets.

The knocking turned into a rude banging that rattled the door.

Sara pushed up on her hands and knees, stared at

the imprint of sweat her body had left on the bed and did not immediately comprehend who or where she was. Then she finally remembered—the beach, Sam, the paramedics, Casparian, the hospital. She groaned and collapsed.

Now someone was slamming his fist against her door.

She struggled to the edge of the bed and groped for her robe. She was extremely groggy, and when she opened her eyes, at first she was blinded by the sun. When she could manage to focus, she read the clock on the dresser. *Ten thirty.* She had crawled into bed just two and one-half hours ago! *Who the hell is banging on the door?* She glowered over her shoulder. It better not be a friend or relative.

"Val, would you answer that?"

Then she remembered that Valerie had been getting ready for school when Casparian had dropped her off on the way back from the hospital. She was alone, then. She cursed, slipped into her robe, and strode out of the bedroom. Before she had the presence of mind to realize that she could be greeting someone who had come to kill her, she crossed the living room and jerked the front door open. When that thought did occur to her and she started to slam the door, she stopped. She was staring at the gold badge of an L.A.P.D. detective. It was held by a large, blond man wearing a dry-cleaned and pressed Hawaiian shirt and neo-Fifties jeans, the cuffs rolled under. He looked to be almost forty. He was grinning like he'd just left her bedroom instead of knocked at her door.

"Allow me to introduce myself, ma'am. Lieutenant Timothy Dodge. Feel free to call me Tim." His eyes swept over her body and undressed her. "Am I addressing Miss Sara Scott?"

She nodded and scowled.

He gestured at his partner behind him, who resembled a barbershop quartet singer. "This is Sergeant Grace." He turned further, indicating a second, heavy-lidded man who could've passed for a homicidal maniac. "And this is Sergeant Palinko. May we come in?"

"What for?"

"You don't trust us?" he asked jokingly.

"Would you?"

"I never thought of it that way before." He nudged the doorjamb with his huarache. "But this is regarding the matter of Sam Gage and his unfortunate possession of heroin, ma'am," he said with relish. "I believe a few questions are in order."

She acquiesced with a curt nod, turned away from the door, and went over and sat on the couch.

Dodge led the way inside, twirling a Panama hat. Like the rest of him, it seemed to be out of season. He sat down across from her, dropped his hat on the floor, and removed a pen and notebook from his pocket. "Sorry we're so late," he said sardonically. "Normally we like to stay on top of things and get an early start."

"Why don't you just ask your questions and get it over with, Lieutenant?" she replied with mock sweetness.

"Thanks, ma'am." He gestured with his pen. "But we've already had our coffee."

She took a Sherman out of a pack on the coffee table. He was there in a flash, his old Marine Corps lighter clicking open and burning steadily. Her eyes met his; they gleamed with accusation. She accepted the light and acted bored. Actually she was terrified. She was dealing with an expert.

"How long have you known Sam Gage?"

"I don't know." She shrugged. "A long time."

"What does that mean? You met him last week or day before yesterday?"

"We go back years together, Lieutenant!"

He smiled. "Ah. An enduring relationship. I'm so happy for you."

She smoked nervously; she was already perspiring.

"I take it you know each other intimately, then? Or do you just shoot up together?"

"We know each other intimately, yes."

"Where'd your boyfriend get the smack?"

"I don't know."

"Who's his pusher?"

"He doesn't have a pusher!"

Dodge smiled smugly. He looked at his companions. They chuckled. "He doesn't have a pusher," the lieutenant repeated. "Sure."

"Sure," the other detectives repeated.

"Where'd he score the junk, then? Sav-On?"

"I don't have any idea!"

"You do know that the stuff was uncut, don't you?"

She nodded. "I figured."

He grinned. "You wouldn't just happen to be Sam Gage's pusher, would you now, Miss Scott?"

"What are you talking about?"

"That would certainly explain the uncut smack, wouldn't it?" He spread his hands. "Now why don't you tell me what went down?"

"You know what happened! You've read the report!"

"No, no. I mean before. Between you and him."

Sara was puzzled.

"Did you have a fight? A junkie lovers' quarrel? Did you catch him with another woman, or what?"

"I don't believe this."

"You don't have to."

The other detectives chuckled.

"Look, Miss Scott, I've been doing this a long time.

I've seen it before." He paused and half-closed his eyes. He raised his hand and gestured as he spelled out the scenario. "You were pissed off at him. You thought you'd teach him a lesson, so you cooked him up some uncut smack, knowing that he trusted you implicitly. He shot up and passed out. You had second thoughts and got scared. You didn't want him to die. So you called the paramedics. Only they surprised you by showing up so fast. You didn't have a chance to fly the coop, am I right, Miss Scott?"

"No." She shook her head, amazed. His story sounded so plausible. "You've got it all wrong."

"Do you use drugs, Miss Scott?" He glanced at her arms.

"No, I don't."

"Glad to hear it. Then you won't mind if we look around the place?"

"Of course I mind!" she replied indignantly.

"It doesn't matter."

On cue Sergeant Grace waved a piece of paper. "We have a search warrant."

Dodge nodded to them, and they left to go through the apartment.

"Why you . . ." She clenched her fists. Her face was hot. *The indignity of it!* "You . . ."

He held his hand up. "Don't say it, Miss Scott, okay? Because then I'll get angry." He grinned broadly. "So if you're not a pusher, then what do you do that lets you sleep in? Hook? Or collect alimony?"

"I'm a private investigator," she replied coldly. She reached into her purse, took out her license, and tossed it onto the coffee table.

His face showed obvious surprise as he inspected it. "Interesting. Very." He looked up and studied her. "Not just another pretty face, hey?" He eased back in the chair and eyed her suspiciously. "What the hell is a licensed private eye doing running around with a junkie?"

"I wasn't aware that he was a junkie," she stated.

"How could you miss, lady? The cat was track-shoe city."

"I hadn't seen him in awhile. I just showed up and found him in that condition."

The assistants returned. Sergeant Palinko was nodding his head, grunting and licking his lips. "I got it right here, boss." He held up a baggie with a minuscule amount of ancient leaf inside.

Sara blushed and looked down. It had been in her spice cabinet for months. She'd forgotten about it.

"Grass." The assistant lifted his coat, took out a pair of handcuffs, and stepped toward Sara.

Dodge waved him off with disgust. "Jesus Christ, Palinko! Weed's only a misdemeanor now, remember? Write her a ticket and let's get out of here."

Palinko scratched in his book like he was doing the Sunday crossword puzzle. He took forever. Finally he gave Sara the book to sign, then tore out the ticket and handed it to her.

Dodge stood up. His companions headed toward the door. He donned his Panama and regarded Sara with a mixture of contempt and grudging respect. "I'll be in touch."

He went out the door, then turned, tipped his hat, and grinned one last time. "If I get anything at all, ma'am—even a rumor—I'll personally be back to jerk your license and take you downtown."

She hurried into the kitchen, picked up the phone, and called the hospital. After an interminable wait she was finally connected to someone in Intensive Care. She was told that Sam's condition remained unchanged. She almost wished she could tell the zealous

Lieutenant Dodge about the Reardon case and walk away from the entire affair—except, if Sam died, she would blame herself. She had an obligation to solve the murders. She had an obligation to find out who had tried to kill Sam. Before, she was bound to Andy by her own promise. Now she was pledged to Sam by her own sense of morality. In this case knowledge did not just equal retribution. It meant fulfillment and release. Besides, if she quit now, she would probably go insane.

She took a quick shower, then called Mrs. Berman and tentatively scheduled routine A in case she was late. Armed with a pack of cigarettes fresh out of the refrigerator, she grabbed her purse and headed for the door.

Her car was still at Sam's place, so she ended up taking the bus. It was most unpleasant. From behind a discarded newspaper she watched all the passengers very carefully. One of them could be an assassin.

Hers.

Three hours later she was driving back toward the city, grateful to be behind the wheel of the old, familiar Pinto. Lured by the smell of seafood at the roadside restaurants, she stopped at a Jack-in-the-Box and filled her stomach with onion rings and tacos.

Thus refueled, she spun back onto the highway and continued driving south at a consistent fifteen miles over the speed limit. A cigarette was clenched between her teeth, her hands fixed with determination on the wheel.

It was Mar Vista or bust.

This time Sara was going to start at the top. There would be no subterfuge, no false business cards. She was going to get some answers. If nothing else, she had accumulated enough sensitive information to buy some cooperation. She relished the prospect of a confrontation, and she wondered how Anna Perez would respond when she asked her if she wanted the wrong people to find out about how the good senator passed the time when her husband was out of town.

"Do you have an appointment?"

"No, but that's okay. I'll wait."

"You might be waiting a long time."

"What's an hour or two in the scheme of things, right?" Sara sat down on the couch across from the desk.

The huge Chicano named Hector leaned back in the desk chair and chuckled. His girth jiggled. He clearly enjoyed playing the stone that blocked the proverbial door. "Senator Perez isn't seeing members of the press today."

Sara shrugged and said nothing.

"Now all interviews are arranged through her press secretary, who is in Sacramento for an indefinite length of time."

Sara stared steadily at Hector, making no attempt to hide her distaste for the man and his bulk.

Hector frowned. "Did you hear what I said?"

"Yeah, I heard you. Who said I was a member of the press?"

His frown became a scowl. "Last week when I threw you out of this office you were a member of the press."

"So? That was last week."

For a moment he was surprised. Then he suddenly found the situation funny. He laughed. "And this week, *hermana*? What is your occupation this week?"

"I'm a private investigator." She leaned forward, handed him a card, and smiled. "And I'd like to talk with Anna Perez as soon as possible. It's important."

Hector was taken back. He read the card, mouthing

the words, then gaped at her. "The nature of your business?"

"Personal."

He thought quickly, then grinned. "I'm sorry. Senator Perez does not discuss business of a personal nature."

"But I'm a constituent."

"So? Move to the valley and vote Republican." He laughed expansively while raising his immense body from his chair. "Now if you'd be so kind as to let me show you to the door?"

Hector rolled toward Sara, his arms outstretched. But before he could grab her, she had La Belle out and aimed at his face, the pistol steady in both hands. He stopped and rocked back on his heels, absurdly shielding himself with his arms. She could see him sweating.

"Sorry, but I must insist on seeing the senator," she said sweetly. "I'm in a very talkative mood."

"Miss Scott . . ."

She walked past him toward the door marked PRIVATE which led to Anna Perez's inner office. She pushed it open and stepped inside. What she saw astonished her.

The room was empty.

Sara turned and glared at Hector. "Okay, cutie, where is she?"

His body filled the door frame. As he leaned against it the wood creaked. He laughed and sweat dripped from his face. His belly shook and he wheezed for breath.

"Where is she, dammit?"

"She left . . ." He giggled. "She left yesterday for Washington, D.C.!"

"*What?*"

"I don't know when she's coming back, either. Honest."

So the joke was on her, was it? She blushed with embarrassment, then put her pistol away. Turning quickly, she strode out of the building without saying a word. For the sake of her self-respect it was the least she could do.

When she got back to her office late in the afternoon, she was still fuming from her encounter with Hector. She poured herself a drink from the pint of tequila she kept in her bottom desk drawer. She sipped and let her anger subside.

She called the hospital to check on Sam. She waited patiently for Dr. Meurer for fifteen minutes until a nurse came on and told her to try again later. Dr. Meurer would not be on duty for another two hours.

In the meantime she decided to take out the Reardon file. She would go through it again on the remote chance she had overlooked a lead. No matter what Sam had said on the phone, something still seemed suspicious about Jorge Martinez. But intuition was worthless without evidence.

She read each page of notes and observations methodically, and then came to the pile of proof sheets and prints. On top were the shots of James Reardon leaving home for work. In the next ones he was entering the Straighten-Up Halfway House. Then came the other photos of the campaign rally. *Ah, yes.* There was Senator Anna Perez shaking hands with Lawrence Conrad, the tall, sandy-haired state comptroller. There was Anna Perez smiling and waving to the crowd. There was a Japanese tourist. There was a smiling *mamacita* with three clinging kids. There was a Venice native lying stoned in the grass. There was . . . She stopped and looked closely at an eight by ten of James

Reardon hurrying away from the halfway house. He had a driven look about him, but that wasn't what captured her interest. She examined the print with a magnifying glass. In the top right-hand corner stood a tall, thin man, slightly out of focus, entering the building through an emergency fire exit. Did he look suspicious?

Suddenly she dropped the magnifying glass and looked up. "Jesus, Sara, so what?"

There were all kinds of people in these pictures. She picked up the print and regarded it with disgust.

The phone rang.

It was Valerie reminding her that she had promised to take her to the hospital to see Sam. Sara apologized for being late, said that she would be right home, and hung up. She finished her drink and hurried to the door. Without thinking, she unlatched the deadbolt and was about to leave when she remembered her purse.

There was a noise just outside the door which she did not immediately notice.

"Damn," she muttered. *The kid just mentions Sam's name, and I get so rattled, I lose my wits.* She went back, locked the Reardon file in the desk drawer, picked up her purse, and turned to go. Then she heard a creaking noise. As if by instinct, she reached into her purse and grasped La Belle. Leaving the room carefully, she gently locked the deadbolt and turned to cross the tiny foyer. She stopped short and a chill went through her. Her outer office door was ajar. She quickly glanced into the waiting room.

Empty.

Had she closed the door securely when she first arrived? Had the draft in the corridor blown it open or . . . ? Through the marbled glass she saw a shadow flit down the corridor. She grabbed the doorknob, jerked the door open, and looked down the hallway, pistol at the ready.

No one was there.

She heard voices and glanced in the other direction. What she saw was reassuring. The two Iranian realtors who had recently taken over the entire third floor were coming down the stairs, bantering in Farsi.

Sara sighed. She waved at them, then closed her door, but didn't take the time to lock it. She wanted to be out of the building before the heavyset Iranian with the broken nose could ask her out again.

Valerie was hunched over, staring out the side window of the Pinto at the smoggy sunset while the car lurched forward in the snarl of rush-hour traffic, taking them to the hospital. She had spent the night on Mrs. Berman's couch, unable to sleep, worried that something had finally happened to her mother, who hadn't called or come home. At seven that morning she had gone back upstairs to get ready for school, once again going through the motions, passing the time. Her mother had staggered in then, pained, exhausted, and ashen-faced. Before Valerie could ask what had happened, Sara told her about what happened to Sam.

One trait she shared with her mother was a strong desire to be alone in the face of tragedy. So, instead of going to school, she had gone over to the park between Main and Pacific near the RTD maintenance terminal. She spent the day there, absently watching the senior citizens congregating, the occasional wino shuffling for the trees, the pairs of hookers taking breaks from the grit of the streets.

No one bothered her, and she reviewed everything that had happened in the last few days. At first she felt she hated her mother, blamed her for the attempted murder of Sam and even for the death of her father. Then her resentment cooled, and she just felt numb. She spent hours ambling along the streets of Venice, watching the people, wondering how long some of *them* would live, then why they were alive in the first place. By the end of the afternoon she felt calmer, and she thought she could better understand what her mother was going through.

Now that she was with her mother in the car on the way to the hospital, she didn't know what to say or do. She remembered that when they told her about her father, she had been confused, then totally bewildered. She was never going to see her daddy again? It had taken her years to accept that fact. Sometimes she wondered if he wasn't alive somewhere and it had all been a mistake, or a giant conspiracy to confuse her. Would she have to go through the same things all over again if Sam died? Sam was her favorite man in the whole world. What was happening, anyway? She fervently wished that someone, somewhere could make everything right again.

Valerie felt her mother patting her on the shoulder and that gentle contact unleashed her pent-up feelings. Involuntarily she began sobbing. She turned, grabbed her mother's arm, and pressed her face against it. "Oh, Momma, why?" she cried. "Why?"

"Not now, Val," she whispered. "Please?"

Her outburst was over quickly, and she felt better. She straightened up in the seat and tried to concentrate on staring out the window again. When her mother asked if she was all right, she just nodded.

Once they arrived at the hospital, Sara left word for Dr. Meurer, then waited outside Intensive Care with Valerie. Soon the doctor greeted them, and Sara could tell that he hadn't slept, either. He reported that Sam's condition had worsened considerably; there was nothing more they could do, and he was not expected to live through the night. The doctor was very sorry.

Sara leaned against the wall, shut her eyes tightly, then took several deep breaths. She slowly turned back to the doctor, who was waiting patiently. "Can we see him?"

Dr. Meurer nodded. "As soon as the nurse is finished." He excused himself and went back on the ward.

Sara and Valerie embraced each other. No words were exchanged. They stood united in grief, and there were no hysterical outcries. Mother and daughter were stronger than that together. They turned and slowly walked down the corridor toward the lounge, hand in hand.

"Do you want to talk?" Sara asked.

"No."

"Do you want to stay?"

"Yes."

Then Valerie pulled away and went into the TV room. She moved a heavy chair up close to the tube, sat cross-legged on it, and stared at the news.

Sara went farther down the hall, leaned against a wall across from a window, and looked out until the dim light had faded to blackness. *Andy. Now Sam.* She remembered the last time she had seen them together, about two years before Andy's death. Sam had just inherited his father's beach house and had invited them up for the day. She had watched them surf for hours. Andy was the hot-dogger, the playful one who had to try every wave no matter what the form, whereas Sam rode the waves methodically, selecting them as a composer would a musical theme. At dinner Andy did most of the talking, full of enthusiastic suggestions about what Sam should do with his house and his life. Real estate! That was the answer for Sam, because there was no apprenticeship. Just pass a test and then make millions! Sam remained quiet through it all and several times Sara caught him gazing wistfully at her. Later, when she and Andy were on their way home, he told her that Sam was the only person in the world he truly envied. He didn't elaborate.

Sara briefly wondered why she wasn't crying. But she guessed it was because she was just too exhausted and numb. Her emotions had been all used up. She didn't know exactly how long she had been standing there thinking, but it really didn't matter. Her watch read six fifteen.

Meandering down the corridor, she came to a bank of telephones. She decided to check in with her service.

"Triple-A answering. May I help you?"

"Anything for one by seventy-two?" Sara asked mechanically.

"One moment." There was a pause. "Yes, Miss Scott, you have two calls. Both from Helen Reardon."

Damn! I should have talked to her long before now. I promised I'd call every day. I wonder how she's doing?

"She says that since she hasn't been able to reach you by phone, she'll meet you at your office at six thirty."

"Tonight?"

"Uh-huh," the operator replied. "She said that she had some very important information for you."

"Thanks." Sara hung up, glanced at her watch again, then automatically fed another dime into the phone and dialed Helen Reardon's home number, intending to cancel the appointment. She couldn't leave the hospital when Sam's condition was so critical. Surely it could wait.

She let Helen Reardon's phone ring fifteen times before hanging up with disappointment. Obviously she was on her way to Sara's office. She cursed. *Some very important information, huh? Why now? When Sam's in such serious condition?* She scowled, weighing the options. The appointment must be urgent. And to be realistic about it, she had to admit her presence here wasn't going to save Sam's life. She wondered what Sam would do in this situation. Or Casparian. She knew. They both would pursue business first and conduct vigils later.

Someone was rapping on the glass. She turned, saw Valerie, and then opened the phone-booth door.

"We can go see him now, Momma."

They stood at Sam's bedside and watched helplessly. Sara could not believe how pale he looked, how thin and tentative. He was inside a transparent oxygen tent, with a half-dozen bottles and tubes attached to his arms and nose. She thought that he appeared unreal—like a synthetic man created by the wizardry of medical technology. She sighed. At least he wasn't in pain anymore; at least his face did not express unspeakable agony. If he died, she was certain he would die peacefully and smoothly. After all, that was the way he had lived.

Sara leaned forward and placed her hand on his leg, now covered by the crisp hospital linen, thinking of the many things he had done for her. *You protected me, Sam. You led me through vast stretches of terror, and you did not even know what you were doing because I never had the courage to tell you about what was going on in my head. What a fool I was. I guess I figured that if I told you, then you wouldn't want to see me anymore.* She shook her head, bit her lip, and held back tears. *No, Sam, darling, that's not it, that's*

*not it at all. If I told you about the dream, then you
would know that Andy still has a hold on me. And
how could I possibly tell you—yes, even when we made
love—that you still had a rival?* She bowed her head
and covered her eyes. *I'll make it up to you, my
darling. Whether you live or die. I promise.*

She straightened up and glanced at her daughter,
who was staring straight ahead, transfixed. She
squeezed Valerie's hand. Valerie lowered her head,
turned, and started for the door.

Sara leaned over the bed. "I have to go now," she
whispered. "I'm sure you'll understand why. If you
wake up and I'm not here, Valerie will be outside."

They left the Intensive Care Unit, and Sara walked
Valerie back to the TV room, explaining that she had
to leave to meet Mrs. Reardon. She told Valerie to
wait there in case Sam came out of the coma. The girl
shrugged and nodded, as if to say that her entire life
was a period of waiting. Sara gave her five dollars for
dinner, kissed her good-bye, and left the hospital.

Sara drove to Venice and arrived at the corner of
Market and Pacific around seven thirty. She circled
the block prudently, making sure that there was no
one suspicious near 71 Market Street. Then she cut
her lights, drove down the alley, and parked in the
lot behind the building. Before she got out of her car,
she looked in all directions, assuring herself that she
was alone. Satisfied, she walked around to the front
entrance. The building was locked up every night at
seven. She used her key to slip inside, then closed and
locked the door behind her. At the foot of the stairs
she stood and listened for a moment. She heard nothing. No voices, muffled or otherwise. All the other tenants must have left for the day. She shivered. She did
not like being alone in dark places. The foyer was

black, too; the night-light had burned out and had not
been replaced. Sara lit a match and held it up so she
could locate the handrail. She didn't want to stumble
or slip on the stairs. If she fell and made a noise . . .
Well, that wouldn't exactly impress her one and only
client. Taking hold of the handrail, she started up the
stairs. The match flickered out. She paused to look
behind her. Nothing was visible except the very dim
outline of the stairwell. Was someone down there?
Her mouth went dry; she swallowed hard. No, it was
only her imagination. The darkness had a grip on her
now; she could not control the fear that made the back
of her neck tingle. She listened for strange noises, but
silence blanketed everything. She was afraid to move
because she did not want to make any sound that
might call attention to herself. Her heart was pounding, the palms of her hands moist. She abruptly shook
her head and swore. How absurd to be standing in the
middle of a flight of stairs waiting for some imagined
horror to materialize! She turned and resumed climbing the steps. The whisking sound of her shoes on the
jute runner caused her to dash up the last few stairs.
Having reached the second floor, once again she turned
around to look behind her. Nothing. No invisible
hands clutched at her.

She crossed the landing and turned down the corridor. A shaft of light was coming from the glass of
her office door. She sighed with relief. That meant
Helen Reardon was already there. *That lady's got a
lot of guts,* she thought. To wait in an empty office
building.

Sara's stride became more relaxed, and she chided
herself for being skittish. After all, this was *her* building. She knew it well. She had come over here before
alone at night. She remembered Casparian's warnings,
but how could she be any more cautious in the future

than she was already? Well, at least there was nothing to worry about right now. Still, she took one last look behind her before opening the door to her office and stepping inside. She closed and locked the door, then turned.

"Helen, it's me, Sara." She emitted a short laugh. "Just so you don't freak out." She crossed the small foyer. "I'm sorry I haven't called." Then strode into the waiting room. "How you doing, anyway?" Suddenly, she stopped short, puzzled.

Helen wasn't there.

"Helen?" Sara frowned. If she wasn't here, then who had turned on the light?

"Helen?"

Sara moaned. Something was terribly wrong. She sensed another presence and was suddenly consumed with fear. She quickly spun around but was thwarted in her attempt to bolt from the room.

Someone very big and strong grabbed her from behind and laid the honed edge of a knife across her throat.

Thirteen

"Helen won't be showing up tonight."

Sara was trembling. She was cold. Her skin crawled. The only thing that kept her from fainting was the slight pressure of the blade on her neck. "What have you done with her?" she croaked.

Her captor laughed. "Helen ain't keeping any appointments because she didn't make any in the first place, you understand? I made the arrangements. You see, no one's been able to locate you, and my guess is that you been lying low. Then I remembered that no matter what was going down, you had the bad habit of always checking in with your answering service. So that seemed like the simplest way to get in touch with you. After I left the message, I called Helen Reardon and told her to meet me at the Marina because I had some information on her old man. That meant that if you called her to confirm, you'd think she was on her way." He gave out with a throaty chuckle. "I was right, wasn't I, girl?"

Sara stiffened and her eyes narrowed. There was no mistaking the voice. She would recognize it anywhere.

The man was her landlord. Spencer Harris.

Just the idea, the thought of it, made her so angry

that she almost forgot about the knife. "You son of a bitch! You son of a bitch!" She struggled. "Let me go!"

"Easy, wo-man!"

She wasn't about to listen. She shrank away from the pressure of the blade and pushed him back until they both hit the wall. She grabbed his knife hand and pulled it away from her throat. He jerked it back with all his strength, intent on slashing her open. She diverted the move just enough and felt the butt of the knife handle grind into her collarbone. The pain was awful. She raised her leg and swung it back hard. Her boot heel smashed into his shinbone. He weakened and his body convulsed. She did it again. He grunted and his grip relaxed. For one glorious moment, she was free of him, but before she could use her advantage, he hit her in the face.

She crumpled to the floor, her head bouncing on the thin rug. She twitched, then lay still.

When she regained consciousness, everything was out of focus. She blinked. Spencer was squatting beside her, rubbing his shin, his face expressionless. She kept blinking, but her vision wouldn't clear. There was something in the way. She looked out of the corner of her eye and gasped. He had the tip of the knife poised a hairsbreadth away from her iris. She couldn't move. Her head lay against the floor.

"Please," she whispered.

He leaned his big face over her, frowning and shaking his head. His gold pendants fell out of his shirt and clanged together. His breath was close. He had the look of a man who had just been granted authority and wasn't sure how to use the power. "You behave yourself, you might live a little longer, you dig?"

She nodded carefully. Her head ached and pounded inside.

"Now we going to do this by the numbers. You don't *move* unless I say so, understand, girl?"

"Yes."

He took the knife away.

"Thank you." She exhaled slowly.

He got a solid grip on her hair, then stood up. "Up!" She rose quickly so she wouldn't be pulled to her feet. He turned her to him and casually placed the knife against her stomach. Then he grinned, now that he had the situation under control. "You something else, you know? Downright dangerous! Uh-huh. I mean, there is bitches and there is *bitches!*"

She stared at him, waiting for some indication. She could feel her face swelling where he had hit her and knew that it would be badly bruised. As if that mattered right now.

"But you . . ." He went on expansively. "You is one of the smartest and the toughest bitches I've ever gone up against. Yeah! And an amen to that, Jim!"

"What do you want, Spencer?" she asked quietly.

"What do I *want?* I don't want nothing!" he snorted. "Nothing except to be left alone!"

"What do you mean?"

"You got bad people on your case, wo-man, bad people and the wrong organization."

"What organization?"

"None of your business, sister!" He gestured with the knife; it glinted in the light. "You see, I owe these folks a couple of favors, you dig where I'm coming from?"

"We could make a deal."

He shook his head. "I'd rather be in debt to the Lord than to them. And they want you dead, girl."

Her eyes went blank. *I don't believe this is happening.*

"I'm sorry, baby, but that's the way it is, and I got

to be looking out for Spencer Harris. He's my main man." He relaxed a little. "Just so you know," he said gently, "I am not a depraved cat. I'll make it quick and easy and clean. You won't feel a thing. I promise. Then in a few days, a week maybe, I'm going to find your corpse right here in your office. I'm going to scream for help and call the police. And then I'm going to tell them that I was walking down the hallway and I ain't seen you come to work in a while and I smelled something real bad and I thought that it was my obligation as a responsible landlord to investigate, you dig?"

She couldn't talk. She shook her head. She felt queasy.

He forced her head back so that she could not avoid looking into his eyes. They were dark and glassy with power. They were her windows to oblivion. "You going to meet your Maker, girl." He nodded. "And you looking at the man who's going to do the introductions."

"Why?" she asked hoarsely. "At least tell me why!"

"Well, according to the chairman of the board, you know too much. You came too close to the truth, whatever that is. He also done told me that they nailed your boyfriend for the same reason, so I guess that explains everything, right?"

"Did you kill Sam?" She wasn't about to ask if he had made the attempt on Sam's life. If they thought that he was dead, then at least he was safe for the time being. And that was a small comfort.

"Fuck, no! What you think I am, girl? An assassin? I am a legitimate man of property! I am merely protecting my investments by liquidating my debts."

"What about the others?"

"The others. What others?"

"Did you kill them?"

"You don't seem to understand, girl. I don't know nothing about nobody named Sam and I don't know nothing about no others, neither. You see, this is a one-time deal for the purpose of rendering accounts paid in full. I am, you might say, a pinch hitter, you dig where I'm coming from?" He chucked her under the chin with the knife. "Now why don't we retire to the privacy of your office so that your last moments on earth will be more comfortable?"

There was no mistaking it. She saw hesitation in his eyes. *Hmmm.* The reason he was talking so much was that he really wasn't an assassin. Clearly, she could see that he was nervous now. She wondered why they had chosen an amateur to murder her? For the sake of convenience? Maybe. More than likely, though, the reason was surprise. She wouldn't expect to get caught inside her office by her landlord when she was looking the other way. They couldn't have chosen a better person. Even if she had heeded Casparian's warnings, she never would have dreamed that Spencer Harris would have set her up. And now she found herself staring at him like a small animal in the grasp of a predator.

He blinked and looked away. He frowned. A line of sweat ran around his neck and down his chest. *He's losing courage, isn't he? I'll stall him. I'll keep him talking long enough to think of a way to escape.* She fought off her panic, then forced herself to speak. "How did they find out about me?"

He seemed relieved that she had broken the silence. "How did they find out?"

"Was it Sam? Did he say something?"

"Why you keep asking me about this Sam dude, girl? I don't know nothing about no Sam!"

"Well, then?"

Suddenly he glared at her maliciously, as if he knew

what she was trying to do. He twisted his hand in her hair, and she gasped in pain. Tears welled up in her eyes. "No more bullshit jive, wo-man, you understand?" He strode out of the waiting room to her office, half-pulling her behind him. "Open it up."

"Wait a minute, please."

"You open this motherfucking door and you open it right now!" He prodded her with the knife point just below her chin. It broke the skin, and she felt blood running down her neck.

"Open it!" he hissed, shaking with nervous rage and anticipation.

"My keys." She gulped. "They're in my purse."

He studied her for a moment and gave a slight twist to the knife, still under her chin. Then he dragged her back into the waiting room and took the knife away so she could bend down for her purse on the floor. *This is it. His hand isn't so tight in my hair; I can't feel any pain. The knife is down by his side. That's as far away as it will get. This is my time.* But just as her fingers went around the handles, he yanked on her hair and jerked her back toward the oak door. She yelped with pain and raised a hand to slow him down. It was all she could do to hang on to her purse.

"Now open it." He placed the tip of the knife on the hollow of her throat just above the collarbone.

She opened the flap of her purse, then slowly, deliberately reached in for her keys. *I'll get hold of La Belle, release the safety, and shoot him through the cloth of the purse.* She read his face. It was intense and murderous. *No way. If I try to use La Belle, I might get him, but I won't survive, either. His knife hand is poised, the muscles coiled. Even as a reflex action, he could easily drive the blade completely through me.*

She lifted the keys out and started to turn, her eyes

asking Spencer for permission. He nodded once and stepped back. She unlocked the deadbolt, then turned the key in the bottom lock. The door clicked open. Spencer shoved her across the threshold and into her office. She faked a stumble and fell to the floor, holding her purse close to her body. He was right on top of her, sighting in over the knife. She had no time to go for her pistol. She looked up at him and smiled weakly.

"What you doing? I didn't shove you hard enough to make you fall down."

"I tripped. I tripped on the desk. I couldn't see."

He did not turn on the overhead switch, so they remained in semi-darkness, with only the shaft of light from the waiting room. She pushed up, turned, and sat against the front of the desk. At the same time she nudged her purse under the desk and out of sight. He stood over her, holding the knife with both hands. It was pointing at her face. He was sweating heavily and seemed serious now. It was obvious that the mechanics of killing had not occurred to him before. His lack of confidence clouded his face and made him angry.

"How much do you want?"

"I said before, I don't want nothing!"

"I'll give you double what they did."

He snorted derisively. "You ain't got a dime, girl."

"Anything," she whispered. "I'll do anything."

"Shut up, tramp!" He reached down, grabbed her hair at the base of her scalp and twisted his hand into a fist again. He dropped to his knees and snapped her head back. "You about to die, girl." He raised the knife and aimed it at her chest. She tensed involuntarily, terrified and dizzy. He hesitated. The moment seemed to take forever. His eyes were dark and hateful. Then she saw a flicker of doubt in them. This was her final chance.

"Don't the condemned always get one last wish?"
He eased back and exhaled hard.

She gazed at him steadily. She began unbuttoning
her blouse. She parted her lips slightly and forced a
seductive smile. It was the most convincing bit of acting she'd ever done in her life.

"What you doing, wo-man?"

"If I'm going to die, I want to go out in style. You
mind?" She took off her blouse and dropped it on the
floor. She stood up, reached behind her, and un-
snapped her bra. She tossed it away with a casual gesture. Then she cupped her breasts with her hands,
offering them to him. He stared at her, fascinated. She
stared back.

"Do I get my wish or not?"

He lowered the knife and sat back on his haunches.
He was clearly amazed. He grinned foolishly, then
shook his head as if to rid himself of the temptation.
But she had planted the seed. The impulse grew and
became plausible. "Come on now, girl!"

"Do you want me or not?"

"You still got to die!"

"What would you do, Spencer, if you were going to
die?"

He gaped at her, astonished, his jaw slack. "You
know, you're fucking crazy, but you ain't talking
trash." He shed his clothes.

She pulled off her boots and socks, stood up, un-
zipped her jeans and stepped out of them. He grunted
approval and gave a low whistle. She felt loathsome,
but her mind raced as she quickly planned the scenario. A sudden draft of cold air raised goosebumps
on her skin. Her nipples hardened. He misread the
reaction and reached for her. She avoided his hands
and lay down on the floor so that her head was near
the desk and her right hand fell under it, touching

the edge of her purse. Despite the nausea in her stomach, she looked up at him and forced herself to smile.

"Come on," she whispered impatiently.

He got onto his hands and knees, the knife still in his right hand. Then he moved over her, chuckling, staring at her body, shaking his head at her beauty. Suddenly he stopped and glanced at her, hesitating.

She had left her panties on.

She held his eyes with a steady gaze, then nodded once and lifted her hips as a sign for him to take them off. He looked down, and she could feel his breath on her stomach. Her skin crawled. She worked her hand under the flap of her purse.

He put the knife down, grasped her panties with both hands, and pulled them off. He half-turned and tossed them away. Her hand found La Belle and snapped off the safety.

Suddenly he stopped. *He heard the click!* He dove for his knife, fumbled, raised it, but before he could stab her, she jerked her La Belle out of her purse and fired.

She was blinded by the flash, but Spencer was hit in the head and thrown back. He rolled once and was dead, an incredulous expression frozen on his face. When she looked at him, she moaned, dropped her pistol, and put her hand over her mouth. Her eyes widened. *Andy was there before her, dead. His body became Spencer's, then Reardon's. The corpse of Alan Rosenus. Spencer's again. Andy. You didn't want me involved, yet there is an eternal bond between us, and my soul is cold. What has happened to me?*

He burst into her office—he had sprinted up the stairs and down the corridor after he heard the pistol shot. One glance told him what had happened, and he knew she must be in shock; she'd never killed anyone before. He grabbed her by the shoulders and began shaking her. "Are you all right? Are you all right?"

Sobbing, she pulled away and cowered by the desk, automatically trying to shield her nudity, quivering, still not quite believing that she was alive. When she realized that someone was with her, she peered up through the hanging smoke of burnt gunpowder and saw his round silhouette with electric hair in the doorway, fumbling for the light switch. "Casparian?" she whispered tentatively.

He turned on the light, then came back to her and spread his massive arms, grateful that she was alive.

"*Casparian!*"

She threw herself against him and hugged him so tightly that he wheezed. Her face was hard and swollen where Spencer had hit her, but right now she felt no pain.

Casparian stroked her hair. "I'm sorry, Sara, my God, I'm sorry! I should've gotten here sooner! I should've figured it out quicker!"

"I'm okay," she uttered, "I'm okay."

He extricated himself from her embrace and held her by the shoulders at arm's length. "Did he—?"

"No." She shook her head. "I . . . I bought myself some time. I got lucky."

"Jesus." He blushed and turned away. "Jesus H. Christ."

She looked down at her body and blushed herself. She had forgotten that she was nude.

"Get dressed."

She nodded quickly, then put on her panties and bra, her hands trembling. She pulled on her jeans, buttoned her blouse, and cast a quick glance at Spencer's body. His color had changed from a dark brown to a blue-gray. His blood was drying in great patches on the old rug. She backed away, suddenly realizing the enormity of the situation. Dazed, she sat down behind her desk, closed her eyes and put her face in her hands. She felt so sick. It didn't matter that Spencer had intended to use her body and then kill her. It didn't matter who he was or what he had planned. She was disgusted and frightened. She had finally been forced to use La Belle. Her strength drained away.

Casparian flipped back his silk-mohair sports coat and dropped his Magnum into his hand-tooled shoulder holster. "I stopped by the hospital looking for you. Your kid told me you was over here." He shook his head ironically. "I wanted to warn you about your landlord because I finally remembered where I'd come across the dude's name before. The man was a pimp who got busted and did a lot of time, maybe for somebody else. They say he took a lot of privileged information to jail with him. After he got out, they tell me that he suddenly had a lot of green. Nobody knew where it came from. They still don't." He paused and reflected. "The dude made some real-estate investments and joined the chamber of commerce." He turned back to her. "He tell you anything?"

She couldn't bring herself to speak; the horror of the scene enveloped her, and she was shaking badly now. She glanced at Spencer's body again. It seemed enormous. Everywhere. She turned away, shuddered with revulsion and fear, recalling his eyes. She gagged. She had come so close to dying. So close. She could smell his death now, and she gagged again.

"Sara, come on! It's over now."

She remembered the tequila, took the bottle out of her desk drawer, uncapped it, and drank. Then she spoke. "He said . . . he said that some bad people in

a wrong organization wanted me dead and he was re-
paying debts."

Casparian shrugged. "Figures. The only thing that
surprises me is that they didn't try to nail you sooner."
He rolled up Spencer's corpse in the rug. "I might as
well take the whole thing," he explained. "There's no
way you'll ever get the stains out."

"Please," she whispered. "Just get him out of here."

"Is there a broom closet or utility room downstairs?"

"There's one at the end of the hall."

He hoisted the body in the rug onto his shoulder,
turned, and started out of the office. She followed him
into the corridor, then down to the broom closet. "I
suppose you'll be calling your L.A.P.D. friends."

"It's too late for that."

She opened the door for him. He lifted his shoulder
and pitched the corpse inside. It hit the wall, bounced,
and smacked down on the floor among buckets,
brooms, and mildewing mops. Casparian stared at it
for a moment. He wrinkled his nose with disgust, and
his normally generous eyes became sorrowful. He
closed the door and ambled back toward her office,
deep in thought.

"What do you mean by too late?" she asked.

He jerked his thumb over his shoulder at the broom
closet. "You just killed the son of a bitch, and we
don't have any answers." He shook his head. "What a
fucking mess. You knock off an assassin who's under
contract, and we don't even know who we're going up
against!"

"We?"

"Yeah. You just got yourself a partner. Ruby ain't
going to be happy about it, either."

"Why? Because it's dangerous?"

"No. She'll be pissed off that I waived the consulting
fee. She's very protective."

Sara's eyes widened with surprise. "Casparian—"

"No, no." He scowled and waved her off. "I insist. You're in over your head, Sara."

They went into her office, and he sprawled in her desk chair. She gave him the tequila. He wiped the sweat off his face, drank, and started to look better. His color returned.

She leaned against the wall. She wasn't so sure that she wanted Casparian's help. Of course he was good and smart and thorough and imaginative. He was probably the best around, but she didn't want him bailing her out or doing her job for her. What about her own self-respect? She frowned. Self-respect? What about the danger? She'd almost been killed! There was the nightmare, too. Lately, it had been recurring at moments that were less than opportune. She knew she should be grateful to Casparian. Still, what about his safety? Did he deserve to get dragged into the Reardon case? She should be honest with him and tell him her doubts. "Casparian, you don't know how much I appreciate this, but—"

"I don't want to hear about it, okay?" He finished off the tequila and stood. "I mean, it's either lend you a hand or take a week's vacation in Vegas. Besides, if anything happened to you, I'd never forgive myself."

She felt a surge of tenderness for him and smiled softly. Her lips stung where they were split, bringing tears to her eyes.

He inspected her with fatherly concern. "Hurt?"

"Yeah. Do I look grotesque?"

"You could never look grotesque." He stepped back. "Let's get the hell away from here and have a drink."

She picked up her purse and started for the door.

"Sara?"

She turned.

"I don't think you should use your office anymore. Not until this is over."

"I hadn't planned on it."

"Or your apartment. I think you should go home, pack your bags, grab your kid, and move out. You can stay at my place if you want to."

"Thanks, Casparian, but . . ."

He rolled his shoulders. "Or a motel. I'm serious. They're going to find out real fast that you're still alive."

The telephone rang.

Sara gasped. The sound cut through her and she felt a rush of adrenalin. Her heart pounded. She froze and looked at Casparian. He stared right back at her, not moving, probably thinking exactly the same thing that she was. Whoever was making the call expected Spencer Harris to answer.

It rang nine times before stopping, and Sara vaguely remembered that her service went off at eight o'clock. Casparian nodded toward the door, and they left the office.

Sara heard the phone start ringing again. They hurried down the stairs. Casparian headed toward the front door, and Sara hesitated.

"My car's parked in back," she explained.

He nodded. "I came by myself. I should leave by myself." He rested his hand on the door. "I'll see you and your kid back at my place."

"Do you think anyone's out there?"

"Maybe." He shrugged. "But if so, they'll be looking at me."

Sara watched Casparian leave. He was the picture of the diligent businessman who had been working late. After the door closed, she heard him whistling as he walked away. A nice touch—almost too obvious and old to be staged. She hurried to the back door, opened it, slipped outside, and slowly closed it so the heavy metal wouldn't bang. She looked behind her, then turned and started up the alley, intending to stay close to the building and cross to the parking lot at the last possible moment. She hurried around the Dempster Dumpster, but ran into a parked car that hadn't been there an hour ago. She barked her shins on the bumper, cursed silently, then looked up and recognized the vehicle. She shrank back in horror. There was no mistaking it this time.

It was the same dark-blue car she had spotted just before she'd arrived at Sam's beach house.

She was close enough to smell fresh metallic paint. She squatted in front of the grille, looking for a trademark. There was none. Sara touched the glistening surface. The dark-blue was not completely dry—the car's most recent paint job couldn't be more than a few days old. She nodded and gulped. The logic was inescapable. She was crouched in front of the same car that had crushed James Reardon to death, and the reason the vehicle hadn't been identified before was that it was a customized car. It had no name. It looked *like* some other automobiles, but only vaguely so. There was, however, a license number. Sara looked down and memorized CALIFORNIA 186 RXF. Her heart pounded. She was afraid to speculate about Andy's death, but she did so anyway. The car had the same Art Deco shape which was etched in her mind. The tiny windows, the curves, the absence of hard lines and corners. The vehicle looked heavy and constipated. Malevolent. It seemed incapable of motion, yet she knew that it would be swift and deadly. She imagined it crushing her. She moaned, then shut her eyes tightly and swayed, waiting for the inevitable flash of the dream.

Instead she heard the muffled click of a rifle bolt. With no time to think, she flattened out on the pavement instinctively and crawled underneath the car. Oil dripped onto her hair and face. It was hot and it burned. She slid away from the leak and strained to peer out from under the car. Her heart was beating frantically. Why hadn't she been more careful? *Close. Oh, so close.* Across the alley in the shadows near her car she saw the outline of a man holding a stream-lined .45 caliber automatic grease gun half-hidden by his coat. He was staring intently toward the street. Then she heard Casparian walking along the sidewalk; he got into his car, started it, and drove off. The man relaxed and spun the weapon with a flourish. Then he lit a cigarette and started to pace impatiently. The only reason he hadn't seen her leave the building was that he had been watching Casparian. She shivered. If the man had seen her, she would be dead by now. If only Casparian had noticed him and anticipated the trouble that she was in. *No such luck.* She inched her way back toward the building, pulled herself out from underneath the car, and rolled against the dank brick. She managed to take La Belle out of her purse and click off the safety. The man across the alley was probably waiting for Spencer. Soon he would either drive away in the iniquitous car or he would attempt to enter the building. And when he did, Sara would be there with her pistol in his face. She would deny him a chance to use his weapon and take him alive. She would walk him over to the lights of Pacific Avenue, where she would hail a passing car. A policeman would not be far away.

She got to her feet, huddled behind the car, and

aimed La Belle over the top at her adversary. She waited. Seconds passed. Something out of the corner of her eye drew her glance to the left. At the end of the block where the alley bumped into Speedway another man was visible inside a lighted phone booth. He had his back to Sara and the phone to his ear. She didn't think that he was speaking because he was not moving. Could he be calling her office? Waiting for Spencer Harris to answer?

So there were two of them.

That definitely complicated matters. If she confronted them, she would have to kill them both. More likely they would kill her. And her object was to question them, not to provoke a shoot-out. She thought hard. Was there an alternative? She shook her head. To try to capture two professional killers was foolhardy. Laughable. She might as well save them the trouble and commit suicide.

Victory would have to wait. She scowled. And just when she was close enough to taste it.

The man in the phone booth hung up, turned, and walked briskly in Sara's direction. He whistled to his partner. They swung together in the middle of the alley and walked toward the car, their rhythmic stride typical of street-gang homeboys. Sara suddenly realized that if she didn't want a confrontation, she'd better flee. She looked around desperately. There was nowhere she could go without being seen except . . . She dove to the ground, crawled to the Dempster Dumpster, and squeezed underneath it.

"Bichocabrón!" one complained. "He was supposed to answer! It was part of the deal!"

"Maybe he was having a little fun, huh?"

"Or maybe something went wrong," came the dark and urgent response.

They ran to the back door. Sara heard them picking

the lock. It didn't deter them very long. When the door closed behind them, she backed out of her hiding place and sprinted to her car. She leaped inside, started the motor, zoomed down the alley to Pacific Avenue, swung north, and accelerated hard.

Once out of Venice, and certain that no one was following her, she turned her lights on.

Fourteen

Sara entered the hospital as if it were a sanctuary. She hurried to the TV room to collect her daughter and was relieved to find her there. Valerie was indignant that her mother had been gone for so long, then gasped when she saw Sara's bruised mouth and swollen cheek.

"What happened?"

"I'll tell you about it in the car." She was eager to be underway—she felt less vulnerable when she kept moving. "How's Sam?"

"The same."

That was good news to Sara. It was her firm, albeit unscientific opinion that the longer he lived, the better chance he had of a full recovery. There was a perverse logic to her thinking.

They left the hospital, crossed Wilshire, and bought pastrami sandwiches to go. But when they got to the car, they both discovered that they were too distraught to eat. Sara explained what had happened, sparing no details.

Valerie was silent for a while, hunched over and staring out the window. Then she turned and looked at her mother, her face wrinkled with great worry. "I wish you'd never taken this job in the first place."

"It's too late to back out now. They think I know too much."

"Well, can't we go away somewhere, then?"

"No."

"Maybe visit Grandpa and Grandma in Hawaii, where no one will be able to find you?"

"No."

"How come?"

"I couldn't live with the fear—knowing that they were looking for me. I'd worry about you, too. I'm having enough trouble maintaining as it is."

Valerie considered what her mother had said, then nodded soberly. "Do me a favor, Mom, will you?"

"What?"

"When this is over, don't be a private eye anymore, okay?"

"Val, honey, when this is over, I won't *have* to be a private eye anymore." She wondered if she were lying.

Casparian lived in an expensive security apartment building north of Montana in Santa Monica, but that was no indication of what the place looked like on the inside. Disheveled was a kind description. Newspapers and magazines were strewn everywhere. Dirty dishes were plentiful. His tailor-made suits and cashmere sweater-vests had been left in piles on the furniture and floor like the droppings of an exotic animal. The smell from uncapped liquor bottles and moldy coffee grounds was pervasive. Obviously Casparian did not care much about his personal habitat.

He greeted them in his undershirt, a glass in his hand, his face wreathed in smiles because they had arrived safely.

"Jeez," Valerie said with disgust. "Is your maid on strike or what?"

256 • KARL ALEXANDER

Casparian did not like to be reminded of the obvious. He scowled. "There's Seven-Up in the kitchen, kid. Go drown whatever sorrows you got, and we won't have any problems."

"I sure won't drink the water," she replied, walking over a stuffed chair to avoid some discarded pizza boxes.

Before he could respond, Sara took him aside and explained that Valerie was afraid and always overreacted when she didn't want to think about something. Casparian nodded as if he were trying to understand. Then Sara took the phone with the long cord to the table in the living room by the window. First she called Helen Reardon. Luckily she was all right. Helen wanted to know why she had been sent on a wild-goose chase and became annoyed when she didn't get an explanation. Sara apologized again and told her that she would call the next day when she had some answers. She hung up, feeling guilty, and lit a cigarette. Then she reached for the phone again and dialed the Department of Motor Vehicles special emergency information hot line, a twenty-four-hour service exclusively for the police. Casparian himself had given her the phone number years ago. Meanwhile Valerie and Casparian were eyeing each other.

"Is this the bathroom?" Valerie asked, pointing to a door that was ajar.

Casparian nodded. "That's it, kid."

"I hope I don't catch anything." She went inside, closed the door, and locked it.

Sara heard the phone ringing at the other end. She glanced at the scrap of paper on which she'd scrawled the license number of the dark-blue car.

A recording answered. "We're sorry. Due to recent staff cutbacks the emergency information service has been temporarily discontinued. Please direct all inquiries to the Investigation Section, which will be open tomorrow between the hours of nine and five. Thank you. Have a nice day and drive carefully."

Sara slammed the phone down in frustration. *Twenty-four-hour service, my ass!* She turned. Casparian was tapping her on the shoulder, making incoherent sounds and gesturing angrily after Valerie.

"Did you . . . did you hear what that kid said?"

"No. We'll have to wait until morning to find out about that license plate."

"What license plate? Who gives a shit about a license plate?" He pointed vehemently. "That goddamned kid said that if she used my john she'd probably get a disease!"

"What?"

"Yuk." Valerie came out of the bathroom and slammed the door.

"Did you say that, Val?"

"There's hair all over the place in there, Mom!"

"What'd you expect, kid? Fur?"

Valerie gave him a withering look. "I wouldn't be surprised."

Casparian rolled behind the bar, the only tidy spot in the apartment, and filled his glass with more Jose Cuervo Conmemorativo. He started to speak, then hesitated, trying to remain calm. He chugalugged from the bottle.

"Valerie Scott," Sara commanded, "you apologize!"

"I'm sorry," she said without remorse. Then she went over to the sliding glass doors and stared out at the balcony.

"Kids." Casparian shrugged and took another drink. He looked at Sara and forced a grin to hide his wounded feelings. "Kids and dogs, you know?"

"I know," Sara sighed. "Valerie, you should go to bed."

"Do I have to?"

"Yes."

"Can't we go and stay with Mrs. Berman?"

"No."

"How come?"

"You know how come."

"Kid," said Casparian, coming around the bar, "go to bed."

"You're not my mother."

He crouched and spread his arms, trying to act friendly. "Go to bed or Uncle Casparian is going to get mad."

"You're not my uncle, either."

"Valerie!"

The girl abruptly turned and marched off toward the bedroom.

"I'm sorry. She's just really worried."

"Mom?" Valerie called from the bedroom.

"What?"

"I can't sleep."

"You haven't been in there long enough to even try!"

"There's sand in the bed."

"So brush it out!"

"All right," came the defeated reply. "Jeez."

"Look at it this way, kid," Casparian wisecracked. "Better sand than fleas."

"I'm not holding my breath, Uncle Casparian."

Valerie was lying in bed, her hands under her head, staring at the ceiling and listening to her mother and Casparian talking in the other room. She couldn't make out what they were saying, but she wasn't sure she wanted to know anyway. She was terrified. Her mother had almost been killed, and now they were both running like fugitives and holed up in an apartment that smelled worse than dirty socks. Tears ran down her face onto the pillow. She felt empty inside; she longed for comfort, but she knew that she wasn't going to get any until this awful time was finished. There were no reassurances; she could end up alone with both her parents dead. Then what would happen? It would be horrible. She would probably get dumped into a foster home where she would have to fight with other orphans for survival.

She heard her mother in the bathroom getting ready for bed. The sounds were so normal. Why couldn't her life be that way, too? She turned over and buried her face in the pillow to muffle her sobs. It was so unfair; she felt so helpless. She wished she could've stayed with Mrs. Berman. At least she would've gotten some sympathy and attention.

After a while she stopped crying and turned over on her side. Her mother went to sleep in the adjacent bedroom, and Casparian was still snoring on the couch in the living room. Hours passed. She tried to fantasize about running away with a boy from school, but the images didn't work because she didn't know any boys she could get along with. They all thought she was weird. She shrugged and supposed that she was, what with a mother who—

A long, agonized wail came from the adjacent bedroom. She bolted out of bed, her ear cocked toward the door, her heart pounding. Casparian snored on uninterrupted, deep in an alcoholic slumber. She heard the sound again, only this time it was higher-pitched and more like a scream.

Valerie ran into the other bedroom and saw her mother sitting huddled in her bed, arms hugging her chest tightly, pushing into the wall. She turned on the light, and her mother was instantly conscious, chest heaving, eyes wide with terror.

"Mom!"

"Go . . . go back to bed, Valerie! Please?"

"What's wrong?"

"Go back to bed, Valerie!" she shouted. "I don't want to talk about it!"

"Can't we do something?"

"There's nothing you can do," she whispered. "Believe me. There's nothing anyone can do."

Sara sat on the edge of her bed and smoked one cigarette after another, afraid to turn out the light and try to sleep again. The dream had seemed so real this time, and she was badly shaken. She stared off into space, recalling Andy's death alongside the horrors of the past few days. But she couldn't lose sight of the bottom line. She had survived. She would make it through this, too. She had to.

The next morning Sara called the hospital. They had attached Sam to a life-support machine in the middle of the night. Her heart sank. At least he was still alive. She must continue to function, even if her world was on the verge of collapse. Her only other choices were death and madness.

She phoned the DMV again and found out that the dark-blue car was registered to a man named Pablo Cardenas. She got his address, then dressed in the same clothes she had worn the day before. In the living room she roused Casparian out of his deep sleep and handed him a cup of coffee. They would have to leave as soon as possible.

Next she confronted Valerie in the bedroom, extracting promises that she wouldn't go anywhere or let anyone inside the apartment.

"Why don't you just take me to jail?" she asked sullenly.

"Come on, Valerie, that doesn't help."

"Well, what am I supposed to do? I don't want to stay in this dump!"

"Why don't you clean the place up?"

"You've got to be kidding!"

"Wouldn't it feel more like home, then? For both of us?"

Valerie crinkled up her face thoughtfully. "Yeah, I guess so." She grinned slowly. "Throw in ten bucks and you've got a deal."

"Boyle Heights, huh?" said Casparian, squinting out the window.

"That's what they said."

"I haven't been here since they started selling paint in spray cans. I didn't recognize the neighborhood."

Sara did not laugh as she drove down First Street looking for Mott Avenue. She was too tense. Pablo Cardenas lived in Boyle Heights, which was a small pocket of Chicano and black poverty east of Los Angeles, bracketed by freeways and blanketed by smog. Generally the neighborhood was a mixture of single-family dwellings, heavy industrial buildings, and government housing projects left over from World War II. Graffiti flourished. So did weeds, broken glass, and hordes of unattended children.

But 267 Mott Avenue was a pleasant surprise. The Cardenas residence was a well-kept bungalow surrounded by flowers and a manicured lawn. A small pearl in a tarnished setting. Sara found it hard to believe that a murderer lived there, but she did not comment, for Casparian was suddenly on edge. She guessed that he was as nervous as she. They were on the brink now—in the vague periphery where uncertainty ruled. They were about to confront a killer, and although their plan was beautifully simple, they had no way of knowing if it was foolproof.

"Should I park?"

"No," he growled. "Cruise around and let me know if you see that car."

She did not.

They parked a half block away from the Cardenas house. "I guess that means he isn't home, right?" Sara asked.

"It doesn't mean anything."

They watched the place for a long time. The stillness was occasionally broken by a barking dog, a screaming child, a stereo playing Mexican music, or a loud truck passing by on one of the freeways. Sara wondered if she should have worn a disguise, then shook her head. They almost certainly did not know what she looked like.

Nevertheless she pulled her hair back into a ponytail, then wrapped and pinned it up on top of her head. She put on large tinted sunglasses that made her eyes seem gray instead of brown. Finally she changed to a light pink shade of lipstick, wincing where she touched cracked skin.

Despite Casparian's disapproving frown, she gave her pistol its usual check. She knew that he suspected her of wanting to indulge in heroics, even though she had no intention of risking her life. After all, she hated pain; she'd always imagined that death hurt forever.

Reaching behind her, she opened the bag that contained the cassette recorder. She took her last two bugs out of the side pocket and preset their stations on the machine. If they caught Pablo Cardenas, then they wouldn't need to tap his phone. If he wasn't there, however, the bug would certainly tell them when he returned. She turned to Casparian and gave him a quick, brave smile. "Okay?" she whispered.

"Might as well get it over with." He grunted and reached for the door handle. "Give me a couple of minutes' head start."

Casparian slipped out of the Pinto and disappeared behind an ancient stand of oleander. Sara checked her watch. In just a few minutes she would knock on the front door while Casparian was sneaking in the back way. She was the bait; he was the hook. If Pablo Cardenas was there, Casparian would surprise him from the rear. If he wasn't there, then Casparian would melt back outside and no one would be the wiser.

Sara left her car and slung her purse over her right shoulder. Her hand was inside, holding La Belle. She walked up a slight rise, went inside the gate, and up the steps. She tried to add bounce to her stride, projecting the image of youthful officialdom. She rang the doorbell and waited for the longest time. Just as she was about to knock sharply, the door opened and the faint odor of Mexican spices wafted onto the front porch.

"Yes?" Behind the pleasant voice was the wrinkled but placid face of a small and stately gentlewoman modestly dressed in black lace. Although probably close to eighty, the lady was extremely attractive, except for a slight yellowing at the ends of her luxuriant gray hair. She was smiling expectantly.

Sara hadn't expected this and was shocked. But she choked back a gasp and returned the smile. She wondered if she were in the wrong place. No, this person was probably a mother or a grandmother. And what was so unusual about several generations living under the same roof? Even if one of the sons was a murderer? Still, Sara just stood there and stared. She was speechless.

"Do you have the right address?" the lady asked in a pleasant voice with a hint of an accent.

"Yes, yes, I'm certain of it," Sara replied in a rush. "You are Señora Cardenas, are you not?" she guessed.

"I am."

"Pleased to meet you." Sara regained some of her composure and showed her counterfeit license, complete with the Los Angeles County seal. "I'm from the Department of Social Services."

"Yes?"

"And we're conducting a survey in the neighborhood—particularly among the elderly—to see if they are currently enrolled in all the assistance programs available to them."

"How nice."

"If you could spare a few moments, I wonder if you would mind answering some questions."

"Not at all."

Sara produced a bogus computer printout.

"Would you like to come inside and have some coffee while we talk?"

Sara's eyes widened with surprise. She hadn't expected either cooperation or generosity. Was she still within Los Angeles city limits? Or was she being set up? She swallowed hard. There was no turning back. "Why, yes, I'd love some coffee."

Señora Cardenas opened the door wide and graciously ushered Sara inside. Her eyes sparkled. "We can sit at the table so you'll have some room for your questionnaire." She led the way.

Sara closed the door and looked around cautiously. She saw no one and heard nothing unusual, so she crossed a living room cluttered with early California antiques and went through an archway into a formal dining room. Señora Cardenas indicated that Sara should make herself comfortable at a long mahogany table that glistened from years of polish. Sara perched on the chair closest to the wall. She felt as if she were in church.

"Just a moment, please." Señora Cardenas excused herself, went into the kitchen, and loudly busied herself with the task of brewing coffee.

What about the killer, Pablo Cardenas? Sara didn't think that he was in the house; he never would have allowed the old lady to let strangers inside. She turned and quickly glanced back at the front door. When would he return? Would he come through that door and greet Sara with a sneer and a submachine gun?

She shook her head, confused. It all seemed so incongruous. The house possessed an air of dignity and charm not associated with a murderer's habitat. Nevertheless she arranged her purse so that the flap was open and La Belle was within immediate reach. Then she studied her surroundings, looking for something unusual or out of place. No luck there. She left her chair, kept an ear cocked for Señora Cardenas, and went looking for the telephone. There were so many antiques in the living room, she had difficulty distinguishing one piece from another. She finally saw the phone on a table across from the sofa. Above it on the paneled wall were several framed pictures. Curious, she went over and peered at them. They were family portraits, typical and rather uninteresting. One group shot showed Señora Cardenas surrounded by a dozen relatives. One of the men struck Sara as vaguely familiar. Then she rejected the notion. Under these circumstances, anyone looking slightly suspicious might seem familiar.

She heard Señora Cardenas collecting china from a

cupboard. She cursed herself; now she would not have time to tap the telephone. Just as she returned to her chair, Señora Cardenas pushed through the swinging door into the dining room carrying a coffee service on a sterling-silver tray. She set it down on the table and smiled at Sara.

"Cream and sugar?"

"No, thank you."

The lady poured Sara a cup and handed it to her. "Now. You had some questions?"

"All due respect, Señora Cardenas, but the person I should talk to is Señor Pablo Cardenas. Would that be possible?"

Señora Cardenas frowned and patted her hair, confused. A bemused smile spread across her face, and she slowly shook her head. "Ah, I am sorry for you, my dear, although it is not your fault. *Las oficinas! Los departamentos!* I believe you call it bureaucracy?"

"I am in the right place, aren't I?"

She laughed and nodded. "Of sorts."

Sara stammered. "Pablo Cardenas. Is he—"

"He was my husband."

Sara frowned. "You have children, then. A son."

"We have no children."

"I don't understand. You say Pablo Cardenas *was*—" Sara touched her forehead. "Oh, of course, forgive me. You're divorced."

"My dear girl. Pablo Cardenas died five years ago."

Sara was amazed. "No, that's not possible."

The señora rose gracefully and went into the living room. She turned and gazed at Sara, her chin held high, her hands caressing a lacquered canister that reposed on the mantle. "My husband wished to be cremated. This urn contains the ashes of Pablo Cardenas." She crossed herself automatically. "May God rest his soul."

* * *

They left Boyle Heights and drove west toward Santa Monica, dumbfounded and frustrated. While Sara had been talking with the widow Cardenas, Casparian had made a cursory but careful inspection of the back of the house. Needless to say, he had not found Pablo Cardenas. Sara was crestfallen. She really thought that they had been onto the fresh trail of a killer. Instead she had discovered that her one and only suspect wasn't even alive. Well, at least now she didn't feel so bad about blowing her opportunity to tap Señora Cardenas's phone. All she would have done was waste one tiny and expensive microphone.

Casparian was glowering out the window and smoking, distant and unhappy. Sara didn't know what to say at this point. She felt like she was confined with a close friend who had suddenly changed into a stranger. She lit a cigarette to have something to do. He grunted and shifted in the seat.

"Drop me at my office, will you? I got things piling up that need attention.

"Okay," Sara replied.

"I got to think this through, too."

"Shouldn't we talk about it, then?"

"I'll be better off noodling it out on my own."

Sara scowled at the traffic ahead. Her face grew hot —more with humiliation than anger. She knew that her cheeks were crimson, but there was nothing she could do about it. So he had given up on her. That quickly, too. And it was her case! *What is it with the male of the species anyway? Aren't I entitled to make a mistake?* Her questions didn't matter. Very simply, she expected more from an old friend, regardless of sex.

When she pulled up in front of his office building, she stopped him before he could get all the way out the door. "Casparian, I think we were in the right place."

"Sure." He nodded sardonically. "Then how come you didn't bust an urn full of ashes for murder, Sara?"

"Come on!" Her voice was small. "There must be a logical explanation."

"What? An eighty-year-old lady jobs out as a hired gun? I ain't buying that."

She didn't know what to say. She punted. "Well?"

"Take a rest, Sara."

She had a sudden thought. "Hey, maybe we weren't in the right place."

"There you go."

"Then that means that the DMV screwed up!"

"How do you figure?"

"One of their computers could be wrong, Casparian! It's happened before, hasn't it? I mean, after all, they've got a car registered to a man who isn't even alive!"

He shrugged. "So his widow never got around to changing the registration. Maybe she doesn't drive."

"Still, license plates don't lie, do they?"

"Nope, but they can be misread when it's dark and you're scared shitless."

"What are you saying?"

"Couldn't the *R* have been a *P*, Sara? Or the *F* an *E*?"

"Hey, wait a minute! You think—"

He got out of the car, closed the door, and leaned in the window. "You got it wrong. All the DMV did was give you the right address for the wrong license number." His eyes sparkled with concern. "Forget it. We all fuck up from time to time. Especially when you're tired. Take your kid to the beach or something. Relax." He walked away.

Sara watched him go, astonished at his remarks. *So*

that's it? The paragon of logic, the champion of deductive thinking just assumes that I made a mistake and slams the book shut and says "Case closed?" If I didn't know, I'd assume that Casparian was a cop. He just bulldozed me the same way the police did when I tried to tell them about the car when Andy was killed. Well, no more. Maybe I can't depend on anyone else. Maybe I never could. She shuddered as she drove away, then glanced compulsively in the rearview mirror and out the windows, looking for the unknown and the unseen. She was alone again. Naked. Was it permanent this time?

When Sara got back to Casparian's apartment, Valerie was dutifully running the vacuum in the living room. She shouted over the noise, "How much longer do we have to stay in this dump, Momma?"

"I don't know!"

Valerie turned off the vacuum and gestured at the result of her labors. Trash was piled neatly in one corner of the room, Casparian's clothes in the other. "Lemme tell you," she commented sourly, "I should've held out for twenty."

"The place looks great."

"Yeah. I couldn't stand the smell, so I had to do something, you know?" She picked up a can of air freshener and resumed spraying. "We're going to run out of this stuff soon. What do I do then?"

"Open the windows."

"The guy's a real slob, Mom. How could you stand working for him?"

"I never had to come over here."

Valerie laughed, and Sara was surprised that she seemed to be in such a bright mood. Maybe something good had happened for a change.

"Did you call the hospital?"

Valerie could not keep a straight face. She grinned. "He's a little better."

Sara went over and hugged her. "That's great!"

"I know, I know, but it's not terrific." She pushed away. "The doctor said he still only has a fifty-fifty chance."

"Doctors are always pessimistic," Sara replied, somewhat sobered. "He's getting stronger though?"

"Yeah." Valerie glanced down. "You have a good morning?"

"No." Sara frowned, then looked at her daughter with a flat, determined expression. "But the day isn't over yet, is it?"

The girl sighed. "I wish I could do something."

"Why don't you make us some lunch? There's sausage-and-cheese pizza in the freezer."

Valerie went into the kitchen, grateful for the diversion, and Sara sat down on the couch. The radio suddenly came on playing bubblegum rock, but Sara was not to be distracted. She was deep in thought, trying to sort through the contradictions of the Reardon case. There was a key somewhere. Something small and elusive.

Her visit with Señora Cardenas was fresh in her mind. The old lady had been gracious and correct; she had done nothing to imply collusion with a murderer. So, either she was innocent or she was a better actress than Sara was a detective. What about the urn containing her husband's ashes? Sara did not doubt that Pablo Cardenas was dead. But the lead still existed.

She closed her eyes and created a mental picture of the Cardenas house, precisely recalling everything she had said and done there. Señora Cardenas had gone into the kitchen to make the coffee. Sara had worried about the murderer's showing up. She had gone into the living room to tap the phone but was distracted by some innocuous family pictures on the wall. Suddenly she remembered something, and her heart started pounding with excitement. That was it, wasn't it? *The man in the family portrait who seemed vaguely familiar.* She looked around frantically for her things, but she could only find her purse.

"Valerie?"

"What?"

"What did I do with my folders and stuff?"

"I don't know anything about any folders," she said, coming into the room with a steaming pizza and a stack of paper towels. "But this, *mamma mia,* is ready!" She set it down on the coffee table.

"Where did you put them?"

"Put what?"

"My folders!"

"I didn't see 'em, Mom! Really." Her face wrinkled up. "Jeez! First you force me to do lunch, and then you scream at me about folders!"

Sara mumbled to herself, shaking her head. She remembered. She pulled on her coat, grabbed her purse, then turned to Valerie, excited and frightened. "Val, honey . . ."

Valerie was confused and astonished. "Aren't you going to eat?"

"I'm sorry. This can't wait."

"I thought you weren't supposed to leave here without Casparian, no matter what."

"This is very important."

"What about me, Mom?" she cried. "How come I have to stay here?"

"Because . . ." She patiently started to explain.

"Don't tell me! I don't want to know! I've heard it

before and I hate it!" She slumped in the chair and put her face in her hands, then shrank from Sara's touch.

"I'll be fine," Sara whispered. "Really."

"Where are you going, anyway?"

"The office."

She parked on the street in case someone had been paid to watch the lot in the alley, eased out of the Pinto, and looked up at the building. Its stately brick looked clean in the afternoon sun, giving no indication that a dead man was stashed on the second floor. She glanced around quickly, then hurried inside. As she entered the foyer she shivered, recalling the chill of the night before. She paused and listened. There were only the muffled sounds of office work coming from various open doors. *Business as usual,* she thought. The tenants were unaware that their landlord was stuffed into a broom closet and would not be collecting rent checks anymore. Instead of reassuring her, the air of normality was frightening. Visitors to the building—murderous strangers, perhaps—would not be noticed. They could loiter in the waiting rooms and corridors, passing as customers while they watched for her.

The stairway was dark even at midday. Sara imagined a faceless assassin coming out of the wall, grabbing for her. She ran up the steps two at a time. When she reached the second floor, she forced herself to stop. She took several deep breaths and tried to calm her imagination. Finally the terror subsided; there were no demons, real or imagined. She strode briskly to her office door. As she paused to unlock it, she noticed the faint yet pervasive odor of rotting flesh in the corridor. It was nauseating. She'd have to do something about that. She took La Belle out of her purse and slipped inside, closing the door behind her and leaning against it. So far, so good. Weapon at the ready, she checked out her waiting room. No one was lurking in the shadows or behind the furniture. She moved to her inner office door, less apprehensive now. It was highly unlikely that anyone could get past the deadbolt. She unlatched it.

She was right. Her office was just as she and Casparian had left it the night before. She put La Belle away and hurried to her desk. With trembling hands, she found the Reardon file, opened the folder, and sorted through the papers until she uncovered the stack of prints and proofsheets. On top was the photograph of James Reardon leaving the halfway house. Once again she examined the right-hand corner through her magnifying glass. She stared at the photograph for a long time. *Yes.* There was no doubt in her mind.

The tall, thin man entering the building by a side door was the same man she had noticed in Señora Cardenas's family portrait.

She carefully circled the face with a grease pencil. He must be the killer. His name wasn't Pablo Cardenas, but Señora Cardenas knew who this gaunt man was. And so did Jorge Martinez. An identification, of course, was a long way from bringing a criminal to justice. Very possibly, neither Señora Cardenas nor the people at the halfway house knew that this mystery man was an assassin who could kill with anything from a car to a syringe full of heroine. Sara stared off at the Cézanne print on the wall. She hated to be cynical, but she had a feeling that others did know. Especially Jorge Martinez, although she was sure that he couldn't be linked to anything more substantial than, say, a delinquent parking ticket. At least for right now.

But there was always tomorrow.

She wondered how she would proceed. The idea of a stakeout at 267 Mott Avenue was not appealing. She didn't want to go snooping around the halfway house, either, because that would be tantamount to committing suicide. Suddenly, she knew. She took a manila envelope out of her desk, put the photograph in it, then phoned the L.A.P.D. and asked for Lieutenant Timothy Dodge. Her call was transferred to the Venice Division and she was put on hold.

Suddenly the marbled glass of her outer office door rattled slightly. She hung up the phone and glanced in that direction, listening intently. Was she being paranoid again?

A soft rustling noise.

No, she wasn't. Someone was coming for her! She dove for her purse. Her hands shook, and she couldn't get it open. She envisioned the man in the photograph swinging through the door, a leer on his face, and spraying her with bullets. She flinched and ducked down, still fumbling with her purse. She dropped to the floor and rolled, but it was too late.

The door was slowly opening.

Her hand found La Belle and jerked it out of her purse. She clicked off the safety, raised the pistol, and aimed around the corner of her desk.

"Sara Scott?"

A hush. Sara dropped her weapon, moaned with relief, and put a hand over her eyes. "Jesus Christ."

"Should I have knocked?"

"That's all right." Sara worked to catch her breath. Nervously she almost laughed. "I wasn't expecting you, anyway."

Judith Rosenus stepped into the room.

"Do me a favor."

"Yes?"

"The next time you come, either make an appointment or wear bells, okay?"

"I'm sorry I startled you."

Sara tried to shrug it off, but when she got up, she was still shaking. She collapsed into her desk chair, waited until she was fully composed, then scrutinized her visitor. Judith Rosenus was wearing a gossamer print dress. Her hair was brushed out curly and full, making her face look childlike. She wore rouge and powder to cover the ravages of sorrow. Though she appeared more frail and winsome than before, the effect made her seem more beautiful than Sara remembered. The young lady wore tragedy well.

She came forward carrying a scrapbook and a box and stood in front of Sara's desk like an errant schoolgirl. "I've been thinking about what you said last week. I want to know who killed Alan and why."

Sara indicated a chair.

"You were right," Judith said as she sat down. "No one seems to care about him anymore. The lawyers say that I have to sell the house to pay off Alan's ex-wife and children." She looked down. "And they didn't even come to the funeral."

"God, I'm sorry."

"The police haven't arrested any suspects yet. I think they've given up."

"That doesn't surprise me."

"They won't even return my phone calls."

"And if you didn't want their help," Sara commented dryly, "they'd probably move in with you."

Judith managed a smile, leaned forward, and handed Sara the scrapbook. She set the box on top and pointed to it. "His address book's in there and some notes that have names and numbers on them. I looked through it all. Nothing seemed unusual, but then again, I'm not a detective."

"Thanks." Sara set the box aside and inspected the scrapbook. The cover was red Moroccan leather. *Alan Rosenus* was embossed on the front in gold letters. She opened it.

"Over the past few months, I've spent a lot of time going through his papers." Judith's voice quavered. "The scrapbook was going to be his birthday present."

"It's beautiful," Sara whispered reverently, leafing through the pages. She was impressed. The gift reminded her of the sweater she had knitted for Andy, now neatly folded in the bottom of her trunk. He'd never even seen it, never tried it on.

Judith automatically took out a linen handkerchief and held it tightly in front of her face. "All the articles he wrote for the *Times* are in there. I arranged them chronologically. There are pictures, too. Before he got completely turned off, Alan used to go to a lot of political gatherings."

"This will be a great deal of help," Sara lied. How could she tell Judith Rosenus that she didn't need any of this anymore?

Judith did not see through the deception. In fact she seemed pleased. "I thought you should have it. You would've liked Alan. He cared about people and he hated injustice."

"Thanks, I . . . I don't know what to say."

"I don't really care about the stuff in the box, but someday I'd like the scrapbook returned."

"You'll get it back just as soon as I find out who killed your husband."

"You'll help me, then?"

"You're helping me, aren't you?"

Judith gazed steadily at Sara and nodded. "I'm glad I came."

"So am I."

"I was afraid to, you know. After what I said."

Sara shrugged and tried to look cheerful. "I've heard worse."

Judith cleared her throat. "Will there be some sort of fee?"

"I'm not worried about it."

"I can afford something."

"If I need it, I'll ask."

They shook hands.

"I'll be talking to you in a few days."

"I'm so very grateful."

"Judith," Sara responded firmly. "I'm not a saint. You should realize that if I didn't have a lot riding on this, I wouldn't be doing it."

"Oh. Why not?"

"Because it's too goddamn dangerous."

"So is your boyfriend still alive?"

"He's in a coma."

"It'll be interesting to talk to him if he wakes up."

"It'll be a relief."

Lieutenant Dodge ran his hands through his blond hair, leaned forward, and grinned. "Why a relief?"

"Because I love him." Sara pushed her chair away from the lieutenant and crossed her legs. He made her nervous.

His grin got wider. He spread his hands and feigned surprise. "You mean you didn't come down here to confess?"

"I have nothing to confess."

"Then to what do I owe the honor?"

"I'm working on a divorce case," she explained, masking her lie with a professional air.

"I don't know nothing about divorce. I've never had the pleasure."

"You haven't tried marriage, then?" she asked, forcing a light tone.

"Naw. It's the pits being a cop. You never have time to do anything except bust people." He chuckled. "Frisk 'em and forget 'em."

"Got to keep that crime rate down."

"You drop by to chat or what?"

"I'd like a favor."

He raised his eyebrows and sank back in his chair. He hadn't expected that. "A favor," he said lubriciously.

She nodded and gulped. "I'd like to look through your rogues' gallery."

He studied her, slowly tapping a pencil on the desk blotter. He half-closed his eyes and weighed her request. "What for?"

"Supposedly my client's wife ran off with a pimp," she lied glibly. "And I'd like to place a face with a name."

"I'll bet you would." He laughed. "Yeah. I'll bet you would." He leaned forward and grinned knowingly. "This pimp just wouldn't happen to deal smack on the side, would he?"

"What do you mean?" she said, guarded.

"I think you know, ma'am. I think you want to find out who your boyfriend's pusher is so you can nail him yourself. I think your story about working on a divorce case is a crock of shit. I'll tell you what, Miss Scott, I'll let you take a look-see at the rogues' gallery on one condition."

"What's that?" she croaked, embarrassed that her story had been so transparent.

"That you show me the name of this so-called pimp if you come up with it."

She thought a moment, then sighed. She really had

no choice. Somehow she would have to trick this disarmingly handsome, slick police lieutenant. "Okay. I'll agree to that."

He was obviously delighted. He picked up the phone and punched an intercom button. "Sergeant, come on in here, will you? I think I finally found something for you to do this afternoon."

Sara was always intrigued by the variety of faces. The first time she'd gone through police files, she had expected to detect a common denominator of guilt and outrage, but there was none. In the faces before her now there was a unifying characteristic, however—resignation.

She had reached the *P*'s, but so far hadn't seen anyone who resembled the mystery man. Which was just as well. Dodge had shut her up in the room with Sergeant Palinko. The sergeant was sitting close behind her, watching her hands and eyes for the inevitable reaction. She steeled herself against this constant annoyance, hoping that when the time came she would be able to suppress a response. As it was, she was having enough trouble concentrating; the sergeant was constantly scratching and the habit was distracting. Suddenly he stopped, and she was able to continue.

Forty minutes later she was flipping through the *S*'s, pausing briefly to read the name below every picture. Palinko had grown bored. His occasional sidelong glances at Sara's breasts were becoming stares.

Then she saw her mystery man.

Her heart jumped. *Yes, this is him.* The light-brown-reddish curly hair, the intense dark eyes, the long, haunted face. There was no mistaking it. *He doesn't look like a criminal,* she thought. *He looks more like a Cuban long-distance runner.* Then she forced herself to continue flipping through the pictures lest the sergeant detect that she had hit the jackpot. At the end of the *S*'s, she stopped, stretched, yawned, leaned back, turned toward Palinko, and smiled.

"I don't think I'm going to find him."

"No?"

"No."

"Too bad."

"Are you hungry?"

"I'm always hungry."

"I'll split a bear claw with you."

"How did you know that we got bear claws?"

"The police always have bear claws."

When he left the room, she quickly went back to the *S*'s, found the picture, removed it from the file, and studied the description typed on the back.

ALBERTO SECO. 6'3", 180 lbs., reddish-brown hair, brown eyes. No scars, tattoos, or other distinguishing marks. Wanted by the LAPD & the DEA for the possession of narcotics for sale. Last seen in the vicinity of Durango, Mexico. Whereabouts unknown. Considered Dangerous.

Sara dropped the picture into her purse, feeling smug and satisfied. So much for interference from the police. She got up to leave.

"Sergeant Palinko is going to be very disappointed that you didn't stick around. He donated a buck to the kitty for your bear claw."

She gasped and looked up. The voice came out of a small speaker. Above it was the telltale lens of a surveillance camera. She was momentarily shocked, then chided herself for not having seen it before.

Lieutenant Dodge came into the room, grinning, his hands spread. "I know, I know, it's embarrassing to get caught shoplifting, so to speak." He pointed at the camera. "You'd think that cops could trust each other."

She sat down, furious with herself.

He held out his hand. "We made a deal, didn't we?"

She took the picture out of her purse, gave it to him, then shook her head with disgust. *Whoopie-fuck. I've just blown it. Now it's going to be a race to get to him first. If they win, all they'll do is try to stick him with a drug charge, and I'll come away with nothing.* Sergeant Palinko came into the room, carefully balancing two bear claws and coffee.

The lieutenant's grin faded. He tossed the picture on the table. "Guess who's back in town, Sergeant?"

Palinko's gnarled face made a question mark.

"Alberto Seco."

"Holy shit. Just when I was learning to like my job."

"I suppose you're going to run right out and bust him," Sara said hotly.

"I wish we could. D'you know where he is?"

"If I did, I wouldn't be here."

The lieutenant sucked his lip and reflected. He nodded acceptance.

"Well?" she asked. "What are you going to do?"

"Oh, we'll put out a bulletin and do the usual things, but I doubt anything'll come of it. He's been at large for five years."

"Am I free to go?"

"Sure," he said expansively, with a quick nod to Palinko that she didn't see. "But if I were you, I'd forget about Alberto Seco no matter what he sold your boyfriend. He's a very dangerous dude."

"He likes to hurt people," Palinko added thought-fully, on his way out the door.

"And he's got lots of good friends," Dodge explained. "*Old homeboys* is too restrictive a term. You see, Alberto Seco is one of the leaders of the Mexican Mafia."

Fifteen

The Mexican Mafia. My God.

Sara was turning north on Lincoln when she saw the familiar unmarked brown Plymouth sedan following her. So Lieutenant Dodge was taking no chances, was he? She thought that she'd gotten out of the L.A.P.D.'s Venice Division a little too easily. Changing lanes, she drove just fast enough to put five cars between her and the sedan. Then she slowed down, deliberately stacking up the traffic. When she could no longer see the Plymouth, she knew that the driver couldn't see her. She made a quick right turn on Marine Street and vanished into the hills of Ocean Park, successfully losing her tail. Lieutenant Dodge had made a serious mistake. He had dispatched an amateur to follow her. Like other men she had known, Dodge had assumed that she was just another woman driver.

She leisurely drove back to Casparian's apartment, opting for the relative obscurity of the side-streets and thinking about the enigmatic Alberto Seco. How was she going to find him? Most likely, if he showed up anywhere, it would be at the halfway house. *But when?* She frowned. Were her options reduced to the standard strategy of a stakeout? She lit a cigarette and blew smoke rings. They hung in the air, then dissipated with her next breath like hypothetical situations. There must be another way.

Back at Casparian's, she carried the stuff she'd taken from her office upstairs and put it on the table by the window. Valerie grunted a hello from the den, where she was watching television, then made a comment about being under house arrest. Sara responded lightly that it would all be over soon and, inanely, that there was nothing to worry about. The words were meaningless, and she knew it.

She called her service, asked for messages, and found out that Helen Reardon had phoned earlier in the day. Sara quickly dialed the number, and her client answered on the third ring. When Sara identified herself, there was a long pause.

"Helen, are you there?"

"I talked to the Santa Monica police this morning," she blurted out. "I told them everything."

"Why?" Sara asked, astonished.

Helen explained that after Sara called her the night before, she got scared and couldn't sleep. She realized that she probably should have told the police what she knew in the first place, but there was Wally to think of.

"Who the hell is Wally?"

"My brother." She cleared her throat, then sighed. "When my husband and I were first married, Wally threatened to kill James because he thought interracial marriages were the work of the Devil. When you told me that James had been murdered instead of accidentally killed, I though that Wally had done it and I didn't want anyone to know."

Sara gaped at the phone. "Then why hire me at all?"

"I thought if I didn't, then either you or the police would suspect me of having James murdered."

"I don't believe this." Sara shook her head. "I *don't* believe this!"

"I'm sorry, Sara, really I am. You're a nice person, but I won't be needing your services anymore."

Sara wanted to scream into the receiver, but she controlled herself. What was done, was done, and anger wouldn't help the situation. Besides, now the Reardon case had a momentum all its own. "You can't fire me, Helen."

"What do you mean?" came the guarded reply.

"I don't work for you anymore," Sara stated flatly. "I'm working for myself."

She hung up and strode into the kitchen. So the Santa Monica police were in it now, were they? Well, the first thing they would do would be to come looking for her, and she figured that it would be downright impossible for them to trace her to Casparian's apartment. Furthermore, she was certain there would be bureaucratic fumbling while the Santa Monica police and the Venice Division of the L.A.P.D. "effected liaison." Still, it was an added pressure, and she knew she didn't have much time. She sighed. She didn't even have time to feel sad that Helen Reardon hadn't had the patience to hang on for the duration. *Such,* she supposed, *are the wages of fear.*

She went back to the table in the living room, sat down, and stared out the window, carefully reviewing her recent discoveries. She knew that Alberto Seco was related to Señora Cardenas. He had been acquainted with Spencer Harris, too. Therefore, he must know some of the others she'd stumbled across during her investigation.

She sat up suddenly and took a handkerchief out of her purse. She picked up the phone, tightly stretched the cloth over the mouthpiece so her voice would sound muffled and unrecognizable, and dialed.

"Hello?" Señora Cardenas sounded pleasant, but slightly inquisitive. Sara surmised that she wasn't used to talking on the telephone, but that was fine.

"Hi. Is Alberto there?" she asked breathlessly.

There was a long static hush.

"Hello?" Sara said.

"I'm sorry." Her voice was hesitant and cold now. "You must have the wrong number."

"Is this 666-8717?"

"Yes, but—"

"Jeez, that's funny." She paused and gulped. "Jorge told me that I'd probably be able to get in touch with Alberto at this number."

"Who?"

"Jorge Martinez. I'm a friend of his, too."

"Why didn't you say so in the first place?"

"I'm sorry. I didn't think of it."

"Alberto isn't here very often, and when he is, he doesn't like to be disturbed."

Sara was not to be deterred. "We were supposed to get together tonight. That's the only reason I called."

"Well, he's not here right now."

"Oh. When will he be back?"

"I'm sorry. I don't know."

Sara pressed on. "Would it be all right if I came over and waited for him?"

"You'd be wasting your time. This morning he said that he was leaving the city on a business trip."

"Can you tell me where he's going?"

"I have no idea."

"Exactly when is he leaving?"

"I'm sorry."

The phone went dead.

Alberto Seco was leaving town on a business trip. He could be going anywhere! She went back to the phone to call Casparian, but stopped and cursed herself. *Call him? What for? He won't know where Seco's going. He might not even know who he is!* She sat down and stared off into space, remembering Señora Cardenas's words exactly. Alberto Seco was leaving the city on a business trip. *A business trip. Of course!* He was almost certainly a professional assassin, so that had to mean he was going to kill someone! All she had to do was figure out who, and then she would know where Seco was traveling to, and she could stop him. If there was time.

Once more Sara opened the Reardon file, its contents now more than slightly dog-eared. She plowed through the material. She even looked at the photographs again, unconsciously sorting out those which did not include James Reardon.

She discovered nothing.

In reaching for a cigarette, she accidentally knocked Judith Rosenus's leather scrapbook off the table, then bent down and picked it up. As an afterthought she placed it in front of her, opened it, and began leafing through the pages. The articles written by Alan Rosenus drew her attention. The progression of his thinking fascinated her. It mirrored the loss of trust and innocence that had blighted the last decade. Four years ago he had praised the current state government as a newlywed would his bride. Gradually he became disenchanted with the administration until finally he had nothing but scorn for every politician and bureaucrat in Sacramento.

Except one.

The Honorable Lawrence Conrad, Comptroller of the State of California. Rosenus had written that he was the only politician in the state who could still wear a white hat without being ashamed.

Sara heard Valerie straggle into the room and looked up, almost grateful for the interruption.

"I'm sorry for ignoring you, Mom."

Sara shrugged.

"Did you get your stuff?"

"Yeah, for all the good it's doing me."

Valerie pointed at the scrapbook on Sara's lap. "What's that? I haven't seen that before."

"Memories of another dead husband. And father."

"Oh." Valerie stared at the red-leather cover, her eyes expressing a morbid fascination. "Can I look at it?"

"Sure." She handed her daughter the scrapbook. "It's not doing me any good."

Valerie took the book, curled up on the floor in front of her mother and began leafing through the pages, pausing to look at the pictures. "So you haven't been having a good day?"

"No."

"What about Casparian?"

"I haven't talked to him."

"I wish this whole thing was over with. I want to go home."

"So do I, Val. So do I." She shuddered, then lit a cigarette. She felt utterly hopeless. Someone was going to die, and she did not have a clue. She couldn't even bring herself to tell Valerie what was going on.

"Momma?"

"Yes?" Sara saw that Valerie was staring at a particular page in the scrapbook.

"What's the story on this guy here?" She pointed at a newspaper photograph. "When I was going through Daddy's old clippings, I saw a picture of him and Daddy at a barbeque in Modesto during the last campaign."

Sara dropped down on the floor next to Valerie, who was tapping the photograph.

It was a picture, now yellow with age, of Alan Rosenus shaking hands with Lawrence Conrad.

Sara's mind raced. She had forgotten that Andy had known Lawrence Conrad, too. She quickly rummaged through her own photographs and found the one of Anna Perez shaking hands with Lawrence Conrad at the campaign rally. She studied both pictures. And then she felt she knew instinctively. Andy. James Reardon. Alan Rosenus. Marta Fontana. Sam Gage. The attempt on her own life.

She sat back. "My God."

"What?"

"Valerie, you may have just solved the Reardon case!"

"Really?" Her eyes shone.

Sara stared at the pictures again, nodding, convinced.

Alberto Seco was going to murder Lawrence Conrad. His "business trip" was to Sacramento, to eliminate the person James Reardon had been going to see when *he* had been killed. She could finally piece it all together. *James Reardon suspected that someone was dealing heroin out of the Straighten-Up Halfway House. He nosed around and confirmed his suspicions. Even worse, the operation was controlled by the Mexican Mafia. James Reardon had gone to an old friend, Alan Rosenus, for help. Rosenus had advised Reardon to get in contact with someone in Sacra-*

mento. Who? The only one with power and influence that he still trusted. Lawrence Conrad. The comptroller knew Senator Anna Perez, who was the chairperson of the board of directors of the halfway house. Also he was rumored to be the governor's closest advisor and confidant. Lawrence Conrad was the ideal government official to inform.

Unfortunately Lawrence Conrad had never been told, because James Reardon was killed before he could keep the appointment. Then Alberto Seco and his cohorts began eliminating everyone else who might have known about their dealings. Sara shuddered. Lawrence Conrad must be the last name on the list. Just below hers.

"So what do we do, Momma?"

"We prevent a murder." She frowned darkly. "If it hasn't already occurred."

"How?"

Sara opened the box of Alan Rosenus's memorabilia and took out his phone book. In a few seconds she found Lawrence Conrad's home phone number. While she dialed she quickly formulated a plan. She would warn Conrad, then have him set a trap for Alberto Seco.

There were two rings, and then a recorded message.

"Hello. This is Lawrence Conrad speaking. I can't come to the phone right now. Either leave a message for me after the tone or try me at CApitol 7-8394, extension three. Remember, you must wait for the tone . . ."

Sara didn't bother. She broke the connection and immediately dialed Conrad's office. The phone rang fifteen times, but there was no answer. She glanced at her watch. The time was ten to six. The state capitol's switchboard probably closed at five.

"Damn!" Would she have to go to Sacramento blind? Only to discover another corpse? It was too late for idle speculation. "Get me the Yellow Pages, quick."

Valerie ran into the kitchen. Moments later she returned with them, and Sara flipped to "Travel Agencies," called the first one listed and asked about flights from Los Angeles to Sacramento. She jotted down the schedule for that evening, then went through the torturous process of phoning each airline and identifying herself as Alberto Seco's secretary, calling to confirm his reservation on flight so-and-so.

According to all the reservation desks from Air California to Western Airlines, no one named Alberto Seco was flying to Sacramento that evening.

Sara was crushed. Could it be possible that Alberto Seco was going somewhere else? Sure, it was possible, only there was no way that she could find out. All her leads were exhausted. She would never have gotten this far except for Valerie's observation. No. More than likely, Alberto Seco had already gone to Sacramento, maybe by car or train, and assassinated Lawrence Conrad. Once again she was probably too late. She supposed that she should call the Sacramento police and ask about Lawrence Conrad. Yes, she must. She reached for the telephone, then hesitated, and looked off in the distance, past Valerie, who was waiting, absently picking at the carpet. Her mind sorted through the little bits of information that had been piling up ever since she barked her shins on the bumper of a customized car-*cum*-murder weapon. *Wait a minute!* The car. The license number. The registration. If it was good enough for the DMV, then why not for an airline ticket?

She dove for the telephone and began calling the airlines again, only this time when she asked to confirm a reservation, she identified herself as the secretary of a man named Pablo Cardenas.

"Thank you for calling PSA. May I help you?"

Sara made her request, then waited, her heart pounding. She listened to the soft tones of the Muzak emanating from the phone, hoping against hope, dreadfully sure that she was wrong.

"That's Pablo Cardenas, spelled C-a-r-d-e-n-a-s?"

"Yes!"

"He is confirmed on Flight 710 this evening, leaving LAX at 8:25, arriving in Sacramento at 9:30 P.M."

Jackpot!

Sara furiously scribbled down the information, then thanked the clerk and hung up. She was proud of her resourcefulness and extremely relieved. Alberto Seco hadn't left yet, which meant that Lawrence Conrad was still alive. Then she thought about her adversary. He was a shrewd operator. No wonder Alberto Seco was still at large. He had assumed the identify of a man who had been dead for five years! If there was a more perfect cover, it would be difficult to imagine. Sara was surprised that such a simple scam hadn't occurred to her previously, *or* to the police, for that matter.

She checked her watch again. Five minutes to seven. If she hurried, she could actually make it to Sacramento before Alberto Seco. Then she could get to Lawrence Conrad's office early and actually *prevent* a murder for a change. And that would be the most satisfying revenge of all.

There was one hitch. Although she was positive that Lawrence Conrad was Seco's next intended victim, how could she be certain that the assassination would take place at his office? She assumed that Conrad was working late, but she wasn't sure. *I'll have to pick up Seco's trail at the Sacramento airport and follow him. Shit. It's a weak move, but how else can I be sure? I'll just have to be ready for the moment of truth. Since I'll be behind him, I'll have to be quicker than he. I'll have to be first. No more corpses this time. I'm going to get answers.*

"Well?" Valerie asked fearfully.

"Wait a second." Sara picked up the phone, slowly this time, and dialed the hospital, only to learn that Sam's condition was unchanged. Then she explained to her daughter that she had to go to Sacramento. Valerie did not ask why; she already knew.

She looked up at Sara, her eyes brimming with tears, and tried to sound brave. "All right, but the same thing'll happen to you that happened to Daddy."

"No."

"That's what everybody says! Nobody ever thinks they're going to die!" She put her face in her hands and sobbed.

Sara knelt beside her and put her arm around her daughter's shoulders. Valerie was right—she really couldn't foresee what she might encounter. She would just have to be intelligent and anticipate danger. However, she was worried about leaving Valerie alone. She felt compelled to leave but didn't really want to. She pulled Valerie close to her. Her daughter was so precious to her. She hated to see her grieve. The girl's sobs shook her body, and Sara bit her lip to hold back her own.

"I don't care about Daddy, Momma! I'd rather have you be okay!"

Sara vacillated. *Yes, what about the danger? Doesn't Valerie have a right to expect that at least one of her parents will be alive to bring her up? I honest-to-God don't know what to do! How can I leave her? How can I reconcile loving and caring for someone with my own sense of self-respect, my own sense of obligation? I promised Andy the day he died that I would avenge him.* If there was an answer, it eluded her, so she just tried to comfort Valerie. At that moment she was considering giving it all up and staying with her daughter.

Until she remembered the dream.

Valerie felt her mother stiffen, so she pushed away. She was angry that it had come to this, but she was also tired of living fearfully and full of resentment. She remembered being a little girl before they had killed her father. Her mom had been a real mother, then. Her days were relaxed and fun, full of long walks and birthday parties, new dresses and Saturday matinees. Yet those days might as well have not existed, for they had been replaced with baby-sitters, few friends, and a haunted mother who could be cooking scrambled eggs one moment and wrestling with invisible demons the next. At best her mother was indifferent and driven, despite the love she always expressed. At worst she was a woman possessed. Valerie nodded. She didn't want to go to bed anymore wondering if her mother was going to wake up screaming in the middle of the night. She wanted her own peace of mind. *Okay. If something happens to Momma, I'll go live with Mrs. Berman. She's a pain a lot of the time, but at least she's all there. Besides, maybe Momma will work it out, maybe she'll find out why and our life will be like it was before.*

She turned and looked at her mother with an intensity that she had never felt before. "It's all right, Mom. I'll be okay. You remember what Daddy always said," she whispered. "I'm a survivor."

Sara was astonished. "What are you saying?"

"It's something you have to do," Valerie replied with wisdom beyond her years. "So go ahead."

"Valerie . . ."

"If you don't go to Sacramento, Mom, you'll go insane, and they'll take you away, and I won't know how to deal with that."

Sixteen

"What the hell did you say?"

Sara raised her voice above the roar of jumbo jets winding down and revving up, almost shouting into the unenclosed pay phone. "I said, you've got to do something about Spencer's body!"

"Can't it wait?"

"It's stinking up the entire building!"

"How do you know?"

"I smelled it, Casparian!"

"I thought I told you to stay away from your office! You're supposed to be holed up at my place! You trying to commit suicide or what?"

"I'm not there anymore!"

"Where are you?"

"I'm at the airport!"

"What the hell are you doing at the airport?"

"I'm leaving town."

"*What?*"

"I'll be in touch."

"Wait a minute! What's going on? What have you done now?" He sounded like a distraught parent, helpless to stop his errant child from self-destruction.

"I really don't have time to explain!"

"Then what the fuck are you calling me for?" he roared. "Just to tell me about some *corpse* in Venice?"

"No, Casparian! It's Valerie!"

"What's wrong with her now?"

"Nothing. I want you to take care of her."

"You want *me* to take care of her?" He was incredulous.

"No matter what happens, okay?"

"Sara, the kid hates my guts!"

"She's only going through a childhood phase."

"Yeah? Well, I have trouble enough trying to understand adults!" He was almost crying. "How the hell am I supposed to handle her?"

"Just change your personal habits, and you'll be fine, Casparian."

"You can't do this to me! I'm not ready to be an acting grandfather yet!"

"She's supposed to start ballet lessons next month." He groaned.

"When you need a baby-sitter, call Mrs. Berman."

"Mrs. Berman? I'm an Armenian! I don't have time for Jewish grandmothers!"

"Her number's on the Rolodex in your office, from before. I gotta go, Casparian."

"Wait!"

"Don't forget about Spencer's body, okay?" She hung up.

She hurried across the vast stretch of tile toward the ticket counters. Off to the left she saw a line of x-ray machines manned by grim-faced security personnel. She had forgotten about them! There was no way that she could get through.

She ran back to her car in the parking lot, opened the trunk, and lifted out her overnight bag. When she was sure that no one was watching, she transferred La Belle from her purse to the bag.

At Western Airlines she bought a ticket on a commuter flight that left at eight o'clock and arrived in Sacramento an hour later. She checked her overnight bag, watched the baggage conveyor carry it away, then ambled toward the airport security check and the departure gates.

She had fifteen minutes to spare.

Twenty thousand feet above the Pacific the 737 leveled off, banked around to the north, and started its run for Sacramento. Sara pushed the recliner button, eased her chair back, and sipped the white wine that the stewardess had served just moments before. Since the plane was almost empty, she had the luxury of a window seat. The night was clear. The lights of the coastal cities gave way to the blackness of the mountains and the San Joaquin Valley.

Sara lit a cigarette and reflected. No longer was she nervous about what lay ahead. She felt confident. Soon it was going to be over, and she could bury her past forever.

Andy crossed her mind and lingered there. For some reason she thought back to their honeymoon. They had flown from Honolulu to Los Angeles, picked up Andy's old VW, then driven down to Calexico. They had left the car there and crossed the dusty border on foot, with a grand total of two hundred and fifty dollars between them and nothing to come back to except some boxes of books and a bed and typewriter left in a friend's garage. Andy would get a veterans' benefits check when he started graduate school, but that was three months away.

Once past the border town they had taken the train south along the gulf coast for the most memorable trip Sara had ever experienced. Five days of beautiful mountains, clean air, the unspoiled ocean, small cities,

and quaint villages. Exotic food and drink for a pit-
tance. The mariachis. Or the sound of a guitar quietly
strummed, the song drifting with the warm night
breezes. It was a time for loving and making hopeful
plans for the future. On a hotel balcony in Mazatlan
with a view of the surf phosphorescent at midnight,
they made love, climaxing when the moon rose, and
when it set, too.

She brushed away tears and felt the familiar ache in
her stomach that she had lived with ever since Andy's
murder. Painful though it was, she couldn't resist wondering how their lives would have been. When he was
killed, they had just started to mature together, to
learn how to balance each other's faults. She had been
happy and satisfied, and she knew that he was, too,
although there was that quiet, private part of him
which she could never crack. She supposed that it was
normal; no matter how intimate a person was with
someone else, he always needed solitude. Besides,
didn't Andy write her some of the most sensitive love
poems during those times?

She'd felt certain that their life together would have
continued on a blissful course. She sighed and closed
her eyes. Excitement lay ahead. She could already sense
it. *Andy would've enjoyed this, the challenge, the excitement. That's the worst of it. The few times I enjoy
myself, the few times I forget myself and try to relax,
I remember him and I grow cold. I've always asked
myself why, and I've never figured it out. It's happened
with Sam, it's happened with Valerie. You have a
good time, and you end up at the goddamn cemetery.
May those days finally be over.*

The stewardess refilled her glass. Sara thanked her
with a demure nod, then let her thoughts wander
once more. *If only you could see our daughter, Andy.
Valerie is twelve now, and I'm sure that she will be*

the best of any of us. She's already intelligent and resourceful, and she's still devoted to you. Yes, you have a fine daughter. Today, in fact, if it weren't for her, I would still be sitting in Santa Monica, waiting for a murder to happen and not knowing where to turn. If it weren't for her, I would still be on the edge of madness. She shuddered. Danger lay ahead. No matter how calm she might make herself feel, until the ordeal was over with, her soul would remain in darkness.

The 737 began its long descent toward the ground. As it nosed into a heavy cloud cover the cabin shook with turbulence. There was a metallic clang and the seat-belt sign flashed on.

Sara obediently strapped in and checked her watch. *8:45.*

The jet broke through the overcast and banked hard. Sacramento lay directly below, blanketed by a low-hanging fog. The lights of the capital city were softened by the fog and merged together, forming a weblike pattern of diffuse illumination. The plane leveled out and dropped from one plateau to the next, heading toward the airport. There was another noise and the no smoking sign flashed on. The flaps dropped. Electric motors whined as the landing gear was lowered.

Suddenly there was an unnatural grinding and a thud. The plane shuddered and listed slightly. Sara looked out the window. The landing gear under the starboard wing seemed to be stuck. It would not fully extend and lock into place. She turned, raised up and anxiously glanced behind her. The stewardesses were exchanging nervous whispers. One ran up the aisle toward the pilot's cabin.

The jet nosed skyward with a great whine and surge of power that flattened Sara against the seat.

"Ladies and gentlemen, we are experiencing a slight mechanical difficulty that may take a few minutes to correct. We'll be a little late into Sacramento, and we certainly hope that the delay does not inconvenience you."

Sara felt sick. She paled and sweat rolled down her face. One of the stewardesses offered her more wine, thinking that she was worried about the plane's crashing. But she just shook her head. There was no point in trying to explain that while they were flying around in circles, PSA Flight 710 was inexorably nosing down the glide path for Sacramento Municipal with Alberto Seco comfortably aboard.

Twenty minutes later, the crew had temporarily fixed a bad electrical connection and could lower the wheels at one-quarter speed. Sara stared out at the landing gear as it inched down, hating to feel so helpless in the grip of a mechanical failure.

Finally the 737 landed. It was 9:25 when they taxied up to the gate. The great engines shut down and the doors clanked, then rumbled open. Sara raced from the plane, dodging through clumps of people until she reached the first TV monitor she could find. Alberto Seco's plane was arriving at gate twelve. She started in that direction, then stopped, realizing that she needed La Belle.

At the baggage concourse the wait was interminable, but there was nothing she could do. She might as well not have bothered to run from the plane. The other passengers crowded around her. She wanted to yell at them to give her room so she could move and see, but she did not want to call attention to herself. She worked to control her growing desperation. Crowded amid the passengers who pressed from all directions, she felt nauseous. She stared at the baggage carousel in front of them. *Suddenly, it was turning, and the bags were dropping down. Andy was there smiling at her, his normal loving self. They hugged and kissed. He lifted his bag off the carousel, and they moved toward the exit. She was filled with joy to see him and started to ask about his trip.*

"PSA Flight 710 from Los Angeles now arriving at gate twelve," the loudspeaker droned.

"Do you mind?" a lady said indignantly.

Sara had just walked into someone. She turned and gasped. She had left the passengers at the carousel and had sleepwalked almost to the door, only there was no Andy. She cursed softly. She didn't have her overnight bag, either, and Alberto Seco had just landed! She fought her way through the crowd to the carousel, trying to ignore the people who jostled her as they moved in and grabbed their luggage. Her overnight bag fell down the slide, coming around toward her. Another crush of people was moving into the baggage room. *Passengers from PSA Flight 710.* She stood on her toes and craned around several men behind her, looking for him. In a knot of people passing by the entrance, she caught a glimpse of reddish hair under a broad-brimmed Panama hat and a tall, gaunt figure draped by a light-tan cashmere sports coat. *Alberto Seco.* He hurried past the baggage concourse, and much to Sara's chagrin went the other way, following the signs that pointed toward the lockers, telephones, and exit. She propelled herself around the carousel, grabbed her overnight bag, then lunged at the faceless wall of passengers. Finding a gap, she slipped through and broke free of the crowd. She sprinted out of the baggage concourse toward the exit, passing the telephones and reservation desks. The doors opened automatically, and as she burst out into the damp, foggy chill she was panting from the exertion. She stopped and looked in all directions. People were coming and going by car, bus, taxi, and on foot. None of them even came close to resembling the shadowy Mexican Mafia leader. She looked down; her hands were shaking. How could she follow Alberto Seco? She was too late. He was already gone.

Thanks to the dream, the recollection.

Seventeen

There wasn't any one set of disappearing taillights to follow, either. Dozens of them were leaving the airport in all directions. Alberto Seco could be en route to anywhere in the city of Sacramento, and she hadn't a clue. Thus she had no other choice.

She would have to trust her intuition.

She hurried across the loading zone and slid into the open door of a waiting taxi. The driver jerked awake.

"The state capitol, please."

"Yes, ma'am." He nodded, started the meter, and drove off.

"It's fifty dollars if we get there in a hurry."

"You know they close at nine."

"I know," she lied. So she'd have to break in. So would Alberto Seco.

He shrugged and turned onto the freeway for the short trip into the city. He stood on the gas and soon the lumbering vehicle was pushing ninety. She leaned back, closed her eyes, and tried to relax, but her heart was pounding with excitement. Once again she recalled how Casparian had told her to always rely on the evidence. *Well, I'm fresh out. All I have left is my intuition. And this once I hope I'm right.*

The trees they sped past were partially obscured by the fog that clouded the freeway in great patches. The taxi driver was concentrating hard on the road ahead. Sara took La Belle out of her overnight bag and dropped the weapon into her purse. The driver swung off the freeway, rocketed north on Freeport, then took a dogleg over to 10th Street. Ahead, the lighted dome of the state capitol rose like a beacon. Sara shouted at the driver to stop when they got to the corner of 10th and L Streets. A chill of fear ran through her as they drew closer. He pulled over to the curb, and she could see the majestic park that lay behind the capitol building. She gave the driver fifty dollars and jumped out of the cab, leaving her bag behind.

She ran down a wide path in the shadows of the great old trees that gave the park its dignity. Halfway across the park she slowed to a walk and scrutinized the vast building in front of her. It was deserted. At least there weren't police cars and ambulances all over the place; Lawrence Conrad must still be alive. She frowned. *If* he was here. Alberto Seco could have gotten inside, accomplished his evil mission, and already left, no one being the wiser. She would know soon enough. She glanced up at the magnificent dome and couldn't help pausing briefly to study it. Through the fog the dome seemed mystical, its grandeur belying the machinations which went on underneath in the bowels of its offices and corridors. Sara reached into her purse and curled her fingers around the comforting shape of La Belle. She moved forward, more carefully now. When she was clear of the trees, she looked in all directions, then ran to the side of the building. She huddled against the masonry to catch her breath. Then she crept along through the ivy that grew thick against the building, looking for a way inside. Finding her way around a giant air conditioner, measuring her steps so she wouldn't make too much noise, she came to a fire door. She removed from her purse the miniature crowbar she kept for such circumstances. She could get through this in a flash, depending on how difficult it would be to circumvent the alarm system. She inspected the door, looking for wires or magnetic devices, then suddenly stepped back, surprised. The latch had been taped shut so it wouldn't lock. That meant the alarm probably wasn't working, either. She gave the door a light tug and it swung open. *I wonder who's behind this little convenience? A clerk? Security guard?* Her heart sank. Did Alberto Seco know someone on the inside?

She stepped inside the building, stopped, and looked around. Her suspicions were confirmed. The small lock for the alarm system on the right wall was in the *off* position. *So he's already here, is he? Well, if so, I'll make damned sure he doesn't get away.* She removed the tape from the door. It closed automatically and locked behind her. Then she took a bobby pin out of her purse, inserted the two ends into the alarm's keyhole and gently wiggled them until the lock turned back into the *on* position with an electronic click. She sighed with satisfaction. If she had to sneak out of the building, she'd merely turn the alarm off in the same fashion and slip out the fire door.

She turned and hurried down a hallway which opened into a broad corridor. None of the names on the office doors she passed were Lawrence Conrad's. Toward the center of the building she found the directory. She scanned it and nodded. Lawrence Conrad's office was on the first floor in the northwest corner, right across from the governor's. Sara turned and was about to continue when she heard footfalls. A security guard was ambling in her direction. She looked around wildly, saw a dark hallway by a bank of elevators, and darted down it. Around a corner the wall came to an abrupt dead end, and she huddled against it. Then she saw the guard's flashlight beam playing on the wall. He was coming her way. Panicked, she glanced around. Across the hall was a ladies' room. She bolted for the door. Fortunately it was open, and she slipped inside just as the guard rounded the corner. She sagged against the enameled wall, her heart pounding, her breathing heavy. Had he seen her? Finally she heard the scuff of the guard's shoes; he had turned around and was headed back in the other direction. After waiting a good three minutes, she crept back down the dark hallway to the main corridor. She hesitated at the elevators, looking in all directions, listening cautiously. She heard the faint sounds of the guard pushing through a door into another wing. Moving in the other direction, she came to the edge of the great rotunda and paused, peering into the darkness beyond. Along with the alarm system they probably only had one security guard per floor; she doubted that she would encounter another one. Still she crossed the area slowly, carefully zigzagging between pieces of sculpture on exhibition. Finally she came to the northwest wing.

Mist-softened moonlight came in through the glass doors at the far end of the passageway. She went down the wide hallway moving carefully, *feeling* the air, gliding along silently. The hall smelled curiously of stale newspapers and mimeograph fluid. Further along that odor was replaced by the scent of furniture polish. Sara looked to her right. She was approaching the end of the wing. The governor's mahogany door glinted in the moonlight. She shuddered. Andy had been here at least once, hadn't he? The governor had talked to him about a job. She wondered how the conversation had gone.

She turned away, strangely uncomfortable with her musings. There was something eerie lurking in the air. The gold lettering on the mahogany door across the corridor read:

LAWRENCE CONRAD
COMPTROLLER

She had to suppress a sigh of satisfaction; her intuition had been correct. A faint glow of light shone from beneath Conrad's outer door.

Someone was inside.

Before she had time to speculate, she heard the low tones of conversation coming from inside the office. *Hmmm.* So the light did not necessarily mean that a diligent public servant was working late for the benefit of California. A meeting was going on. *Why now? When the rest of the capitol's locked up tight? Does it have anything to do with the latch of the fire door having been taped shut? Something's weird. Something's happening that I didn't anticipate. Maybe Lawrence Conrad doesn't wear a white hat anymore. Maybe no one does.*

She went back to the door next to Conrad's office. In her wallet she found her overdrawn Master Charge card, which she regarded as an appropriately feminine device for breaking and entering. She slid the card between the door and the jamb. With two quick motions she popped the bolt from its socket, turned the handle, opened the door, and slipped into the room. She quietly closed the door and stood still, waiting for her eyes to adjust to the blackness. When she could distinguish shapes, she recognized desks, typewriters, and copying machines. Files occupied one entire wall. This was a nuts-and-bolts office where the drudgery of bureaucracy was performed.

Across the room was a door. Sara went over to it, paused, and listened. The conversation was just as indistinct here as it had been out in the passageway. She needed to get closer. She opened the door a crack, saw no light, and sneaked into a rectangular chamber with richly paneled walls. It was a reception and waiting room. Following an inner-office hall, she found her way to still another room. There were two desks and some antiques; Conrad's personal secretary probably worked there. Without asking herself why, she automatically crossed to the telephone, took a tiny electronic bug out of her pocket, and slipped it under the phone, magnetic belly up.

Then she turned and peeked farther down the hallway. A scant six feet away was Conrad's door. Light blazed from underneath. She tiptoed to the door, put her ear just below the PRIVATE sign, and listened. She frowned. The conversation was still inaudible, although she did recognize Conrad's distinctive tone. Who was the other person? She wouldn't know until someone came out, and she didn't have the time to wait. Suddenly, she had an inspiration. *Wait a minute. Hadn't she noticed an intercom by the secretary's phone?* Sara turned, retraced her steps across the plush carpet, eased behind the desk, and looked closely. *Sure enough.* By the telephone was a small speaker, an *on-off-listen* button, and a volume control. She turned the volume to zero, pushed the button to *listen,* then slowly increased the volume until she could just barely make out the voices.

"How much did you get?" asked Lawrence Conrad.

"A couple of ounces," a man replied in an accent that was unmistakably Latin.

Sara had heard that voice before—in the alley behind her office building the night she was almost raped and murdered. *Alberto Seco?* The comptroller of the State of California was having a clandestine meeting with a leader of the Mexican Mafia! And she had thought that Lawrence Conrad was a target for murder?

Her analysis hadn't been cynical enough. No one had taken things far enough, including Alan Rosenus and James Reardon. Including Andy? She sat down heavily in the desk chair, mouth agape. She just listened to the intercom.

There was a rustling sound, and then a very slight, sandy thud. It sounded like something had been dropped onto Lawrence Conrad's desk. Next she heard a crackling noise.

"Only a couple of ounces?"

"Hey, man, I've been busy, you understand?"

"I don't know . . . The way he's been going through it lately."

"That's his problem. Tell the dude to slow down and forget about the White House."

Conrad laughed sarcastically. "Sure." More crackling sounds. "Is it any good?"

"Better than usual. The best."

"Colombian?"

"No, man! It's pharmaceutical! From UCLA!"

Conrad sighed. "That's something, I guess."

Seco snorted. "That's something, I guess. Sheeit!"

"Where's Marta, anyway? I thought she was right behind you."

"She didn't come, man."

"Oh." He was clearly disappointed. "I was really looking forward to seeing her again."

"Marta won't be making any more trips to Sacramento."

"Why not? I thought she was reliable."

"She was. I mean, she set up the Reardon job just like I wanted it. She picked up his briefcase just like she was supposed to, but she got curious and made the mistake of reading what was inside. She knew everything. I didn't have a choice. I had to kill her."

"But she was on your side!"

"Nobody's on my side but me."

A pause. "Jesus. With friends like you, who needs enemies?"

"Hey, I didn't get the chance to grow up hanging out on a surfboard, remember? I didn't graduate from SC Law School, either!"

Now it was Conrad's turn to laugh. "Come on, Seco! Don't sing me the ethnic blues! You've had a damned sweet ride!"

He sighed nervously. "Okay, okay, let's get on with it. I was going to send Marta's replacement, but I thought I better bring this myself."

Sara heard a cassette clatter onto the desk.

"What's on this?" Conrad asked sarcastically. "The 'La Cucaracha Disco'?"

"Fuck you, man! Just play it! Play it and see how close you came!"

A desk drawer opened. A cassette was ejected from a tape machine. The one in question was clicked into place. A button was pushed, and over the intercom Sara heard the beginning of the conversation that had taken place in the Malibu-by-the-Sea Motel. A man who must have been James Reardon was talking very fast, incoherently at times—but he said enough to sketch the outlines of a giant conspiracy to his reporter friend, Alan Rosenus.

ROSENUS: I just can't believe it!

REARDON: Every halfway house in the state is run

by the Mexican Mafia! The entire drug rehabilitation program is a front for the biggest heroin operation in the world!

ROSENUS: But why would the state government want to do business with the Mexican Mafia?

REARDON: Come *on*, Alan, surely you've heard about marriages of convenience! There's peace on the streets and in the fields, the junkies are happy, the middle class keeps working, and the governor's a hero!

ROSENUS: Okay, okay, suppose it's true. Who's behind it, then?

REARDON: You want me to name names? You can start with Jorge Martinez and a man who calls himself Pablo Cardenas.

ROSENUS: How did you find out?

REARDON: It started with one of my patients at the halfway house. I was analyzing his dreams. They played like Hollywood movies. One thing led to another. I got curious, and I started hypnotizing him. Over a period of weeks, it all came out.

ROSENUS: But that's no proof at all!

REARDON: I saw a drop, Alan!

ROSENUS: What do you want me to do? I'm just a reporter!

REARDON: Talk to somebody who *can* do something, for Christ's sake! I'm your friend! Go to the state government!

ROSENUS: (sighs) Well, I don't know. One of the few people in Sacramento I can think of would be Larry Conrad. He's the only one I'd trust with anything sensitive or potentially scandalous.

There was static for a few seconds, rendering the conversation inaudible. Then it continued.

REARDON: I swear to God, man! I wouldn't lie!
ROSENUS: That's impossible! That's the most ridiculous thing I've ever heard!

The tape clicked off, and the amazed sound of Alan Rosenus's voice was replaced by Lawrence Conrad's. "When James Reardon called me, I couldn't tell him that he was signing his own death warrant, now, could I? Especially after I'd come so highly recommended!"

"So what did you tell him?"

"What else? I set up a meeting with him and told him that the attorney general would be there to take a deposition. Then I phoned Jorge Martinez, and you know the rest."

"What did that dude Rosenus call you? Trustworthy?"

"I am," Conrad replied, his voice suddenly cold.

Sara heard him move around the room, then open a cabinet and take out glasses.

"Would you like a drink before you leave?"

"Sure, man," Seco replied.

The drinks were poured.

"I know it's a little late, but I congratulate you on your resourcefulness." Their glasses met in a toast. "You made James Reardon's murder look like an accident."

"Not to mention the others."

"I don't want to hear about the others."

"That's the privilege of your position, counselor."

Conrad emitted a long sigh of satisfaction. "Is it finished, then?"

"Except for one more. And she's running scared."

"Who?"

"Some pussy who calls herself a private investigator. She's disappeared, but sooner or later she'll be out on the street again, and I'll find out where she is." Seco paused and reflected. "How the hell she got involved, I'll never know."

"What's her name?"

"Sara Scott."

"Sara Scott?"

"Yeah, that's it. You know her or something?"

There was a hush. Then Conrad spoke slowly and with deliberate calm. "I know how she got involved. She's Andy Scott's old lady. I thought we were done with him a long time ago."

"Who the fuck is Andy Scott?"

"Don't you remember him? The greedy one? That was your first job for us. You cut your teeth on that pushy bastard."

Sara remained perfectly still in the chair, her arms straight out in front of her, hands grasping the desk. *Greedy? Pushy bastard?* What did that mean? She stared at the intercom, unable to move. The darkness was oppressive; it seemed to be crushing her. She remembered how the night used to make her feel infinitesimally small when she was a little girl. She had been terrified then, totally helpless and adrift in a sea of blackness. The memories made her want to scream.

Instead she kept silent. Gradually the tension eased, but she felt strangely empty, even though now she knew. *Finally.* Andy had somehow been connected with this evil business. He had died by the hand of Alberto Seco.

Why?

Her muscles tightened, and she swelled with courage. She was surprised to find a sudden source of strength, for she had no brilliant ideas or insightful plans. But she was caught up and made resolute by the moment. The events themselves would motivate her.

She took a deep breath and leaned closer to the intercom. The clacking sound of the cassette meant the tape was being ejected from the tape machine.

"I think we should destroy this together," Seco said.

"Why destroy it?"

"What do you mean?"

Conrad just laughed.

Sara straightened up. She took La Belle out of her purse and eased off the safety. She rose. *The cassette. That will end it. The explanation is on tape. That's all I need to bust this whole thing wide open. For Andy's sake, God bless him. Yeah, he had a story all right. Someone's going to print it, too.* She crept across the room, priming herself for what lay beyond the door marked PRIVATE. Her skin tingled. Her body coiled.

At the door she transferred her pistol to her right hand and stood poised a few feet back. She concentrated on making her breathing even, then waited, her eyes riveted to the door handle. She heard the sound of soft footsteps; someone was approaching the door. When the brass knob turned, she threw all her weight against the door. It slammed back and sent someone sprawling to the floor. She pivoted to the side and backed against a couch, La Belle leveled at an astonished Lawrence Conrad, who was standing behind his huge polished-oak desk. He sank into his chair, visibly shaken. She glanced at Alberto Seco, now on his knees, holding his face and moaning. He was bleeding from the nose and mouth.

"Get up slowly, please." Her voice sounded tiny and far away. *"Very* slowly."

Seco looked at her and blinked. His hands dropped down loosely at his sides. Blood was flowing freely down his face, dripping onto the crushed Panama hat on the floor. "Fuck!" He motioned with one hand without raising his arm. "It's her!"

"You stupid son of a bitch!" Conrad hissed. "She followed you!"

"No," Sara stated. "I didn't have to."

Conrad looked at her, trembling. His face was helpless and confused. The former surfer's complexion now matched the streaks of gray in his blond hair.

"It was only a matter of time. You made more mistakes than I did."

Seco got to his feet, watching her carefully. She kept her pistol aimed at his chest. He let his arms hang suspended away from his body—he had observed scenes like this before and knew how wise men behaved in such situations. He dutifully obeyed her quick gesture and backed against the cabinets where the comptroller kept his Cate School golf trophies.

Sara glanced at Conrad. He sat stiffly, his hands on the desk blotter. On the desk next to the cocaine sat the tape cassette. It was a mere ten feet away. She gulped. All she had to do was scoop it up and get out of there alive. Conrad leaned back slowly, letting his hands drop onto the arms of his chair. He exhaled with a whistle and studied her, his fingers twitching compulsively. She resolutely strode forward, reaching out for the cassette.

Conrad saw what she was about to do and held up his hand. "Don't you want to know about your husband?"

She picked up the cassette and gestured with it. "I've got his story right here." She dropped the tape into her pocket.

"Don't be too sure."

She stared at him and gulped, her eyes locked on his. "What do you mean?"

He rose easily from the chair—almost as if she didn't have a pistol pointed at his belly. "I'll make a deal with you. You go your way, we go ours. And that buys the final memory of what went down with your old man."

"You'll tell me anyway," she replied almost cheerfully, "because if you don't, I'll blow your brains out."

He paled and seemed to hesitate. "I don't think you have the guts."

"I don't have anything to lose, either." She spread her feet, held La Belle with both hands, and aimed between his eyes.

"Tell her, man!" Seco blurted out.

Conrad glanced quickly at Seco. Intent on Conrad, Sara did not see the assassin's conspiratorial nod. Conrad looked back at her. The beads of sweat on his forehead shone in the light, and he seemed uncertain. Sara saw the desperation in his eyes. She had used her weapon only once before, but there was no turning back now. Only how long could she wait? She was spared the decision.

"All right." He dropped into the chair, exhausted.

Sara eased back, almost gasping for air, but she knew that she could not relax. Seco was studying her, waiting for an opening, his eyes glittering. She felt her fine edge slipping away, and with it her advantage over them. *If I could just sit down.* She shook her head and stiffened, resisting the temptation.

"He found out about us," Conrad said slowly.

"I already *know* that!" she cried, her voice quavering. "And that's why you killed him! Isn't it? *Isn't it?*"

"No," he replied flatly. "Your old man wanted in."

Sara's eyes widened with astonishment. Her knees sagged, and she gaped at Conrad.

"We said, sure, you can have a job on the staff and a hundred grand. He said no. He wanted a million, or he was going to tell his story to the world. We didn't have that kind of money. We pleaded with him. Instead of listening, he gave us the weekend to consider it and flew to L.A. The rest is history." Conrad shrugged. "We really didn't have a choice."

"No!" she exclaimed. "That's not true! That can't be!"

"Hey." He spread his hands. "Why would I lie to you?"

She blinked. *Andy was beside her in the VW, holding her face, studying her, whispering. "Don't make me lie to you. Ever." She felt him kiss her, then watched him get out of the car and walk in the shadows toward the front of the Taco Bell. Suddenly everything froze. There was an explosion.*

The image of her husband shattered, and the jagged pieces seemed to slice through her soul.

Sara was looking down at the floor and sobbing when she came back to reality and realized that Conrad had taken La Belle out of her hand, twisted her arm behind her back, then placed a .38 Special against her head. She was too weak to make a sound; she was utterly destroyed.

"I don't know what happened," Seco said, bewildered but immensely relieved, "but you sure blew it, lady."

She tried to move away from the voice—just to go somewhere, into madness perhaps—but Conrad jerked her back toward him, and she knew that they were going to hurt her. "Please. Don't kill me," she whispered. "I'll do anything you want."

"And it won't make any difference," said Conrad, propelling her forward through the outer office.

"Where we going to take her?" Seco asked.

"The river."

"Please?"

"One more sound and you won't live to see the moonlight outside, understand?"

Sara nodded and swallowed, but her throat remained dry. She gagged several times and began shaking with fear. Conrad tightened his grip on her arm, and the pain made her weaker.

Seco opened the outer office door a crack, listened, then nodded. He led the way into the corridor. Conrad followed, pushing Sara in front of him, and they silently moved through the northwest wing.

The cruel news about Andy had left Sara numb, desolate, without hope. She briefly wondered what else she didn't know. Then memories of him surfaced and lay heavily on her mind, mocking her. She was a burnt-out case now, a victim. There was no way she could reconcile the truth about him with her images of the past except to . . . embrace madness? As if it mattered, for soon death would resolve all things in her life.

She walked mechanically now, dazedly, except that she could not ignore the annoyance of the pistol at her head or the throb of her twisted arm. She scowled. Feelings returned. Anger. *God damn you, Andy Scott, God damn your petty, corrupt soul! I lived with your nightmare! You had no right to deceive me! You had no right to tell me that you never wanted to lie to me when your whole existence was a lie. Should I pity you and feel sorry for your memory? No. I cannot. Not after the haunted years, the obligation I felt to you, so obsessively. Not after the pain. I gave you my essence, and you betrayed me. You left me nothing to believe in. And now, because of you, I am going to die.*

They had crossed the rotunda now and were waiting

by the elevators while Alberto Seco scouted ahead, looking for the security guard. Then the gaunt assassin returned, nodding and motioning them forward. Conrad nudged Sara with his pistol, and she moved forward, her anger giving way to waves of fear. She didn't want to die. She was determined to survive, and if she played it correctly, she might have one last chance.

Conrad twisted her arm higher, tighter. She gritted her teeth, then leaned to the right to ease the pressure. Had he sensed her resolve? They were in the narrow passageway now, silently heading for the fire door by which both Sara and Seco had entered the building. Conrad quickened his pace. She stumbled and gasped, held up only by his grip on her arm. The pain was excruciating. She scrambled up and continued, her chest heaving.

When they reached the door, Conrad paused and took one last, nervous look over his shoulder. Sara held her breath, her eyes fixed on Seco, waiting. She tensed. He grasped the door handle with both hands and pushed.

The door clicked open and set off the alarm.

The staccato clanging muted Seco's shouts of surprise and echoed through the building. Conrad's grip slackened for an instant and she spun away from his pistol. He fired, and the bullet ricocheted off the door into the wall. Sara jerked free and sprinted back down the hallway, off balance and staggering. She got only fifteen feet away before he fired again. The bullet creased her breast, ripped through her side, and buried itself in her shoulder, splintering bone. The impact spun her around.

"Oh," she grunted, and dropped to the floor, shocked and dizzy. The pain was instantaneous, overwhelming, consuming her and making her sick. She whimpered with fear, realizing how vulnerable she was, but she didn't have the strength to get up and run away. *I'm going to die, aren't I?* She managed to look back and saw Conrad trying to shove Seco aside so he could get out the door.

"The cassette, you fucking idiot!" Seco cried. "She's got the cassette!"

Conrad stared at Seco, dumbfounded. He glanced down at his .38, then tossed it to the floor and shook his hand as if he had burned himself. Muttering curses in Spanish, Seco ran back to Sara and reached into her pocket, fumbling for the tape. She could feel his hot, desperate breath on her face. He found the tape, jerked it out of her pocket, and straightened up.

The lights went on.

Seco backed away, cringing at the illumination and reaching inside his coat, but before he could get his weapon out, a lithe gray-haired security guard vaulted into the passageway, dropped to one knee, and fired three shots. The first one hit the ceiling. The next two caught Alberto Seco in the chest and lifted him off the ground. He went down, his breath whooshing out. He half-rolled and twitched. A chrome-plated, long-barreled .44 Magnum slipped out of his hand. His eyes glazed over; he wheezed for air. Blood bubbled up through the holes in his chest and formed a crimson sea beneath him.

The security guard hurried past Sara and leveled his service revolver at a paralyzed Lawrence Conrad. She looked at Seco. His eyes opened briefly, and he acknowledged her. He grimaced, then stiffened. Sounds of agony came from deep inside him.

"Viva la fraternidad," he managed to utter. They were his last words.

She turned away. Her shoulder throbbed now. She wanted to cry, but she hurt too much. She knew what had to be done. Immediately. She gritted her teeth, then forced herself to crawl over to Seco's corpse, take the cassette off the floor beside him, and stuff it into her jeans. *Just in time.*

"Hold it!" someone screamed.

Almost delirious, Sara looked up and found herself staring into the barrel of a revolver. She froze. Two men picked her up, carried her back into the main corridor, and sat her down on a marble bench. Her vision cleared for a moment. She was aware of Conrad's being handcuffed, then heard the gray-haired security guard on the phone, shouting for the police.

It was over.

She was free now. One of her lives had ended—not as she'd expected, not even as she would have wanted —but ended just the same. And now another was about to . . . She felt giddy and lightheaded despite the raw pain in her shoulder. *How the past dies, the future will become. Finally I am victorious.*

There were sirens in the distance. She welcomed the sound. Someone would treat her wound, and the pain would go away. She would be whole in body. She was certain that someday soon her spirit would mend, too. Drowsy, she envisioned herself traipsing across a meadow searching for pieces of her soul. Would she ever find them all?

She tried to open her eyes but could not. She swayed back and forth. Everything hurt so much. She wept. She was agonized, then was suddenly euphoric; sorrowful, then ecstatic. She was coming apart, slipping away. She was fluid. She could do nothing. The sirens were . . .

The sirens . . . She pitched forward off the bench and sprawled onto the floor. Vaguely she sensed someone running toward her. Then she went limp. Her head lolled on the cold, smooth marble, and she was enveloped in blackness.

Epilogue

No more screams, no more tears.
Finally Sara seemed beyond the nightmare and its memories. No longer did she feel haunted, teetering on the edge of madness. No longer was she a dead man's puppet. She slept peacefully now, safe with dreams of herself and the future. The dark side of Andy had been exorcised, and only a vague shadow remained. A reminder. Yes, someday she would tell Valerie the truth about her father—when she was sure that she could handle it.

The sun broke through the overcast and shone in the bedroom window. It was hot on Sara's face, and she turned away from it languidly. Her hair made a floral pattern on the pillows and sparkled where the sunlight hit it. She shifted slightly to ease the dull ache where she had been shot. Her skin itched under the bandages, too. But those were only minor discomforts. Yes. She was going to be all right.

The same could not be said for the governor of California. After the shoot-out at the state capitol, there had been hushed staff conferences and phone calls to the governor from the comptroller's office about the packets of cocaine on Conrad's desk and how to best cover up the scandal. The tap Sara had placed on the secretary's phone recorded it all for posterity. As a result the governor had taken an extended leave of absence from his reelection campaign and was fighting hard to stay out of jail.

Already in jail, Lawrence Conrad was trying to exchange a full confession for immunity and wasn't meeting with much success. Sacramento was in chaos. Accusations, subpoenas, and indictments were falling thick and fast, sparing no one—not even Anna Perez. No one believed her tearful claims of innocence, although she was offered a three-picture deal for a million per by a Hollywood studio. Her boyfriend, Jorge Martinez, had burned the Straighten-Up Halfway House to the ground the night before and had escaped across the border into Mexico.

Sara rolled over and kicked the covers off. She sighed deeply and slept on, sharing the space with Sam's beige cat, who took up half the bed. Vaguely aware of the pleasant and predictable pounding of the surf, she smiled.

Sam was still in the hospital, but he was going to be all right.

She had come up to the refuge of the beach house just hours after the story broke, for she had neither protection nor anonymity. Her apartment had been overrun by a media crush unprecedented in Venice. She had been holed up here for days now, mainly sleeping but also enjoying solitary strolls along the beach and quiet nights in front of the great stone fireplace. She liked becoming whole again; she liked the sense of freedom she had now found. Four years was a long time to live with a broken past, constantly reminded of death.

Cooking odors drifted in on the salt breeze. She started to open her eyes but once again succumbed to sleep. The sun warmed her thighs and belly now, and the sensation was pleasantly erotic. She stirred.

"Mom?"

Sara stretched, yawned, and sat up. Disturbed, the cat gave her a look of disdain, jumped off the bed and sauntered away. She smelled freshly brewed coffee, bacon, and buttered toast. Her mouth watered. "Be right there." She got out of bed and started dressing.

Valerie came into the bedroom, wearing a sweat-shirt and cut-offs. "You got a thousand phone calls."

"From who?"

"You want me to skip the people who wanted to know how to get here?"

"Yeah."

"That leaves two."

Sara laughed, strolled into the kitchen, and poured herself some coffee. She ignored the twinge in her stomach signaling that it was time for a smoke.

"Some guy named Don Barrett was the first one. He wanted to tell you that he was getting married."

"Really?" She blushed. "How did he get the number anyway?"

"The same way everybody else did. From your service."

"From my *service?* I didn't give them this number, I gave them . . ."

"Casparian's." Valerie nodded sympathetically. "He called to say that he had referred them to this number because he was tired of taking messages for you, es-pecially after he dumped Spencer's body where no one'll ever find it."

The telephone rang. Valerie shrugged. "It's been like this all day." She turned and automatically an-swered. "Hello?" She paused and listened. "I don't think so, but I'll ask." She held her hand over the mouthpiece and looked at Sara. "Some guy wants to talk to you about his wife who disappeared last year. Shall I tell him to get lost?"

"I'll take it in the other room." She turned and left the kitchen.

Astonished, Valerie dropped the phone and followed. "Mom, you're *not* going to be a private investigator anymore, are you?"

"Valerie, honey—"

"But you *promised!*"

"Val, I *didn't* promise! All I said was I didn't know." She turned and placed her hands on the girl's shoulders. "I had to find out about your father, but at the same time I discovered that being a private eye isn't such a bad way to make a living."

"Jeez!" Valerie pulled away. "Why can't I have a normal mother for a change?"

Sara crossed the room and picked up the extension. "Hello?"

"Is this Sara Scott?"

"No," she said. "Not anymore."

"Huh?" came the puzzled reply.

"I'm changing my name back. The name's Martin. Sara Martin. Now what can I do for you?"